PRAISE FOR NEODYMIUM CHRONICLES

"...this intricately plotted outing ups the already sky-high stakes of Finelli's turbulent space opera series, setting up the board for a bombastic finale to come."

—*Publisher's Weekly*

NEODYMIUM SACRIFICE

THE NEODYMIUM CHRONICLES
BOOK 3

JEN FINELLI, MD

WFP
WordFire Press

EBook ISBN: 978-1-68057-392-3
Trade Paperback ISBN: 978-1-68057-391-6
Case Bind Hardcover ISBN: 978-1-68057-393-0
Library of Congress Control Number: 022946477
Cover design by Janet McDonald
Cover artwork images by Adobe Stock
Kevin J. Anderson, Art Director
Published by
WordFire Press, LLC
PO Box 1840
Monument CO 80132
Kevin J. Anderson & Rebecca Moesta, Publishers
WordFire Press eBook Edition 2022
WordFire Press Trade Paperback Edition 2022
WordFire Press Hardcover Edition 2022
Printed in the USA
Join our WordFire Press Readers Group for
sneak previews, updates, new projects, and giveaways.
Sign up at wordfirepress.com

DEDICATION

Dedicated to Brian, Gabi, Jordan, and SPC Yoshikawa.
For saving my life in 2019.
I don't always believe I was worth it, but your belief in me then still
keeps the spark alive now.

CHAPTER ONE

Lem

IF ONLY EVERYONE COULD SPEAK THEIR OWN TONGUE.

The tunnels of the Beryllian mines echoed with crunching rocks, a constant baseline to one of the premier research facilities in the galaxy, where hands-on learning and work experience attracted almost everyone with a pulse. Along the rough hallways, through bubbling laboratories, lively classrooms, and bustling forges, teenagers of all species chirped, gurgled, or otherwise laughed or complained, chattering to each other in their various accents.

All in the same filking mandatory language, though.

Lem Benzaran shook bitterness and sweaty hair off her forehead with a violent toss of her head as she swung the pickax in the darkness again. Here in the shadows of this hidden shaft she couldn't afford to use automated mining equipment herself—but she could hear it running in the lit tunnel outside, and its whir annoyed her as much as that one girl's grating voice.

"Bla bla bla boys. You sound just like a lieutenant I used to know, Kym," Lem muttered, tossing the pickax to the side again to get her fingers around cool stone. Still stone. Still not earth. Not that she expected real soil here on Beryllia, not dark and rich like the jungles back home, but she hoped to hit red dust and pebbles at some point soon.

Jei's waiting.

It had been a couple of weeks since Lem's last communication with either her former sparring partner Jei Bereens, or her Biouk adopted brother, Cinta. She missed Cinta's giant, expressive furry ears, and she wondered if his fangs had started to grow at all. Shyte, she hadn't even seen his face in almost a year, since he had to kind of keep their long-distance conversations under wraps after—well. Cinta now had to travel all the way off post, back to the Biouk village where they'd grown up in the treetops, to place short calls to her. Even Jei, once every commander's golden boy, couldn't reach Lem without sneaking off to find an open network in whatever civilian city he happened to be in for whatever mission, and from what Lem understood, the Frelsi's top bigwigs had him on a short leash with lots of time-out in between.

No one *else* really wanted to talk to her these days.

Lem shook her head to snap herself into focus. It didn't matter. It didn't matter what anyone else wanted or said. What mattered right now was getting out of this idiotic school back to the real world. Lem's palms sparked in the darkness as she gripped the boulder in front of her and pulled—*come on, come on, dislodge—think backward, think harder, get that electromagnetic nervous system powered up, pull—*

No good.

She paused, glancing over her shoulder out of habit as she panted with the taste of iron in her mouth. There was no one else here. Far behind her, only the faintest ring of light outlined the rock that hid the entrance to her secret mine shaft from the people in the main tunnel. She was safe here.

Lem resented the forces that made her watch over her shoulder anyway.

The former Frelsi cadet no longer had to hide her thoughts, but she'd kept her powers secret all this last year. Couldn't have word getting back to the Growen that she'd turned up on *the* center for learning in the galaxy. Theoretically Beryllia was a pretty good place for a human Lem's age to blend in: with high security and ample research programs, most young civilians spent some time here at one point or another.

Most young civilians didn't get sent here after living most of their lives with a militant freedom force, though. Shyte, it was harder getting along with people here than undercover with the filking gray kid-killers. Lem gritted her teeth as she swung the pickax again. She resisted—*swing*—resisted—*crash*—resisted the urge to snarl. At least in the Growen torture camp she'd had a battle-buddy. Shyte, even disguised in Growen uniform at least she'd had a purpose. Most people like Lem ended up in refugee forts with the Frelsi, so most people *here* either sympathized with the Growen, or just knew nothing about the galaxy beyond "do your homework and get a good career." If Lem had to hear one more teacher remark about the "Contaminated extremists ..."

Lem grunted as a pocket of dust exploded under her next blow. Sure, Growen soldiers talked like that, too, but Growen soldiers actually had to cash the checks their tongues wrote. And most soldiers didn't have time to actively spread nonsense to impressionable young civilians.

Impressionable young civilians ... listen to me, like I got age on them or something. But the numbers didn't matter. Everyone here seemed like little kids to Lem.

Lem straightened, dropped her pickax, and pulled her mace off her belt with a fierce exhale. Eh, she had nothing on the other civvies here. She was one, too, now. She wasn't Frelsi. She wasn't fighting to save the galaxy from homogenization. Gossip and accusations from Frelsi Command and former comrades alike rang in her ears, as if carried on the vibrations of the machines in the tunnel outside. She was erratic, they'd said, possibly even a traitor. She stopped moving for a moment, like her body had forgotten what she was doing—like it was locking her forever in that dark, curtained conference room, looping over and over through last year's shyte hearing.

Lem shook herself off, spinning her mace with a frustrated grunt and a deep breath. *I knew what I was getting into when I went undercover with the Growen. It's fine.* She flicked a groove on the mace to switch it on; red laser washed across the staff, rippling around and avoiding her fingers to blossom into a spiked orb on one end that danced like the ancient models of the atom. With clenched teeth she leaned in to the wall, pressing the spiked orb of light into the stone. Lem didn't want to damage the staff casing or its DNA-sensing components by whacking it against rock over and over, but the controlled plasma could carve a good-sized chunk with gentle pressure ... there, now the rock began to heat, crumble, and glow under her push. She'd alternated between this, the pickax, and her em abilities for the last few hours.

It was fine. She'd just figured she'd die before getting disgraced. She kinda wished she had.

Of course you don't mean that.

Oh, Njandejara. A cool draft in the darkness answered Lem's thoughts; the still voice of her invisible friend sounded far away today, as if shouting into her thoughts from down a deep, deep tunnel, or from the distant past. *You don't mean that*, it said—it, because he sounded like an it, today, just a sentient flicker of temperature in the stone. *What about Jei?*

Well. Yeah. Lem huffed, breathing through her effort. That was worth the stupidity of being alive. Her sparring partner was free from that *witch* because Lem hadn't died.

"That wasn't all me, though," she grunted back. Jei could take down a filking regiment with his bare hands now. Lem grinned, despite herself, remembering the sudden lurch as he, deaf and blind, ripped her ship out of the sky in rebellion against his lady's mind control. Lem had no doubts that Jei would have taken out his tormentors on his own eventually.

But—as a tiny rivulet of sweat began to trickle down Lem's

spine, the voice, or the coolness, or perhaps simple logic, rebuked her—she had to admit it wasn't likely Jei could've then escaped with his life. Killed everybody, yes—survived, no. Not against two Stygges with that kind of hold on him.

She was glad, at least, that she'd been there—that, at least, was not a waste.

And if she could get through this filking planet crust to the extraction point, she could finally see him again.

Suddenly the boulder hiding Lem's secret tunnel *straight-up exploded behind her.*

The sound of the blast threw Lem's nerves into high alert; sparks lit around her in a forcefield as she whirled, mace raised. Splintered rock fragments like knives shot past her as a beam of light hit her face.

"What the bloodseas?" Lem exclaimed.

The silhouette of a shocked civilian stood at the entrance to Lem's secret tunnel, his hand outstretched like a claw, jaw agape. Lem couldn't see any explosives or mining equipment on him —had he—?

"Did I just—did—did I do that?" he gasped.

Yup. He'd blown up the rock with his bare hand.

CHAPTER TWO

Lem

NOW? RIGHT NOW? REALLY?

Lem strode over to the boy who'd blown up her secret door
with a low growl, her own surprise lessened under the insistent need to *act* to cover her tunnel back up. The guy stood
stiff, his hand outstretched, as if still leaning on the rock that
was no longer there. Decorative cloth wristbands dangled and
danced as he trembled, tracing tiny circles in the air, the only
motion around his frozen form. Lem recognized him from the
class a year below hers: Laaru, his name was. Not insufferable
—actually a really sweet kid. Lem ate lunch with his crew
sometimes.

"Anyone else with you?" Lem called; mostly she didn't want
to deal with any soft chicks just itching to report unauthorized
mining to the Administration. Like Kym.

"I—what just—am I dying?" the civilian stammered, gripping his own wrist with his other hand.

"No, but you're killing me," Lem muttered, trotting to
clamber over the rubble to reach him. She wasn't too surprised
about the explosion; back in the Stygge training center, where the
Growen tried to create super-soldiers, Lem had heard of a
trainee who could blow up rocks with his mind. This was differ-

ent, but close enough: powerful em-chemistry could manifest anywhere, in almost any species.

But it sure was filking inconvenient for this little shaggy dude to suddenly discover his talent the day she needed to escape. She'd reached the opening now where her once-hidden mineshaft joined the main hallway, and Laaru wasn't alone. His two best buddies were trotting over, and it wouldn't be long before others further down the tunnel looked up and saw them gathering here.

Oh, how Lem missed just knocking people out. *Not his fault, just a civilian ...*

"Get in here, now," Lem ordered. "I need this to stay hidden. Yeah, you two, also." The three humans looked at her, stiffened by her tone. Lem forced herself to smile. "Please."

"I—I think I need to go to the medic's office!" Laaru stammered.

"No, you super definitely don't." Lem could see shadows further down the lit hallway starting to stir. "You do that, and they'll round you up."

"Round me—*what*?"

Lem didn't want to *grab* a person just discovering his abilities —wouldn't really do to scare him and then *explode*—but a sudden silence threw her heart into palpitations: someone had shut off the automated mining equipment down the hall. *They're coming this way.*

"We've had a good school-year, right, guys?" Lem asked through a strained voice. "Like you all don't hate me, right?"

Xunst, the almond-eyed black-haired human who didn't say much, shook his head. "What? No, we're cool. We're friends."

"Okay then friends, check out this completely unauthorized tunnel I made!" Lem stepped back with a stiff flourish and a tense laugh. "Please come in. Watch the carpet."

"Should you be joking around right now?" Curly-haired ever "practical" pale boy Nevik pointed at Laaru's trembling hands. "We heard the cave-in—is he okay?"

Footsteps approached, boots and skittering claws on stone. *Aaaaaaaah.* "Laaru," Lem stepped one leg back, down into her hidden tunnel with her elbows on her front knee so she could meet the guy's downward stare without bending. "Laaru, you are more than okay. Just don't touch anything and I will explain what is happening to you. But you *gotta* listen to me and hide in here *right now* or they will ship you off."

"What the hell are you talking about?" Nevik asked. "What happened?"

Xunst was already in the shaft, admiring Lem's handiwork—he didn't need a second invitation to adventure. Laaru looked up into Lem's eyes through the hair falling over his face. "How do you know?"

Lem threw her fingers in the air and let sparks fly. "I know."

Everyone's eyes widened.

And that was how a disgraced ex-military freedom fighter lured three civilians into a dark hole, and then had to figure out what to do with them.

First things first: *hide.* It took Lem seconds to carve out a rough chunk of rock wall with her mace; with a grunt, she shoved it over the cave entrance atop the rubble of the exploded boulder.

"Hold on, how can you lift that thing?" Nevik asked. Despite his small stature and youth, his ultra-deep voice brought a sense of authority, almost accusation, to the question. "And where'd you get the laser staff?"

I'm one of those Contaminated monsters you keep hearing about, Lem wanted to snark, but her brain stopped her from blurting things these days. Some things, anyway. "One question at a time," she said. "Laaru, you're electromagnetic, and—follow me this way, please, everybody—and if you tell anyone, you'll get scouted by the Growen."

Xunst kept up with Lem, but Nevik and Laaru picked their way over the rough rocks with such tenderness she wanted to beat them both. *Hurry up, I need to meet Jei!*

"I'm electromagnetic? That's—that's impossible," Laaru protested, hands up in the air. He shied away from his friends, who still didn't know why. "None of my parents—hey but wait, how—" His voice squeezed into a near-squeak. "Blowing up rocks has nothing to do with magnets."

"You blew up a rock?" Xunst paused and looked up from his tunnel inspection.

"It's not always hereditary," Lem answered Laaru, "and without some kinda tissue analysis, you kinda gotta assume it's controlled by *some* alteration in your nervous system. You did it with your hands, right? I knew of a guy who did it using intense ultrasonic waves at some frequency we can't hear. He was probably a chemosynth, of course, with some kind of calcium-build-up-organ-thing or something but ..." Lem tilted her head, listening for voices outside as she raced to her dig site at the end of the tunnel—as much "racing" as you could do trailed by someone who'd just discovered they're living dynamite—*hurry, hurry*—

"That's impossible," Nevik protested. "Humans can't generate that kind of biochemical energy."

"Just like blind people can't develop the ability to echolocate?" Lem smirked, flickering sparks around her fingers again to emphasize her point. Her brain danced through escape scenarios. If someone opened the tunnel ... it was dark here, at the end, so maybe ... "The nervous system is strangely adaptable," she added.

"Adapting what's there is one thing—suddenly growing new systems out of nowhere is something else," Nevik panted. "You're comparing a firefly to an atom bomb. There's a reason no one believes in punctuated equilibrium or abiogenesis anymore."

"I don't know what to tell you, guy," Lem said, trying to estimate how much further before she would've reached soil uninterrupted. "Ain't science supposed to be about understanding the world as it is, not trying to make it fit what already makes sense?"

She laid her hands on the rock. Was it realistic, to try to—

"Okay, playing along here, and not trying to challenge you—you clearly know something we don't—but how do you know he'll get scouted by the Growen? And I mean, is military service even a bad thing?" Nevik asked.

Lem scowled, glad the kid couldn't really see her face by the light of her mace. "I was tracking them a couple years ago when they were actively hunting people with electromagnetic abilities for their Stygge Army. Things have cooled since we shut down their training center, but they still keep an eye out for new abilities."

"Oh come on, that's a conspiracy," Nevik laughed. "Some hidden mountain prison in the middle of a Revelonian national forest? No way. You must have misunderstood the situation."

"Must have. Guess I *misunderstood* the months I spent getting tortured there. Just some miscommunication." Lem managed an angry smile as she waved Xunst back a few steps from the wall. "Laaru, come here and put your hands on this rock."

"O-okay." Laaru obeyed, holding his hands up like they were dirty. He placed his palms, and Lem stepped close to his shoulder.

"Whatever anyone tells you," she said in a low voice. "Don't let them show you to anyone until you're ready. You can't take the risk that I'm telling the truth."

"How do I—how do I make sure I don't hurt someone?" he whispered back. Poor guy—sounded like he was whispering to hide the fact that his voice might break otherwise.

"What were you thinking about when the rock exploded?" Lem asked.

He dropped his head. "I—don't want to talk about that."

"Cool." Lem waved Xunst and Nevik behind her, and powered up her body's energy field to protect them. "Do it again. You gotta learn what triggers it."

Before Laaru could even answer, shards of rock exploded past Lem again. Xunst hit the deck; Nevik yelped, a low cry like a choking sabertooth cat.

"Everyone okay?" Lem asked, grinning wide. She'd found a faster way to tunnel.

Laaru panted. Nevik stood jaw agape, and Xunst's eyebrows raised, but neither was hurt. Lem kind of wished she could've prevented them from seeing what their companion could do, but after a year here, getting back to Jei mattered more to her right now. The main hall outside rumbled as the mining equipment started back up again. No alarms yet ...

"Keep going, Laaru," she said. "Just straight forward and up. You'll want to learn how to control it, but for now just focus on firing it again and again. Learn the 'on' button. Wear it out." To the other two: "While he works off that energy, I'll answer your questions."

But Nevik had lost his ability to ask anything. He shook his head and blew his breath out with an overwhelmed whistle, both hands in the pockets of his baggy work pants.

Xunst tilted his head, rising, and brushing himself off. He was calmer than Lem would've expected. "So you're Frelsi," he said. Lem was astonished by the lack of judgment in his voice— just friendly curiosity. *I'd bet money he's secretly Contaminated*, she thought.

"Yeah," she said aloud, forgetting that she actually wasn't Frelsi anymore. "But that's not important right now. I know you guys are all pretty good friends. It's pretty filking crucial that you don't out him. It'll start as what looks like some kind of scholarship opportunity. Sometimes they'll pretend to get you out of a bad situation. But once they know you've got the thing they're looking for, they will try to turn you into a weapon."

Nevik found his tongue. "Isn't that—what you are? If you're Frelsi, and electromagnetic, then you're like—like that guerrilla fighter who tore up an entire Growen supply center with his bare hands. On Luna Guetala, I think it was? Bloodseas, I thought that monster shyte was fake, but—"

"Aw, that? He was just worried about me, that's all," Lem joked, dismissing Jei's infamy with a flippant wave of her hand.

It wasn't at all like her, and she almost laughed out loud, tickled by the stiff, awkward silence as the other two tried to process what she'd implied. She sobered: "I'm kidding. What's important is that you understand a lot of the information we get out here is pretty twisted. The people with money make the news—that's just how it is. There's a difference between being enslaved as a super-soldier to kill kids, and using your powers to defend the people you care about. And until you know the difference, it's best to keep all this shyte hidden. Oh—Laaru stop, stop right there—"

Pebbles were starting to fall into the tunnel. Laaru would break into the meeting cave up in the upper crust any moment. "Laaru, I'm gonna touch your shoulder, okay? Don't freak," Lem said. She pulled him back and set him by his friends, guiding him with her touch so she could look him in the face. "How do you feel?"

"Crazy," he said. But he was speaking, not whispering, and his voice didn't break. He took a deep breath. "What if I think of *it* when I'm not paying attention?"

"Then either you'll blow up whatever you're touching, or this only works on certain materials. Let's not test that right now." Lem patted the side of his arm, steering clear of his hands but trying not to look like she was. "You should see if gloves protect you, man."

"Okay," he said. Lem gave him another pat and turned toward his work. The faintest blue glow flickered through the red silt and small rocks now trickling down into the shaft: the meeting place with Jei lay just through there. A twinge of guilt tugged at Lem—poor Laaru. He was just discovering this whole new universe without anyone to guide him, and she'd *immedi-*

ately used his emotional distress as a shovel. Very practical. Very Growen.

She'd gotten used to feeling that background shame; she swallowed it, and threw on a cocky grin. "You guys need to get out of here," she said. "You got classes still, right? The rock slab at the door isn't as heavy as it looks—the three of you should be able to pull it back without exploding it or knocking it down on yourselves."

"Wait, where are *you* going?" Nevik asked.

"I'm graduating," Lem grinned. She gave Laaru what she hoped was an encouraging last nod, and scrambled through the loosened dirt to the cave above.

CHAPTER THREE

Lem

THE EARTH SQUEEZED AROUND LEM'S SHOULDERS AS SHE PUSHED through it, breath held and eyes squinted. She gripped cave floor as rock scraped her ribs—the hole wasn't exactly as big as it needed to be—and huffed through her nostrils as the ground birthed her. Grit scratched her skin and dust threatened a sneeze and through itchy near-blindness she focused on the blueish glow, and now the large cavern, the shape of a ship over there, and kicking, kicking, squirming—

A firm hand gripped her forearm, and together they pulled her up.

"Let's go," Lem coughed, stumbling forward as she blew sand off her face. She could hear that the distant hum of the mining equipment had shut off again. They needed to get the hell out.

"Roger that." His familiar light bootstep punched the cave floor behind Lem as she sprinted for the long silvery needlecraft parked nearby. The two-man fighter glittered in the dark cave, the blue glow of its ready and waiting engines beckoning like—like home?

Did she have a home?

Thoughts of thick velum on enormous leaves and Biouk fur

in a treetop nest all faded under the anticipation of swinging herself into the black back seat and getting forever away from this land of insipid monotony. She dove toward the needlecraft's side wall—

"Whoa whoa whoa!" An invisibility tugged her backward, and now Lem saw Jei for the first time so far, running behind her in a loose black jumpsuit. He caught up to her with his hand outstretched and closed his fist; the unseen tug stopped as he powered down his em-pull. "Come on, I haven't seen you in forever! Let me get the door for you," he said. But as he placed a palm on the ship's side, and the wall slurped open, Jei winced. He was trying to play it off as joking chivalry, but Lem knew what he actually meant: the polymerwall on the side of the ship wouldn't take her DNA anymore since the Frelsi had canned her, and instead of phasing through the ship wall, she'd almost face-planted into it.

Lem played it off just like Jei did. "Psh, you *better* get my door, son, you're filking late," she grinned, ducking down to clamber into the gunner's seat. Dim lights pulsed on the floor as she sighed with the comforting give of the cushion. The rough embrace of the worn straps across her chest, the little click as she hooked the security mechanism shut—well, it felt like a kind of home.

"'Son'? Lem, I'm two years older than you. I was the one waiting for you. Always am." Jei chuckled from the pilot's seat just in front of her as he slid his palms across the compuwall control system to activate it. The back of his chair pressed so close to Lem he was almost sitting between her legs, but she'd always felt safer in small spaces like this anyway. She didn't love all the physical contact of cramming into a one-man blastercraft or a Growen Maggot, but this narrow needlecraft, with the walls just wide enough for elbow room, the cushioned chair between them—this was the safe closeness Lem missed. Everyone here on Beryllia kept such a distance from each other physically that Lem constantly felt cold.

"Age is nothing. Girl brains mature faster than dude brains," Lem retorted.

Copper-colored space-ready panels outside closed around the whole ship with a heavy clunk. There was a moment of complete darkness; everything vibrated for an instant as the engine revved; then the dim floor-lights shone constant, and the tapered front wall flickered once before lighting up with a steady view of the cave outside. There was a soft floating sensation as Jei drew his palms up the compuwall in front of him and the ship rose under them—gone were the days when he used to jerk them off the ground for takeoff.

"I think you might be the exception to that," he quipped back. It didn't really matter what they said, just that they were talking, and they both knew that. The ship turned right, away from the small hole Lem had squeezed through—it looked a bit like a sand lion's trap from all the way over here—and the cave walls spun around them, and then a dark opening yawned ahead. The ship shot into the darkness, its front light casting eerie shadows through the chasm. It was said these upper crust tunnels belonged only to predators and lost souls.

Jei wove through the narrow twists and vast pockets, his palms dancing across the compuwall as the ship moved with his fingers. They picked up distance from Beryllia's livable terraformed depths, and the compuwall turned orange to show the atmosphere outside thinning—*come on, come on*—

Lem found her knee jittering. Shyte, finally, soon: real natural light. Finally about to get out of this drab mole-world. *Hurry up!* Here, so close, it was so much worse—she ached to leave so much she couldn't breathe.

At last they broke out into space, diving out of their dark hole into the deep.

Lem cringed, and gasped.

Wow, it was big. And vast. And swallowing, with light and color and naked darkness and *no walls at all*—

"Breathe," Jei said.

Yeah. Yeah her pulse was way high. "Filking heart tryna dig a hole in my sternum," Lem laughed, but it was for show, for his benefit, not a true emotion, because she knew he shared her fear of open spaces—another side effect of the Growen torture chamber that supposedly never existed. She breathed, and rubbed her fist against her knee, and laughed again. "Crazy shyte, huh?"

"I figured it might be worse after you've lived underground for almost a year." Jei spoke in a low voice, almost a whisper.

"It's not worse," Lem said. "Look, see?" She held out her hand. "Barely shaking. It's much better. I hate that place so much, man. I missed space."

"It is strange. I've always loved space. I don't get triggered as long as I'm in a ship."

"Have you ... had to do a lot of ... spacewalk maintenance? Outside?" Lem asked—also in a quiet voice. She didn't want to draw him into uncomfortable thoughts, but she also knew since his severe demotion Frelsi Command had given him more unpleasant duties, and—it wasn't like watching a crash, not morbid curiosity, more—she had to know what she'd left him with. What her work had cost.

"I've been fine, Lem," Jei said. "I feel like a prisoner all the time with the constant checks and calls and monitoring and repeated lie detector tests every time I go somewhere—but I mean, I'm still doing missions. They need me."

Yeah, they needed him. Not her, though. Lem chewed her lip as her chest tightened; Jei immediately backpedaled: "They need you too. They're just afraid of you."

"Psh, they're not afraid of me. For all they know I'm second-string leftovers," Lem grunted, turning to the wall with her cheek on her fist. "They don't know what I can do. Shyte, they don't know that Sterba coulda deflected their missile easy if not for my brain-worm, and they don't even know for sure Morda existed. They'd all be dead without me but they've got no clue."

"I told them in my debrief—"

"I know, we've been over this a thousand times," Lem growled. She saw his shoulders stiffen in front of her, and she softened her tone. "It's cool, man. They couldn't possibly keep me. They didn't believe me before I went AWOL, they couldn't trust me after my Growen time—I mean, *you* get it more than anyone." Before he could wince at the memory of his own manhunt against her: "And you know I don't mean it like that. We're cool."

Jei sighed. His hands pulled back from the compuwall, and the ship slowed, then stopped, floating now amidst the stars. Beryllia lay far, far beyond them, just an ugly scarred fruit-pit turning in space. Jei unbuckled and turned to sit backward in his seat, facing her with his arms folded across the back and knees just outside hers. Flaxen hair fell across his dark tan face, and his clear eyes almost seemed to glow in the shadows.

"They really are afraid of you, Lem," he said. "It's not that you're not needed."

"Meh. I don't think I coulda been a good Frelsi cadet anymore anyway," Lem said. "Don't get me wrong, please, but that Growen uniform, it—it's heavy. There are people I still think about who could've been good guys under the right circumstances, who just never got the chance." She looked away from him at the wall for a moment. "Doesn't excuse what they do, though." She shook herself off, and with a stiff-upper-lip kind of grimace turned back to him. "But all that monitoring you're under? Nah, not for me. At least Command thought I'd be safe on Beryllia. That's an okay goodbye present."

"I heard there's a lot of pro-Growen educators in Beryllia's school system. Has that—affected you, at all?" Jei looked away, clearly ashamed of the question, but Lem felt it—the scar, the distance between them they couldn't cross again even sitting here knee to knee. The hint of the possibility that she could still become a Growen secret weapon after all. It stung.

But before Lem could answer, Jei corrected himself with a curse. "Bloodseas, of course not. Sorry. I'm sorry I keep doing that to you." He, too, shook himself off and put on a strong face. "Let's talk strategy."

Lem nodded, but the sting remained, and intensified, because she didn't want to talk strategy. She wanted to know how he'd been—wanted to ask about her family, her brothers and sisters, her parents, her dear Cinta—"Sure, yeah. So I'm like, your consultant?"

"Yeah. I just got full authorization to use civilian resources again, and that's you. You don't have Frelsi fort access—your DNA won't work with any polymerwalls—but no one can stop you from helping me liberate Retrack City. That's not even Frelsi territory. There's no claim there."

"Technically I'm still ordered to safety exile on Beryllia, though, right."

"That's made-up shyte. There's no regulation that can keep you anywhere once you're cut loose. What are they gonna do, put you on staff duty? Make you swab the mess hall? Gonna be hard to inflict discipline when they can't even contact you." He nodded to her left wrist, where not even a faint tan line remained in her chestnut-bronze skin: she no longer had a Frelsi wristband. Jei's, on the other hand, now bore a metal security cover to keep him from cutting it off or tampering with the vitals monitor.

"Never thought I'd hear Mr. Perfect Record Jei Bereens talk like such a rebel," Lem murmured, leaning her chin into her hand to hide her grin. "That why you're wearing black now, instead of that combat uniform you used to keep so sharp?"

"Never thought I'd hear Lem Benzaran worry about uniform protocol," he teased back. "What was it you said? It's an army, not a fashion show?"

Lem laughed. That seemed so long ago.

"Have no doubt, I'm still me," Jei continued, pivoting back toward the compuwall up front to pull up map readouts and mission briefs. "This whole operation's entirely above board. I've worked my tail off to get that kind of trust, and I've convinced them I can handle you if things go sideways."

"Can you, though?" Lem asked the wall. She didn't move from where her chin lay in her hand, elbow resting on her seat.

"Can I what?" Jei turned back toward her.

"Handle me." Lem didn't meet his eyes.

CHAPTER FOUR

Jei

THERE'S NO SOUND IN SPACE.

But inside the needlecraft, there were tinkling dings as tiny bits of rock and ice bounced off our hull. There was the hum of the biosupport system. The soft beep of the onboard computer. The rustling, as I shifted my weight, of the plain clothes I wore now instead of the uniform that constantly reminded me how painfully I'd lost my rank. Our breathing: her, the rebel too off-script for the rebels, and me—whatever I was, now.

Louder than all these sounds echoed the words I'd said to her last year. We might as well be there now, bathed in the burnished-orange glow of the underground tunnels thick with the sweaty scent of clay as the bomb vest wires slipped under my fingertips and my jaw gnashed on the acrid meal of certainty that she'd joined Diebol and he'd double-crossed her anyway and I was surrounded by her lies, Morda's lies, bloodseas, lies from Njandejara himself, it felt like, as my self-hatred for caring bored through my midsection while I *filking saved her life anyway*, and the longing to punish her for starting it all just slipped out between my bitter lips.

Last year.

I was the one who told her the heat death secret she *wasn't* supposed to hear—who turned her vision of herself from hero in waiting to villain in embryo.

"Can you?" she asked me now.

"Can I what?" I turned back to face her. I wasn't going to help her remember this.

"Handle me. If things go sideways."

This wasn't her standing challenge to spar, eyes sparking like the red mace that used to twirl over her wrist right before our boots hit the forest floor with a blast of earthen scent and flying leaves. Her eyes now stared dead at the wall as she slouched in her seat, chin in hand, brooding far too much like our mutual archenemy. "I asked Cinta," she said. "It was true, what you said. That I'm supposed to end the universe somehow."

I forced my shoulders to stay loose and my face assured. "Lem—I'm definitely not in a place to question your relationship with Njande, or with your adopted brother, but to my understanding, all that stuff's kind of vague, right? You run the risk of making it self-fulfilling. The point of the story was to bring you closer to Njandejara, keep you from cracking, so what if it's a metaphor? An *internal* universe?"

"A metaphor would be a shyte thing to get tortured about." Her grumble was muffled in her fist. "Cinta lost his claws over it."

"Maybe you don't understand what your internal universe is worth," I answered.

She almost scoffed—I saw her consciously hold her breath to stop herself, and the uncharacteristic cynicism perturbed me. Her eyes stayed on the wall; her mouth still hid behind her cupped hand as she leaned on her elbow.

"Diebol believes in the heat death," she said finally. "Bricandor's finding a way to make it happen."

Heat flared in my tone. "Diebol is a liar, and Bricandor? The old man talks to himself, and lets his top officers kill each other off in the name of 'moral natural selection.' Bricandor is *literally* insane."

"And yet over and over again he's eons ahead of Frelsi diplomacy, sucking planet leaders into his orbit with the *gravity of his mere personality*." With a flair of lavish vocabulary, again more like our mutual enemy than herself, Lem sat up and met my eyes. "Jei, he's got pacifist educators preaching kid-killing—people who won't even raise a shoe to squash a bug." She pointed behind us toward the mined-out hollow planet. "There's this whole parents' rights movement on Beryllia right now where young civilians think it's progressive for parents to euthanize kids who might be Contaminated. Or disabled. Or just inconvenient to career goals. I don't think you realize what a feat of mental gymnastics Bricandor accomplished to pull that off. You have to really know how to package this mercy killing shyte to make people believe it, and that kinda manipulation requires a *solid* grip on reality. He's not crazy." She pulled a data chip from her pocket, and slapped it into my hand. "Look at this."

I turned the chip over in my fingers. Hmm. Civilian made, one of the newer models about the size of a fingernail, with silvery-blue lining, and four prongs. I snapped the small compatibility viewer off my wristband—couldn't plug unknown chips directly into the Frelsi network—and slipped the chip into the viewer.

An image appeared on my palm: an educational grant document, addressed to Beryllia's top education officials.

"The Growen want to fund hands-on material science engineering classes for youth?" I narrowed my eyes. "That's awfully charitable. In exchange for what?"

"In exchange for nothing. No strings attached. Look at the terms. It's not weapons research. But look at the curriculum." She motioned with an upward jerk of her chin, and I scrolled down.

"So—they want people to dig for large crystals." I tilted my head. "With ... very specific neodymium impurities." The skydancing warrior who now haunted my dreams used to use her mace's neodymium crystal to focus her abilities. We all did it, but no one quite like her … I shook my mind back to now. "You think they're upgrading the Stygge super-soldiers?"

Lem shook her head. "Nah, they can make neodymium laser cores for super-soldier maces from any industrial ore, and look! They're asking for intact, natural neodymium crystals. There isn't even anything in the curriculum about YAG doping."

YAG—yttrium aluminum garnet—was the sister compound to neodymium in the crystal cores of most lasers. Aside from industrial magnets, Nd:YAG crystals were the only practical neodymium use I knew….

Lem pointed at the document displayed on my palm. "This is a *huge* amount of money just to find naturally-occurring neodymium crystals," she said. "And it's not just Beryllia. Online there's a *surge* in bounty hunters and treasure-seekers looking for precious gems with neodymium impurities. And I happen to know the Frelsi are monitoring another Growen search for something that sounds a lot like these same crystals on Forge."

I tapped my finger in the center of my palm to copy the document, then squeezed the compatibility viewer to spit the chip back out into Lem's hand. "I get that you've been reading hunter forums, but since when do you know about Frelsi missions I don't?" I asked.

"Since they hired bounty hunter Lark Scrita to escort a clandestine Frelsi operative to Forge yesterday," Lem said.

Ah, that made sense. I'd never quite gotten a read on Lem's relationship with the Bont lizard mercenary, but I knew they had an understanding that involved a lot of sharing. Lem gave me another upward nod: "When was the last time Command wanted something so incognito they wouldn't send their own special forces?"

"The Spaces Treaty, Lem," I answered. "They can't have our guys getting caught in Uncontested Zones, you know that."

"So why didn't they send *you*? Don't give me any bull about disgrace or treaties. You're cheaper than a civilian mercenary, you still do illegal retrieval missions for them all the time, and here they trust you to take out an entire city's worth of Growen opposition on your own." She leaned in, her eyes on fire. "No, Jei, the last time they brought in the Ebon Shadow and Lark Scrita it was because *you and I were not available.* You were AWOL, I was Growen. For whatever reason, for the purposes of *this* neodymium mission, they can't trust you. Wonder why?"

I leaned back, chewing my lip as my fingers tapped on the leather of my pilot's seat. She waited while I finished her analysis: "You think Bricandor's building something that will focus and amplify someone's powers to accelerate the heat death of the universe. You think Frelsi Command has reason to believe that someone is you, and that I'm too close to you to trust." I shook my head, but made sure to keep my tone kind. "Lem, I'm sorry, but you're neither a god or a devil to these people—if they really thought that, they'd be hiring someone to assassinate you."

She became much smaller now, her knees tucked up by her chest. "No, I know. I don't think they know it's me. I think they know Bricandor's doing something weird, and they're trying to figure out what it is. And I think they left you out of it because they think it has something to do with electromagnetic powers, and after last year, they know what people like you, or Sterba, can do when pushed." She swallowed. "No one suspects me. I don't think Bricandor even knows it's me. But if the trail does lead back here … if it looks like I'm going to ruin everything …" Her big eyes seemed to glow in the dim light, focused on my face with painful earnestness. "I need you to take me out."

I wanted to shake her. They weren't delusions of grandeur— not coming from someone who'd foreseen the Frelsi nightmare last year—but—shyte, this was premature. "Lem, you don't know what kind of super-weapon he's building. We can look into your theory, but I'm not going to kill you before you've done anything wrong."

"That's not what I'm asking. I'm just asking—"

"You don't need to ask, then." I looked outside for a moment as my face heated. "After last year you know damn well I'd take you out if I had to."

"No. You saved me from the bomb. Even as your enemy."

"That was Njande, not me," I said.

Njande. His name on my lips lit up my mind with a memory from an ancient text—*where two or more are gathered with my name, I am there.* I'd invoked him. Summoned him, if you could "summon" a being that existed outside of the timeline, *around* time, even—like a feathered cat curled around a toy. I couldn't feel him anymore—after last year, I couldn't even hear him—but he was here, and the tightening in my chest softened with a solution to Lem's angst.

"Lem, Njande already told you how to get around this whole issue," I said. "Just stay close to him. That's it. Maybe it's not that dramatic, anyway. Maybe there was some tiny action from you that was supposed to set in motion a bunch of other actions toward the end of time, and since you didn't give way in the interrogation center, that future's already changed—no more heat death. Either way, you can just stay close to Njande. Should be easy enough, right?"

She ... didn't answer? She fidgeted, dropped one knee, and looked back at the wall.

Shyte.

It shook me that she didn't find this easy anymore. Her confident love for her invisible one was so core to her *identity* that it'd annoyed me in the past. And now? It was as if the sky was wondering whether or not to stay up. I gripped the back of my head. "Bloodseas, did I do this, or did it happen gradually while you were on Beryllia?" I asked.

Her shoulders slouched. "I just ... I'm not convinced Njande wants me anymore. And ..." I recognized a faint hollowness in her eyes as she turned back to me. "Something else does."

I laid my chin down on my crossed arms. Shyte, I knew Lem had been plagued by a dark interdimensional force while working for the Growen, but she hadn't mentioned in our distant communiqués that it still haunted her *now*. "That what you mean by the weight of the Growen uniform still on you? Heavy?" I asked.

She nodded. "Yeah. But on Beryllia everything's muffled. Like by believing it enough, the population's willed the ba-eaters, and Njande, all far, far away, almost out of existence. So now instead of a pounding voice from the Accuser, it's just this constant vague thought that maybe I'm the enemy ... like I was supposed to take up Sterba's cloak or some shyte. Stupid shyte. Like Njande hates me."

"At least you can still hear Njande," I said. There was no bitterness in my voice, but she cringed now.

"You haven't been able to fix it?" she whispered.

"Even went with Cinta to one of the Biouk healers." I wasn't angry about it, just ... sad, like I'd sold all the color in my vision and all the music in my ears for a cheap win, and now couldn't go back on it. "I think there's a genetic component. The Admiral stopped hearing Njande over thirty years ago." I still didn't call my biological father *dad*. "He was always kind of against me hearing. Like tolerant, when I came out to him about it, but like he knew it would just be a phase. I think there's a deformity in the part of his brain that picks up theta waves."

"Theta waves?" she asked.

"When you meditate, or pray, or you're in a deeply relaxed state of mind, you give off theta waves. That's how you connect with interdimensionals. You know how Diebol thinks Njande wants to use our brains as a portal to enter and destroy our universe? The theta waves are the energy frequency he thinks Njande will use." I smiled, and shook my head. "I'm surrounded by crazy people with apocalypse theories, and I might be the one with the actual brain problem."

"I'm ... so sorry." Lem looked down at her boots now. Oh, Lem. Emotional, hyper-readable Lem.

I reached out for her shoulder with a soft punch. "It's okay.

It's why I've been memorizing those ancient texts like crazy now. I can speak to him through them. It's like getting a letter from a friend, in another time."

She leaned into my fist, and dropped her head on my forearm with a sigh. We were quiet for a moment.

"It's good to see you again, man," she said. "We're gonna get you hearing Njande again, I promise."

"And you're not going to destroy the universe," I said. "Not even a dent."

She chuckled, and finally looked like herself again, crouching on the chair as she nodded toward the compuwall behind me. Her eyes blazed with excitement over a dangerous, toothy grin. "All right. Enough talk. Show me how we're going to take revenge on the city that ruined your lady's life."

CHAPTER FIVE

Diebol

JARED DIEBOL STROLLED THE FACTORY CATWALK WITH HIS HANDS IN the pockets of his studded leather jacket. The secret service guards in the doorways below glanced up at him every now and then with eyes full of curiosity. Or fear. Sometimes fear. He stood out, certainly: their pressed uniforms and silvery body armor looked nothing like the ragged black vest and pocketed pants he wore. But they didn't need the same kind of mobility he did.

Around them automated conveyor belts crisscrossed the factory floor, punctuated by scientists in gray lab coats and robotic arms injecting samples or sealing packaging. Chemicals bubbled in a large sealed tank in the far corner, the heart of the production.

Diebol leaned his forearms on the cold railing. "How many?" he called down.

The lead scientist didn't stiffen, or snap to attention—Diebol liked this about him. The hoary man stood straight already, as if waiting for the question, and met Diebol's eyes with calm self-assurance. Without even glancing at the compupad in his hands he answered: "Two thousand samples by tomorrow. Enough for a trial run. We'll stop production to avoid waste until we receive your results, but we're poised for immediate ramp-up afterward."

"You're my favorite for a reason, Sanders," Diebol grinned. Several soldiers tensed—he rarely grinned—but Sanders gave him a short nod, and turned back to his work, unperturbed by the half-smile that sparked everyone else's imaginations.

If you see the smile, you're about to die, the rumors said.

Diebol had something to smile about, though. He'd bottled the essence of the female Stygge like a fine perfume. He swung himself over the rail and landed on the story below with the light footfall of a feathered cat. With a flourish he plucked one of the finished delivery systems off the assembly line. It was rounded dart like a rubber bullet, but lighter, and rough, with tiny hooks, much like the seeds of plants that spread by falling onto animal pelts.

They'd had a lot of issues testing the delivery system so it could be fired at an unsuspecting target without punching all the way through vital organs, or bouncing off. The goal was to stick, stab, and cleanly deliver the first burst of neurotransmitter into the target before he or she could attempt to remove the device. They'd devised two ways to keep any helpers from removing the device, as well: one, it would deliver an incapacitating electric shock when it began to lose skin contact, and two, if lodged in the cervical spine, it could latch on to the spinal cord so removal would cause death or permanent paralysis.

They'd also struggled to maintain the radio signal to the delivery system from each main control panel—affordably—and Diebol still needed money. But the new efforts on Bijou should take care of that.

"What are we calling these, Sanders?" he asked, turning the little seed around in his fingers.

"Whatever you like, of course. We've been colloquially saying stingers. Or freedom pills," the scientist smiled.

"A little on the nose," Diebol laughed. "May I?"

Sanders nodded, although really he had no choice. Diebol

pocketed the device and whirled to leave the room, stopping in the doorway to give his favorite scientist a friendly joking salute. "You will receive orders about the first target shortly," he said. "Give me an hour."

"We are ever at the ready."

"Of course."

Diebol took five steps down the silvery hallway, then ducked into the nearest janitor's closet, phasing through the polymer-wall entrance as it sensed his DNA and softened with a slurp. He waved his hand over the lock on the inside to guarantee a moment's solitude, and took a seat cross-legged on the floor between two trash-bots.

Diebol had played the long game, and now he finally almost had the win.

The young Growen leader closed his eyes, tilted his head back, and stepped into the hallway in his mind that he shared with his archenemy, lilting along that electromagnetic bond forged in captivity together so many years ago.

In his mind, Diebol's hallway was long and white, with pristine matte walls. They'd been reflective once. He'd ended that two years ago after his "father" tortured him last.

Diebol's boots made no sound as he strolled down the hall toward the abyss at the end. He could see the wooden cage floating in the darkness now. It reeked of fearful sweat, and blood, and cedar.

Comforting, in that old, twisted familiarity.

Diebol crossed the darkness and opened his cage door. It creaked as he entered. That creak had heralded food, punishment, human contact—everything in his childhood followed that creak.

He stretched out his back, then his shoulders, and took a deep breath, feeling his ribs expand to their limit as he took a seat on the floor to lean against the bars.

The shadowed figure in the ivory hallway opposite his began to move now. It shambled with a limp, each step measured and painful. Diebol's heart beat faster—this felt like fear, but bled with anticipation. He clenched his teeth; the shadow reached its abyss, crossed, and found its cage door.

Jei Bereens stepped into his side of the cage and slumped to the ground, covered in rivulets of blood.

"Hey Jared," he winced.

"You appear so quickly these days," Diebol gloated. He'd discovered he could usually summon Jei back here on command now after what Morda did to him.

"Well, you need me, so," Jei shrugged. It seemed casual, but his eyes burned: Diebol couldn't escape him, either. "I'm your only path to Njandejara."

The name brought bile into Diebol's throat. "Whatever twisted alliance you've made with the Contamination from Outside," he sneered. "I'm not part of it."

"Yeah, except I was thinking about that," Jei blew wet hair out of his face, shifting position with pain to lean his head back against his cage door. Agonized sweat gleamed on his forehead. "If it weren't for you, I wouldn't know Njande the way I do."

"I did everything to save you from It. I've tried," Diebol hissed.

"But everything you did just made me want him more," Jei chuckled. "We always want what we're not allowed to have. The glittering facets of the rare mineral in the museum. The neighbor's wife. The colors of the worlds *distance* says we'll never see ..." Jei wheezed, the rise of his chest ragged and jerking. "It's so strange. Since Mera deafened me I can't stop thinking about his voice. About what it's like to live outside of time—to play history like the keys of a musical instrument. To ... feel ... everything. And care about everyone. It's—"

"It's sick, Jei," Diebol snapped. The tortured man before him turned his gut. He hadn't done this. It was the Being's fault. They'd *had* to—

Jei coughed, and closed his eyes for a moment.

With his eyes closed, Jei's face bore the features, just for a moment, of the little boy who once stood between Diebol and his violent "father," jaw firm but lids squeezed shut to lock out the terror: *"Leave him alone! Take me instead!"*

How long had they known each other now? Twelve years?

Diebol rose, and crouched beside his enemy. "Jei," he said, reaching for firmness but unable to hide his gentleness. "I can make you better. All this struggle, all this—attachment. You're being torn between two universes. I really can free you from it." He closed his mouth before saying how. If only he could make this voluntary, though—!

Jei chuckled, eyes still shut. "Free me? It won't be that easy to take me out now."

Diebol tilted his head. Ah. Jei had a bodyguard. "She's back, isn't she."

Jei's lids fluttered open now. He sighed. "What do you want, Jared?"

It was her fault, too, that Jei suffered like he did. Diebol wished they could measure her Contamination like viral load, or radiation—wished he could prove how much she'd poisoned the young "Paradox Warrior." He should've shot her in one of his dirt tunnels underground. Let her bleed, then suck out her last breath with a kiss—

But she, too, served a purpose. A something. A kinship. And a brightness ...

He ached, and it made him furious. *Sever the attachment that causes pain*—he asked the next question with a cold sneer dripping in mockery. "How are her spirits these days? After all of you betrayed her."

"What do you want, Jared?" Jei repeated. Not angry, not triggered at all. Just tired, and firm.

As if talking to a mere child.

How dare you.

Diebol struck him on the jaw.

The crack echoed. Jei's head snapped to the side; pain flashed across the muscles of his cheek, his neck, but his eyes did not flinch, and his gaze returned to Diebol's face with something that looked like disappointment. Or teasing? Was it compassion, or pity? Something Diebol couldn't read, and something he hated, because of late the Paradox Warrior he had always controlled through anger no longer *reacted*.

"Can you feel it, in real life?" Diebol hissed.

"Yeah," Jei answered, adjusting his jaw, and wiping blood from his mouth. "But I know you can't help doing it. You're sinking; it's not going well for you."

"I'm not sinking! It's all very well, I am winning!" Diebol snarled. "I have everything I ever wanted. I am *days* away from a final conquest that will seal every Frelsi fool in a prison of their own bodies, in a—" The intent, listening glimmer in Jei's eyes stopped Diebol's mouth. Shyte, he was being played. He was never the one to be played.

Diebol forced a laugh. "You're getting good," he said.

"I'm always here to listen when you need it," Jei grinned— the enemy grin of old, the teasing Diebol felt comfortable with.

Diebol kicked him, enjoying his enemy's spasm, and backed away to his own side of the cage. Enough distraction. He'd summoned his rival to make a decision, not to gloat. "If you could vacation anywhere, between Bijou, Forge, and Luna Guetala, where would you go?"

Jei heaved himself to his feet, gripping the bars of the cage. "What are you doing, Diebol?" he asked.

"Bijou?" Diebol watched Jei's eyes—no blink.

"What are you deploying?"

"Luna Guetala?" Diebol asked. Ah, a flicker of pain in Jei's eyes—no, too much memory there. He was likely headed there now, but wouldn't stay long.

"You don't have to do this anymore, you know. I know you're tired."

"Forge?" Hm. A twitch in the corner of Jei's left eye. Something there intrigued or worried him. Diebol only had to plant the seed of suspicion to ensure he made the appointment. "I'll see you on Forge, then," he said.

With that, the young Growen leader slammed the door of his cage behind him. He awoke back in the janitorial closet with his good mood shattered. No matter. He would feel better once he ended this war.

CHAPTER SIX

Lem

FIRE FLASHED OUTSIDE THE NEEDLECRAFT AS IT PLUNGED TOWARD Luna Guetala's atmosphere, diving away from the cool of space with a panicking spin.

"Jei?"

The needlecraft's pilot didn't respond. His head drooped down his chest. There was some kind of murmur?

No time for murmurs. Lem ripped out of her restraints to climb over the pilot's seat in front of her. She slammed her hands onto the smooth compuwall and rubbed the panel clockwise to slow the ship's descent, hooking her knees under Jei's seat so she didn't go flying backward as the force of the fall punched her belly through her spine—

"Yo, Jei, you okay, man?" she asked, eyes forward as she directed the dive through the flashes of heat and bursts of clouds. Shyte, she hadn't flown a spacecraft in over a year. Gentle pressure—now firm, to the side—whose airspace had they just plunged into? Over the ruins of Fort Jehu she would've asked for permission to land, but she wasn't allowed on that hallowed ground. They were somewhere near Retrack City now —couldn't land there, either, that was Growen—landing somewhere in the woods—?

She glanced at their destination coordinates on the top right of the viewscreen in front of her and held the ship on course as planet surface rose toward her. She wanted so badly to look, to check Jei's pulse, but if they crashed he definitely wouldn't have one.

Warmth—his scarred hands came to life over hers. "Bloodseas, Lem, get back in your seat," he grumbled.

"You sure? You good?" Lem asked. She'd love to punch him in the head for his tone, but hurtling through the sky wasn't the time for ego.

"Yeah—yeah, I'm sorry—hold on."

Lem unwound her knees from his seat, trying not to elbow him in the face. She clawed the back of his chair to keep herself from slamming against the back wall—the force yanked at her fingers—she snatched her safety belt—sparks flew around her as she focused her neurons on pulling, attracting herself like an electromagnet to where she needed to go—

She got herself seated and strapped in.

The ship turned with Jei's palms now, and he spoke—order restored, dangerous or not, when you did something every day you could multitask. "Thanks for grabbing the controls."

"It was just a couple of seconds. Maybe a minute," Lem said. "But you know as well as I do that a minute during atmosphere re-entry—well. That's death."

"Yeah. There's no excuse. I'm sorry."

Lem understood in his tone what had happened. He'd been sucked into the portal in his mind, leaving most of his brain on auto-pilot—almost a complete blackout. "You gotta break that connection, man," Lem said.

"I've had it all my life. It's part of my brain, my abilities—I don't think I can."

"Maybe you're just afraid to try."

The jungle canopy reached toward them now; verdant shamrock, emerald, and purple leaves shuddered under their wind as they sailed over. "Maybe I'm afraid he'll go insane,"

Jei said. "There isn't much keeping him from what he could be."

"What, you think his abilities will unlock or something? You're like a fuse breaker?"

He put his shoulders and elbows into controlling the ship as if lifting weights; the ship shook as he swerved over a river, fighting for a landing zone. "I don't know. I think actually Njande can get to him through my brain."

Lem gripped her arm-rests—oh man, *so long* since her last space travel. "You never cared about that before. You want him to die as far away from Njande as possible."

"Yeah, I did. But Njande wants to ... save him."

The river basin opened up in front of them as they shed altitude. The needlecraft wove between two large Bangla trees; branches cracked off; everything knocked forty-five degrees to the right; Jei's knuckles whitened as he pressed on the compuwall, one hand rotating, the other swiping right.

They slid into their landing, waves splashing across the viewscreen and river boiling under their glide as the reverse thrusters fired to slow their momentum. Lem's mind echoed her adopted space-lemur brother: *Such good fishing area wasted ...*

"How do you know what Njande wants if you can't hear him?" Lem asked.

"It's there. It's in the ancient texts." With the ship now resting on the riverbank, Jei shut off the engines and cracked his knuckles. A waterfall thundered beyond them. Outside, singing day-lizards called to each other under the caws of parrots, the laughter of canopy dogs, and the squeaking of baby peacock-feathered guinea pigs chasing their mothers. Lem sighed and unbuckled, aching to smell the humidity, the earth, and the plants.

Jei turned; his elbow draped over the back of his seat as he tapped her knee. "It's also in the texts that you were right, by the way," he said. "Njande didn't allow ancient people to cut down fruit trees for siege works, or take both generations of an animal while hunting. War's supposed to be between people, not against the land, and even what we eat is supposed to be in harmony with the universe."

Lem smiled. "Jei Bereens, saying *I'm* right? Psh, never."

He laughed. "Ready to come home?" He unbuckled, yanked a lever to release the space-worthy walls with a large clunk, and pressed his hand through the polymerwall, holding it open for her. The wall split and dribbled under his palm like water, and suddenly, staring out at the brilliant colors as hot breeze blasted Lem's face, she felt … nervous. Her heart raced, and she didn't know why.

"Is it home?" she murmured, slipping out through the gap in the wall.

CHAPTER SEVEN

Jei

THE SUN WAS SETTING IN BLAZING PINKS AND ORANGES AS I clambered atop the needlecraft to sit cross-legged on its warm roof and meditate.

Lem's demeanor had me worried.

My worry wasn't just personal. I'd pulled her into this operation as much for her confidence as for her tank-like fighting power, and ... well, I had kind of hoped to plug into her effervescent, burning connection to Njandejara, to connect with what I could no longer hear on my own....

Didn't look like that was happening.

Lem was right about my connections though. Bloodseas, Diebol had never summoned me during an atmospheric re-entry before, but I wasn't about to let that happen in another high-risk situation. I was going to infect Diebol with the Contamination, or cut the connection out of my brain.

Could I?

My chest began to tighten.

I could start trying again?

I forced myself to focus on the brilliant greens rustling below and around me as I breathed to calm the pounding behind my sternum. Yeah, the idea terrified me. Like ripping out a major blood vessel. Or killing a brother. But I wasn't about to let him and what he was becoming—

But wouldn't he become *worse* if I couldn't reach him?

"Njandejara, help me, please," I whispered into the wind.

I inhaled deeply … let my stomach expand … tightened, then relaxed my throat to warm and control the air as it passed … and let my muscles soften as I exhaled. Then, instead of waiting for an answer I couldn't hear, I flipped through the scans of old, withered manuscripts on the viewscreen of my wristband. Over the last year I'd discovered a system to analyze what messages Njandejara might have hidden for me in the distant past. He could do that—weave me a message in stone, waiting for the moment I'd be born to dig it up. He sounded young when he spoke, but Lem and I figured he was at least as old as our universe, if not the oldest being of all.

So to decode his messages, I'd start with the literal meaning of each archaeological text, then the allegorical meaning, then its meaning in its cultural and historical context, and then finally I'd meditate on it, trying to connect to the mystical personal meaning. Four layers. Sometimes in the meditation at the end I'd almost think I heard him again … but it was important to keep in this order, since I couldn't actually hear, and we humans had a tendency to make shyte up if we didn't start with the facts first.

"*Peshat, remez, derash, sod,*" I repeated my focusing mantra now, starting with the words before my eyes. The breeze flicked at my forehead as my chest relaxed.

I am an alien on this world

Don't hide your instructions from me….

Hidden One. The ancient languages didn't lose much in translation to Grenblenian, but I'd learned to cross-reference the various lexicons put together by Biouk space-lemur scholars to catch the nuances I missed. I'd come to enjoy these detective journeys through the past even more than I'd once enjoyed poring over technical readouts for ships. I still did that, but I'd come to realize I only ever studied tech out of compulsion—

because I wanted to have a leg up on our enemies—not out of pleasure. Same with air-rider tinkering, or training my powers … over time it had all just become the next way to beat Diebol. In some ways, this history study was my first actual hobby.

"Diebol's kind of always had me on a leash, hasn't he?" I said to Njande. The brilliant sunset seemed to cast flames over my black jumpsuit as I shifted my position now, chin on both fists as I gazed over the horizon like I could see my friend beyond it. "I don't know what I'd do if Lem and I hadn't uncovered more of these texts. Not that I cared about them before. It took last year to … well. You know."

Before I was afflicted I wandered away; but now I become guardian over all you say.

"This, exactly." Words mattered now. The "Contamination" wasn't just in theta waves. Every school of meditation from the dawn of time, good or evil, had attributed importance to sound, and silence, and often recorded them both. This was how infection spread through history, from one time to another, from one brain to the next—through words.

Aha.

I smiled. "He's going to be so pissed." I leaned back, laughing into the sky, and I faded into my mind with a gleam in my eye.

It was difficult, these days, to reach the channel I shared with Diebol directly; my mind passed first through the freshest connection, the one forged by chemical intoxication, and I wandered for a moment through an imaginary field of bamboo. I couldn't see anything but shadows and stalks in the pale mist, but I knew I was now atop a distant forest mountain that overlooked the brilliant lights of an unreachable, magical version of Retrack City. My bare feet swished against grass, and soft, spongy earth. There was a cottage near here, in my mind, where Mera—

Mera was dead. This was only my body missing the relaxation hormone she produced, the pheromone that put you into a quiet, receptive state for her neurotransmitter sting to take control of your movements. She was her own good cop and her own bad cop, and the good was so good.

But I couldn't stay. This didn't exist anyway. The stalks stretching above my head always took on this eerie pink, perhaps painted in the permanent twilight of a blood moon, or a setting sun; either way, this place was empty, and no one would walk here with me ever, in this dream of the future that could have been, and so it smelled like blood and burning gymnasium.

I sighed, and moved on with an ache in my chest.

I made it into the connection Diebol and I shared, the two white hallways with a dark abyss between them housing a dimly-lit wooden cage.

A pen materialized in my fingers as I appeared in my hallway and proceeded to make it anything but white. In large scrawling letters along the floor and each wall I poured out memorization after memorization like one of the Retrack City dancers spraying paint—crouching, bursting, stretching for the ceiling in wide bold swaths all the way down the hall.

Then I filled in the spaces between my wild signs with small precise strokes, weaving uniform tiny sentences around and around my giant letters like spellcraft.

Now for the darkness, the abyss of our familiar terror at the end of the hallway, just before the cage we shared in the middle. Here I began to write on the blackness, my words hanging in the air like laser light—

"Holy ..."

There were things here in the shadows. Things I'd always rushed by on my way to the cage. An old table? I bumped my knee against the corner, and something rattled. Shyte, my mother's Burburan shellfish, open with pearls in it ... one of them rolled off the table, and further into darkness.

I thought for a moment I heard a growl.

Shyte.

I didn't dare look away from the darkness. In my periphery I could see my waiting cage, glowing beyond the abyss. I could hurry into the cage, like I always did. I could write the rest of my script there, and weave my infected messages in the air so thick Diebol couldn't breathe without inhaling ideas.

No. There was something else in here that needed to be written on.

It was too dark in that back corner to see anything. I waited still for my eyes to adjust, and they did not.

I almost couldn't breathe. I crouched, feeling for the pearl along the floor, my other hand clutching the pen like a knife.

A bony form lifted its head, and opened its eyes.

Oh shyte.

The gaunt face spread its lips in a snarling smile. Fangs glowed through rotting holes in the cheeks.

It was my mom.

Not as she looked; not as I remembered her. Just the essence of what she left me. A hungry ambition without words, or reason. Something like revenge, but before the inciting incident, predictive hatred in a cyclical timeline.

It was the event I couldn't remember. The reason I wouldn't call the Admiral my father anymore. The secret he kept. Whether she had left us, or whether I'd watched her die, I didn't know.

Was this how I saw her? Did I once watch her change into someone else, or was this only a child's memory of a bombed-out corpse? My tongue clung to the roof of my mouth, thick and dry; my throat closed.

Looks like we needed some spring cleaning in here after all. A lame joke flashed to mind, but my parched, trembling lips would say nothing.

It stared at me. Unmoving. The smile seemed to widen beyond the point of a grin to a grimace, but with the pained glee of rigor mortis you could never tell.

I clicked my pen.

It leapt at me.

I slashed in the air.

It hung above me, dripping, impaled on glowing letters, floating in the air as if lying on a glass window-shield.

You are good, and do good; teach me your rites.

That was the root of me, wasn't it? The question—could my invisible, powerful energy being, really be *good*, given everything that had happened to me? Beyond what I knew of interdimensional biology—that he was too radioactive to touch us directly without killing us all, that he could see the myriad time-streams impacted by each butterfly's wings, that he had to choose the least evil timeline even before all of our competing reference frames hit go—beyond all of that, when it came down to just him and me, this was the root. Was he good?

This was the thing in my darkness that made it impossible for me to trust anyone.

Knowing that suddenly made it very mundane. Everyone had lost someone in this war. I might not even have lost my mother to war—could've been divorce, for all I knew. I'd seen worse than this grilled demon in a hundred waking nightmares.

"I'll see you later, Mom," I said, as I continued on my writing way. I couldn't make her disappear, and I probably couldn't get rid of Diebol's connection, either. They probably formed who I was. But I could write all over them with ancient magic words, and transform what had happened into what was to be.

CHAPTER EIGHT

Diebol

OH, JEI THOUGHT HE WAS CLEVER, DID HE?

Diebol heard the whispering even before he blinked into the hallway in his mind. It had been a long day prepping for the offensive on Forge. Diebol always had his go-bag ready so there was nothing to pack, but with personnel to brief, ship inspections to double-check, flight plans to approve, and of course, the safety of the all-important cargo to ensure—well, when not stalking through someone's office or a cement hangar bay, he'd been texting, calling, or manning the intercom non-stop to fix everyone else's errors.

Now, after sprinting through the warm Alpino prairie in a dusty windstorm, he'd ducked into a janitorial closet for a moment of rest and recuperation.

But as he tilted his head back against the nearby trash-bot to close his eyes, he heard them. Evil ideas and wicked spells whispered just beyond his hearing. He couldn't quite make out the words, but he hated them already.

"Jei, what did you do …" Diebol grumbled aloud.

He stepped into the hallway in his mind.

All that pristine ivory was covered in words. Not just

Diebol's hallway, either. Jei had painted his own hallway, and the cage, too.

"Ech." Diebol tried to wipe the wall off with his sleeve. It stained like blood, and glowed. Diebol's skin crawled with something moist … he shuddered, but resisted the urge to rip the words off himself. Couldn't let Jei take pleasure watching him come undone. He paced forward, struggling to keep his eyes away from the words everywhere. Trite, pithy sayings at the best; slurs in support of interdimensional tyranny at worst.

Oh, it got worse.

The darkness that surrounded the cage between Diebol's hallway and Jei's? That change. That was worse.

Glowing words illuminated ugly truths: over there on Jei's side, some kind of blackened corpse floated in a dusty corner, and ugly jewelry draped across old furniture that cluttered a space once hidden in clean onyx shadows. Shyte, had this room always been so small? Even from here in Diebol's hallway, that dead body seemed close enough to hit with a stone's throw. Diebol had always thought the abyss between himself and Jei much bigger.

And here, as he reached the end of his own dirty whispering hallway …

"Jei …" Diebol growled.

By the glow of an inane phrase scrawled in some ancient language—"*Ani hu ha ohr*"—Diebol could see Bricandor's hooded cloak floating empty in the shadows. It waited for him, and he despised it. Bricandor. The Growen leader who manipulated the universe with decoys and politics instead of coming right out and saying why he fought. The traitor who promised to stamp out the interdimensional Njandejara while cavorting with an interdimensional of his own. Diebol stepped into the darkness with his head low and shoulders hunched.

"Die," Diebol muttered.

But the cloak followed him, bobbing in the air, a phantom of the future, and now he could see whips and electric wires littering the floor all across his side. He'd always rushed through this space with the sensation of something following him, and didn't appreciate the obvious revelation Jei forced upon him. Yes, he knew. He knew he lived in Bricandor's shadow. Thank you.

Diebol didn't even reach the cage. Oh, he wanted to. He wanted to summon Jei, to punish him. Work off some steam. But he couldn't stand it in here anymore. He would come back later to clean it off. Right now, though, he needed to leave, before the infected air cursed him, too.

No matter. He would see Jei in person soon.

LEM

A light breeze filtered through Lem's puffed hair; her dark coils frizzed out of control in this humidity, but she'd take that over the cold of Beryllia any day. She didn't love the sweat dripping down her spine, though.

Retrack City sprawled below the two Paradox Warriors now, a tangling cluster of metal and noise in the center of the bustling jungle. From here, atop the water tower on the hill, they could see the white spaceport hub stretching for the sky like a Revelonian cloud tree, long spindly metal branches sprouting into wide landing platforms. Ships buzzed around the spaceport like hummingbirds flitting along white flowers.

Jei's eyes strayed toward the art district, and the colorful airships that floated there trailing tiny silhouettes on rope. The girl he'd fallen in love with had been a sky-dancer.

Lem laid a sympathetic hand on his shoulder. Jei said nothing, but his back seemed to relax under her palm.

Shyte, for some reason this made her miss Cinta, and being a little sister cuddled up with all that fur in the Biouk nest years and years ago.

"Let's roll," Lem said.

Jei sighed, and they got to work. He crouched to begin sawing open the water tower with the laser edge of his mace handle; Lem shimmied down the tower leg with an explosive remote in her mouth and a backpack full of bombs.

Retrack had always posed a problem for Frelsi invading forces because of the spaceport: with the thick jungle almost impossible for landing, both civilian and military ships came through the spaceport, so either you bombed it and took out a bunch of interplanetary civilians, or you left it, and the Growen flooded the city with reinforcements. Retrack's tightly-woven streets and alleyways left no room for tanks without significant civilian casualties, either, and there was always the risk that no matter what you did the Growen would carpet-bomb the citizenry and blame it on the Frelsi to the media. They needed to separate the enemy from the civilians.

There was one break, though. Retrack City had a civilian curfew—in about an hour, no one without a military permit would be out in the streets. So that was a good time to set off some explosions by the water tower. Bring out soldiers only, and all that good shyte. That didn't solve the problem of the spaceport reinforcements, but Jei had a reputation that would bring every last blitzer out to him: no need for any all-out firefights in the streets between Growen and Frelsi armies. Frelsi ships couldn't land in the spaceport without being shot down, and a heavy ground force couldn't get close unnoticed, but Jei could, and a light Frelsi air-rider battalion could wait for his call far enough back from the perimeter to avoid detection until he called for them to occupy the city. Plus, Jei's powers magnified with every opponent, so the more soldiers they could muster, the more power he had to take them out. At his baseline, Jei could em-pull about his weight, but when powered up by opponents, Jei could throw vehicles, smash buildings, hurl entire armies in the air with a pull, or a push.

Lem was here to make sure the spaceport closed to reinforcements—and test a new weapon. She'd always wanted to try an actually nonviolent solution to mass warfare, but they'd never had enough power to make it happen. You could stop a little kid from doing something stupid or evil because you had longer arms, but when you fought with someone your own size, you had to play dirty, and maybe kill, to protect your family. The solution to war, then, was to become so much bigger than your opponent that you didn't even need to hurt them to stop them.

So—paralysis.

But not like shock-cartridges and stun blasts, since that required, well, aim, and put you at a disadvantage against the people trying to kill you. One of the Burburan expats at the Frelsi Hiding Place had created a paralytic that worked on liquid skin contact, so you could literally spray a rioting crowd, and put them all to sleep. Growen blitzers wore full space-ready armor, but they also had their laundry schedule standardized across the force—one of those small, insignificant details Lem had learned during her time with them.

Insignificant like the new weak spot in the underarm seam of the uniforms.

Lem slid down the hill of the water tower, soil and moss spraying around her boots. She vaguely remembered it wasn't very Biouk of her to leave a scar in the dirt—more human, maybe even more Growen, than anything—but as she tumbled toward the bushes at the bottom she shook the thought out of her head. The city rose before her in tall mud rectangles and silver spirals. A glance behind her—Jei was well hidden at the top of the tower, and the guards asleep at the bottom of it remained propped up and unconscious, as they would for the next twenty-four hours. This now-tainted water tower supplied the western district, where the Growen barracks—and laundry— were located, by the foot of the spaceport.

Lem crouched to plant her first explosive in a shallow hole at the base of the hill, almost without stopping her slide. Twirl to the side, run along the hill—next explosive—all right—another couple meters—Lem counted paces with sawing breath, a bit weaker from her time on Beryllia despite her regular exercise regimen.

Aight, explosives done, time to cross the city. Jei should have delivered the sleep toxin into the water tower by now. "The field's yours," Lem said into the borrowed black communication pendant around her neck, diving out of the underbrush into someone's yard at the edge of town. A hissing alarm sounded as she crossed the manicured lawn of perfectly round purple leaves —but alarm was kind of the point. Lem dashed to the nearest wall, a tall, mud-brick affair, and threw her electromagnetic pulse downward to propel herself up like a rocket.

"Roger that," the pendant answered with a crackle. "You clear?"

"I'm clear." Lem dashed across the roof and leapt to the next flat housetop. Twenty minutes to curfew. The last bus to the skyport would pass by the next street in five … four … three …

Lem jumped into the air, arms outstretched like a sky-lizard's limb-sails. Her body slapped against the low-flying bus with a stinging thwack; sparks glittered around her, reflecting off the pink and silver surface—"Come on, stick, stick, pull," she muttered, skin tingling and cold—her fingers clung like gecko feet as her biological static shock made her like a magnet. Hot wind battered her cheeks. She clambered under the bus's left wing, behind the bulge of the engine turbine, to stay hidden from any blitzers they passed on the street.

And there were *tons*. From scouts in slim, heat-friendly light cloth with bare wrists and ankles, to standard blitzers covered toes to hair in atmosphere-modifying spacesuits, the city streets looked almost like a straight-up Growen base as the civilians crawled into their homes.

Well, it wasn't really like a Growen base. Not with all these different buildings, the mud-towers and spirals, and the colorful ships. Growen outposts always looked either industrial or sterile to a girl who'd spent her formative years in the trees.

Dusk raced toward the bus as the base of the spaceport tower approached. Just in time, too—Lem's fingers grew weary of the tingling, her biceps burned, and the hot wind in her face had her tearing up like a baby's funeral.

Behind her, the explosions went off right on schedule.

"I hope I get a chance to see your work this time, Jei," Lem chuckled.

"I hope not, it's ugly," he said. "Good luck on your end."

"Psh, luck? Never had it. Never needed it. See you on the other side."

CHAPTER NINE

Jei

BRILLIANT BLUE EXPLOSIONS LIT UP THE HILLSIDE BELOW ME AS sprays of dirt and moss splashed sky-high against the fiery orange fading sunset; across the city, the spaceport loomed like a bony finger silhouetted against the red heavens, waiting for Lem.

Here atop the water tower, I stood tall and raised my hands. A knot rose in my throat—that nervousness, as always these days, that my powers might fail me, but I swallowed it as blitzers poured through the streets toward my hill. We had enough people to trigger my powers. We had a backup plan and an escape route. I'd slept the night before to charge up. I hadn't used my abilities for a couple days. I even had a lightning rod I could orbit and throw to draw close-range electricity away from me—that was in case anyone here knew that you can turn off an em-warrior's abilities completely by shocking their nervous system. Over the last year I'd brought my recharge time down to about twenty minutes, but twenty minutes without abilities against an entire army simply meant death. So, instead, I'd learned how to levitate the rod enough distance away from me that I wouldn't get hit by electric splash, and so far, it worked well, in practice.

All that was left was to trust and make it happen—the rest was beyond me.

Beyond me. It was so unlike me, letting anything *be* beyond me.

"Njande, make it good."

I took a deep breath and reached out for the air-riders shooting toward me up the hill. I clenched my fist—

Oh, there was no reason to be nervous.

When my palm closed all fifty flying vehicles crunched under their drivers with the screech of bending metal. Blitzers fell out of the sky into the bushes in a hailstorm of armor. A mere swat of my hand grounded a gunship; it smashed into the jungle with a burst of flapping birds and fleeing day-lizards. My mace floated by my right hand almost without thought, spinning into a force-field to deflect the multicolored swarm of oxidizer death cartridges fired by panicked blitzers; at a distance to my left I levitated my lightning rod to draw electric off shocks.

Soldiers scrambled to set up rocket guns at the base of the hill. I couldn't see them clearly through the smoke of the bombs, but I could almost close my eyes and *feel* every nervous system down there. Just follow down their arms under the rustling of the fabric and trickles of sweat to the hot metal, and—yeah, I found the guns.

Another closed fist, and the huge barrels pinched shut before anyone could load a single rocket.

It looked like the laundry tip had worked out for us. The frightened cries about unanswered calls to the barracks seemed to say as much. Given a normal Growen response time, I'd expect at least double the troops here now. Since we'd gotten the temporary paralytic into the western water supply with enough lead time, it looked like everyone trying to suit up found themselves knocked out by their freshly-cleaned uniforms.

A successful test.

But now came the hard part.

Deep breath. Mostly just ground troops now, charging up the

hill. A few more air-riders zipping in from the left—crush those vehicles, lower the pilots into the bushes—bloodseas, all of these distractions from the actual weapons test. I needed to get the chemical past the armor; if I couldn't, I'd have to kill these guys. I'd done that before—shyte, last year I'd crushed them by the droves while Mera and Diebol squabbled over how to get me to stop—and they were child-killers after all. But the idea of a universe where we ascended to a power beyond simple warfare, that evolution, it needed a first technological step, and—

I just needed a small leak in each uniform. Lem had told me the weakness at the neck that we used to aim for was now reinforced; we wanted to try for the underarm seam with only cloth between the plates of body armor. Could I tear—

Too many targets. It felt like I had too many limbs to keep track of. One invisible hand spun my mace; one invisible hand gripped my lightning rod; my fingers flicked soldiers down the hill to try again as another invisible hand now plunged into the water tower, trying to draw out the liquid using the polarity of the negative oxygen molecules in water—

Stop. Too many details. I dropped the water back down in the tower underneath me and tried to refocus on the people swirling around the crown of the hill. Another gun team set up a cannon to my left, and two more air-riders flew in above me—

A hot breeze sucked sweat off my neck. Maybe I didn't have the power to do this. Maybe I was only good enough to destroy. They deserved it anyway.

But something ached within my core as my eye caught the empty space where the art district's airships had flown earlier. My sky-dancer traipsed through my mind, ribbons trailing from her wrists and ankles, hips swaying with the happy wires bouncing under her toes kilometers above the bustling city—

But her eyes, dark and slanted, cried.

The sunset blinked red with the memory of her death in my arms. My chest burned with grieving fire. I could feel her, and I could feel her in every one of *them*. Lies and circumstance, genetics and society, tragedies and privilege, these stories created the enemy when just a breath of change, a butterfly wing in the right era, could have created someone else. She'd mused once that perhaps ghosts were just a place's memory of the people who died there; if so, then her traces lingered in this city's every magnetic field, because here, before I ever met her, was where she really began to die.

My limbs now moved on their own under her shadow. My fingers flicked open; shards tore off the top of the water tower. Liquid rose around me without touching me. My palm lifted, and then shoved forward like an open-hand punch: the bits of tower whistled through the air like arrows with water for tails. Every blitzer's weakness seemed to glow in the dark for me, and all down the hill hissed the sound of tearing cloth with the rush of flying water.

And as the hill became quiet in the dusk, I couldn't feel them, or her, anymore.

They were asleep, stilled by the toxin splashed through their torn uniforms.

My mace fell into my hand; the lightning rod clattered to the top of the torn water tower, and I had to step on it with my boot to keep it from splashing into the contaminated liquid. I could feel a headache starting to come on, just a little burn in the back, as I pulled leather gloves from my belt and slipped them over my hands. No more powers; if anyone was still awake down there in the shaded bushes, they were just one or two people, not enough to keep me at full throttle. And I'd likely drained all my battery anyway. It felt like it. My skin tingled. My lungs strained against a weak chest. I wanted to sit down.

But we weren't done. "Lem, I'm calling in the Frelsi," I panted into my wristband. "You all set to block reinforcements?"

There was no answer.

"Benzaran."

No answer.

And a lightning storm was brewing around the spaceport.

CHAPTER TEN

Lem

ACROSS THE CITY LEM SQUEEZED TIGHTER BEHIND THE ENGINE turbine of the bus as it lumbered through the air just above Revelon's clearing streets. The spindly white spaceport, Lem's target, loomed just ahead. The hot wind died as the ship slowed. ...

Not a moment too soon. Her fingers burned, still gripping the underside of the bus's wing with her static cling. *Hurry up.* Her elbows shook. Blood rushed to her head, pulsing in her face. *Hurry up and land, you slow ass civvy pilot.* It wasn't electromagnetic skill at this point, just a straight-up test of muscle failure. Lem breathed, trying to speak patience into the churning rush in her belly—

Except—uh-oh.

Lem expected the bus to turn up toward one of the spaceport's landing platforms—to the "branches" of the metal "tree" reaching over the city.

But the bus didn't turn at all. It was heading straight for the spaceport's stem. The stalk. The trunk. Like, collision-course.

"Oh shyte, Njande, it's a polymerwall," Lem grumbled. She was getting tired of not being able to get into places.

Lem eased her cling to scuttle across the wing, over the top of it, scanning for somewhere else, anywhere else, to climb. The ship began to penetrate the wall—

There was nowhere to climb. The spaceport wall ahead was perfectly smooth, above and below—and oof, a long way down to the tiny city streets and that *huge* ventilation port in the ground, fan blades spinning spinning spinning behind that giant grate.

Uh … well, Lem could probably hold on to the trunk with her static cling, but actually reaching the nearest platform stories and stories above would take hours she didn't have—and what happened if her muscles gave out or her powers flickered?

The wall had swallowed half the ship now. Its edge slurped across the helm in slow motion toward Lem.

"Do I just cut a hole in the tower, Njande?" No, she still needed to stay incognito to keep troops away from here and focused on Jei—

But she needed to shut this place down *now* to keep the Growen from summoning new ships.

Oh shyte. The wall oozed across the bus's dorsal wing; Lem was standing on the edge of the back tail now—*need to decide, need to decide—*

A crashing crackle sounded across the city. Over her shoulder, Lem could see the blue explosions lighting up the dark edge of the jungle under a zipping rainbow of oxidizer cartridges. She couldn't make out Jei's distant figure on top of the water tower, but she knew she was now late.

"Filk it." Lem whipped out her mace and smashed the polymerwall, surfing the back of the bus into the spaceport through a cloud of rubble.

Time to bring the chaos.

An alarm screamed. The huge hollow white tube stretched for stories above and below Lem. She had seconds to take stock of the vehicles buzzing around—a few other squat-winged buses, a handful of moving elevator platforms—and moments to stop the whirring alarm. Where was it? Lem's balance shifted as the bus under her boots turned upward—where—where—shyte, the bus was almost vertical now. Lem crouched and stuck a hand on the bus tail, rubbing it up and down to ensure static stick. The proximity alarm?

"Filk it." Lem fired an arc of electricity from her finger back to the wall. The bolt danced across the tube, bouncing back and forth along the crumbling hole Lem had entered, illuminating the whole huge panel of damaged material. The shock took out the panel's sensors; the alarm silenced.

Not that it made much difference—after that alert Lem now had less than two minutes to stop all outgoing transmissions and seal off the landing platforms.

But—*oof*—her torso slammed against the back of the bus as it climbed stories; she hung vertical now, her entire body-weight dangling on static cling from just one palm. Well. She did need air control at the top of the tower. She'd just planned on taking an elevator, not flapping around like a leech on a sabertoothed cat. There was a hand-crank-powered rescue lift that didn't require DNA access—for emergencies and power outages—parked on the lowest spaceport platform, where she and Jei had thought buses landed. That's what she was supposed to be riding right now. There was another crank-lift lying somewhere on the tower floor far, far below her now, but that meant less than nothing …

Ooh, but there was another elevator on its way up now: an automated white service platform carrying four Growen blitzers in gray cloth uniforms. Lem hurled herself forward, ran up the back of the bus, and leapt for the platform in a ball of sparks.

The blitzers panicked—apparently not used to girls hurtling at them through the air—two of them raised weapons to fire, two yelled about damaging the tower, one fired anyway, the cartridge swerved around Lem's electrical field, and Lem slammed against the side-rails of the elevator gut-first. She grunted as the air burst out of her, *almost* unaware of the pain as she flipped herself up and over the railing to hit two blitzers in the face with her boots.

"No armor today, guys?" she asked. Her voice sounded like a cough: wow, that bar took more out of her than she expected. She ripped the gun off one of their belts, yanked back the slide while her finger clicked it to stun, and *bzip, bzip, bzip-bzip*—

All four blitzers hit the deck unconscious. "Shyte, I shoulda used the thing I brought with me," Lem remembered: she still had the gun on her belt with the inky sleep capsules.

Thirty seconds. Thirty seconds to seal off the landing platforms and stop all outgoing calls. Lem snapped her mace back onto her belt and ripped a small black button transmitter off the jacket of the guy closest to her.

"Attention, this is an emergency transmission," she spat into the button as the elevator flew toward the ceiling. "There is a biological weapon incoming. Seal off all landing pads immediately."

"Message received, this is the tower—who is this?"

"General Johnson, Control Number 3-215," Lem recited her dead former Growen identity code from memory, with a pompous voice to match: "And dammit, you imbecile, this is an emergency! Did you not hear the alarm?"

"Well, I'm going to need to verify that, sir or ma'am, we have a situation at the end of town and we're in the middle of calling in reinforcem—"

"Oh, shut up," Lem growled. Fifteen seconds and the elevator still wasn't near the traffic control center yet. Lem looked around for options, eyes narrowed against the rushing air blasting down from above—but there wasn't a faster ride than this one. With most of the civilians in curfew, and most of the Growen forces dealing with Jei, the buses had all parked, and except for a few elevators this place was mostly empty. And it wasn't like she could scale the tower on her own. So then what?

"Show me something please, Njande," Lem growled.

A large water pipe ran up the side of the tower.

Press in case of fire, said a pale silver button on the elevator control panel.

"All right, I guess we have a fire." Lem said. If she remembered right, the spaceport also drew water from the western water tower they'd polluted. She yanked her atmosphere hood from her left cargo pocket and slipped on some gloves. Skin covered, she punched the button.

Massive sprinklers burst throughout the tower. Lem heard cursing through the transmitter—and then silence.

No one would be calling in reinforcements in their sleep.

"All right then." The contaminated water struck Lem's masked hood with a heavy pitter-patter that reminded her of huddling under giant leaves with Cinta, hunting for mud-grubs. Shyte, this whole planet made her miss him. Hopefully his mission was going well on Forge—

Uh-oh. The elevator platform didn't seem to plan on stopping as it neared the ceiling. "Ceiling's a filking polymerwall, too, Njande," Lem grumbled. The guards could phase through to the room above with their DNA as keys, but Lem was about to be squashed like a mud grub in Mali's protein flour. She whipped out her mace again and thrust the glowing bulb above herself—

Too slow, bad angle, not enough room to swing! The ceiling resisted with such force Lem's shoulder was yanked out of joint. Pain shrieked down her arm as she slipped with a curse—

But her mace wedged at an angle, spikes in the ceiling and handle on the lift floor, temporarily stopping the elevator. She was un-squashed for now.

Not for long, though. The elevator's boosters whined; the surface under Lem's boots jittered as the lift's gears ground and rockets struggled against her mace. Railings whirred and folded beside her, trying to prep for docking. The ceiling cracked, and oozed, super-heated by her weapon's spikes; a horrid chemical smell stung Lem's nostrils as the staff began to melt through the elevator floor, too.

Shyte, the floor was breaking faster than the ceiling. "Yo, Njande, I need to stand on this!" Lem cried out.

She almost thought she could feel him chuckle.

He wouldn't.

Would he?

You're going to get him killed.

Oh man, not now.

He's going to die because you're too slow.

The hissing threat pulsed through Lem's brain in time with the stabbing throb of her dislocated shoulder. Lem felt cold fingers reaching through her back, into her chest, as if squeezing her lungs—

It's just the Accuser. He's a nobody, she forced herself to breathe—

But her body panicked and with a strangled roar Lem gripped the mace in her other hand and *shoved* her way through the ceiling. The elevator slammed in place beneath her; inertia sent her tumbling forward into the center of the tower control room.

Finally.

Lem was surrounded by three hundred and sixty degrees of computers and windows. Sleeping bodies lay on the floor in puddles of azure liquid, glowing in the soft shadows cast by the monitors and the setting sun.

Lem had to close those platforms and prevent reinforcements. She scrambled forward for the emergency lock, a huge red lever jutting out between two huge computing towers—she dropped her mace, gripped with her good hand, and yanked.

A pre-recorded emergency message blared over the speakers and flashed on every computer screen, warning nearby ships to stay away. This emergency message would override any other outgoing transmissions on all frequencies within a 10-kilometer radius. Outside, a clear dome closed over every platform, sealing off every branch of the metal tree. Quarantine procedures: no one in or out of the port.

Lem breathed a sigh of relief. Okay. No reinforcements. Everyone in the spaceport showing even the slightest skin now lay unconscious—all the armored units guarded the landing platforms outside, so anyone still in full spacesuit was now locked in one of the sealed domes.

"We're almost done. We did it. Kind of," Lem said, half to Njande, as she allowed herself a weary stretch of her back. "Just gotta tie up the sleeping beauties in here." She bent to pick up her mace …

Oof, something *burned*. Lem looked down.

Shyte, a melted bit of floor had seared a hole in the shin of her pants leg. Her gloved hand shot out instinctively to wipe the hot gunk off her leg—

Oh, shyte, now she had blue liquid on her skin.

"Filking fantastic," she groaned. Shyte! She wasn't done yet! She didn't have time to get paralyzed or fall unconscious or whatever happened first—

Things not going well?

Lem looked up, and saw her nightmare.

CHAPTER ELEVEN

Jei

THE JUNGLE BEHIND ME SWARMED WITH FRELSI SOLDIERS NOW; THEY poured past the water tower under me in color-shifting camo, skittering and stomping through the underbrush and zipping by on shadowy air-riders, down the hill and into the streets of Retrack City.

I'd called them in without Lem's confirmation because, well, we didn't have much time to occupy the Growen barracks before the remaining blitzers there recovered enough to sort out the mass fainting of their comrades by the laundry pods. And Lem *had* closed the spaceport—even from here I could see clear quarantine bubbles now encasing the landing platforms, and my wristband showed an emergency override on all communication frequencies accessible from the tower. Incoming civilian ships circled a few times before diverting south to the next port town; military ships would have to land in the treacherous jungle, where we could fight without civilian casualties. Sure, there did seem to be a—hole—or something—in the spaceport stem? But Lem always came through, however she did it.

What had me worried was the *lightning* coming from the top of the port tower.

Bloodseas, I was dizzy. The grip on my gloves squicked on

the wet metal of the water tower ladder as I leaned away from it, squinting—I couldn't actually make out the control center windows across the city, but the lights there flickered on and off. I shook my pounding head with a hiss, focusing on each boot-step and each ladder rung on my way to the ground.

"Operations, I'm heading to the spaceport to recon ahead of your attack squad," I spoke into my wristband. I'd found they tended to loosen my leash more when I stated my plan, instead of asking for permission.

"Negative, Alpha-Twelve, you're—hoooly shyte in a sand-basket, what was *that*?" Sergeant Strong's deep Hoernig-amphibian voice squeaked at the end of his sentence, and I took comfort in that.

Because I wasn't the only one who suddenly remembered the destruction of Fort Jehu.

A power surge blasted from the spaceport. The entire block of buildings around it flickered, the glow of life through their poly-merwalls struggling against the encroaching night for just a moment—before the streets went dark.

I don't know what Sergeant Strong remembered, but I suddenly heard water that wasn't there, hissing from a shower head that became a weapon when every computerized system in our lives turned against us under Sterba's control. My skin remembered the scalding; children's screams echoed in my mind under mechanical whirring and wild flayer fire.

That destruction in our memories? It had started with a black out.

"I think you want me down at the spaceport, Sergeant," I said, and he didn't argue as I swung myself onto a Frelsi air-rider and took off across the city.

LEM

Terror surged down Lem's spine in bolts of what looked like lightning, and she had no idea why.

It's all in my head. It's all in my head. I'm having a bad reaction to the sleep drug that got spilled on my leg. I might even be asleep right now. It's all in my head.

But she could now see her own energy field: not just sparks, definitely not the invisible electroencephalic signals an EEG machine might read, but an actual spreading wall of blue electricity blooming into an enormous orb that enveloped first her, then the nearest computers, now the control room with such brightness she couldn't see outside it.

See? Not real. I know my abilities: static shock, static cling, and an innate field of charge that repulses metal shot at me. This—giant—dome-field—isn't real.

A shadow appeared just outside the crackling wall of light— Lem's heart raced, and something moist soaked her underarms—

A familiar figure parted the wall and stepped into the ring.

Whoa.

"I killed you before," Lem said, shivering as if freezing. "Why would I be scared of you now? If you *were* here."

"Because unlike fear, terror is biology. You can't control your biology," answered the figure. Lem recognized the words—the "voice," if an energy being that invaded your thoughts could be said to have a "voice." This was just the Accuser she'd picked up during her time with the Growen.

But the image didn't match the voice. The form that stepped into the ring belonged to a patchwork human sewn together from thousands of pieces, long blond frizz jutting around her head like lightning. Her violent blue eyes glowed brighter than even the walls of light around them, with a piercing depth to their hue as if someone had punched two portals to another world through her skull.

"You're looking better, Sterba," Lem quipped. "Very ... put together." She couldn't stop shaking. She heard her teeth chattering.

"The one person who actually understood you, you killed." In three strides Sterba crossed the space between them; her hand shot out to Lem's throat. Lem moved to block, and found her fingers moving through the air as if through thick honey, in slow motion. Claws dug into her jugular—

Long adult space-lemur claws. Reality blinked, and sped up; now Lem was on her knees, gripping her throat as burning crimson liquid trickled between her fingers. No more Sterba. A space-lemur flashed around her now, first kneeling in front of her, chuckling, then behind her, beside her. She didn't recognize him.

But she did recognize him?

What a nonsense-burger question! It's not real. I'm asleep. Have to remember to report this crazy nightmare reaction. The test studies didn't have anything like this—

"Test studies? You're so stupid. Don't you see what's going on?" the space-lemur laughed in the throaty consonant-filled Biouk tongue.

Lem squinted. Where did she know him from? Long, flowing black fur, with chestnut highlights, and the outline of a light brown triangle tracing his ebony forehead. Adult fangs jutted from his muzzle, down to his chest, and one of his giant, face-sized ears bore a sharp tear. Like a Cinta palette swap, but with scars, and muscles—bigger, and older. Alternate reality Cinta.

"I'm not Cinta, you idiot!" He laughed—that wonderful hissing, snarling Biouk chuckle, not like the loud, wide, vowel-filled laughs of humans. It was strange how sinister and *good* he sounded all at once. Like coming home finally, only to see it full of ghosts.

"Going through some serious effort to filk with my head, Accuser," Lem grunted. It gurgled in her bleeding throat.

"Ha! I'm not even the Accuser!" He put her face between his

leathery paws, squishing her cheeks like a baby. She reached up to grab him, but he was already on the other side of her electric field, like a blink, or a computerized glitch—a shadow silhouetted against the spreading wall of light.

Lem tilted her head, struggling to rise to her feet. Shyte, she was losing a lot of blood in this dream.

But the palette-swapped Cinta-guy wasn't lying: it was true, he didn't sound like any ba-eater she knew, and definitely not the Accuser. This dream had started with the Accuser's voice, sure, but *this* voice? This voice was different. Her brain itched with the certainty that she knew it from *somewhere*, but she couldn't place it in that face, behind those fangs.

"Okay, fine," she gurgled, standing now. "Who are you?"

He leaned close; blood still dripped from his fangs. "I'm you," he whispered.

That made sense. The voice, the swagger, the easy way he picked up her mace and spun it over his head—yeah, it seemed like her. The self she'd always wanted to be as a little girl while she watched the other space-lemurs play, or even later, when she felt alien among the other humans.

"The self locked inside," he finished her thought.

"I don't think I locked you anywhere," she said. "I've tried to live like the person I wanted to be, I—shyte, why am I so terrified?" Her heart fluttered so fast she thought it might just explode, aching and flopping and flittering behind her sternum. She pounded her chest with one fist, trying to force herself to breathe. "What the hell?"

He laughed again, pouncing here and there on the tips of his toes as her field continued to spread. Now the control room, now the landing pads, now the city streets ... the people in the quarantine bubbles screamed in this dream. She could see the city around them now, outside the tower, in the eerie light of her electric field, cut off from the jungle and the moonlight. Houses lost power, and the streets seemed barren of life.

"So you're mad at me," she said, palms on the windows.

"Mad doesn't begin to cover it, *Jaika*," he said.

JEI

I leaned into the evening wind as my air-rider whined through the narrow city streets, weaving past colorful blue, red, and green mud-brick slums, through sculpted gardens behind chic metallic spirals, and down the main dirt causeway toward the towering spaceport. All the culture and wealth of one of the most important cities on Luna Guetala seemed washed out, ghostly, in the blue light of the electrical dome spreading from the spaceport like a skirt woven of lightning. It buzzed, louder and louder as I drew nearer, and a scent like meat frying, or rubber burning, beat against my face in the breeze. A wave of darkness went ahead of it, heralded by flickering lights at the surf's point; I could feel static in the air, and hear crackling under an eerily-muffled cacophony of distant, distant screams.

Other Frelsi air-riders scattered around me toward their disparate objectives, some rushing west to solidify our hold on the city, others on my course, overhead, with their own orders to secure the tower. I clocked the field as it spread—at this rate in about twenty minutes it would cross the threshold of the western district to engulf the city's famous hospital, and in thirty it would have a third of the civilian population inside it. Okay, what was the voltage and the amperage here? I'd seen Lem fire targeted electric shocks that could sting, but I'd never seen her kill with them. So could I hope for a wall of stinging, stunning energy? The biggest threat seemed to be something like an EMP blast emanating in that wave of darkness ahead of the wall—definitely bad news if it reached hospital generators.

Was this Lem, or someone else?

It just *looked* like Lem, for some reason, and no matter who was causing it, something had gone wrong.

Gah, I was well and truly drained of power myself. My head rung like the vibrating core of the stabilizer in an air-rider. The dizziness rocking the world reminded me of my first time in space.

One of the Frelsi air-riders racing toward the tower began to surpass me overhead—

"Slow up!" I yelled to the pilot.

She didn't. She zoomed toward the field with her lips pursed like she could taste the medals of honor already—and her air-rider shut off abruptly in mid-air.

I swerved upward as she fell like a stone; my hand shot out to snatch her collar, yanking her off her seat; her air-rider dropped out from between her legs and crashed below us with a floral explosion.

"I told you to slow up, soldier," I said, zipping a ninety-degree turn and swooping my vehicle down toward the street. As soon as the over-eager hero's feet touched dust, I released her collar, and leapt down off my air-rider, leaving it idling on the ground just outside the wave of darkness. Other small vehicles were falling out of the sky like flies around an electric zapper. We both trotted forward into the darkness, and looked up, up, up at the towering wall of light.

"Is it the Anomaly?" my unwanted companion yelled, coughing and rubbing her neck as she recalled the nightmare of Sterba's power in Frelsi slang.

"No," I said. But I didn't know any more than she did. I looked at the street around me, and at the items on my person. I didn't have any juice left for electromagnetic shenanigans....

A leaf fluttered by my boot in the dust. I stomped it, picked it up, and held it out into the lightning.

It wasn't lightning. The leaf didn't singe. It sparked, and stuck in the wall as if in a spider's web. *It's some kind of a photon-emitting static surge.* My lips tightened. *This is Lem's.*

"You mind getting stung, Captain Seria?" I asked, turning to the fallen air-rider pilot who I just now recognized.

She raised and cocked her flayer rifle. "Only if you do," she grinned—the kind of grin that told you she *just knew* she looked cool in the eerie shadows, with her bangs blowing about her perfect sweaty face. The grin of the Miss Perfect who'd won the promotions while the rest of us got screwed for the cause, of the overachiever who'd leave you bleeding if you failed Frelsi excellence. She'd constantly tried to get with me before I fell into disgrace—and then she'd gone far, far out of her way to find evidence for Command to exile Lem, to convince them that our version of last year was too sick to believe. A ribbon-hunter and show-stopper, *she was what I was once*, and I'd never act on it, but for a split second I wanted to shove her into the energy field to exorcise my past self.

"Your flayer rifle's dead," I said instead, nodding to the core of her weapon, darkened after the EMP wave. Her action hero pose deflated, but I didn't have time to take pleasure in glimmers of petty payback. The field washed over me.

It did sting, like the strike of a whip during my first captivity, or the shock waves Diebol used to power me down—bloodseas, these memories—but it wasn't for long. I shoved forward, swimming through energy, and with a pained grunt and a breath found myself inside the sky-high dome of electricity.

It was hollow in here, as bright as a searchlight, with everything cast in stark shadows. The buzzing stilled. I didn't have time to guess why—some wave canceling out some other wave in phase—but the almost muffled quiet seemed pregnant with doom.

Seria stumbled in after me without flinching—hate her or not, we were still surrounded by Growen housing here, and I needed her warrior's scowl at my back. I signaled with two fingers above my head, and she dashed to the right side of the street to get some cover. I ran to the left side to keep my back to the nearest building. Heads on a swivel and dead weapons raised for bludgeoning, we crossed the rows of winding alleyways toward the base of the tower. I didn't bother to report in on my wristband—Faraday-protection or not, even that little green screen lay dark against my skin.

Our footsteps seemed muffled. Sweat misted my jumpsuit—I kept expecting the buildings to burst open with mechanized horrors. It was quiet, like this, back then. *Make it happen already, stop putting it off,* my nerves yelled. I told them to shut up. Across the street, Seria's shoulders hunched, and her knuckles blanched with the force of her grip on her weapon; her hardened steel face just *dared* memory to filk with her. She rubbed her throat where her collar had given her a friction burn after I snatched her off her air-rider to save her from crashing. As much as she angered me ... well, she was one of the last fighting-age survivors from Fort Jehu last year. It wasn't for nothing that she'd pushed hard to get rid of Lem.

A sudden pounding vibrated the wall at my back—the loss of power had sealed the polymerwalls shut. Inside, blitzers not poisoned by laundry found themselves in the dark surrounded by comatose bodies. Powered down, none of their weapons could break the expensive seals they themselves had double-reinforced.

"Help! Someone help!"

But we didn't. We knew what it felt like: the confusion, the strange betrayal when a helpful everyday object turns on you—in that moment, you find yourself believing in possession and poltergeists.

It was why everyone needed a scapegoat in the em-powered traitor who was AWOL when our world went to hell.

CHAPTER TWELVE

Lem

LEM WATCHED PALM TO PALM WITH HER REFLECTION IN THE CONTROL tower window as the electric field ate Retrack City from the spaceport out. There were two of them now, in this dream, one on each side of her.

On the left, in a long blue gown, hair frizzing like a halo of lightning over translucent patchwork skin that seemed to glow like kintsugi at the seams, stood proper Stygge Sterba, taller than Lem, back straight as an arrow, and hands folded.

On the right, leaning back on his haunches, muscles deceptively relaxed while light glinted off his sharpened tusks, crouched the impish Biouk that was, apparently, also Lem. One leathery black ear perked up toward her, and the other, torn, lay horizontal, twitching here and there. It was like a smirk, or a challenge. He was laughing inside.

"I get it," Lem said. "My conscience is doing a guilt-trip three-way with past, present, and future. This whole imaginary spreading energy thing—some kind of metaphor for the heat death?" She tilted her head toward Sterba. "And you're here because I got you killed but can't prove it. You're not really her, though. You're the Accuser, right?"

The image of Sterba stood silent as death.

"What about me?" asked the Biouk imp.

"You're a weird dream from when I was little," Lem said. "When I used to want so badly to *be* Biouk, and I didn't fit in with the humans. I don't know why you're mad at me. Am I seeing you because I'm back on my home planet, but since I'm out of the Frelsi it feels like home is mad at me? Why am *I* mad at me?"

"*Ratschica!*" The imp slashed at the window with his claws, spitting a curse Cinta had always forbade Lem from using. As soon as the word left his muzzle, a sudden pleasant tickle welled up inside Lem—a sensation of *fun* she could only compare to stealing food, or tripping someone in a fight. Lem met the eyes of her shorter self, and saw with the gleam there that he knew. But he didn't say as much; instead, he said: "You're stupid. You're not mad? We became what the Frelsi *humans* wanted for over a decade. Put up with all their names and weird glances, the interspecies compromises, the rules. Then you became Growen for *the worst* five months imaginable, and it was like I was being boiled alive in the community grub-brew. And all that *suffocating*, all for what?"

Lem stammered, incredulous. "Dude, we had a year underground in Beryllia to work this out. Why you doing this to me now?"

"Because then in Beryllia you stuffed down the warrior spirit, hid the electromagnetism, like a filthy non-hunter. You plan to do this again with the next chapter of your life, hiding, hiding, hiding? Nah, *bika*," he dropped the slang for a mating age female who couldn't afford a canopy home, "I'm seeing my shot here, and I'm taking it *now*."

"Look, tiny teeth, no one is more real than me. I—"

The icy woman refashioned from stardust cleared her throat. Lem and the angry Biouk fell silent immediately, waiting for their superior to speak. Lem found herself suddenly overwhelmed with the desire for Sterba to turn her head and look her in the eye. Sure, she could see the woman's face in the reflection here on the window as they watched the field spreading outside —but if Sterba turned her head, would that face decay, maggots in every socket? Or would ice crystals crackle across her face from the dead of space? But she hadn't had a chance to freeze solid—they blew her up. Would her face melt off, then?

The curious terror swished through Lem's belly as if her intestines hung outside her body, dripping onto the floor. Lem didn't like it. They'd had so many nightmares about each other long before meeting; it seemed like they knew each other—out of place in their own worlds, isolated and odd and too intense for everyone around them—and for a brief moment Lem had hoped they could both live. But they could not, and now she wanted to see those blazing blue eyes again that no longer appeared in her sleep.

But Sterba's icy form stared straight ahead and didn't grace Lem with even a glance. "You do not feel bad because you killed me," she said at last. "You feel bad because you *didn't*."

"Yeah I did. Dude, you just said I did! Just because no one believes in me doesn't make it true."

"Perception is reality," laughed the lemur.

"No," said the woman in blue. "You did not kill me. Burbura, Skraeli, and Fort Jehu—those actions were me. We are what we do. And you didn't prevent them."

"I was the first one to try!"

"Say that to the dead," Sterba said, her voice as cold as if she herself wished someone had stopped her genocide.

"I had to do it the way I did. I was never going to get anyone to believe me. You were literally a dream. That was my only intel —a dream." Lem growled. Something she hated more than either of these specters had begun to well up in the corners of her eyes, and she brushed it away to snap: "How do I get out of *this* dream, now?"

The reflection of the patchwork space woman, and the reflection of the rebellious Biouk, looked at each other knowingly.

The world flashed again. A furry ball of mass impacted Lem's torso as the Biouk sprung at her—with a sonorous metallic ring her back hit the floor. Lem raised her hands to fight—the Biouk leaned close with a precocious toothy grin.

"What if I told you," he twirled a necklace of teeth around his long foreclaw. "It's not a dream?"

"What?"

The world flashed a deeper shade of blue, and Lem sat up to find herself alone. In the control tower. Surrounded by unconscious bodies as the water from the sprinklers continued its prattling trickle against her atmosphere hood. There was no Accuser. There was no Sterba. There was no angry nega-self, whatever that had been.

There was only the spreading electrical field that was very, very real.

"Holy shyte, the city!" Lem cried out, jumping to her feet. As she did so the field burst outward, engulfing another row of buildings, and brightened. "Oh shyte, oh shyte—I'm doing this. I'm doing this how?"

She wasn't trying. She wasn't pulling or pushing or thinking of out—she certainly wasn't thinking of *eating* all the power in the city. "Okay I have a static repulsion field that powers up when I'm in trouble, repels cartridges and shyte. Maybe this is a version of that. Okay so just sit down, calm down—"

Stilling her heart rate and slowing her breathing did nothing. The orb continued to spread. She saw at least two hospitals in the distance. She saw Frelsi air-riders zipping around the edge of the light. She saw, for a moment, a future where she destroyed *everything* and she didn't want to and she didn't want anyone to get hurt and that was the whole point of this exercise and the new weapons test and she'd been trying not to be *so angry* these days and oh shyte—

Was that it? Was the angry Biouk with the torn ear her internal metaphor for this?

She tried to meditate, to get back into the dream to talk to him, to do *anything* to come to grips, to fix it, to get control—and no matter what she did, the field continued to spread.

JEI

The spaceport towered above us now, a vast ivory cylinder sealed with reinforced polymerwall. I didn't know how we'd get to the top with the elevators out, but I'd have to improvise later —we had less than ten minutes before the field left the western district. I drew my mace to smash through the wall—

It wouldn't power up. Bloodseas, my mace's power cell was Faraday-shielded, and it usually worked even after EMP blasts, so why—?

"Didn't think so," Seria grunted just behind me. "Wristband's not even working."

Yes, I know. But my mace had never failed me. I felt naked without it.

But naked or not, we needed to get in, and I began to trot around the tower, to the left, looking for—should be—

The hole about halfway up the spaceport's trunk, left by a hasty Lem Benzaran, looked as small as a tree-borer's nest from down here. Too far for a grappling hook, if I could even find a downed blitzer to steal it from—gear like that was too expensive for standard Frelsi issue. Bloodseas, how would I get up there?

"Help me, Njandejara," I heard myself mutter with clenched teeth. *No, stay calm.* I loosened my jaw and breathed. "Help me."

I fastened my mace to my belt again, and closed my eyes, trying to remember all the openings to this building from the readouts. There was the street entry here—sealed shut. Lem was supposed to get in through the landing platforms via bus—also sealed shut, and anyway even the lowest branch lay at about double the height of the hole she'd left, so far above even the rainforest canopy that it almost hit the clouds.

"Give me something," I breathed.

From one of the old manuscripts in my mind,

The mountains will be made valleys, and the valleys lifted up ...

"Yeah the world's on its head. So down. I'm going to go down." I sprinted back the way we came with Seria trailing me. We hadn't even considered it with the electricity on—the hundreds of huge fans in the ventilation ports here would make a red mist of you before you even felt it—but that was the beauty of this mess, now, wasn't it? It was opposite day.

The huge grate into the earth lay within eyesight of the hole in the tower—Lem probably saw it from above when she came in. The small service hatch in the grate was heavy, but didn't have a lock on it. Whirring spinning death blades were deterrent enough.

"If the electricity comes back on, we're dead." I made sure to meet Seria's eyes as I said this. I wasn't exactly offering her an out, but there were other ways to help.

"Always wanted to be a red cloud," she shrugged.

We climbed down into the ventilation pipe, pushing blades out of the way like forest leaves. It wasn't a deep hole—just big, and wide, no taller than my height—and the fat pipe turned immediately toward the spaceport tower, but the fans were packed so densely right behind each other it was excruciatingly slow going stepping through them. The darkness stank of rust and cleaning solution; even our soft boots made loud hollow clangs against the floor, punctuating each sluggish minute in arrhythmia. Feel the cold steel through my glove—rotate the whole fan, like lifting a vertical sliding door—bend down under the one blade while stepping over its neighbor to just fit through the angle—

Seria's curse behind me almost had me jumping into a sharp blade. I stiffened, fists clenched. "You good?" I asked.

"Fine. Just cut myself on this thing. We have ten minutes until it takes out the city's largest hospital, by the way."

"Tracking."

"Sure hope no one's on life support over there."

"Tracking, thanks."

Dim blue light checkered through the inside entrance just ahead. Just about five more fans. My back didn't love ducking while stepping over things, not with this dizziness pulsing through my scalp. So close. So close and *so slow*. Just—wanted to —tear everything—out of my way—*breathe. Rushing and cutting off a hand does no one any good.*

I heard myself growl with agonized impatience anyway. Just two more—rotate—step through—

I threw the grate off above us like a man tearing water-boarding cloth off his face, scrambling into a sprint before I'd even gotten to my feet. The emergency crank-lift was right here, a thick brown and red metal platform hooked up to a hydraulic rail system on the side of the tower. Seria kept up—still too slow for my taste—I urged her aboard with a firm pull and slammed the release lever.

The millions of gallons of water pressure held back by that little lever gate surged into the hydraulic rails, shooting us into the air with the speed of a slingshot. I stumbled, and almost fell off; bloodseas, the world was spinning.

"No warning on that start there, at all," Seria coughed, gripping the hand-rail and scowling up at me from her forced seat on the floor. I shook my head, and looked away, afraid I might hurl right on her face. The whole living weapon display left me *so weak*, and I wished someone else could do this—hell, I wished me of an hour ago could do this—but if you hesitated, if you didn't *commit*, people died. There wasn't time for doubt, or misery.

Shyte, I really might vomit, though. There was a time where this would hurt my pride more than anything else. I was over that now, after Mera.

At least the wind of the ascent soothed the heat on my face. Even at this height, as pressure loss slowed us down, the crank-lift climbed almost as fast as an automated elevator. And the control center floor—our ceiling—had another tell-tale smashed hole in it—

"You need to hold the brake," I said, pulling Seria's hand to the lever. "When we stop under that hole, you need to stay here and guard the platform."

"Guard the platform? From *what*?"

"You'll see," I said.

But I wanted to find Lem alone. And Seria's glare told me she knew that. She'd flipped out when she heard I selected Lem as my civilian resource, and she wanted nothing more than to punish the traitor we couldn't trust. Call it tattling or call it intel, she wanted to see what had gone wrong.

She couldn't voice that, though. If I needed back-up guarding our transportation, I needed back-up guarding our transportation, and whatever lay in the control tower, it was far above her combat level.

I just hoped it wasn't above mine.

CHAPTER THIRTEEN

Lem

THE FIELD WOULDN'T STOP SPREADING, AND NOTHING LEM DID mattered. So it couldn't be hers, then, if she couldn't affect it? She didn't have that kind of juice?

But if she moved, it moved with her, and it pulsed with every beat of her heart, and every increasing breath. An unpleasant freedom held her captive, as if an uncontrollable current had swirled her into an ocean so vast she couldn't see the surface, or the sea floor, no limits, no boundaries. She didn't feel her dislocated shoulder, or the burn on her ankle. She wanted to. She wanted to stop this. She wanted to feel what she was supposed to feel.

Lem gripped her head with her fists. She was going to kill everyone. She'd done everything possible to become a hero, but like an asteroid sucked into a planet's gravitational field, she was damage incoming.

"Hey, soldier, where's your mace?"

It was Jei's tenor timbre, cool and even, but gentler than she'd heard before. Lem didn't know if she should tell him to go away or not. She couldn't see him. There was only this empty room of sleeping enemies in the light of her spreading field....

Footsteps creeping to her left sent painful prickles down her arm—she wanted to lash out, but she didn't want to wake up to find out she'd killed someone she shouldn't, right? She trembled, belly churning, and swallowed, crouching with both hands outspread—

"Lem, you can't see me, can you?"

She shook her head, afraid her voice might betray her.

"I'm going to put a hand on your wrist so you know where I am. I'm going to pick up your mace—"

No, it'll burn you—

"—it's not on, so I'm going to open the core and take out the neodymium crystal."

That didn't make any sense. She'd left it on, and didn't have a chance to turn it off when the liquid hit her ankle. Invisible fingers did encircle her wrist, and even though he'd warned her Lem almost screamed. Nothing made sense.

"I was thinking about your theory, earlier, with Bricandor and neodymium crystals? I'm going to put your crystal in your hand."

Lem looked down in expectation, and saw nothing. A warmth passed over like an invisible shadow, and then something cold, and roughly cylindrical, like a hard uneven icicle, lay in her palm—the Neodymium-YAG crystal from the core of her mace. She closed her eyes and gripped it, recalling its reddish-purple form.

"I'm going to put this one in your other hand, too, okay?"

That had to be the one from his mace. Laser crystals were pretty standardized, but this one was smoother around the edges than hers, with a more uniform girth. She still couldn't see it. This was too trippy, too weird, standing here alone in this dark room with the artificial rain on her atmosphere hood, lit only by the expanding dome swallowing the city while she heard and felt things she couldn't see. Maybe the whole thing was a dream, still. Maybe Jei was talking to her on her wristband, or maybe this was her mind's way of trying to calm itself down.

"So I don't know how it's possible for the magnitude of

power either you or I generate to exist in one organism," Jei said. "The theory Mera came up with about me is that I'm somehow drawing on the combined electrochemistry of everyone attacking me. If it's true that you have something to do with the thermodynamics of entropy—heat death—then maybe anisotropy matters to you like EEG signals matter to me. After all, heat death is essentially just the perfectly isotropic arrangement of all matter in the universe."

Lem never thought about entropy that way—people always talked like the force of decay was chaos—but Jei was technically correct: chemically, the drive for lowest energy ultimately created the most homogeneity. A universe in one uniform whole, all molecules evenly spaced, all matter the same, all movement stilled, *was* the lowest energy state, in which no more chemical reactions could take place. Heterogeneity—diversity—required energy, unequal spaces, cell membranes, boundaries between this identity and that identity—like life.

She just didn't know what this had to do with anything in the middle of a crisis.

"Nd:YAG crystals are isotropic, and maybe neodymium's magnetic potential can play into that, too. I don't know exactly how it all ties in to the electric eel capacitors in your nerve endings, but—ah—look, we'll—later with that. Focus your electric field into these two crystals."

Lem would've given him an incredulous eye if she could see him. *I can't do that!* Rough hands gripped her knuckles, moving her fists parallel out in front of her.

"Aim up toward the ceiling, think of the color green, and fire into these crystals like you're simulating an em-push."

But those were all his things. Green was his meditation. She didn't even actually em-push. She didn't modulate electromagnetic polarities in the cations and anions of her neurons like he did—she just turned static shocks on and off. She had capacitors along her nervous system like an electric eel to create voltage differences and discharge that energy into shocks, and she'd learned to control those voltage differences to create like a static cling or repulsion. That was all she did. She didn't even know how she was doing this whole thing. She just wanted to turn it off.

It didn't make sense.

"Lem, can you hear me? I know maybe you don't want to push your powers right now—you just want them off, repressed. But I think you can redirect the energy. Sublimate it. Fighting it hasn't been working, has it?"

It was like she'd told Laaru back on Beryllia, maybe. Wear it out. But it was spreading like crazy across the city—this wasn't just some kid blowing up rocks in a tunnel, this was—hell, if it was this bad when she *wasn't* trying, how horrible would it be if she actually tried?

"I don't know if you can hear me. But when electricity or light energy is pumped into a solid-state neodymium crystal, the neodymium cation enters excitation—it collects electrons on its outer orbitals. But it doesn't want to stay there; it wants to lose electrons, drop back to the lowest energy state, an Nd 3+ ion. So it releases that energy again as light, but because of the shape of the crystal, the mirroring, when the energy's released this time, it's focused, all together. That's all a laser is—an energy converter, from electricity into light. And that's what I'm asking you to do. Take all your power, and use the solid-state matrix to focus it. Just like a laser."

Was this even real, or was she going to kill someone, though?

In the pause the grip on her knuckles tightened, and gravel rolled under Jei's voice. "Hey Lem? You've got two minutes to make it happen before I knock you out."

Oh, yeah, that was Jei. This wasn't just her brain.

Lem mustered herself and clenched her fists, firing a shock as hard as she could into the two crystals in her sweating palms. Two blinding red beams shot through the spaceport roof and straight into the night sky. A painful spasm shot through her spine, and she ground her teeth—

And then it was over. Just like that, that simple. Pain flashed back into her shoulder; one hand clutched it and the other hand dropped. The crystals clattered to the floor. Emergency lights flickered on. *I've made a huge mess,* Lem suddenly thought in the harsh yellow light: disheveled bodies scattered everywhere, bulbous melted polymerwall deformed around the fractured hole in the floor ... It wasn't raining in here anymore. Maybe that had stopped a while ago already, and she just didn't know it. She could see now.

A black glove reached down to pick up the crystals; Jei looked more gaunt than usual, with a tightness at the back of his jaw Lem recognized from bad days at the interrogation center. He wiped off the crystals with a clean cloth from his pocket, and clicked them back into the short bamboo-like staffs he had tucked under his arm. He handed Lem hers.

"I'm so sorry," she said.

"We stopped it before you reached the civilian sector. Just scarred a bunch of blitzers for life, which isn't undeserved."

Lem looked outside at the Frelsi air-riders now circling the bottom of the spaceport. Night had fallen full force, but the lights across the city blanked out the stars.

"It's not about what happened. It's what could've happened," she said.

"They don't need to know that. They know very little anyway."

Her wavering gaze fell now over the hole they'd both come in through—where she could just catch a glimpse of a Frelsi uniform waiting down on what looked like the emergency crank-lift. She sighed. She thought she might just pass out if she had to talk to anyone.

Jei followed her eyes and shook his head. "No. We're done. If they can't take it from here there really is no helping them." He nodded toward a different automated lift in the far corner of the control room. "Let's go."

CHAPTER FOURTEEN

Jei

HER NORMALLY CINNAMON-AGATE SKIN WAS PALE, AS PALE AS THE stream that used to flow from the industrial laundry center at Fort Jehu, bubbling and frothing with silvery cleaning chemicals that bleached the earth. One of her shoulders hung lower than the other, the bone bulging forward with a deep hollow above it —a tell-tale sign for dislocation. Dark circles like bruises ringed her eyes. Her irises still glowed a strange pale blue, but she could see me now, and their normal deep chestnut color was beginning to seep back through in streaks.

We disappeared into the jungle without much fuss. There were a couple of alleyways behind the spaceport, and the other Frelsi were pretty busy now. If anyone saw us, Lem had her atmosphere hood up, and most people knew better than to bother me when I looked like I had somewhere to be. Most lower ranking soldiers and cadets sympathized with me against command anyway—even before discovering this massive power-up last year, my skills had saved enough lives that everyone not trying to control me genuinely listened to me.

Which was … a weird thing. I'd always gotten along best with my superiors. I was the kind of person you might even accuse of being a privileged pet if you didn't watch me excel every day of my life. And now I was walking a wide berth around my own team in the dark, rustling underbrush like a newly minted cadet shirking off work to pick herbs while I plotted a diplomatic excuse to my commanders.

Bloodseas, I missed Captain Rana. I even missed Colonel Win —he went out guns blazing against ten of our own tripods the day everything went to hell at Fort Jehu. And that was *after* rescuing two full barracks' worth of soldiers, carrying them out of the haunted halls on his back one at a time. They said he still went back in even after being shot eight times. And he kept going back in until every single living person was out.

Sergeant Strong was kind of unbearable after losing his best friend. He was another one who'd pushed for Lem's exile. But he was also smart enough to recognize her practical value, and that was what I needed to lean on, because now I needed to get her out of here. An uneasiness screeched within me: Diebol's cryptic message lined up with Lem's suspicions about Bricandor, right before she blossomed into an electric flower? Not a good set of coincidences. We had to get to planet Forge.

Gah, the metal casing around my wristband really itched in the heat, all wet and hot. They'd designed it to shock and power me down if I tried to rip it off, but it was more symbolic than anything; they underestimated me, and I could live with being powered down for an hour or so if I had to remove it. It was just this constant reminder that they didn't trust me anymore, that they feared me, that I wasn't one of the "good" ones—that mental shackle was more soggy and itchy and frustrating than anything. I only wore this filking thing so they could feel safe.

"We're up ahead to the left," Lem said. Even without a space-lemur nose, even in the dark, and even after a year away she knew this forest like most humans knew their bedrooms, and we'd fallen back into our old roles: she always found our way on the ground, I always found our way in the air. I hadn't even paid attention as we walked, and we were already breaking out into the clearing with the gurgling waterfall, where the needlecraft parked on the riverbank sparkled in the light from Luna, Gueta-la's twin in the sky.

Lem dropped down onto the riverbank with a quiet groan; her back made a splat in the mud.

"Unless you want to knock out everything that drinks in this clearing you need to neutralize the stuff on your suit," I said, tossing her the can of powder from one of the pockets hanging on my utility belt. She nodded and caught the can, but set it down next to herself, and sat up to wrap both of her wrists around one knee with a wince. With a quick jerk backward and a *clunk* she set her shoulder back in place and then lay back down, breathing hard but otherwise giving no indication that the maneuver hurt like murder.

I gave her a moment, and dusted myself down, pulling my gloves back off and undoing my jumpsuit. The heat blasted me as soon as the atmosphere-controlled material peeled away from my chest and arms, but after draining myself with my own power surge earlier, even my undershirt seemed heavy. I wanted to sleep....

But I wanted to get into space first.

"Whatever that was, it happened after I got some blue on me," Lem said.

"Makes sense. It comes from an erythroidine, I believe. Like an atropine anticholinergic paralytic, but mediated by nicotinic receptors. That's what allows the skin delivery, but then there's the GABA component for central nervous system inhibition."

"Wait, but that stuff paralyzes people and puts them to sleep. So this is the opposite of making sense," Lem said.

"It's a paradoxical effect. As long as sedatives have existed some people have the opposite reaction to them. Probably something to do with the biological capacitors in your nerve endings," I said. "Or maybe inhibition was just the wrong thing for you. Maybe your spinal reflex system or higher control is always keeping your abilities in check, and the inhibitor turned off that control mechanism. It's not unheard of. Medications for hyperactivity disorders never worked by inhibiting the brain, but by strengthening and exciting the brain's natural inhibition neurons. This would be like the inverse."

"Hm." She had her atmosphere hood and jacket off now, and powder all over the riverbank next to her, and all over the tunic she'd tossed aside, and on her sleeveless undershirt, and smeared on her ankle—

"Bloodseas, Lem, you don't need to inhale it," I teased. Shyte, I was so tired.

She didn't laugh. Her still-glowing eyes trained on me in the darkness like one of those electric sabertoothed cats you never wanted to run into out here.

"We're going to Forge to check out your lead on Bricandor's new rock-collecting hobby," I said. "And see if I can find you a relaxation aid."

The glowing eyes narrowed. "I'm not broken."

"You're the one who's worried about some kind of doomed fate. I'm going to find you a backup solution just in case."

"What's on Forge?"

"Diebol will be. Do you remember the experiments I told you about, that Diebol was doing with Mera's blood? I—have a bad feeling that he may have made progress. But Mera's abilities had two parts: one a calming pheromone, and one a pulsatile series of neurotransmitter signals. Maybe the calming pheromone could help you get control." I rubbed my palm against the back of my neck; oof, it was the first time I'd said it aloud.

Lem didn't like it. "Are you filking kidding me? She poisoned you for months and you want to give me some of her stuff? From the hand of the guy who literally drugged us over and over 'til we couldn't see straight?"

"Just because she was wrong doesn't mean everything about her was worthless," I said. I kept harshness out of my voice, even though something hot welled up inside me with the memory of the dying soul in the burning building. "What she had—what she could do, how her mind worked—she could've been amazing for a lot of people."

"And I'm sorry, but I'm not here to give some kind of post-humous purpose to her life, Jei," Lem said. She too, fought for a strained kindness—she'd had a somewhat different experience with Mera than I had.

"I know. Maybe there's nothing for you there. Bloodseas, Lem, I'm obviously not trying to put you under some kind of mind control for Diebol. But whatever we do, I think it's time we at least tried to hunt down some answers for you. And whether that's by uncovering Bricandor's new obsession with neodymium crystals and heat death, or by breaking Diebol's mind-control experiment, I think we'll find something on Forge."

"I don't want to, but I don't know why I don't want to, and I'm too beat to disagree. So let's go," Lem said. She heaved herself to her feet and trudged across the shallow river, splashing with every weary step—not like the "leave no trace" space-lemur child at all. When she reached the bank, she turned back, glowing eyes piercing the distance between us: "I don't think I want to see Diebol again. I have a bad feeling, like a—final—feeling. I think you shouldn't see him either." She turned away, and threw her hands up in the air—well, one halfway in the air, still obviously sore. "But I don't have any logic for it, so let's do this."

SHE WAS ASLEEP BEHIND ME IN THE GUNNER'S SEAT, SNORING LIKE A day-lizard choking on a peacock-feathered guinea pig. The front viewscreen of the needlecraft showed Luna Guetala floating below us, two colorful marbles in a dance around each other against the backdrop of stars.

And I was arguing with Sergeant Strong on my wristband.

"It worked, didn't it?" I said. "I got you Retrack City. What's it been, ten years under Growen control? And let's not pretend I don't know why you were willing to trial the nonlethal control. This pacifist shyte looks *great* for the media blitz. You and I both know how big this is."

"You're in space! I can see on your read-out, you filking horn-muncher, you just up and went into space without signing out!" His Hoernig roar peaked over my speakers.

"I figured you wanted me to make *absolutely sure* we didn't knock out the power grid of the whole city, sir," I smiled through my teeth.

"And what if *your* power's knocked out, spine-kisser? It looked like standard EMP protection didn't matter, so what if you don't even have backup life support? You're in space, you brain-dead vegetable-cruncher!"

"Well better me than an entire city, I guess," I said. "Unless you're saying I'm worth more than that? If that's the case, well sir, your very expensive super-weapon needs to request temporary duty to investigate a lead on Forge that could shut us all down."

There was a silence—a rare thing for the volatile leader. "How did you find out about that?" he asked.

Lem was right. They didn't want me to know. "It would be helpful if you would send me the mission files on the Forge neodymium investigation, sir," I said. His new promotion honorific still didn't quite sit right in my mouth. "In the interest of full disclosure, I've also received more intel from Diebol that I think is relevant to the biological control experiment he started last year."

Another long pause punctuated by wet Hoernig breathing. "There's no reason you can't do that alone," he grunted. "Something's up with you, space-singer. Either you and Miss Crazy planned that whole heart-attack-in-the-sky today, or you lost control of your asset. You're good at what you do. But you're young and hormonal and you make bad decisions."

"I'm not going to argue with that," I said. "But I still stand by the assertion that if Lem had felt anyone would believe her, she wouldn't have had to desert, and maybe she would've prevented the Anomaly."

His voice rose again to violent, speaker-blasting peaks; it was a testament to Lem's exhaustion that she didn't wake up. "Are you blaming Colonel Win for the Anomaly?" he seethed.

No, but I might be blaming the Admiral, I thought. Aloud, I said: "No. I don't think it's useful to find a scapegoat, sir. I think it's useful to find things we all could've done differently so we don't screw up moving forward." I was done. I wanted to sleep. I was starting to wonder if I even needed command's good graces anymore. How were they going to stop me if I wanted to do something? What army would the waning Frelsi forces send against my power? The shock in my wristband would only give them about three hours to catch me. I'd bowed and kowtowed to their disciplinary fronts for a year, but in the end, they couldn't afford the loss and the only thing giving them sway over me was my guilt, my own personal penance for my role in slowing down Sterba's assassination. I carried the weight of three planets on me, and so did Lem, but in the end, we were the only people actually taking responsibility for something everyone had caused.

Strong's screaming faded in the background of my thoughts, and his words only stung in theory, in memory. I'd always wanted the glory and the stripes and the accolades; I loved to win, to succeed, with a biological, *primal* competitive drive; and I'd loved the approval of people who maybe represented my father in some shadowed way. But I saw them all now as aching wounded animals like myself, and I showed them respect only out of kindness for their shared suffering. I wasn't going to desert them, or ignore their words, like I did last year. I let them think they had something over me so they wouldn't be afraid. And I let Sergeant Strong finish chewing me out.

But then I set my autopilot on a course for Forge, leaned back in my seat, and fell asleep without a backward thought.

CHAPTER FIFTEEN

Laaru

THE CAFETERIA CAVERN IN BERYLLIAN SECTOR CGS-STFRD ECHOED with the clatter of plastic trays—an unchanged feature of schools everywhere for millennia. Here, under the watchful eye of teachers posted cross-armed in the doorways like prison guards, the hundreds of students spent their one truly free period of the day devouring the bounty of Beryllia's aquaponics systems. Everything grew here, from Alpinoan Smungworms to Luna Guetalan Lechichi to Burburan Twilightfish—a diversity in sustenance rivaled only by the self-proclaimed diversity of the students, who despite a number of lectures on interspecies unity, universally self-segregated by shape and color into their own tables during lunchtime.

Laaru was lost.

The young first year heard his two companions pitching ideas back and forth for the new interdisciplinary project on neodymium crystals—one had it in geology class, the other in chemistry, both in history—but their words sounded distant and ... meaningless? It was like he had died, and as a ghost, these things in the living world seemed misty and transparent. Or he'd awakened from a dream, but the dream hung about him still, fading before his eyes. That split second, when his hand blew up an entrance to a secret tunnel? Everything now revolved around that moment. There was pre-explosion, and post-explosion. They might as well not be in the same reality.

Laaru poked his salad with his chopsticks, watching the deep green and blue leaves bruise and bleed. He lifted one stick and twirled it; light gleamed off the black utensil between his gloved fingers.

It had worked, what Pele had said. If that was even her real name, which … it most likely was not? His new—uh, explosions —only worked on collections of minerals. Hardness seemed to matter, too, and some kind of force conductivity? Organic material disrupted it. He'd tested, over the past few nights, in the chemistry labs just a couple halls down from his bedroom. No one could enter the main tunnels at night without a permit, but with his new ability he'd made his own tunnel within minutes anyway.

Once you were here, the school owned you. That was generally accepted. Any research you did, any championships you won, all brought glory to the school. Fair exchange for feeding you and educating you, right? Laaru had heard of wealthy kids who paid for room and board and owned the copyrights to their creations, but in general everyone in the galaxy came here for Beryllia's famous work-study service. Which worked, right? The brightest minds in the universe graduated from here, with work experience and connections.

Did they own this new ability, too?

"Did anyone ask you about the graduate?" Nevik was asking.

Laaru looked up from his thoughts—it took a second for him to realize Nevik was staring at him pointedly from behind that curtain of long curly hair, referencing Pele's escape last week.

"The—oh, uh, no," Laaru looked back down at his salad. "We don't know anything anyway, right?"

"You're technically an accomplice," Nevik said, voice low.

"No, I—"

"Ooh, what's Laaru up to? Accomplice to what?" Kym's slender form slid beside Nevik. The way her long dark hair fell over one eye left her looking permanently sultry, and Laaru had wished since day one to see her unfurl those iridescent Draconian wings around those slim curves. She, like many of the other humanoid females, had undergone surgery to make herself look more *Sapiens* standard, so she lacked the sharp teeth, pointed tongue, and temple scales of her sub-species, *Homo Sapiens Draconius*. She'd likely also had a rib removed and eyelids adjusted, leaving her looking like something out of a story—like a fairy, or an angel.

Laaru still remembered that really awkward argument Kym and Pele had not more than a month ago. *"You ever get any work done, Pele?"* Kym had asked.

"No. Don't wanna hurt your feelings, but to tell you straight I think you're under the psychological bondage of homogenization." Pele was so—blunt—about something that she didn't experience.

"What backward planet are you from?" Kym had smirked. *"It's a woman's freedom to look like whatever species she wants."*

"Is it really freedom if you're thinking someone else's thoughts for so long you don't like your own skin?"

"Easy for you to say, born Sapiens."

"No. I get it. Grew up with a species I didn't fit into. I'm just not gonna let a culture of homogeneity put thoughts in my head and someone else in my skin."

Pele hadn't gotten along well with the other girls. She'd always seemed kind of socially awkward, like she didn't under-stand a lot about the world. Odd. Weird.

But not, like, run away with school property, part of an evil militant force kind of weird! They'd all signed the work-study contracts, right? No one really read them—well, Nevik and Xunst had, but Laaru hadn't—but for four to eight years, they all belonged to the government of Beryllia, to the school. Right? Breaking the contract ... what even happened if you broke the contract?

And what happened if someone thought you were an accomplice to truancy?

There was one more worse question, one Laaru didn't want to ask.

Laaru stood to leave. He'd kind of heard the conversation meander away from him into jokes, and he trusted both Nevik and Xunst to keep quiet, at least until—until something changed? He didn't know what, exactly. For now. "I'm gonna go to chemistry class early," he said.

"I'll come with," said Xunst. The dark haired humanoid photosynth was a guy of few words, but when he did speak, everyone listened, and the others at the table looked up.

"Is there something going on I should know about?" Kym asked.

"They're behind on a project," Nevik said, with another pointed look.

Laaru checked the large pocket in the side of his tunic pants for his compupad and his baggy breast pocket for his holo-pen. He and Xunst both had good reputations with the teachers, and they waved him on down the hallway with just a quick flash of the pass chip hanging around his neck. He appreciated that Xunst walked with him in silence.

What if he'd aided an actual terrorist in some ... he didn't know, some kind of plot or something?

"That's not something you see every day," Xunst nodded down the hall. Laaru followed his eyes—

Huh. He'd never seen soldiers here on Beryllia. The education industry maintained control of the livable tunnels with robotic defense systems, and he'd seen the occasional overweight security guard in gray slacks, but these? *These* were armored space-men with giant rifles strapped to their backs, faceless under silvery helmets so polished it seemed like they had portals to a mirror dimension where their heads should be. They swaggered like giants, and Laaru could see the outline of huge muscles even through their thick protective garb.

"They're Growen blitzers," Xunst said. "Wonder why they're here."

"Probably just some kind of science thing. Beryllia's an Uncontested Zone."

"Lots of armor for a research trip."

"They're probably always a target for terror attacks." Still Laaru eyed the thick pistols strapped to each thigh as he passed. And the rifles strapped to their backs? That was ... so many guns. This, right after discovering a Frelsi operative, made the Contested Zones seem a lot closer. He didn't have any reason to be afraid, but something churned in his gut, and his new gloves seemed to burn. Was he afraid that they really did hunt down new electromagnetics like him to turn into soldier-slaves? Maybe. But that wasn't the question that defied words, that raised the hair on the back of his neck.

What if the whole world, all worlds, wasn't at all what he thought it was?

CHAPTER SIXTEEN

Reise

THE HANGAR BAY OF THE FRELSI FIREBASE ON ALPINO BUSTLED WITH the tinkles and clangs of mechanics' tools, the mumbles and shouts of pilots running pre-flight checks, and the thunks and thuds of cargo loading. Weapons clicked and chattered as inspectors checked them; boots on cement and clanging metal kept rhythm under the high-pitched melody of the cool breeze whistling though the enormous rectangular entrance and echoing in the back corners of the building.

Reise Benzaran wiped his brow, sweat evaporating in the wind that never stopped blowing here on this continent of open plains. Even dripping inside a huge concrete garage full of hot engines, the Luna Guetala native felt cold.

He didn't miss Luna Guetala at all, though. The action here was twice the fun without any of the worry for family.

Fun? Reise smirked as he hefted another crate up the gangplank of his team's ship. Yeah, filking fun. People like his parents, and maybe his older sister, might think him calloused or insensible to imagine diversion in a galaxy of death, but he'd never known anything else. In a life as short and brutish as theirs, to borrow terms from an old philosopher he'd read, one could only be merry with the time one had—especially now that his youngest siblings were safe.

Reise paused his travail to gaze out the huge hangar entrance, toward the smoking volcanoes across the plains ... almost his entire family lived in the Hiding Place now, somewhere safe, far beyond there. Even his parents had followed after escaping Fort Jehu, apparently smuggled out by his sister's Biouk family. Reise had so much family when so many of his friends had none; it felt strange, oppressive even, to have so much to lose. Better to have his adventures far away from them while they remained safe.

In the meantime Reise had fun, and the best filking squad he'd ever had. Militant refugees were usually grouped into squads by biological family, but since Reise and Jake had none here at the Firebase, Command had assigned them both to a new squad with their two other teenage Sapiens companions from Fort Jehu, Nathan and Gideon. The two adults who rounded out the squad were a pair of lively Draconian newlyweds, Lev and Nefesh: energetic, chill mentors who both knew when to give the other four squad-mates space. All they asked was that the other guys clear out when they needed the room alone, which was all too easy. Shyte, life was like what Reise imagined civilian school parties to be. He'd only ever had one other squad in his life—his family—but facts were facts, and he denied himself any guilt for enjoying his current situation more.

"You ever been to Bijou, Reise?" Gideon didn't even grunt as he carried crates of medicine two at a time up the ramp into the small boxy cargo ship.

"You know I have not," Reise said, trying to hide how much he struggled with just one. "What secret life do you imagine me living?"

"Psh, I don't imagine *you* at all," Gideon's eyes strayed to the parking spot across from them, where a human female pilot was head-first inside the guts of her triangular blastercraft, rump out.

The sound of someone loudly clearing their throat made Gideon jump. "I wasn't doing anything!" Gideon protested.

"Of course. You were just counting the stitches on those back pockets," said curly-haired Nathan as he stepped out from behind a stack of crates in the far corner of the ship. The small human held his knife in his mouth as he used both hands to tighten the straps stabilizing the supplies.

"Engine grease just looks good on—"

Nathan's eyes turned on Gideon. He took the knife out of his mouth, and his hands paused in their work. Gideon was at least three times the size of the older kid, but Reise saw him really take a moment to think—not his usual course of action. They both knew Nathan would never harm a teammate, but no one wanted him filing more paperwork for disciplinary retraining, and his stance now just *dared* Gideon to keep talking.

Gideon dared. "I mean, I'd be flattered if she said the same about me," he said.

"Oh, I know." Nathan turned back to his work, apparently placated by the pause. "Not everyone is you. Some people get really uncomfortable with that stuff. You don't know her history. If you want to get to know her, tell her to her face. And if she says, 'gee, I really wish men would talk about me behind my butt,' then go right ahead I guess."

"I think she's in our same platoon. I can't be open about it."

"There are *forms*." Nathan pushed the other two out of the cargo bay, and slammed it shut behind them.

Reise and Gideon shared a look. Reise had half a mind to go correct Nathan for his infringement on other people's eyes and minds, but Gideon's shrug stopped him.

"He's in a better mood today than usual!" Gideon's cream-colored cheeks widened in a grin as he locked up the outside hydraulics after their companion. "Sensitive guy, I'm glad he keeps us straight. One of these days I'm going to make him snap, though." He whacked the door like a drum with a silly laugh and trotted off to finish the refueling.

Hmm.

Reise checked his wristband—he'd already finished his own pre-flight checklist, and with everything loaded, it looked like they were just about ready to go. Where was—

Oh, there. Jake was running through the small door that led underground, on the side of the hangar opposite from where the ships came and went. His limp had improved a lot over the past year. He'd had physical therapy most of this life, but something had changed after they'd gotten lost in the plains together. Perhaps he was more motivated these days. He trotted now with their extra rations pack on his back and his hand near his new holster—this was his first official offensive as a fighting-age cadet.

A large male Draconian stepped through the door behind the running thirteen-year-old and then took to the air over him, flapping giant red bat-wings as he glided over to Reise's crew.

"Let's roll," said Lev, his blue eyes twinkling under the shadow of his sharp ridged forehead. Slight scales blended into soft mammalian skin along his temples, framing his gentle sharp-toothed smile in sparkling crimson. "Ah, can you hear space singing her siren song?"

Reise couldn't hear any sound in space, since vibrations don't transmit without air particles, but he appreciated the sentiment. Lev was about six years older than even Nathan—coming up on the average life expectancy for a Frelsi soldier—and often said such odd things Reise wondered if he'd been a poet before joining up; all in all, Reise didn't feel as much kinship with the man as with his fellow Fort Jehu brethren, but still Lev had his respect, and Reise waited for his thumbs up before climbing into the ship's cockpit. The Draconian was technically team leader today, with Nefesh manning intel as their handler from home; the pair alternated these supervisory duties between them, while weapons management, logistics, and repair rotated between Gideon, Nathan, and Jake.

But Reise was always the pilot.

The cockpit lights bloomed as Reise settled into the worn leather pilot's seat, soft after carrying so many heroes before him. Reise undid the chip that hung around his neck and plugged it into the ship to start up the AI co-pilot he'd programmed—named *Phoenix Anomaly* in homage to the ship he'd lost during Fort Jehu's destruction. A firm press of the faded speaker button—it stuck a little—sent the AI's feminine, tinny voice back into the cargo bay to warn the other crewmates to strap in for imminent takeoff. Reise could just as easily call over the intercom himself, but he liked her voice better. She added a soul to the ugly, boxy old body of this cargo clunker. He glanced at the video feed and the weight distribution graphs— yup, everyone was strapped in. A quick listen as the crew sounded off over the intercom—sweet, good to go.

The sleek compuwall glowed under Reise's palms, smooth and warm under his caress as the ship hummed around him, purring like a pet. He drew his hands upward as if conducting a musical swell, and she rose off the hangar bay floor and danced with him out the garage maw into the sunny blue sky. Reise's voice recited the clearing procedures and communication codes into the console without even thinking, his mouth just another controller and his words another step in the dance.

They'd run a number of supply missions like this, delivering medications and food to isolated people groups in need, and their work had even helped diplomatic missions and recruiting among independent nations. Most of these areas were so distant and safe Reise never got to utilize his sharpshooting skills, but he enjoyed flying to new parts of the twin solar systems anyway. Someone had to do this stuff—people would die without resupply, and all the older pilots were too busy killing and getting killed by the Growen. While technically all Frelsi were supposed to be lethal defenders, it was no secret Command still tried to give safer, happier jobs to the younger pilots.

Today they would do a quick drop on Bijou: a distant, almost uninhabitable planet where a loose colony of Alpinoan and

Burburan Frelsi had joined with locals to start construction on a new trade and communications outpost. With the exception of the unusual binary star system housing Luna Guetala, Alpino, and their neighbors, each solar system in the galaxy's most stable arm only had one or two habitable planets, and in Bijou's case, it sat right at the edge between unlivable and survivable. Anyone on Bijou had it hard, but some people felt that maybe out there the oppressors would leave them alone.

The windows of the cargo ship misted as it burst through the clouds. Reise loved the 180 view, but shyte he missed the gorgeous clear top-shell of the tiny blastercraft he'd trained on. So easy to see your enemies above you ... oh, and atmospheric exit in a blastercraft! Agh, such a beautiful fiery burst, like a phoenix from planet Skraeli ...

In his mind, anyway. He'd never visited Skraeli.

Reise kept an eye on the distance from the hangar to the perimeter of the Firebase. Alpino was a Contested Zone, like Luna Guetala, but with a lot more Growen control, so Growen one-man fighters—usually Maggot ships—often patrolled space above the Firebase, waiting to pick off Frelsi supply ships. Reise had to break out of the atmosphere before even reaching that danger zone. He released pressure under his palms and brought them together to tell the ship to rise....

"You're clear for atmospheric exit, Reise," Nefesh's high, sharp voice crackled over the ship's computer. Her severe tone was a not-so-subtle reminder that Reise was supposed to check with her about Growen patrols even after takeoff, even though she knew he'd checked the safety forecast and the command tower twice.

"Yes ma'am," he answered. "Sorry ma'am. I was just about to verify."

"Next time you'll check earlier," she said.

"Yes, ma'am. Over?"

"Over."

The colorful flashes of heat and light, the rumbling, the

struggle to keep his hands steady, and the sudden drop into the twinkling vastness of space had all become so familiar to Reise now. He almost felt a glimmer of pride as he turned on the artificial gravity to let his passengers out of their seats. *Almost* a glimmer of pride. Nefesh's tone had prevented that. Reise was now remembering his first space trip, full of incessant vomiting, and worse, his first time in the cockpit, when a quick distraction almost caused him to crash. So much scolding. He shuddered. Gah, it still made him feel so stupid. He was stupid.

Once you got into space, though, everything became easier. You could set a course, and frictionless inertia would take it from here. Reise would just need to keep an eye on the proximity alarm for ships or stray debris. He leaned back in his seat, opened software on his wristband that projected a blank surface onto his hand, and began to draw a picture of a warrior with an enormous hammer. She bore some resemblance to the girl Gideon had pointed out earlier … Reise glanced over his shoulder to make sure Nathan wasn't around, although Reise had plenty of words for him about freedom of expression if he was.

CHAPTER SEVENTEEN

Reise

WRAPPERS DISCARDED FROM REISE'S DEHYDRATED RATION PACK crinkled under someone's foot by the doorway to the cockpit. Reise jumped, one hand on his pistol and the other over his drawing.

"Now Nathan—" he began.

"Not Nathan," Lev smiled, peeling the sticky wrapper off his boot and snatching other bits of trash floating in the air around him. Shyte, Reise hadn't even heard the splash of the polymer-wall when he came in. The Draconian craned his neck—"She looks like a badass," he said.

Reise shrunk a bit, his cheeks warm as he uncovered his drawing. "It's just a sketch. I was thinking maybe she's the leader of a revolution against a robot army that follows the philosophical tenants of nihilistic utilitarianism, and try to—uh, her name is Valkry."

"Why were you hiding her?"

"I wasn't." Reise paused, and adjusted his pilot's goggles as Lev floated into the co-pilot's seat beside him.

"I don't think Nathan has anything against badass women with giant hammers," Lev's blue eyes twinkled. Reise felt teased, but in a way that made him want to laugh, too. "But nihilistic utilitarianism, huh?" Lev didn't comment on how out of place Reise's vocabulary was in a mouth his age. "What've you been reading this time?"

"Right now I'm working through Jaheenson and Voltran."

"You might like the works of Uesugi, then," Lev nodded.

Reise doubted it—he felt no interest in Luna Guetalan philosophers, and preferred to dissect the rise and fall of civilization here on Alpino. He tried to respond as tactfully as he could: "A lot of Guetalan thought tends toward the celebration of outdated traditions that weaken sapient advancement. That's ultimately why there's a strong Growen presence there."

"Mm, there's a whole planet of work you can't paint with one stroke," Lev balled the trash up and tucked it into the recycle chute. "Uesugi spends a lot of time dismantling the concept of communal responsibility for individual actions, and the impact of that concept on justice and economics. I'll lend you his first file when you're done with Voltran—gosh, Voltran's dry, if you can get through that reading anything else is like watching an action flick where everyone's wearing pink leather." He laughed, and looked out the window. "What a beautiful universe looks down on us boring sapients and our books. Can you hear her siren song?"

"Why do you say that so often?" Reise asked. "I understand it's technically a metaphor, but—"

"Oh, you think so? No, it's not a metaphor," Lev smiled, tapping his fingernail on the glass now. "Just because we can't hear in space doesn't mean there's no sound."

"There's no air to transmit vibration to the eardrum," Reise countered.

"Mmmhmm, but you know as well as I do that space isn't truly a vacuum—I mean, just the routine maintenance we have to do on the ship to clean up after solar wind debris—! There's plenty of stuff in space to transmit vibrations, just not vibrations our ears could ever pick up." Lev leaned back with his boots on the dashboard and his hands crossed behind his head. "Those vibrations still exist, though, whether we can hear them or not. Silly people who like to talk about trees falling in empty forests —they try to define sound specifically as the movement of your eardrum in response to sound waves—as your *experience* of the vibration—but I've never seen any physics textbook define sound that way. The waves of kinetic energy transmitted from one vibrating molecule to another—that's sound, and that still exists in space. Stars and planets are vibrating, and sending those vibrations along into all the little particles of floating space stuff … singing a song."

"How do you know?"

"Satellites and monitors pick up those vibrations," Lev said, closing his eyes now. "I used to work in a civilian astronomy center before I joined up, and we'd sometimes make weird beats with the sounds we recorded when we were bored."

"So when you ask if we can hear space singing, what are you really asking?" Reise asked. "If we've got em abilities we don't have or something?"

Lev cocked open an eye and rubbed Reise's hair. "Nope. I will say, though—it's not space's fault we can't hear her sing. We're always wearing suits to protect ourselves from her. Even in low orbit, even at the edge of atmosphere and gravity where air's wisping away, it's too cold, and the pressure's too low, for us to survive without suits, and you know it's hard to hear anything in those things."

"So …" Reise narrowed his eyes. "You're asking if we're brave enough to go out with nothing on? Metaphorically speaking?"

Lev chuckled, and rose, floating up out of his seat and back to the polymerwall. "Mm, who knows. Have a good night, Reise."

"Well presumably *you* know," Reise called after him, but the man was gone.

After a day or so Bijou appeared, a white, almost translucent orb shimmering in the darkness. The frozen surface couldn't support life, so Bijou's inhabitants lived in tunnels criss-crossing underneath a ceiling of ice. Reise and his crew would need to drill through when they landed, so Reise armed his astronomy toolkit now, watching his spectrometers for a thinner patch of ice without any heat signatures directly below it—or water, either—

Lem lived in tunnels now, didn't she? On Beryllia? What a nightmare. Reise's claustrophobia didn't like imagining miles and miles of rock between him and the sky. Of course on Beryllia, the only area suitable for terraforming—and the only heat— lay closer to the core. For some reason, though, the idea of tunneling underneath Bijou's comparatively thin, translucent layer of ice didn't bother him at all. There would be light, and you only needed a good ice pick and an hour or two to find sky. Juju's new androids could probably do it in twenty minutes.

A *thunk* interrupted Reise's daydreams. The ship tilted for a moment—shyte, had something landed on the wing? The proximity sensors hadn't gone off ... Reise put his head on swivel, trying to see out the windows to either side, and adjusted the rear-view cameras to get a better look at the top of the ship. Shyte, they'd iced over, somehow? That didn't make sense. What ...?

The white surface flashed in front of Reise, much closer than he'd anticipated. "Focus!" he told himself. No distractions— they'd entered the atmosphere now, and he could kill all of them if he didn't pay attention to his landing. Stupid!

He forgot about the *thunk* while he found a stable place to put down the cargo ship.

The other guys burst into jubilant action the moment the engines shut off, as if the safety straps were bonds and the ship herself a prison. Reise couldn't hear their words through the door and short hallway separating the cockpit and the cargo bay, but Gideon's whoop and Nathan's scolding carried through any space. A large hatch creaked as they opened the bottom of the ship, and then Reise heard a *screeeeech* as someone—probably Gideon—dragged the drill along the floor—

"Hey, I'm signed for this ship!" Reise yelled over the intercom. "Don't scuff up my tiles!"

Gideon's "sorry" was cut off by an "I told you—" from Nathan, and a laugh from Jake. Lev was the only one of the crew who never announced himself by sound. Reise shut off the intercom and leaned back in his seat, feet up on the dash on either side of the compuwall as he finished up his picture. He'd do his post-flight safety checks in a moment, and then go help the guys unload crates. He liked the curve around his girl's hips, but her eyes seemed off …

It was *really* quiet suddenly. Reise heard the drill humming away, but nothing else.

Probably just—

Just what? There was no such thing as "just." Reise glanced at the camera—shyte, there was some dark liquid on the lens? He reached for the intercom—no. Bad idea. He closed his picture and stood up, hand on the flayer pistol strapped to his thigh. *Who am I kidding? Better just pull it out.* He raised the weapon with one hand while the other reached for the polymerwall. Shyte, it was *really* quiet, and even through the sealed cockpit the cold had begun to reach her icy tentacles into his skin. *Breathe, one—two—three—*

Reise burst through the polymerwall and dodged left—

His back hit the cold wall of the dark stairwell. Nothing shot him or jumped him. There was definitely something wrong though. He still heard nothing but the drill.

And a—skittering—

Oh, shyte on a stick.

Reise inched down the inky stairwell, two *violent* heartbeats at a time, each soft bootstep silent on the grated metal, back sliding along the wall—he wanted *so badly* to rush the polymerwall at the bottom—*No. One step at a time, don't announce your presence*—

Shyte, what if something was killing his little brother?

Reise leapt and tucked into a dive-roll through the polymer-wall at the bottom of the stairs, landing in a kneel with weapon raised. He had a split second to see an enormous—something—with its proboscis in the back of his brother's neck. He fired before even seeing it fully. The thing screeched and dashed back into the shadowy maze of stacked crates.

"Holy shyte, what are you?" Reise cried. Spindly legs—except for two front paws with wicked claws—giant clear fly-wings and disgusting compound eyes—

"What the filk!" He heard himself panicking, but everything seemed frozen, far away, as his brain refused to process the four unconscious bodies laid out around the drill: Gideon, Nathan, Jake, and Lev, each with a tiny dribble of blood coming from the back of their necks. "How the filk did that hideous abomination get the drop on all of you? What, you couldn't see it? It's filking—"

Oh. Like that.

There was a lightning-fast flicker, and Reise tumbled to the ground under stinking fur, freezing limbs, and furious, buzzing wings as a sucking proboscis with a razor-sharp tip plunged toward his eye.

There was no one to hear him scream.

CHAPTER EIGHTEEN
Cinta

Cinta heard what he should not hear.

The young Biouk noticed this first while ambling on all fours through the colorful mineral sands of the planet Forge, his muzzle covered with a soft mask to protect him from silica lung disease. He could still feel the grit, and small rocks, despite the space-gloves on each paw. It did not trouble him much. It did not even trouble him that his ears had gone over a year now since last hearing anyone call him "Biouk," in his native tongue, instead of the silly human term, "space-lemur."

Only two things troubled him these days.

First, the question of his mission: what did the Growen want with natural neodymium crystals here on Forge, and how could he disrupt their economic supply line or steal their weapon constructions? He had found good fortune, in volunteering for this, and obtaining permission to enlist the two mercenaries he liked. Fortunate—for he had his own worries that the Growen patriarch Bricandor needed crystals for something more sinister than mere firepower or money.

Only imaginings, he tried to tell himself.

His second trouble lay in his little-big adopted sister. She should have found Jei Bereens and escaped her civilian school by now, but she had not yet contacted Cinta to tell him. Strange, that, when she could finally now speak using Jei's transmitter. While she lived at her school Cinta could not speak to her over Frelsi networks—security risk, Command would say—and to call her he had had to creep off to civilian network cafés while on mission. Her lack of contact now made Cinta worry, given her last sad words …

A voice interrupted his thoughts. It seemed as if someone grumbled right in his ear. "We're never going to get a good deal on a ship in this two-bit town!"

Cinta's ears twitched. The words came from the wide, flat air-rider zooming like a bug along the horizon. It did not surprise him that he could hear the whooshing engines, even from here—Biouk ears sucked in sound like whirlpools drowned swimmers—but a voice so quiet he should not hear from here. Cinta glanced over at his companions.

"Did they shout at us?" Cinta asked.

"Hm? Who?"

"The—nothing." Cinta shut his muzzle, falling back into a trot beside the reptilian mercenary Lark Scrita and her mysterious human partner, the faceless Ebon Shadow. Even covered head to toe in that gleaming black armor, the latter showed no sign of discomfort in the beating sun. Cinta imagined a human cooking inside that metal statue, but of course, this man's technology knew no equal in the galaxy, and his suit likely possessed some measure of atmosphere control.

Cinta could not say the same for his own itchy, Frelsi-made utility belt and weather cloak: his skin *dried* so quickly here in this world of sands. His body liked even the cold, bitter plains of Alpino better than this wasteland, and of course many rotations had passed since he had last seen his jungle home on Luna Guetala.

Still, all places bore a beauty—ancient fingerprints left by his friend through space and time, Cinta thought—and the young Biouk enjoyed the oranges and reds painted across the sky, and the pinks, and pale turquoise-greens of the sand in this area.

It was not the worst place in the universe to hunt magical rocks.

"Think he'll show, mate?" Lark Scrita grunted, the gravel of her lizard voice muffled in the tinny, metallic microphone in her mask.

"He better," said the Shadow.

Lark Scrita had found them a contact who claimed to know the reason for the Growen crystal hunt. The contact would not talk more over networks, however, and wanted to meet in town.

"Still wish you coulda flown us a little closer to the settlement, mate," Scrita grumbled presently.

The Ebon Shadow did not answer. Cinta had never heard him repeat himself, and he had already said he would not pay for parking near town when the dunes cost nothing.

"At least we are there now," Cinta said. He checked the time on the wristband on his left forepaw, and glanced up at the tents and booths now trickling into the scenery around them. Such was the illusion of the shifting horizon that as the earthen city began to sprawl around them like a living thing it seemed as if it walked up on them, instead of them on it. Cinta's ears perked this way and that, sifting through the scattered conversations that built around the trio … sifting for talk of treasures, mines, construction sites, and electromagnetic powers. For now, he heard only artists debating the merits of first or second century tapestry versus sand art; a few mothers corralling wild children around their shop stalls; and haggling, lots of hungry haggling.

Their destination lay—there, up on the right, the building with the three mountains painted on its front face. Cinta nodded his head, pointing with his ears. The two mercenaries followed him, and they ducked out of the bright, dusty sun, into the cool darkness of the mud-brick saloon.

Cinta blinked as his eyes adjusted to the dim light, scanning the dining area for the red scarf that would identify their local contact in this quiet crowd of Vibrant Insectoids, Bont lizards, and humans.

Then he blinked again.

"Wait—is that—" Cinta's ears stood straight up on his head as he looked over at his companions to correct his deceitful eyes.

His eyes did not deceive him, however. The Ebon Shadow and Lark Scrita stood beside him still, hands on their weapons at their belts. Yet in the far left corner of the saloon sat an exact copy of the Ebon Shadow—only this one lounged with drooping, relaxed muscles, a postural opposite to Cinta's rigid, controlled ally.

The air hung thick, suddenly, with the scent of human tension. The sounds and sights of the saloon—soft music, chatter, clanging of dishware, humming of the trash-bots and living tables—faded in the background as the breath caught in both of his allies' throats, and their muscles spring-loaded at the ready.

The faux-Shadow raised a red scarf with a cocksure tilt of his head, and let it flutter to the floor.

The doorway erupted in explosion.

"Everybody get down!" roared Lark Scrita, ripping her orange glow-whip off her waist and dive-rolling down the middle aisle as the doppelgänger fired on them. Cinta leapt left —his paw-pads touched cold matte wall—he bounced off, grabbed the head of the first civilian he saw, and shoved it under the table—

"What a bad place to fight," Cinta muttered, pouncing to the next table. He wove back and forth through the crowd on shoulders—heads—bar banisters—knocking as many people as possible down out of the line of fire. His left forepaw unclipped his flayer gun from its holster as he tried to flank the copycat.

"Ooh, what a party!" The copycat whooped, literally cartwheeling along the back wall as he fired at the Ebon Shadow. "Boom, boom, boom!" With each repetition he pointed a remote at the windows and doors; a detonation followed each cry. The air filled with the tangy scent of ash and flint. "Smoke and chaos and favors for everyone!"

"Nutty show-off," Cinta heard Lark Scrita cough. He could no longer see her, but her glow-whip sliced through the smoke in an arcing snake; green and pink pistol fire flashed from her direction, but it seemed she couldn't get close to the acrobat in black. Somewhere back near the door Cinta's Ebon Shadow cursed: the bulk of the explosions, and the *stream* of death cartridges from the doppelgänger seemed focused almost entirely on him. Cinta had seen the man wade through fire-storms like nothing in that armor, but these shots bore an eerie silvery-blue color, and maybe the Shadow knew something he didn't.

Cinta, then, had a better chance of getting close than anyone. He dropped to the floor and dashed, weaving around fearful patrons huddled on the floor and past the shins of those still trying to flee. These inconsiderate mercenaries, could they not have their fight somewhere else?

"I thought you'd be better at this by now, brother mine," the double laughed, whirling now to twist his own arm behind his back while he fired trick-shots into the drinks atop the bar. He seemed to enjoy keeping the Shadow pinned down in that far corner.

Cinta's nostrils flared: almost there. He could see the man's boots through the legs of this chair. Honestly, if the dancing double would stop—dancing—and—talking—he probably could've killed the three of them already, but Cinta did not plan on giving tips to the human with the repeating machine-gun.

The breezy performance was still dangerous. An explosive flew just above Cinta's head, kicked by the doppelgänger after an extended juggle—Cinta flattened to the floor, ears down on his back. What an utter fool, this one! Cinta aimed his pistol, searching for a crack in the armor. He had not exactly asked the Ebon Shadow for a list of his weak points. The neck, though?

Cinta took a guess and fired.

Perfect aim. The kill cartridge sizzled against the seam of the man's armor.

Then the smooth, faceless black mask turned toward Cinta unharmed.

Oh dear.

The doppelgänger cracked his neck; Cinta heard a smile in his voice. "Oops, *there's* our little rat!"

That arm raised faster than reflex; Cinta saw the reflection of his own death in the man's shining mask as his mind's ear heard the report of his enemy's pistol.

Then Cinta blinked, and time rewound.

Before the gun fired *someone yanked the masked man out through the wall behind him*. Rubble sprayed everywhere; Cinta yelped; a red mace glowed in the settling dust. A familiar fist raised in the air, silhouetted against the sunset, and then dropped—and the doppelgänger slammed against the ground with a puff of orange sand.

"Oooh, spicy," the doppelgänger groaned with a laugh, hand darting to his belt—

"I'd reconsider that course of action," said the silhouette. A breeze cleared the dust, revealing a flaxen-haired dark tan youth in a slim black jumpsuit.

Jei Bereens closed his fist, and the doppelgänger's machine-gun and pistols crunched in on themselves. Bereens was not alone: firm chestnut-bronze hands held that red neodymium mace to the double's neck—and brighter than the glow of that spiking metal ball flashed the fiery hazel gaze of Cinta's human sister, Jaika or, as the bipeds called her, Lem.

Cinta's lungs became metal—or his heart sank, as the humans said—to see her. Something dark hung under her eyes, and she seemed to slouch as if she carried a moon on her shoulders, but no longer cared.

"This yours?" she asked Cinta, not even looking up.

"Yes—yes, he was to give us information," Cinta said, head low between his shoulders as he looked from the enormous hole in the wall to the disaster inside the saloon. Oh, the poor restaurant owner. Cinta's two mercenary partners emerged to pounce on their downed attacker, one pulling off his helmet and the other immediately slapping a restraining collar around his neck.

The captive shook long dark sweaty locks around his face with a little smirk and a wink in Lark Scrita's direction. "Hello there beautiful," he said.

The Ebon Shadow stiffened, and Cinta could almost swear he saw the man's normally emotionless grip quiver around the pistol he lifted to his captive's forehead. His thumb brushed the side, and the chamber hummed with a live cartridge—

"Hold hold hold!" Cinta cried, up on his hind legs now. "Yes, it was a trap, but he still may know things!"

"He's too dangerous to keep around," grunted the Shadow.

Lark Scrita growled and pushed the Shadow's gun down. "Blast it all, will you blokes calm down? That's the old you talking, lad, and if memory serves you've already killed your brother twice now anywhut. We need to move, mates. We can't restrain him right here." She threw a slit-eyed sideways glare at the two mace warriors: "Not to mention you two nutters just made your presence very clear. You always have to muss everything, don't you?"

"*You're welcome.* It's not like we couldn't hear your shoot-out from five kilometers away," said Jaika—no need to call her by her human name now after the Frelsi had cut her off from the other furless bipeds. Cinta scampered close to her leg, wishing he could take his tiny four-year-old cub sister back into his arms and tell her everything would be okay.

But she was no longer a cub: she was a giant warrior three times his height who did not have time for comfort. Jaika yanked the captive to his feet, and Scrita said no more to her, apparently begrudgingly content to focus on disabling security on the doppelgänger's armor.

Cinta sighed, his ears drooping down his face. He had hoped

that they would finally have a lead into the crystal market here on Forge, and instead, this.

Well, there was some consolation, at least. Before they left for the dunes, the Shadow stepped back through the hole in the wall to bark: "Barkeep!" After a pause, a short Bont lizard, her scales bright-yellow with terror, poked her head out from a back room whose polymerwall now lay melted on the floor. The Shadow tossed her a square pay-chip—a Burburan currency marker worth double the cost of her establishment. Burburan central banking issued pay-chips of different shapes based on the amount of encrypted currency each chip contained, and one could not amend a pay-chip's amount once purchased. Cinta had never even seen a square one in real life before.

So not everyone was worse off when the five allies hastened away through the colored sands, back to the mercenaries' ship with their prey.

CHAPTER NINETEEN

Cinta

STARLIGHT TWINKLED ON THE SURFACE OF THE SLEEK OBSIDIAN spaceship planted alone in the dunes, a black gem beckoning thieves like a slime-spider's trap invited swamp-wolves. Like that muck-dwelling arachnid, the Ebon Shadow did not bother to hide his home, for he preyed on predators. Even if an errant criminal managed to avoid triggering the nerve gas perimeter or the hull's shock field, the cockpit of the *Huntress* would admit no visitors without a word from her master; if you entered, and attempted to turn into the polymerwall any more, or any less, than twelve paces from the loading elevator, the walls would fire without impunity, and your ashes would wash into the bilge, leaving the universe without a trace of your former existence. Still better to die in the approach than succeed and meet the hunter living inside: if you survived, it was because he wanted your price.

Nevertheless, despite several weeks living inside the *Huntress*'s safety, Cinta always found himself checking the windows during meals—and he saw Jaika, and Jei Bereens, do the same now. Frelsi pilots would almost never park their ships out in the open like this. *We're the lone target for kilometers and kilometers....*

The conversation around dinner had lulled. Cinta stood on his haunches on the small black table in the middle of the room, both paws wrapped around a feeding straw of fruit. Below him, on the floor, crouched Lark Scrita, her large reptilian thighs tucked under her as she drank a pink slurry of meat protein from her own sustenance straw. The Ebon Shadow sat in the pilot's seat, which he'd swiveled to face the rest of the large cockpit, as his suit fed him through hidden tubes inside his mask. To anyone who did not know, it would appear as if the Shadow were doing nothing—only staring into space with his hands on his lap. Apparently long hunts without pause had left him most comfortable with this habit of feeding in effortless stillness, like a tree. Whatever food coursed through the secret reserves of that suit, however, Cinta could not imagine it tasted good.

The two new visitors ate, but seemed focused elsewhere. Jaika lounged on a side bench just under the port-side window, staring out into the night sky with her back against the rear wall as she twirled her now-empty sustenance straw between her fingers, elbow draped over her knee and boot on the thin grey cushion. Beside her—taking up much less of the bench, with his feet on the floor like a civilized human—Jei Bereens alternated between pretending to check his wristband, and pretending to like the nutrient paste in his half-finished tube, while his eyes swept every joint and panel in the room.

"You won't find the *Huntress*'s hardware specs in any database, mate," Lark Scrita said, wagging her snout at Jei.

Jei shot a sheepish look over at the Ebon Shadow; the bounty hunter showed no sign of reaction to Jei's technological snooping, but Cinta doubted he had not noticed. "Sorry," Jei said. "I don't usually see ships this ..." He trailed off.

"Fancy," finished Jaika, running a long finger along the porthole.

"It's not fancy," the Shadow grunted. The Shadow only ever

spoke in a grunt, a few words at a time, but Cinta could hear offense in this grunt. "It's practical."

"It's expensive as shyte, is what it is," Jaika laughed. "Maybe with the clients you used to roll with you think fancy is some luxurious-ass floating beds with the long silky tassels and booze or whatever—but to me fancy is a good security system and a sexy engine."

"What she said," Jei agreed. He pointed at the security feed on the dashboard that showed the Shadow's doppelgänger down in the hold chained to the wall in a forcefield. "What's your plan with him?"

The Shadow grunted in displeasure, and swiveled his chair to face forward.

"It's a tough one, that is, mate," Lark Scrita translated for the human of few words. "They've been killing each other for years. That's just about the only way they know how to deal with each other, ain't it? But now the Shadow's got your Grey Ghost all up in his head, and he can't decide how to swing this right. Cold blood execution without a trial's one thing, but on th'other hand no prison'll hold this one."

"Grey Ghost?" Cinta heard Jaika ask.

"It's what she calls Njandejara," Cinta told her in Biouk.

"What do you mean they've been killing each other for years?" asked Jei Bereens.

"Not actually dead, of course, laddie. They always think so; they check bodies and all, but between DNA-psyching, corpse-switching, and neurotoxins that fake pulselessness, they've got nine lives each, they have. Evenly matched brothers and whatsit. No one else even knows the Ebon Shadow is really two people; they've been fighting over that name since before I got into the huntin' game." The Bont lizard tilted her head, her wide snout flushing a subtle, cheeky purple. "Well, no one knows except I suppose the twelve people in that bar today, and you. Normally the cost for knowin'd be death, it would. But our man's changed, and the other one's, well, you know. Not gonna do anything about it now."

The Shadow rose abruptly and brushed past all of them, plunging through the polymerwall down into the hold. *"Stop spilling my life out to strangers,"* Cinta heard him growl.

"Eh, what's your deal today?" Lark shouted after him.

Cinta's ears dropped horizontally in confusion. "Did you not hear him?" he asked.

"No, he must've been mutterin' then—hold up a moment, though." Lark rose, and followed her partner. Cinta watched them both on the dashboard camera as they argued near the body of their captive ... strange. He thought the ship's walls blocked sound better than this. He could hear their conversation all the way down in the hold as if right here in his ears.

"Come off it, Hampt, what's the problem now? I can tell somethin's amiss, mate."

"You're dumping privileged information."

"Oh, blow that, an entire bar saw the two of you together."

"No one will believe yokels from nowhere. But Frelsi operatives —"

"Yeah and the Frelsi operatives saw 'im too, so it's not like you're going to leave here with them thinkin' there's just one of you now, is it?"

"This is true."

"Yeah, you're stupid when you're mad, you know that?"

"Even so, the Frelsi are clients. Not partners."

"Look mate, you've got to trust me about the people things. You're McShooty Intimidation Man, but I've got the silver tongue, I have. Hunters like me without money and power get by on words, lad. And I'm telling you, one liar to another, this is a time you wanna be tellin' plenty o' truth." The animated lizard paced as she spoke, and emotional colors flashed across her snout.

But the stone-cold human turned his back on her, staring into the field where his smirking double lay in artificial sleep.

"Ah, Carl, why won't you just relax?" Scrita reached her claw to touch him on the shoulder—

He jerked away, thrusting an accusing finger at their sleeping captive. *"Because that's your pen-pal!"* he growled.

"I had no idea!" the lizard protested. *"What, you think I like getting my beans roasted by your nutty twin, mate?"*

"No, I think you'd check your lead before we show up to die."

"Oh, come off it, we lived, didn't we?"

"He was playing with us. And even playing, it took an electromagnetic to put him out."

"I wish we could hear what they're saying," Jei sighed.

Cinta startled, and looked over his shoulder to see both Paradox Warriors leaning toward the grainy video feed from the hold, squinting as they tried to read lips on faces turned away from the camera. "How can you not hear them?" Cinta asked.

"Since when can you hear through noise-canceling tech?" Jaika asked, an eyebrow raised.

"Noise-canceling?"

Jaika pointed to Jei's wristband; he held it up to show the rough schematic of the ship he'd been drawing. "He's got noise-canceling fiber and a white noise generator down in the hold so his captives can't hear what goes on in the cockpit," Jei said.

"How do you know that?" Cinta asked, ears straight up on his head.

"Our man here does in fact see ships this fancy," Jaika said. "Jei writes schematics for civvy models on recon all the time."

"It doesn't take a recon officer to put two and two together," Jei said. "You can see the white noise generator in that camera shot, and this—" He rapped on the floor with his boot. "Only one composite sounds that dull in a double-decker swoop."

Cinta did not understand half of those words, but now it seemed his ears would twist off his head with confusion. "But I can hear them. Maybe it is not made for Biouks."

"Mmm, I think the Ebon Shadow's prepped for all sapient mammals. This is rated even for vibration-sensing species," Jei said. "What do you hear?"

Cinta summarized the conversation with some hesitance; the

two Paradox Warriors prodded as he spoke, and finally he waved them off with his paw. "It is their private fight, and not useful for the mission anyway."

Jaika shot a look over at Jei, and then back at Cinta. "You know I didn't actually ask aloud what Grey Ghost meant earlier, right?"

Cinta's ears fell into a quizzical L-shape. "Yes you did."

"I mean, you coulda guessed I wanted to know, probably." She looked at Jei with the comment even as she addressed Cinta, as if arguing with him internally. The other human gave a curt nod as Jaika went on: "But then why'd you answer in Biouk? Wouldn't you guess that Jei didn't know what she meant, either?"

"You are the only one who asked out loud." Cinta's muzzle wrinkled. He did not like the sensation that the two Paradox Warriors knew something he did not.

"I didn't ask out loud. And you did the same thing the last few times I called you from Beryllia without cam on, too."

"What has camera to do with anything?" Cinta's ears started to flatten a bit against his skull.

Jaika shared another wary look with Jei, who leaned forward to pat Cinta on the shoulder. "It's okay, cadet. Do me a favor. I'm going to turn around—can you repeat to me what I say?"

"O—okay, I guess." Cinta tilted his head as the male human turned to the wall. Cinta looked to his sister to tell him what this meant, and why, but Jaika watched her partner's face.

"We need to consider the possibility that even if the Shadow-double is brokering local trade deals for the Growen, he doesn't know more than he told us when we first caught him."

Cinta repeated Jei's words. Jaika raised an eyebrow, and Jei looked at her, and then back away and continued.

"Most of the networks Cinta's already checked here have sold their crystal stores to the Growen through a third party—but even if the Shadow-double is that third party, he might not know why. Cinta could—"

"Why do you talk to me about me—why say 'Cinta' instead of 'you'?" Cinta asked.

"What did he say?" Jaika asked, and again, Cinta repeated.

"So while the mercenary stealth team continues trolling through local contacts, it might be best for Lem and I to take a more direct approach."

Cinta repeated. Jaika's eyebrows continued to raise.

"Also I've been thinking a lot about my dad lately."

Before Cinta could open his mouth this time Jei turned back around with a hasty laugh. "Yeah, okay, I think that's enough! Don't repeat that."

A grin crossed Jaika's cheeks. "Ooh, Cinta, please repeat it!" she begged.

"Lem, stop," Jei threw up his hand. Jaika punched his palm.

"Aw man, no pretty sky-dancer stories for me," she pouted. What? Sky-dancers? Could she not hear what he had said about his father?

Jei chuckled, then shook his head and looked Cinta in the eye. "Well, it's settled. You have Bricandor's gift."

Jaika scowled. "Ew. Why's it gotta be Bricandor's?"

"Who else has it? It doesn't mean anything. Even Bricandor's got good traits."

"You're so enlightened now that you kissed a Stygge." Jaika's eyes showed regret almost before the words left her lips. "Oh shyte, I—"

"It's fine."

"No, that was out of line, I—"

"Hey!" Cinta barked in Biouk. "Hey will one of you furless giants tell me what's going on already?" His patience had expired.

"You can read minds, Cinta," Jaika said. "You heard Jei's thoughts when his back was turned; he didn't say anything out loud."

"But then why did I not know what you two were thinking about me just now, in your lookings at each other?" Cinta asked, in Grenblenian now in case Jei had something more reasonable to add. "I wanted to know very much."

"Because it's a passive ability, so trying to turn it on is like switching off your ears, or trying *really hard* to go to sleep. It doesn't work with active intent. You gotta chill," Jaika said. She paused when she saw Jei grinning. "What you laughing at, man?"

"Nothing." He looked away, still almost laughing. "It's funny how easy it is when it's not you, huh?"

"I don't think it's funny. I coulda killed a buncha people."

"Well, now you know to turn it off you have to turn it on. So to speak."

"The mind is a filking paradox," Jaika grumbled. The grey circles under her eyes seemed to intensify as she stood. "Let's put this to good use. Maybe sleeping beauty can talk to us in his sleep after all."

Cinta threw out his forepaws in exasperation. "What? You cannot just tell me I can read minds, say some nothing about paradox, and then—what do you want me to do?"

"Read the detainee's mind for information about the Growen interest in neodymium, obviously," Jaika said, stepping toward the exit.

"I—I do not know if I know how!"

"Best way to find out is to practice." Jaika jerked her head toward the door with impatience. "Catch up, here, isn't this your mission? Or do you just play saloon superhero and then call it a day?"

"Jaika!" Cinta stomped his back paw. "Why this?"

She leaned against the doorjamb with a low growl; her shoulders slumped. What was this, with his little-big sister? Jaika seemed to *need* this. Cinta had thought nothing of it earlier when she peppered the captive with questions before even starting the walk into the desert—that was standard Frelsi procedure. He remembered Sergeant Strong's interrogation lectures: *"Now listen up, flower-kids, you'll always get the most intel within the first ten minutes of a capture, before the enemy's got time to come up with a good lie."*

This was more than procedure, however. Jaika's fist clenched against the wall, and every muscle tensed like she might leap out of the ship.

"If I can read minds, why don't I know why you're so unhappy?" Cinta asked in Biouk.

She sighed, and left for the hold without answering.

CHAPTER TWENTY

Jei

I STAYED BEHIND IN THE COCKPIT ALONE WITH CINTA FOR ABOUT AN hour, coaching him on his abilities—poor guy seemed so lost and worried. We found out pretty quick that his brain only began to unconsciously "listen" when he couldn't see the target's mouth, so for now it didn't seem like something he could do on purpose if he knew the target couldn't talk.

"I wish you had not told me. Maybe it would have worked if you had lied instead." He perched now on the headrest of the pilot's seat, curled into a ball atop it. "What is the point of an ability I cannot use? Also, how did this happen to me?"

I shook my head, fiddling with the hem of my pants as I leaned back in the upholstered bench Lem had vacated. "Do you remember two years ago, when the Growen were starting their Stygge program, there were a couple of people they hired as Awakeners?"

Cinta nodded. "I met Okl, the Bichank."

"You were a captive, then, though." I kept my eyes away from his paws, where Diebol had ripped out his claws to get to Lem. I knew what it meant for a Biouk male not to have claws. "Okl wouldn't have wanted you to have abilities." I tilted my head. "But you had moon Biouk family, right? Did you ever meet Trchikio?"

"He killed my cousin."

"She killed him, too, though, right? You never met him?"

"I met him before. Jaika—Lem—and I visited the moon tribe years before. I do not know how long he worked for the Growen. We never liked him."

I squinted at the wall, as if I could see through it into the past. "Nah, that timeline doesn't work. He wouldn't have a reason to try to Awaken you if you already kind of supported the Frelsi."

"None of my parents read minds," Cinta said.

I stretched, and glanced at the monitor, where Lem was in heated discussion of some kind with the mercenaries. It didn't look like she needed me, and her adopted brother definitely needed someone after the bomb we'd dropped on him. "The theory behind Awakening is that they can't give you something you don't already have. It's not like some kind of magic mutation. They improve something you can already do by changing something in your nervous system. Sometimes painfully. You know how muscle mass grows when it tears, right, and lactic acid stimulates hypertrophy? Like that, but with neurons. It's supposed to be some kind of pheromone they give off that alters neurogenesis."

"Oh like something with NDMA metabolism, then?" Cinta asked. I forgot, often, that he used to work as a biomedical scientist.

"Maybe? I don't know. But maybe during a time of stress you've been in contact with someone who doesn't know they have the pheromone. Maybe someone you, Lem, and I all met within the past year and a half, since her abilities are going crazy too and I'm—well, I'm basically just the Frelsi's living nuke now."

Cinta didn't need mind-reading to hear the slight tinge of bitterness in my voice there at the end. "I am sorry they have done this to you," he said. He climbed down the chair, and sat on the bench beside me. He paused for a moment before getting too close to me, his nose just by the edge of my forearm—I knew Biouks did physical contact differently, and much more platonically, than most *Homo sapiens* did, and I imagined he probably missed that part of space-lemur society as much as Lem did. So I raised my arm to make room for him and show I wasn't uncomfortable with his proximity, and he cuddled his snout against my ribs and curled up, warm and furry, under my elbow.

"What if it is not us that has changed, but the world?" he asked, his voice muffled against my shirt.

"You mean like we're not more powerful—everything else is just more sensitive to biochemical change?" I leaned my head back against the wall. "Not sure that makes sense."

"It makes as much sense as the idea that any one person can tilt the thermodynamic balance of the universe."

I looked down at him. "Well, that's different. The butterfly effect is proven."

"We would have no control group, since we only have one universe, to know if reactions happen faster now—if entropy itself has changed. We would only have time."

"Time is so subjective, though. Whenever someone says things were different 'in their day' it always feels like they're just selling a story for control."

"We all want control. That does not mean that person's change-sense is broken."

"Mm, still." I let my finger scratch behind his ear, since I'd seen Lem do that, and the fur on his head puffed in pleasant response. My head tilted back against the warm metal wall. We sat in silence for a little while, and I almost fell asleep, but ... last year's fight between us nagged at me.

"Jaika is not replaceable!"

"Maybe if you hadn't told her she's supposed to save the universe from some kind of heat death, she wouldn't need to be replaced. I know you're the one who filled her head with thermodynamic fairytales, cadet."

A harsh space-lemur laugh. "You know half of nothing. Jaika is the heat death!"

I'd weaponized that information.

The word I needed now stuck in my throat, and I couldn't say it, so I did what I suddenly realized Lem did often, and doused that word in extra informality to separate it from me. "Hey, man, I'm sorry about last year," I said.

"No, I am sorry. I should not have told you."

"You think it'll be our fault if it does happen?"

"No. Everything and nothing is our fault. We each have our own butterfly wing, but so does everyone else, and so does Njandejara, from the first one at the beginning of time."

Njandejara. Cinta could hear him better than anyone—even before becoming a mind-reader Cinta had always possessed special intuition into everyone's voices. "Hey, uh—" I cleared my throat. "He's always talking to you, right?"

"He is always talking to all of us."

"Could we—" Bloodseas, this was hard to ask, but I was so tired of posing. "Could we talk to him now, and you—translate —for me?"

"That is dangerous. It does not work like that, and I am not his mouth. I make mistakes."

"I have my manuscripts. I can fact check you," I said, and added, for my comfort, a gruff: "Soldier." Then, as if he might disagree again: "It says in the old writings that where two or more of his friends are, he is. Like his energy's intensified with more—portals, if that's what we are. I'm not expecting any miracles, or asking to hear. I'm just asking you to—talk and I can—agree. And maybe if he says something, then—then you can share."

He shifted, and I could feel his big, glassy eyes on my face as his ears picked up. "We can try."

LEM

Lem climbed the stairs back to the cockpit with her hands in the pockets of her Beryllian coveralls and her shoulders hunched. She hadn't learned much. The mercenaries had infiltrated a number of local trade rings, and only discovered that crystal *age* mattered—the older the better—and that the Growen paid premiums for quicker delivery. That only meant Bricandor had a deadline, and Lem didn't like that at all.

Shyte, what if it was *soon*?

You're crazy. You really don't matter as much as you think you do.

Yeah, that sounded right, too. Shyte, she thought about herself way too much. She was starting to *use* people, and she didn't like that. She hadn't done Laaru any wrong exactly, or Cinta either. But still the *how*—something was—something wasn't right.

Oh, she'd also learned that a lot of natural neodymium crystals had some baseline radioactivity. She knew their colors, now, too: bastnaesite could be pale pink to colorless, parisite brownish yellow, and monazite light purple.

Ugh, so what? She pressed her fist to her forehead—

Something twitched in her periphery. She jumped, her breath frozen—

Just her own shadow on the stairwell. Lem shrugged her shoulders higher against her ears with a low grumble. Shyte, she—

Was that the angry Biouk self behind her?

She whirled, and saw nothing, but thought she heard a laugh inside her chest. Oh *shyte*. What if she went off, here? What if—

Focus. Channel the power into—into—

She drew her mace and gripped it just above its neodymium crystal core without turning it on. The laser flickered for a moment in her hand. Nothing else happened. Good—that was good, right? She could always turn the energy into focused light. She sighed, and the tension, the wheel spinning in her chest, slowed. She compressed the mace back to a short bamboo staff, and hung it on her utility belt again.

The wheel only slowed—it did not stop. For whatever reason she found herself thinking about the hearing last year again. Especially Seria's filking nothing testimony. Seria was that skinny pale Alpinoan in Lem's old Frelsi unit—the one who had major hots for Jei back in the day. Lem had caught a glimpse of that little snake at the Retrack City tower this week, and just—

It was in tunnel vision, the memory: everything in the dim hearing room blurred while the trembling lower lip, the downcast eyes, the wavery voice shone in focus: *"I was there during the Anomaly, on Fort Jehu,"* Seria had murmured. *"I—I'm not convinced Benzaran won't do something like that, wasn't part of that. She's erratic—dangerous."* Lem remembered struggling to keep her jaw from dropping in disbelief. Who the hell was that sadsack? Seria was never sad, always tough and boisterous, chatting with all her friends, or bubbly and bold with whoever she'd marked as her next conquest. Shyte, there was a tasking years back where they'd both been assigned to load the dying into transports for Dr. Loylan—Lem had trouble sleeping that night, but Seria, her tent-mate, slept like a rock. The next day, when several soldiers in agony wondered why the doctor hadn't returned to them, Lem had tried to come up with a plan for lightening the doctor's load or getting more help, but Seria's solution was "they should be taught to have different expectations."

Such a polite way to say "shut up their whining."

Point was, Seria was professionalism embodied. If she cried, she did it in private. And Lem wasn't stupid. They'd both taken the training about how to give testimony for the Frelsi cause to news networks. Just—that no one else could see through the trumped-up emotions—*I mean, they didn't know, but they should have known me, known I would never*—the fact that they believed—

And as it turned out, hey, maybe they were right! Lem was uncontrollable. Everyone around her was in danger, constantly.

She couldn't trust herself anymore. But it was their fault, she'd left to save them, she could've saved them all if she'd just had some filking help, if someone would filking listen and—

Shut up! She needed to get away. They couldn't stay near people. She was down, one hundred percent down, to take as much of Morda's poison as needed to keep this under control.

Lem burst through the polymerwall at the top of the stairs, ready to get Jei and make a plan to ditch.

But as she entered the gleaming black cockpit, the wheel stopped spinning in her chest before she could blurt her plan.

Jei and Cinta were both asleep: the human with his head tilted back against the porthole, lips just slightly parted for slow breath, and Cinta all curled up under his arm into a ball, nose tucked into Jei's side. Shyte, her two favorite people in the universe. Jei always furrowed his brow just a bit while he slept, as if sad, or as if even in dreams he needed to fight someone— Lem still remembered overnight missions where he woke up in a cold sweat, reaching for his mace. Cinta always twitched his left ear—there it was—and shifted with little snuffles that had woken her up often as a little one in the family nest.

Shyte, she'd missed them both so much, and hadn't let Cinta know, at all.

There was always going to be another battle to fight. There was always going to be a new mission. But these two, they wouldn't last forever. Jei had about four more years to live, most likely, and while Biouks fared better than humans in the war-zone stats, that didn't mean Cinta's life was guaranteed, either.

Lem turned toward the polymerwall behind her—not the entrance to the stairway back down to the hold, but the hidden polymerwall beside it to the galley. She didn't know how best to show affection, but she figured everyone likes to eat. The Shadow had programmed her DNA into certain areas of the ship so she could pass, and all Frelsi youth learned survival cooking. She phased through the black goo, and started digging through cupboards for something she could prep for tomorrow.

CHAPTER TWENTY-ONE

Diebol

DIEBOL DIDN'T FLINCH AS HE PULLED HIS MACE OUT OF THE YOUNG Bont lizard's skull.

"You're free now," he whispered as he knelt, and cut the Frelsi wristband off the dead hatchling's wrist. The whisper was more for him than for the dead. He still recalled vomiting the first time he had to kill someone this young.

He also recalled the beating from Bricandor after said vomit.

Colored dust flickered through Forge's dry air, swirling around Diebol's boots, and painting his black vest with flecks of neon as he knelt to close the lizard's eyes. "Your death won't be in vain," he said. They'd be done with this barbarism soon enough.

It had become a common tactic. The Frelsi would almost never leave a child, so many a successful ambush revolved around … this.

Today, however, there would be no ambush. Diebol would wait in the open to test Morda's legacy. Then, the Frelsi search party under his control could return and open the shields for his blitzers to deliver the rest of the load directly into the base without arousing suspicion. In his dreams, he'd imagined sending the child in with the first dose, a tiny ghost infiltrator to set everyone free, but in real life such a thing would never have worked. The Frelsi would have stopped the kid, tested her blood, and obtained the weapon.

He rose, stepping back from the reptilian blood seeping into the sand at his feet. With luck, this would be the last little one that had to die.

REISE

Reise gripped the throbbing proboscis with both hands, screaming as he tried to push it away from his face. Deafening buzzing pounded in his ears; the huge creature on his chest flailed, struggling to stab him with its face. A tiny sharp gleaming tip flicked in and out of the proboscis like a tongue, right above Reise's eye—Reise's boots thudded over and over against its thorax, knocking it—

A *schick* like knife blades—sharp pain plunged into Reise's ribs as the creature rammed in its claws to get a better grip. Reise heard himself shouting for all kinds of gods, legends, interdimensionals, governments, and whoever else—he heard the crunching of his boots against his attacker's belly and the ringing gong of his heels against the floor, but only saw that one droplet forming on the tip of that proboscis—his arms couldn't compete with the force of the creature bearing down, down, toward his eye—

It suddenly occurred to Reise this wasn't his first time wrestling with someone stronger than him.

Fake out. Reise dodged his head to the side and released his hands. The creature's face smashed against the floor. In its stunned split second Reise yanked the knife off his belt and stabbed the thing in the eye. Blue sprayed everywhere. The buzzing crescendoed in whatever passed for rage for this animal as Reise stabbed again and again and again and everything was wet and hairy and searing hot and—

At last the abomination collapsed atop Reise, stilled. Reise heaved, his face wet, and for a moment he thought he'd started crying. Shyte. Oh shyte. What the hell? What the filking hell …? Shyte, the sweat and blood on the frozen metal floor was so cold. He squeezed his eyes shut as if he could make it all go away …

But the claws stabbing his sides and the cold stabbing his back followed him even into that darkness, and this was not going to go away until he made it go away. He opened his eyes, jaw clenched, and gripped the bristly paws jammed into his sides.

A scream filtered through his closed teeth as he drew the long yellow claws out of his side, centimeter by tearing centimeter. Shyte, oh shyte, oh shyte …

At last he shoved the thing off him. Gasps burst from his throat as his head fell back against the floor, chest heaving like the workshop bellows back at the fort. Oh, what he would give to be there now.

"Have to get up," he muttered to himself. It took a moment. His muscles seemed to ooze, instead of contracting, as he crawled to his brother and flipped him over.

Jake was breathing, his violet eyes half-open, but clearly not awake. His nearly black skin shone with beads of freezing sweat. The darkest of the eight siblings, Jake looked so much like Mom suddenly.…

"Okay, you're alive for now," Reise said, his numb fingers on the tiny bit of warmth fluttering in his brother's neck. "Shyte, it's cold. I must seal this and re-power the ship."

He crawled first to Gideon, and Nathan, and found them both alive, but both in the same unaware state, with their eyes half-open; Gideon's pale lids twitched a bit over his baby blues, and Reise suspected his size gave him an advantage against whatever toxin they'd received. Lev looked the worst of all of them, with a strange cyanotic tinge forming around his lips. Well, Reise would get the med computer loaded, and—

What if there were more—*things*—somewhere? He should secure the scene first.

But secure it against which threat first? The cold would get them all soon.

An overwhelming desire to recheck Jake's pulse threaded across Reise's neck, itching, and strangling him.

What the galaxy should he do first?

The fire decided for him.

"Oh, bloody filking shyte," Reise cried out. A flickering shadow was forming in the far back corner of the hold, illuminating sparking electrical wires behind the supply crates. "Filking creature!" The rest of his exclamation—about how the monster had dashed into the back when he shot it, about flammable materials and flayer cartridges and he knew he hadn't missed—came out in a garbled stream of non-words as he dashed for the fire extinguisher—

"What the—" The fire extinguisher was torn out of its place, and leaking. "Filking animal!" Reise grabbed the canister anyway, ran back to the corner, and sprayed.

A weak dribble of foam came out, as ineffective as spit. The fire pounced on one of the medicine crates with an explosion that almost knocked Reise off his feet.

"Holy—"

He dimly recalled some heart medicine was explosive. Shyte, all the crates had a little of it, but wasn't there one crate *full*?

Reise jittered. There was no time to think—he reflexively dove toward the drill hole, shoved the drill out of the way, and started dumping his companions out of the ship, down into the ice cavern below. He snatched a medkit off the wall and jumped down with them, trying not to land *on* them. His boots crunched on the hard ice and a sharp jolt shot up his shins even as he bent his knees and tucked and rolled—hard to roll with people in your way—he groaned, his feet slipping in the ice as he put his back into pushing and pulling them as far away from the hole above as he could. The light from the fire lit up the dim blue cave walls with shadowy patterns that looked like living beings flowing through the solid translucence; the cave glowed brighter and brighter as Reise tried to hide all the bodies behind a large outcropping of ice and then the explosion—

Even through the ice wall behind him, Reise could see the column of fire shoot down into the cavern. The air seemed to suck away for a moment; an arm of flame curled past the outcropping, as if searching for the escapees, but unable to see them.

And then it became quiet, but for the distant crackling.

Reise waited before trying to return to the ship to salvage anything. His bare fingers trembled against the rough, heavy-duty canvas bag of the medkit as he tore it open for the small medspider inside. Shyte, had he done the wrong thing? Should he have found the one heart medicine crate and shoved *it* out instead? He had no guarantee he would have found it in time, but if he had, he could have saved the ship, and—shyte, was this his fault? Had he missed and shot something flammable some-how, or did the creature cause the fire? He could swear he saw his shot impact center-mass. He didn't usually miss. Did he—

The medspider hummed to life. The cool white ball clicked, and eight limbs popped out, reaching with almost sentient eagerness as Reise lifted to place it—

No. His instincts wanted to assist his brother first, but Lev looked sickest.

No one would know, though?

"Filking shyte," Reise muttered. He yanked Lev forward by the arm; the Draconian fell almost into his lap, and Reise stuck the medspider to his neck. He waited until the legs engaged to stab into Lev's partially scaly skin on either side of the puncture wound, and then Reise propped the Draconian up again. He needed to arrange them all leaning against each other, with the least body surface against the ice, and the most surface area against each other, to stay warm. Once the medspider analyzed for poisons and gave him instructions for each person, Reise would get it to sew up his own—

Reise wished he hadn't thought of his sides. He looked down to see six red blotches in his pilot uniform, and his stomach churned as the stink of rotten meat and the buzzing seemed to echo in his senses again. Gah, he'd need to disinfect. Who knew where that abomination had stuck its claws before.

Don't lift your shirt to check. Don't lift your shirt. Conserve body heat until the medspider's ready for you.

He wanted to, though. He could feel each open hole screaming, nerves *panicking* at the loss of tissue integrity. He *should* lift his shirt to check if the bleeding needed stopping, actually. He did so, and saw already drying, freezing rivulets tracing the folds of his doubled-over belly, and the lines of his sharp ribs. The holes gaped, to his eye, oozing dark red, but they did not gush. *It's not that bad. That's what Doctor Loylan would say. Only flesh wounds.*

Stabbing creature legs skewering his skin …

Life-threatening or not, Reise still needed to keep all his warm liquid circulating *inside* if he could. He pulled a roll of soft white gauze from the canvas bag, wrapped it around his midsection, dropped his shirt, and wrapped again, creating a tight embrace around himself, his eyes ever on the medspider. It crawled across Lev's face, now, the words *male Draconian* glowing in blue on its spherical body; Lev's vitals flashed just below his genetic ID. Most of the numbers glowed a safe green— but his heart rate hovered in red, at the very low end of normal even for an athlete. Under that string of numbers flashed a small starburst symbol that indicated a foreign molecule in Lev's bloodstream.

"When do you intend to give me instructions, imbecilic contraption?" Reise grumbled under his breath. People always told him he lacked patience. He felt now, as every other time, that *they* just lacked speed.

The medspider went as fast as medspiders do, scuttling and stopping, scuttling and stopping, injecting needles here and there for blood samples, or perhaps some of the antidotes that came preloaded inside it. In the meantime, for now, everyone's chests rose and fell evenly; everyone's pulse felt about as normal under Reise's cold, thick-feeling fingertips as his own did; and the slow loss of feeling in his toes turned him to a more pressing matter.

Reise checked around the corner of the ice outcropping. The whole cave had grown dimmer now, and with only a dim glow wavering from the hole above. They would need heat; best try to rescue any remaining supplies he could, and steal some of the fire before it died.

Reise's teeth chattered as he rose and crept to the hole above, his stiff fingers opening and closing near his empty holster out of habit and cold. He stood under the hole and looked up … no sign of immediate fire or enemy, but he circled, trying to obtain a view from all angles …

"Up," he grunted, swinging his arms to jump. His fingers caught the edge above, and without much difficulty—lightweight had its advantages—pulled himself back up into the hole.

The warmth in here stunk with the rotten scent of melting plastic and the sweet savor of cooking meat. The artificial lights had died, of course, so now dark shadows hung over every corner not kissed by dying embers of fire or cold white sunlight stabbing through torn ship walls.

The crew couldn't stay inside here—if the slow fire didn't spread overnight the chemical fumes would kill them instead; Reise himself shouldn't spend more time than necessary grabbing supplies. The mission still mattered, and if they could drop off at least some of the medications for the colonists, they succeeded. Reise would spend the next few hours saving what boxes he could in between moving the medspider from buddy to buddy.

First, though, he needed to take some fire out to the others—

No.

Before any of that, Reise turned to the smoking corpse of the creature he'd christened an ursa-fly in his mind.

"We're going to eat you," Reise said, kicking it out the hole, too. "So filk you."

CHAPTER TWENTY-TWO

Lem

A COUPLE DAYS HAUNTING THE MARKET STALLS IN FORGE'S colorful sands had taught Lem three things.

One, she definitely hadn't missed nutrient sludge while on Beryllia. Say what you wanted about the controlling, self-deluded, career-focused bureaucrats, they knew how to eat fresh. The Ebon Shadow's sustenance straws were way higher quality than the ones she'd gotten used to with the Frelsi, but damn did they have her craving greens.

Two, Forge artisans colored their complex tapestries using chemicals in the sand. That was cool or whatever. Their kids liked to use little fans clipped to their heels to make sand-patterns kick up behind them.

And three, she was doomed.

That last bit had started repeating in her head every other hour or so. Ever since getting dosed with that paralytic, Lem felt like she was pulling a sled with two hooks in her shoulder-blades. Or maybe it was since leaving whatever zone of interdimensional silence surrounded Beryllia. Just this heavy angry *thing* in her brain that wouldn't *filking shut the filk up*.

She didn't want to sit near Cinta at all with this happening. She didn't know what he could hear or not. She just wanted him to filking read the sleeping captive's mind *right now today* so she could find out what Bricandor wanted random-ass crystals for. Shyte, Cinta could apparently read things even Jei didn't want him to, so what the hell was so hard about an unconscious dude?

She hated that she thought this way, and wanted herself far away from Cinta right now; she could *feel* him watching her, worrying, even from the bounty hunter's ship way over there as she burnt off energy out here in the dunes.

Lem roared and spun her mace in another violent figure eight to slam it down against the sand. The colorful cloud of red burst up around her like she'd made the planet spurt blood; she dove through it to roll into a long lunge with a side-swipe, then leapt left to flip into a hand-less cartwheel. Her breath roared in her own ears; her heartbeat pulsed in her face; her lungs sawed through her chest. Sweat seemed to cool in the wind of her constant motion. *Die die die die die* screamed her brain; she beat it into silence the only way she knew how right now.

"Can I get next?" someone asked behind her.

Lem whirled, half-expecting to see Sterba, or the weird little inner-Biouk.

Jei stood there leaning on the staff of his mace, a black cloth respirator covering the lower half of his face. His eyes had always been so *bright* in his burnished skin, and the darkness of that half-mask made them seem to shimmer blue now. He didn't scold her for not wearing hers like she should out in this toxic dust—he just tossed one to her with a gentle em-push that made the material flutter like a living thing.

Lem snatched the mask out of the air, and it died.

"Yeah, sure," she said, masking up and stepping back into a pre-duel attention stance. He mirrored her, and they both bowed.

Lem always attacked first, the moment they came out of the bow, no chance for him to think—she slid to the ground and charged at his ankles with a low swipe. He answered with a leap and a downward slash. She jerked her mace upward to block, then exploded out of her crouch to shove him out of the air. Next he'd roll, then come up with an oblique slash—

Huh?

He didn't. He stayed in the air, held up by an em-push thrown behind him, his mace levitating out of his hand.

"Let's stop playing normal people games," he said.

Suddenly she found herself thrown up into the air. She startled, and fired a faux, em-push-back to let herself land, directing her static charge out like a punch. But wait—he needed multiple enemies to charge up and reach his max, and—"It's just you and me," she protested.

"Exactly," he said, landing with a backward slide that sent red sand splashing up around him like two waves. His outspread arms said there was nothing around for anyone to break.

"Shouldn't I be keeping my abilities *down* so I don't—"

He flicked a finger and she went flying into the air again. "I think we already tried that," he shouted up to her.

"Ugh, stop throwing me!" she growled, pulling herself back to the ground again.

"Make me," he laughed, flicking another finger.

"You asked for it," she grumbled as she spun mid-air. A quick electrical shock would power him down. She pointed at him—

He laughed and rolled to the side, tossing his mace in the air. It split, releasing a metal rod that drew her charge away from him.

Shyte, that lightning rod would make it impossible to power him down. Lem threw out a hand to snatch it toward her with static cling—his much more powerful magnetic pull held it firmly in his orbit. He dropped his palm hard; another em-pull slammed Lem toward the ground.

"Whoa!" she cried out, shoving both hands down to cushion her fall with another static push.

"Ignoring it won't make it go away," Jei called, much further away now atop another dune. Sand swirled around his silhouette against the sky; he was a rising sun, and his mace and his lightning rod spun around him like two planets.

Lem shouted in frustration and hurled both fists down by her side. A cloud of sparks burst out around her. She stomped on energy, throwing herself forward like a rocket at Jei.

He drew his pistol and fired.

"What the hell?" she yelped, tumbling into the sand with a puff of red. The shots careened past her, repulsed by her innate field, but—"Filking shyte, did you just shoot at me?" The cartridges glowed the signature yellow of stun blasts, but they both knew never to point a non-training weapon at someone during sparring.

"I told you, we're not pretending to be normal anymore!" he called back, somersaulting over her in the air to land behind her.

Jei was having way too much fun.

And she resented him for making her think so! She was the one who loved this wild shyte. But not anymore—did he *want* to get killed? Lem whirled to fire an electric shock—Jei floated around her, back behind her again, gliding over the surface of the sand as if he weighed nothing. Lem swiped, and missed, and swiped—

Agh! Lem roared with something that frightened her; a dome of sparks burst out around her. Jei crossed his fists over his face, landing, and Lem's energy divided around him like he was a rock in her stream.

"What took you so long?" she saw him whisper; his lips drew into a grim line as he pushed his way into her dome. She could *feel* the ripple of energy, as if she and Jei were pushing on opposite sides of a thick block of gelatin—

Jei raised his pistol—a strange, iridescent bubble had formed around it, and his mace. Shots rang out around Lem as Jei fired again. Instinct made her raise her mace to spin it into a forcefield —good instinct, because this time, the shots slowed, but didn't divert. They pinged against her spinning mace like music. *Why?*

Why didn't they swerve? Was it because they'd started inside her dome of sparks, within the same energetic field as their target? Okay, so—so if she could pull back the dome, could she—

The dome shrunk as she thought this; Jei fell outside it, and his volley of cartridges swerved around her again, missing in all directions. He lost his balance for a moment—Lem fired a bolt of electricity—

It diverted into that pesky lightning rod floating above his head. Lem leapt to dive for it; Jei jerked it out of the way, sliding back out of range again. He was going to force her to use her abilities more. She growled and threw out a hand, switching from the dome of sparks to another static pull, yanking him toward her.

He stopped just out of reach, that stupid metal stick just an arm's length away. She could feel the full weight of his magnetic force against her chest, pushing her back with one hand as he pulled the lightning rod with the other hand. She leaned in, her breath almost a wheeze as she strained for that dumb thing, resenting every loose thread, every rustling strand of hair, every grain of sand whistling between them—"They didn't challenge you enough on Beryllia," Jei panted. Sweat traced his eyebrow. Lem pushed harder into almost a scream.

A click of his finger on the gun—the pressure released just a hair—Lem snatched the rod and fired an electric shock just as something sharp stung her thigh. She heard Jei yelp, and wanted to laugh except that she'd made a very similar sound: he'd fired a shock from his pistol just as she finally powered him down. They both collapsed into the sand.

Lem's back hadn't even hit the ground before Jei had opinions.

"So your EMP field can't shut people down," he panted. "You need a direct electric shock to overwhelm the nervous system. *But* if you'd kept the EMP field out at the same time you could've shorted out my pistol so you didn't get powered down."

Lem stared up at the crimson evening sky, her chest aching as it tried to catch up with her breaths. "The dome—you sure that was an EMP field?" she asked. "Why'd it seem like you were pushing it? And that—bubble, around your gun?"

"I was protecting my pistol with a small em-push. Figured I could become kind of a Faraday cage if I could divert your charge around me."

"Man, that was some nonsense-burger," she breathed. "But yeah, I can try doing both things at the same time. If nothing else, that'll blow out some of the—whatever it is. Energy or whatever."

"Potential energy driven by entropy I think, is your thing. Like empathy is Cinta's. Or anger is mine," she heard him say. She almost laughed. Anger? As if he could hear her surprise in her breath, he added: "Like enmity. I feed off enmity. I think whatever happened to all of us, we just became more of what we were."

More of what they were ... Lem wanted to know Laaru's trigger now, the thought he was ashamed of. Poor kid. She would go back and help him at some point. Maybe when he graduated. When she had her own shyte together.

"Hey, that doesn't make any sense." She turned her head to face Jei. "All chemical reactions are driven by entropy. It's not my thing. It's everyone's thing. Every*thing*'s thing."

He didn't look at her; his eyes reflected the sky above. "I don't know how to say it," he said. "You seem to have something built up inside you, like when you carry something to the top of a hill, and it's just itching to roll down."

"*Repression* is my thing? That's not cool."

"Mine isn't that great either."

Lem sat up and whacked him on the knee with a laugh. "You're thinking of the dark side of everything, you dummy. Your thing is *justice*. Standing alone in front of a storm is where you belong. Enmity or cold anger or whatever is just the bad side of you; righteous silent wrath fueled by the energy of your enemies is your win condition. And mine is *freedom*. I'm entropy, I turn order into chaos."

"Maybe, but then the metaphor's wrong, because entropy isn't actually the same as chaos. That's overzealous primary school teachers trying to explain Le'Chatelier to kids. Entropy technically leads to the *most* ordered state in the universe: everything at its lowest energy state, evenly distributed."

"Oh. Right." Lem deflated, eyes on the sand. The most ordered state, with everything drained of all energy, still, and silent? Heat death.

She wasn't going to get away from that, was she?

CHAPTER TWENTY-THREE

Lem

LEM WASN'T ALONE IN HER DOOM, THOUGH: SHE FELT JEI SIT UP beside her, shifting in the crimson Forge sands to gently knock his sweaty head against her shoulder. "I'm the worst person to cheer you up," he sighed. "For a second there, you were you again. I'm kind of a technical wet blanket. I'm sorry I don't know how to say things."

"Eh. I don't need to be coddled," she grumbled. She felt him looking at her as if he wondered if he should leave, and she quickly added: "I mean, I'd rather you be real, you know? Like just now. With all that." She made a pew-pew sound and pretended her fingertips were guns. Jei laughed.

"Happy to shoot you any time," he quipped.

"Oh, I know," she said. They were quiet for a moment. It was strange that they could joke when last year it might have actually come to that, or it might actually come to that again. Everything about them was strange.

Lem caught him squinting at the left heel of her right boot. "Oh," she said, turning her foot for a better view of the red ribbon. "That's a toy. I was trying to get information from this one booth, and felt like I should buy something."

Jei raised an eyebrow. Shyte, he looked like he might laugh.

Lem smirked, and knocked her heel three times against the dune —one short, one long, one short. Colored sand sprayed up in whirlygigs and curliques around them.

"Pretty, huh?" she said. "It makes me feel a little better. Dunno why."

"Maybe because it's different," Jei coughed, waving color out of his face. It clung to his sweat in flecks of purple, blue, and red. "Another little difference the Growen haven't erased yet in their 'unity.'"

She tilted her head. Maybe. She didn't want to think about it too much. "Hey, you tell anyone I'm wearing a kid's dancing ribbon I'll kill you," she said.

"Your secret's safe with me," he chuckled. His face darkened a little. "Safer than Cinta's was, anyway."

For whatever reason, she appreciated the macabre almost-joke. She huffed half a laugh toward the horizon.

Jei sighed, and made as if to rise. "We better go back and— oh, man," he sat back down with a groan. "Bloodseas, Lem," he hissed, stretching out muscles that probably hurt all over from her shock. Lem wasn't even going to try to stand up her sore self: without their powers up, those charges would've knocked them out instead of powering them down.

"Sorry. I guess you're stuck here with me for a moment," she said.

He batted away the sorry and flopped back into the sand with a puff. "Eh, I asked for it. And anyway, this beats fielding a million questions from Lark Scrita in there about why you and I aren't together."

"I mean, we are."

"Not in the way she means. Most people who aren't Biouks don't have soul pledges outside of marriage and sex. You know that."

"They can all filk off," Lem muttered. She was tired of people having opinions about what should or should not happen to her body just because she cared about someone.

But she looked up at the sky for a moment and a twinge of sadness pierced her solar plexus. Soul-pledge or not, she wanted him to—be happy. "Hey Jei?" she asked, turning to him.

He answered with his eyes only.

"Are you—ever going to be able to have those things, you think?" she asked. "A mate, I mean."

He tilted his head with a wry little laugh. "I'm fine, Lem."

"Are you, though? There's this gentle—thing—about you that—you never used to have."

"What, if I'm not being a jerk I'm broken?" he laughed. "You can go back to calling me by my rank instead of my name if you want. Or I can electrocute you again."

He was deflecting, and it was dumb. Lem narrowed her eyes. Jei sighed and sat up again, gazing off into the horizon with his chin resting on his folded arms, on his knees. "Yeah. I don't know, Lem," he said finally. "I really miss her."

Lem had to fight to keep her teeth from clenching. "She basically forced herself on you."

"Not really. It's complicated."

"It's not complicated. It's not 'yes' if you're making the person say 'yes' with drugs and shyte."

"I know, and I knew what she was trying to do before she did it, Lem. I didn't care. I didn't care about anything she did wrong because I—I just wanted to love her through it. I wasn't going to let her just—I told her—I wanted to—"

Whatever memories rushed through his mind right now tumbled too fast for his tongue to keep up, and he had to stop, and try again. "She did some evil shyte, and I called her out on it. But I believed—I still believe—in her actual self, and not the manipulative thing they'd turned her into. She was *hiding* everything that actually mattered about her, Lem, awesome, beautiful things she'd locked away because she thought no one could love her for them but—*bloodseas* if you could've heard her talk about ghosts—!" Jei smiled into the sunset with so much pain on his face it looked almost like a grimace and Lem wanted to *never ever*

ever ask what he meant. She wanted to erase everything or bring his girl back to life, and couldn't do either. "I thought I could—help her," he added. "I just—I almost did, too. She just—I don't—why couldn't *my* mind win hers over, why did it—" He winced, and closed his mouth before his voice could crack. His face hid in his forearms for a moment, and Lem heard a deep sigh. She wanted to hug him, but there was something isolating about this pain he carried—something only he could carry, like a forcefield between the two of them, something words or touch would only mock. *Please be kind to him, Njandejara,* her heart cried.

As a tendril of sand blew past her masked cheek like a rough kiss, she realized this inner cry was the first honest thing she'd said to Njandejara in at least a week. There was a sad promise on the horizon that she didn't like, as if an answer lingered there that she didn't want to hear.

Jei turned his head presently. "I really think she could've helped you, Lem—could've saved your universe, if you want to put it that way. And I think you would've liked her in another life."

"Hey, I liked her. Wasn't even mad when she stabbed me in the back. I liked her right up until the moment I found out she was drugging your ass."

"Diebol called you my bodyguard for a reason," Jei smiled, leaning back now with his palms in the sand and face arched to the sky. He seemed so carefree, even in pain. It was so strange to see who Mr. Too-Military-For-A-Name was becoming. "What about you, Lem?"

"Me?" Lem shuddered suddenly; something twisted in her belly, and she almost choked before speaking. "I, uh—I'm—eh, I'm too busy for a mate," she croaked. "Shyte, I gotta destroy the universe or some shyte."

He leaned on one hand and looked at her. "You okay?"

She didn't know how to explain it. It wasn't that she didn't notice attractive people—she was definitely a red-blooded mammal—but after always having to worry about whether or not some blitzer would decide to have some fun with you before killing you—well, it just—just kind of turned her stomach to think about a mate. Made her breathe faster, too, like she needed to flee, and sent blood pounding into her temples. Diebol always came to mind. She'd even dreamt about him once and—shyte, she hated herself for that, too. She didn't want abuse. She couldn't think of sex as anything else, though. Filking—ech, her whole body wanted to just crawl into itself and hide and—

"Hey." Jei said. "I'm sorry."

"No, I asked so you asked. If I can't handle it I shouldn't dish it out," she grunted back. She looked away at the ship gleaming in the distance like an obsidian gemstone against the blue sand. "I don't think I'm going to live long enough anyway. My parents had no problem getting busy with everyone filking dying around them, but I'm just—I mean, they were alive before the war, so maybe that's why. I know to them it's important to fill the universe with us, so the Growen can't wipe us out. That's cool. Maybe I'm selfish, but at least until the war's over I just don't want to—risk—I dunno, like, the Growen could take your kids or your mate and—more than that, just mating itself requires a really open—risk." She looked back at Jei, expecting him to say something, and he didn't, just looked at her and listened. "I know it doesn't sound like me, avoiding … risk."

"No, it does," he said. "I still remember the time you almost ripped out Diebol's throat when he said you belonged to him."

"Shyte, that feels so long ago," Lem chuckled. She shook her head, and then elbowed him. "And you weren't so innocent back then either, Mr. Take Off Your Own Shirt."

"Wait, I said what?" He sat up straight with concern. "I'm so sorry, that—"

She waved her hand. "You weren't being scary, I was in on the joke and joking back. We were both high on adrenaline and about to die."

"I mean, I'm not blind, either. Maybe if it hadn't been for …

well. We are what we are." They both watched the horizon again. He didn't need to finish his trailed-off thought. They didn't need to talk about what could have been if he hadn't almost crushed her with an em-push last year. If she hadn't killed the girl of his dreams. There were no guarantees for what could have been *anyway*, even without those things, or even for what *would* be in the future. Lem was pretty sure they would have chosen this brother-sister soul-pledge regardless. Maybe fifty years from now the war would end and things would change and they'd somehow both be alive and decide to go for each other, or maybe they'd get crazy lucky and he'd magically find a new Mera and she'd magically find her own, or maybe they'd both die horrible painful deaths in an hour. Lem doubted all of that; none of that felt right, like mating with a sibling, and none of the maybes mattered anyway, because at this moment, here, watching the sun set as the brilliant sands painted the air and ache and sweat radiated off them both, this *now* was very pleasant—maybe the only pleasant thing in the whole universe, something quiet and warm and clever and wild all at the same time, like the feeling, a long time ago, of playing with Cinta in the nest of Mali and Pali's tree-hut without a clue about what loves and wars waged outside.

CHAPTER TWENTY-FOUR

Laaru

DEEP WITHIN BERYLLIA'S EDUCATIONAL MINING CENTER, THE RUMBLE of machinery and late night study-parties faded away, and all the hallways grew dark, patrolled only by security bots and the very occasional researcher with a laboratory pass. Here underground, the entire planet slept, and only a dim, pale cerulean light illuminated the hidden passageway Pele had built before she left.

Laaru always kept it as dark as he could. He was paranoid that someone might discover this place—and not just because then they'd know to check the security cameras in the next hall over to see who'd been with "the graduate" when she split.

Laaru needed this place to practice, and he didn't want anyone asking how he did what he did.

Laaru was trying now to figure out if there was a way to do the palms-explode-rocks-thing without the thought trigger he hated. He didn't like the memory, or the shame. He couldn't even name it in his head. There had to be another way. No one could know this about him. He laid his hand on the rock wall again, closed his eyes, begged the stone to break—

Not even a crack. He sat down with his back against it and

sighed. Not a bead of sweat; not a twitch of a muscle. His body just didn't react without that one thought.

Maybe it was just as well. Why did he need this ability, anyway? Even Pele herself said it might draw the wrong kind of attention. As long as he could keep it in check, and keep the gloves on, he'd be fine. He'd found it was really only his palms, anyway—he could even have fingerless gloves, and that looked pretty cool, so. Yeah.

Laaru rose, stretching out his back to survey his nexus of tunnels. He couldn't move the stone at Pele's entrance by himself without damaging it, so he'd actually burrowed in from his bedroom, adjacent to the tunnel into the lab. The carpet under his bed was actually just covering a huge hole, and if anyone bothered to look under the bottom panel of his workstation in the lab they'd find the same thing under there. No one ever *would* check under his workstation: he'd very carefully replaced the wood panel each time. But still.

It was crazy imagining a good kid like him building a secret tunnel system, wasn't it? He always got good marks; he was in one of the top talent programs Beryllia had to offer, with enough wiggle room to choose any literary or scientific pathway he wanted. He'd never rebelled against his parents, and that was saying something: they were both pretty strict, both lawyers. No one would ever believe he'd done this. Or that he'd met an illegal. Wow.

"Someone is in here."

Uh. Laaru hadn't been sweating before, but now? Yeah. Sweating a lot. Were those heavy bootsteps outside the tunnel entrance?

Oh no, what would happen to his grades if someone caught him?

Laaru dashed back into the branch that led to his room.

Well, but what if they followed him? They could follow him. No no no. He dashed back out into the main tunnel, his shoes making scratching sounds in the dirt as he twisted this way and that in indecision. What to do?

"We can probably move this rock, then, sir."

"Do not delay."

Okay. Okay he could cave the tunnel in, so even if they moved the rock, they found nothing.

He ran forward as the boulder began to shift with the grunts of what sounded like several very large people. Light—dangerous, unwelcome yellow light—began to stab into the pale blue darkness as the crack around the doorway widened.

Oh, he hated this!

Laaru shoved his hands up above his head—leaning forward on tip-toe so falling debris didn't crush him—grabbed two fistfuls of solid ceiling, and thought the thing. He thought it so briefly it *almost* didn't register in his mind, and he *almost* didn't feel the sharp pang of shame—

But *almost* wasn't the same as *didn't*. The ceiling dropped with a thundering crash right in front of Laaru, close enough that pebbles shot against his shoes, and pants. He yelped more at the pinging impact than from pain, and fell back on his butt. *That* hurt. His involuntary yowl brought another flood of shame—he shoved his fist over his mouth. Oh, he was going to get caught, he was going to get caught, and what would his parents think?

He scrambled to his feet and threw himself back into the tunnel that led to his room with just another hesitant backward glance to ensure that yes, it was now absolutely impossible to break into Pele's abandoned escape route without hardcore mining equipment. He would cause another cave-in behind himself here to hide his side-tunnel, in case the Administration did break out the big drills—he flinched, squeezing both eyes shut—the rocks thundered under his fingers—

Oh, he was going to get caught so *hard*.

But Laaru's heart calmed down as he walked back toward his room. Walked, right? He'd been running, stumbling in the darkness with his hands on the walls. But no one would find him now, right? He'd make it back into his room with plenty of time to finish his calc assignment before going to bed. It made him a little giddy, actually. Look at him, sneaking around like some kind of action hero.

The earthen-red light from his carpet, under his bed, shone up ahead. He could almost skip and dance. He reached his fingers up above his head, under the rough, thin carpet, and shimmied up out of the hole, his feet kicking messily against the stone walls. This part was the hardest—just—eech—he panted, squirming out from under his bed—

There was a knock on his door. It startled Laaru—he scraped his back on the bed trying to get up and *dayuaaaaah grrr* clenched his teeth to hold back some kind of squeal-groan-growl as the sharp pain raced up his spine like hot lava on a diaper and *why* would anyone want anything with him at this time of night? They couldn't know, could they? Laaru made it to his feet—what should he—where should he—his shoes scratched the tile floor as he shifted in his indecision again, turning toward the compuscreen with his calculus still loaded on it, and the little cooling chute on the wall that delivered his evening drinks, and the rustic but comfortable stone bed with the soft feather mattress—what should he look like he was doing when they came in? Well, definitely not standing here with dust all over his clothes! He ripped off his pants and shirt and threw them under the bed, rubbing his hand furiously through his hair to get the shower of rocks out before—

So the door opened to Laaru panicking in the middle of his room in his underwear.

He yelped, as did the silver-robed Administrator who stood dumbfounded halfway in the open doorway. "Why the galaxy did you not say something, young man?" she cried, shielding her crimson eyes as if blinded by his pale body. "'I'm changing,' 'hold on,' 'just a moment'—any number of appropriate warnings!"

"I'm sorry," he squeaked. He hadn't even considered speaking. He just wanted to hide and protect his grade point average.

"For the sake of all that is good in the galaxy, child, clothe yourself! There's a diplomat who's taken interest in your school record and would like to speak with you!"

Laaru complied. His stomach no longer pitted in panic, but still—at this time of night? Well, diplomats had busy schedules. They didn't have time for students and scholarships during the day, right?

Laaru soon wore clean blue school clothes like a respectable human being; their thick, simple weave rustled comfortably against skin sore from pebble-pelting and floor-crawling. He smoothed his hair to the side and hoped the black fingerless gloves didn't seem *too* out of place against the polite loose slacks and blouse.

The Administrator didn't seem to like waiting. As soon as Laaru emerged from his room she stepped off into a brisk, businesslike pace that forced Laaru to trot to keep up, his baggy pants swishing and hissing like a hurried whisper. Against the Beryllian woman's chest, elegantly framed by her red, vein-like skin growths, glowed a white pendant, its signal protecting them both from the automated security systems that roamed the dim fluorescent hallways: no one could leave their rooms at night without the escort of an Administrator.

Was Laaru in trouble for bypassing the security bots with his tunneling?

No, of course not. She'd said a diplomat wanted to chat about his record.

But Laaru's palms warmed, his leather gloves moist as they rounded the corner to one of the guest conference rooms. Two huge space-soldiers stood outside the engraved conference room door. He had no reason to fear them, right? Or their ... many shining gray ... pistols ... or the long rifles on their backs ...

Every firm step of the Administrator's heels against stone

floor sounded like a punch to the temples as they neared the door—and the soldiers. Laaru averted his eyes like they couldn't see him if he couldn't see them; his reflection in their fishbowl-looking helmets creeped him out. It just seemed like they didn't have faces. Like they could swallow his soul if he stared too long? That was silly, but it seemed like that, kind of?

He kind of hated his own indecisiveness about every thought he had.

"You seem like a young man who needs some confidence," said a gentle, elderly voice as the huge mechanical stone door creaked open before them.

Like everything on Beryllia, the conference room was simple, but advanced. An enormous stone table took up a third of the space, its edges ragged and unfinished, but its top shimmering with the latest-model compuscreen embedded in its surface. In front of the table, arranged in a casual sort of circle, stood four rough stone chairs, each decorated with precise machinework and upholstered with plush synthetic fiber that felt like a firm embrace for Laaru's backside as he sat down—across from the oldest human he had ever seen.

"Do you agree?" A wrinkled, hunched specimen with gentle eyes, the thin man seemed like he might shrink into his enormous brown robe, never to be seen again. Laaru was so nervous he didn't know what to say. He'd never met a diplomat before. His shoes fidgeted against the smooth burgundy rug.

"I guess, sir?" he squinted. How did his academic record demonstrate lack of confidence, though?

"I just have a way about these things," the old man chuckled, waving his hand as if dismissing the unasked question. "I can see a clever young man who just needs a push."

Laaru looked around. They were alone; the Administrator had left, and the soldiers stayed outside. "She—uh—the Administrator told me you wanted to talk about my—academic record, I guess?"

The old man nodded. "Yes, among other things. I know you've been doing well in the interdisciplinary Neodymium Projects, and I am, quite frankly, interested in offering you a scholarship." He leaned forward, blue eyes sparkling in his ashen face. "I asked for some privacy, since I am aware you don't want to reveal your gift at this time."

Laaru's eyes widened, and his gloves threatened to slide right off his palms in the river of sweat. "I—how did you know about that?"

"An associate of mine taught you about your gift, very briefly, didn't she?" the old man answered with a question.

Oh. Pele? Pele had told him, maybe? "I thought she was—like a Frelsi terrorist or something?"

"Oh no, not a terrorist. Just very misunderstood. And misunderstanding herself, I'm afraid." The old man leaned back with a slow groan, sighing with his hands on his back as he shifted in his seat. Laaru thought a fragile stick-limb might snap off at any moment. "She had not been feeling well," the diplomat went on. "She endured so much trauma during her time undercover with the Frelsi, I am afraid she's become quite sensitive."

Hmm. Yeah, Pele had been pretty sensitive about issues that really didn't bother anyone else. "So she was actually working for you? Where did she go?" Laaru asked.

"Back on assignment, most likely. But the wilds of space are not a good place to be alone, and she's lost her transmitter, so I'm unable to pick her up as originally planned. I hope she makes it back safely." The old man shook his head, looking off at the wall as if he could see through it to a sad, sad past … "At any rate," he interrupted his own musing. "I apologize—I don't mean to concern you with these things. We are here to discuss *your* future, not my worries."

Laaru pinched his lips together, trying to think, but finding himself not only overwhelmingly sleepy, but very—just very eager to make this kind old man happy. "Thank you—I wish I could help. She didn't say anything about where she was going, though."

The diplomat tilted his head, still facing the wall, as if listening to the silence after Laaru's words. Satisfied, he looked back at Laaru's face. "That's fine, young man. Now. Let us discuss the terms of your scholarship."

CHAPTER TWENTY-FIVE

Laaru

"Counselor Bricandor offered to pay for your schooling?"

The suspicion in Xunst's voice seemed to echo in the empty science lab; Laaru wanted to hush him even though no one else was here. The three guys sat on the lab tables now, unsupervised, eating parrot and sauerroot sandwiches, with their compupads laying forgotten beside them, chemistry homework still lingering unfinished on their screens. Beakers scattered behind them in various states of full and empty as their test samples spun in the heavy-duty centrifuge or cooked in the processing forge. Only Xunst's station was clean.

"You're totally going to take it," Nevik said through bites, pointing his sandwich at Laaru like a lecturing rod.

"This is literally what Pele said he *shouldn't* do," Xunst said.

"Well—he seemed to know Pele," Laaru demurred. "Said she was like undercover or something? It was—confusing. But he seemed nice."

"Yeah, Pele didn't seem to think you should trust the Growen," Xunst furrowed his brow in a way that reminded Laaru of his dad. "She was *pretty* clear about that."

"Well, not trusting someone isn't the same as taking their money," Nevik said. "I mean, if he can get off work-study he can focus on what he wants and Beryllia won't own his work. That means he graduates to the work force with all his projects and patents under his belt, way ahead of the rest of us. Creative control is *everything*."

"We know how scholarships work," Xunst said.

"I'm not so sure you do if you think this is something he can just turn down like *that*," Nevik snapped his fingers. "I mean, Laaru, you said he knew Pele, right? So what if he was the one who paid for her school?"

Xunst held up both hands now, his food long abandoned beside him. "I'm pretty sure she was on work-study, and if he *did* pay for her, that's even *more* reason to worry about the whole 'don't become a soldier-slave, hey look, I'm running away.'"

Nevik's long curls bounced as he shook his head. "Look, I liked Pele, too, but don't you think it's possible we don't understand her whole deal? I mean, undercover or runaway, there's clearly this whole other story we don't know, and I for one am not arrogant enough to assume I know exactly what she meant."

Xunst dropped a laugh of disbelief that bordered on scornful, not at all like himself. He was normally a pretty quiet guy, and it was strange to see him so passionate about this thing. He looked away, sandwich back in hand, but it almost seemed like he might hurl it into the trash.

"I appreciate you both being so—you know. Caring and stuff," Laaru piped up. "But it's kind of my decision, so like— you guys fighting over it won't help."

Nevik tried to lighten the mood. "Psh, we just haven't tried fighting hard enough yet. Wait 'til you see us in a cage match. That'll solve all your problems."

Laaru chuckled; he couldn't imagine diminutive Nevik or slender, perfectionist Xunst in any kind of fight. They were all three pretty nerdy and kind of weak, and Nevik, though he might instigate with questions, would never keep up even the most benign argument for very long.

"At least show the contract to your parents first," Xunst said finally.

"I … kind of want it to be my decision." Laaru looked down at his shoes, kicking his heels against his lab table. He didn't want his parents to ask why this had happened. He wasn't a great liar. He didn't want anyone to think he was messed up, and he definitely didn't want anyone to ask about the awful trigger.

"My guy, you have two free lawyers at your disposal," Xunst cried out. "I think it'd even be worth *paying* lawyers to avoid possible magical slavery. Free money isn't free."

"It is his decision, though," Nevik said in an almost holier-than-thou voice. He stopped himself and laughed: "Wow, I sound like a tool. I mean it though." He paused, tilting his head as he looked to check the time on the centrifuge beside him. "But to be honest, Laaru, even I would ask my parents, and they're not lawyers. Isn't there a military service stipulation?"

"Yeah, it's that, *or* I have to use my—well, rock-busting—to speed up my research project. They really want the new damage-free detection system I'm working on." Laaru didn't look up. "I think I'd choose the military service instead."

"What?"

"Are you insane?"

Both Xunst and Nevik exclaimed out loud, Nevik almost laughing and Xunst looking seriously concerned.

"I just—don't really want any of our classmates to know about—what I can do," Laaru said. "Or anyone. If I can put off the reveal, that's best." The shame of the trigger just—just—no one could know right now.

"It's your life," Nevik shrugged, downing the rest of the blue electrolyte fluid in his canteen.

Xunst's piercing look yet again reminded Laaru of his dad. Laaru felt like he had to defend himself. "It'd mostly be an office job, I think? He explained the rank system to me. Groups like the Frelsi make everyone slog through the same ranks, but the

Growen let you skip directly to like an analyst position, as an officer, if you have enough schooling."

"So you'd skip straight to leadership over people who kill kids, instead of doing the killing yourself," Xunst said.

"Whoa! Whoa whoa," Nevik suddenly stood, hands out between them both, his face panicked by the highly-charged accusation. "Let's not bring politics into this. We don't know any of that for sure. Most major news networks on this planet don't even report on that conflict, and even if they did, political arguments—like really harsh ones like that—never ever end with anyone changing their mind, just two mad people more entrenched in what they believe. This can't be about ideology. It's got to be about supporting Laaru through this really—weird—and hard situation." He walked over to check his sample through the window of the processing forge now. "Besides, you know we're not supposed to talk controversial subjects during school hours."

"And we can't talk at all after school hours, because we can't go out in the hallways, and digital chats are monitored for inoffensiveness." Xunst got up with a sardonic grin. He walked over to his own samples. "Either way, Laaru, you better be sure you believe in the cause before you sign up for any kind of military."

"I think I just don't know enough to know for sure," Laaru muttered. He kind of just wanted to hope for the best and not think about it. He definitely couldn't see the kind older gentleman killing people, whereas Pele, with sparks out of her fingers and that unpredictability—

Well, that was unfair of him. He knew war happened and stuff, and he shouldn't make assumptions about people.

But he was pretty sure most soldiers on all sides nowadays just sat up in offices anyway. People didn't actually *fight* except on really remote, backward worlds still stuck in the past. The modern era didn't work like that. Discrimination, hate, real poverty, intrigue, all of that existed in the past, not the enlightened present except in the minds of conspiracy theorists.

Speaking with Counselor Bricandor had calmed a lot of the nagging fear that Pele had planted in his soul.

Still ... guilt tugged at him, and for some reason he couldn't stop thinking about the moment he'd caved in Pele's tunnel last night. He felt, somehow, like he'd been caught, and didn't really know what that meant.

CHAPTER TWENTY-SIX

Reise

EVEN THROUGH HIS GLOVES, THE COLD HAD SO STIFFENED REISE'S fingers that bending them felt like pushing through clay; his numb fingertips shook as his knife slid through gleaming fascia and blubber under the stinking, bristly skin of the ursa-fly. It would be easier if he turned on the laser edge, but he wanted to save power, so frigid steel would have to do. He hacked off another strip of muscle, stabbed it with a broken bit of crate, and handed it to his brother to roast over the fire.

It was quiet except for the crackling of those flames, some chewing, and Lev's slow, still unconscious breathing. Even the medspider had quieted, laying dormant with a needle still in the Draconian's cubital fossa.

"Yo Reise what'd you call his front elbow again? The place where blood draws from?" Gideon asked.

"Cubital fossa," Reise said. "And it's not my term, that's standard medical anatomy."

"Yeah well. You don't think his fossa or whatever's like losing a buncha heat with the metal of the medspider and shyte? Like especially if blood flows through there." The burly guy pointed a meat-skewer at Lev. He was the first person to talk for a while; Nathan was messing with his wristband, trying to correspond with their handler, Nefesh, back home, and Jake was shivering wide-eyed right up against Reise's shoulder, obviously contemplating some fresh terror as he looked this way and that over the wall of boxes Reise had saved from the fire. Slim Reise, always more cold-blooded than his muscular younger brother, definitely appreciated Jake's body heat. Still, lest his own shivering be taken for fear, Reise struggled to hide the chattering of his teeth as he answered Gideon: "I want to be able to see the medspider in case it comes back on with something for us to do."

"It'll hum if it wants you," Nathan said, reaching over now to tuck Lev's arm under a bit of hide. They'd opted to cuddle Lev up with the half-skinned corpse of the ursa-fly, peeling back the bristly fur to fold it over their leader like a blanket. He was the sickest—he was the only one who hadn't woken up after a dose of antidote from the medspider—and he needed whatever warmth they could muster to help his body survive.

But the resulting image was quite grotesque. With the bristling fur touching Lev, the bloody side of the hide lay up, so he looked like he was wrapped in a disgusting meat burrito, with the unrecognizable flayed anatomy of the ursa-fly attached to him organically somehow as if he, and it, made up two heads of a mutated blob.

Reise focused on skinning. They needed more heat, they needed protein, and they'd need whatever poison sacks he could find in this thing for the medspider to analyze. In the meantime they'd wait until the settlers came to pick up their medicines and outfit them with a new ship. If the settlers even had a spare ship. There was a reason they'd needed outside help for supplies like medications.

Shyte, he hoped Lev would be okay.

"It moved so fast," Jake said finally, sniffing as he glared at the light blue shadows on the cave walls. "I hate this planet. I hate it."

"Nefesh is asking how it got in without triggering proximity sensors," Nathan said. Reise hated the way he made eye contact with him.

"It came through the drill shaft, obviously," Reise said, looking back to his knife with a feigned shrug. Shyte ...

"One of us would have seen it."

"You didn't?" Reise looked up.

Gideon shook his head. "Lev and Nate and me all had our backs to the medicine crates and eyes on the drill. I saw Jake open his mouth, and then—" He mimicked a squelching syringe with his mouth and a penetrating finger motion. "That's all I've got."

"It was already inside, behind you, this big—shadow," Jake said. "It—stabbed all three of you like a machine gun. It was just a second, not even a second. Tick, tick, tick—" He shuddered, clenching his teeth.

"Shyte, if you saw it, why didn't you warn them or scream or something?" Reise asked.

"My throat—stuck." Jake's eyes averted with a still-terrified rage.

He'd frozen, then.

"Shyte." Reise tucked his own eyes in his elbow with a sigh. "We filking suck." Before Nathan could bother him with more questions, Reise added: "I don't know. I heard a thud at some point during our landing, but focused on ensuring a safe atmospheric descent. The external cameras were obscured—I suppose by webbing or slime, now that I consider it—and the proximity sensors never triggered." If it somehow entered through an exhaust vent or something as soon as they'd landed, and then gnawed through the fuel line near some wires, that would explain the fire....

"Maybe that's how it hunts," Gideon said. "It's learned to blind cameras and crack open the metal oyster for the treat inside. Maybe saw the whole ship as like a shell or a nest."

"Maybe. It certainly didn't seem sapient, anyway," Reise said. Gideon's tone made him feel—better—for some reason, like no one was in trouble, like this was another passage in a holo-tale or level in a video game.

Nathan was watching Gideon intently, Reise soon realized, with something that might have passed for curiosity on that small, pointy, stoic face.

"What?" Gideon asked.

Nathan shook his head, and turned his deep-set eyes to Jake. "If it weren't so cold, I'd have you take a walk with me to cool down," he said, his normally soft, high voice even softer. He rose and stepped over Gideon, who scooted over without a word, and made himself useful checking Lev's vitals on the medspider once more.

It was quiet for a moment, as Nathan sat beside Jake, thin fingers twirling against each other in bony black gloves. Presently, the older cadet tore off another bit of crate to add to the fire, and staring into it, he said: "What happened to you wasn't abnormal, Jake. I hope you know that. People teach two biological responses—fight and flight—but the truth is, there are three. It is possible for your nervous system to be forced to shut down and freeze. Literally go limp, or rigid, either one. It's even possible for you to have what's called a vasovagal, where the balance between your parasympathetic and sympathetic nervous system suddenly shifts, and you pass out."

"Fainting," Gideon said.

"Yes." Nathan continued, poking the fire. "That's less of a terror response and more of a blood or pain response, usually. Either way. Different from freezing. You froze, right? You didn't mean to, but you couldn't move?"

Jake nodded, his face red.

"There are all kinds of automatic stress responses." Nathan continued in a low tone that, along with the crackling of the fire, and the embrace of the cold, almost threatened to hypnotize Reise into sleep. "You know, Jake, there are even some mammals on the human homeworld who have this ridiculous jump response, where any danger will make them jump straight up, instead of out of the way. When your adrenergic neurotransmitters kick into overdrive—"

"That's your nerves' 'upper juice' flooding your blood," Gideon interjected.

"Yes," Nate nodded patiently. "When that happens, sometimes there's no telling what your body will try."

Reise knew these things himself from some of his basic combat medic courses—the ones Dr. Patti Loylan used to teach back on Luna Guetala. Reise'd had a freeze response for a long time, too. But he'd trained himself out of it. No one wanted a freezer on their team. He'd been told that enough times to feel ashamed of Jake for doing it.

"You're not any worse of a person, Jake," Nate went on, as if reading Reise's mind. "Fight and flight aren't necessarily better, you know. Fighters can hurt their own teammates without thinking, and of course flight's often out of the question when you're trying to obtain an objective. Taking a deep breath to think is often faster than either."

"Freezing isn't like pausing to think rationally, though," Reise interjected now. "You can't think—almost can't breathe. It's useless in imperilment." He looked up at Jake. "You have to get rid of it."

Jake glared at him; Reise didn't know why. "I couldn't do anything!" Jake repeated, his teeth clenched.

"Yes, I heard that," Reise stated. "Which is why you have to start conditioning it away. So you *can* do something."

"It wasn't my fault!" Jake floundered for words: "You—you ignored the thud on the ship!"

"You try landing a moving vehicle at thousands of kilometers per hour hurtling from outer space," Reise hissed. "There are courting-age adults who can't do it even after training their entire lives." Adult … ah, shyte. Reise's heart sank and he struggled to keep his voice steady as he stabbed into the ursa-fly's face to find those *filking* poison sacs. His words came between panting and clenched teeth as he wrestled that stupid carapace.

"And we were—supposed—to be a team that could be relied on. To get meds to these settlers. We failed. We filking failed and we have to do better." He stabbed the face in frustration. "Failure means death. I don't know what's so hard to understand."

"I. Couldn't. Do. Anything," Jake growled.

Nate's soft voice silenced them both. "What happened, happened," he said.

What a stupid thing to say. Of course what happened happened, or it wouldn't be what happened. Reise hated expressions like that, but this filking difficult faceplate around the ursa-fly's proboscis had most of his attention now. He assumed either the sacs were near the proboscis, or somewhere deeper in the face, and either way he didn't want to cut the delivery line and spray toxin all over himself. He needed to focus.

No. It was difficult to focus. Really difficult. Something about his brother's story bothered him. Not its veracity—just the nature of the whole thing, of Jake's fatalistically deterministic "I couldn't" ruining, in Reise's mind, his chance for redemption in the future. Something was *wrong* and Reise needed it to be *right*.

But before he could speak again, Nathan did.

CHAPTER TWENTY-SEVEN

Reise

"The first time I froze like that, I was a couple years younger than you." Nathan poked the fire again; in the lengthening evening shadows, the splintered piece of wood he held seemed like an extension of his bony finger. "I'm a chemosynth." He looked up, as if quickly gauging his teammates' reaction to this, before looking back into the fire. "On my home planet, the females are larger than the males, like with spotted hyenas, or baleen whales, so—"

"That's weird, I thought testosterone always makes male mammals bigger," Gideon interjected.

"Size is more related to growth hormone," Reise explained for him. "Testosterone and estrogen alter muscle distribution and fat consumption—they're related to size, but not solely responsible for it."

"Yes, whatever. It's not important why," Nathan's tone was still patient, although his words carried a hint of annoyance. "Whether it's through natural selection as our cultures preferentially chose to mate only with larger women, or just a naturally different growth hormone and testosterone distribution in our ancestors, or a mix of both—it's not important why. Just our strain of Homo sapiens, *H. sapiens egetus*, the vast majority of our societies are heavily matriarchal. Depending on the country, males might be sold like property, second-class citizens, or just treated like porcelain dolls that might break. That's not the point, just a detail." He looked up at Gideon. "I grew up with a lot of staring and comments."

"You're hot, where you come from," Gideon grinned.

"Smoldering. It wasn't a good thing." Nathan looked back at the fire. "All that talk is only fun if you're in control, if you've got equal power. The whispers behind your back are better than groping, but you fear the whispers, because even whispers carry the omen of the hunt. There are so many games and tricks the hunters employ—you have to watch your back, at all times, and as the prey you just wish they would speak straight to your face so you know what to watch for. The nice ones are trying to buy you half the time." He looked up at the ceiling with a sigh. "I froze with a nice one. She was just two or three years older than me. About your size, Gideon. I thought we were hanging out because she liked spending time with me. But when I wouldn't kiss her, I found out she thought I owed her. Because she'd spent money and time on me, so like a bad investment, I didn't pan out when I didn't kiss back."

Reise looked at Gideon. The *foreignness* of what Nate was describing was taking such a twisted turn that Reise almost thought he or Gideon might laugh, not out of humor, but out of discomfort, and confusion, with this weird squeeze in his belly. This couldn't be real. There at least had to be more to it, another side.

"I was so injured after the beating I almost died. There was a metal rod involved," Nate swatted his bony hand and shrugged like that explained the missing details. "I wanted to run. I wanted to fight back. But I couldn't do anything. I wondered why for a long time, and I *felt*, for a long time, that I wasn't a person, and that was why, like that trophy, that crown jewel, I did nothing." He shifted with a sigh, hugging himself against the cold. "Of course, the better-looking you are, the more rumors people spread about whether or not they've had time with you. There's this precarious dichotomy where they either say you're easy or you're frigid, and you're punished for both. I can't say the talking at school was worse than the incident, but—in some ways it was? I just slowly started going crazy. You know I was actually grateful when the Growen invaded my town?"

"What? Why?" Reise scowled. That seemed unbelievably selfish, and not in a good, self-interested way, but in a stupid way, from a brain that didn't understand value systems and equivalent retaliation.

"I don't know why, really," Nathan said. "I just had this overwhelming sense of relief. I don't think I saw the Growen as liberators, even though most of them were men, with male leaders. I mean, I lived in a country where theoretically men were equal. Wages weren't equal, and social power wasn't equal—men were still more likely to be forced into something physical than women—but men could vote, at least. It was a good country, in many ways, and it wasn't like the Growen made things better by oppressing everyone equally. Seeing the Growen decimate our military and put men in charge of our government didn't make me feel better or anything, if that's what you're thinking, like I had some kind of revenge-complex against all women. I didn't.

"So I don't know why, Reise. I used to feel guilty about it. But the fact was, I was relieved. Something was over." He turned back to Jake, shaking himself off, as if breaking a spell. "Anyway, none of that's the point. The point is, it took me a long time to be okay with what happened when I froze. People talked about me a lot because I froze. I must have asked for it, or enjoyed it, in some sick way, because I didn't fight back. It took me a long time to learn that it was biology, just as much my biology as my maleness, and you can't drag someone for their biology."

Reise's jaw clenched, and something nauseous lingered in his throat, but he barely noticed it. Nate wasn't playing fair with the stories: uncomfortable emotions aside, Jake needed change, not coddling. "Whatever happened, it's still true that biology can be hardwired and adapted," Reise said. "The brain is the most amazing self-programming computational device. Shyte, some people's biology is naturally under-stimulated so they tend toward being murderers—doesn't make *that* okay. You can't choose the biology you're given at first, but you can choose what behavior you wire into it after. I know. I used to freeze, too."

Nathan seemed to ignore him, and leaned straight in toward Jake. "Jake, you know what I learned over time, and why I sleep like a baby while half the other Frelsi refugees still have night terrors?"

"Why?" Jake breathed a spellbound whisper, his dark eyes almost glowing in the sad firelight.

"I learned, Jake, that there was likely nothing you or I could have done anyway. And even if there was, there *is* nothing you or I can do about the past now. There is only what you and I can do in the future."

"There, okay, you're just proving my point," Reise said. Finally.

Gideon threw a stick at him.

"Hey—"

"My guy, shut up, I want to hear more about planet Amazon-woman-power," Gideon said. "You can be right later."

Reise didn't understand. That wasn't how right worked. If you were right, you were right in the present—time did not change your right-ness.

But more importantly, he heard something crunching. With a hiss he held up his right fist to signal alarm. *Silence.* Gideon, who could see the furthest into the right tunnel, craned his neck—and then blanched like bark left in the sun on sand.

Holy shyte it's like twenty blitzers, he signed.

Well. Technically military sign language lacked expletives, but Gideon's face filled in the words in Reise's mind.

Hide him! Reise waved at Lev, slipping past Jake to take up a position behind the outcropping of ice that had shielded them from the ship's blast. Automatic rifle cocked against his shoulder, he leaned his cheek on the cold barrel, eyed down the sight —his finger found that comfortable trigger—

He saw a head, he saw a neck, and he went for the kill. Unlike most of his peers, Reise's accuracy meant he didn't have to care how much the grays reinforced those neck joints—they were still joints, and that still meant cracks. Breathe—a flash of black undermaterial—

Trigger pull. Flash of orange light. Dark blood spurted across the ivory-blue walls.

There was that moment just before the others realized what had happened, that infinite half-second, where the blitzer clutched his throat and fell back out of view, around the bend in the ice, against his comrade.

And in that half-second, Reise saw the comrade's neck, too, for another hit.

"It's an ambush, cut them off round the other tunnel!" Reise heard a blitzer's tinny, mechanical helmet-voice. Shyte, the other tunnel? The guys were about to be trapped.

Reise tapped Gideon hard on the shoulder and handed him the rifle. Gideon took over suppressive fire, and Reise slid over to help smaller Nathan shove the ursa-fly back against the ice, hiding Lev fully under that flap of hide.

"We need to divert them away," Reise said, stomping out the fire and trying to move medicine crates out of view, too. There was no really hiding these big boxes, but at least if they were tucked behind the ice, maybe they wouldn't draw attention. Maybe.

There was no maybe about Lev, though. If the guys lost their fight here, the blitzers would execute Lev before he had a chance to wake up.

"Someone's gotta stay with him or he'll freeze anyway," Nate said.

Freeze? Reise met Nate's eyes for a split second, and then slapped his little brother's shoulder. "Jake. Take this," Reise said, shoving his pistol into the boy's hands. "Get under this fly."

"I—"

"You will shut the filk up or you're going to die," Reise said. He didn't sound mad. He wasn't. It was just a fact as cold as the breath forming icicles on his hood. The ursa-fly's weight was filking substantial, and its fetor reeked, but Jake would be better off under there than frozen in a firefight or slowing down their run with his limp. Jake squeezed under the creature, wedged in there by Nate's shove. Reise gripped his brother's hand—"Lev's counting on you," he heard himself say—and then he was already sighting down the hallway again beside Gideon, watching for the moment for their break. Gideon added another dead blitzer to the gathering pile at the chokepoint—

"Run for it!" Reise yelled, loud enough to make sure the blitzers heard, and just slow enough that they saw as he, Nathan, and Gideon raced down the right tunnel into the dim blue light.

CHAPTER TWENTY-EIGHT

Cinta

SOMEONE SCREAMED IN THE CLOSET.

Cinta's ears perked, and he lowered his fruit-paste to look around at the others in the room with him. No one else seemed to hear anything. Jei and Lark and the Ebon Shadow all sat eating and discussing leads in various stages of lounging and sitting, half-dress and overdress. Cinta understood why the humans wore clothing, with all their sensitive dangly bits ever kissed by air, but the Bont woman seemed unnecessarily covered given her tough scales and the manner in which reptiles distributed heat for homeostasis. Clothing seemed like it would harm a reptile. It wasn't that cool in here, either: Jei had his black jumpsuit top off down to his undershirt for good reason.

Clothes and missions and oddities aside, Cinta's ears swiveled like satellite dishes as he looked from face to face to see if perhaps he had picked up on one of their inner sufferings. No —he could see the movement of their mouths. These words did not belong to them.

Oh, Jaika.

Without a word, Cinta crawled from his bench-seat beside Jei down to the floor. His clawless paws made not a scratch or a tinkle on the flawless black floor as he walked through the polymerwall into the hallway, careful not to turn to an unauthorized right or left and trigger the wrath of the ship. He found his way down to the hold, where the enemy bounty hunter lay suspended in chemical sleep, floating in a forcefield inside an iron cage reinforced with electrocuting polymerwall. Cinta paused for a moment, facing away from the captive with an ear toward him, just to confirm whether or not he could hear the man's dreams …

He could not. Jaika would remain disappointed in him.

Cinta prowled over to the supply closet in the corner of the large storage room, and rested on his haunches outside it, waiting, and listening, in case he should not interrupt. Perhaps she spoke right now to Njandejara, pouring out her soul, and did not need his intervention.

"You're doomed. You're doomed, you're doomed." The dark childish sing-song tingled across Cinta's spine like the claws of a hundred arachnids. "You're doomed, you're doomed, you're doomed. Heehee!"

Oh no, very much not Njandejara. And his sister was screaming back: "Shut *up!*"

No one could hear this, really?

"Jaika?" Cinta hit the closet's doorframe with his forepaw.

Neither voice answered him. The sing-song continued, and Cinta's throat began to dry.

"You're doomed, you're doomed, you're doomed, haha!"

"Shut up! Don't you have anything better to do? Shut up!"

He did not want to embarrass her, but oh goodness it just *scratched* the inside of his ears like a parasite devouring his eardrums and he feared it would eat his brain. He *must* make it stop—

"*I see you, too, you know,*" it said to him.

Eeep! With a terrified snarl Cinta dove through the polymerwall into the dark closet. He tumbled atop the human curled inside; the motion sensor turned on the light, but *move, move,*

move—Cinta did not want to stay in here with that thing! He gripped Jaika's wrist between his teeth with a sharp tug.

She yelped; as a small child, this grip had kept her away from many a stolen lechichi fruit or dangerous fall, and as a large nearly grown human it still forced her to follow him, if only out of habit. She half-crawled out of the closet after him, protesting. The black polymerwall seemed to cling to his fur as they broke through it—

Once outside the closet Cinta dropped her hand and scampered backward, crouching on three limbs low to the ground as if ready to pounce, ears flat against his back. Jaika scowled and sat up, leaning back against the doorjamb with a quizzical look as she rubbed her wrist.

"Hey idiot, what weather took your sense?!" she snapped in Biouk slang.

Cinta realized he had his breath held, as if the ba-eater might enter his lungs. He released the breath, and sat up on his haunches, ears still laid flat. "You have a—"

"I know what I have," she interrupted, eyes dark. The *hissing* around her—how could she stand it?

"Why didn't I know?" he asked.

"You did. I told you he didn't leave after I left the Growen." She swirled her hand in the air as if motioning to some kind of palpable cloud; Cinta could not help but duck as if to avoid a burst of poisonous wind mixed by her fingertips.

"He? It has a sex?" Cinta asked.

"Might be a she. I don't know. Sounds like a he to me." A wry, tired grin crossed Jaika's face, as if she found this funny.

"I didn't—I didn't understand," Cinta stammered. "This is the same voice I heard in the cage back at the interrogation center two years ago. The one that wanted to eat your partner."

Jaika's head drooped, and Cinta could not see her expression anymore. Her wrists dangled against her knees as she sighed. "That sure ruins hunting season," she muttered, again in the slang they had both grown up with. Her chest rose and fell with great effort, as if bearing ribs too heavy even for her great musculature. She tilted her head back again, staring at the ceiling. Her throat tensed as she swallowed; her lips pursed together—

Cinta realized she had a wet mist in the corners of her eyes, as if very, very tired, or about to leak, like humans did sometimes when sad. It seemed a very long time that her eyes turned upward, struggling to pierce through to the sky.

After a few more swallows, Jaika said: "I thought it might be Jei's ba-eater. I kind of hoped it wasn't. I don't want to be alone, Cinta."

Cinta's ears twisted, one up and one sideways. He did not know what she meant.

"Do I really have to leave, then?" she asked, her head lolling to the side to look him in the eye as if too heavy for her neck. "So it doesn't get him?"

Ohhh. Oh poor little sister. "No, Jaika, you do not," Cinta hummed, slipping over to her side now, again overwhelmed with longing to wrap around her small-past-self and keep it safe from the present. "It is not—contagious, like that. These things spread through ideas and vacuums and acceptance. You talking about it wouldn't even give it to him, especially not as—*covered* —as he is with Njandejara these days. Njande's scent *on* him must make the creature sick. And it cannot defeat you, either, as long as you do not give up."

"I'm so tired, Cinta," she said. "I haven't slept since we landed on Forge. Like, really slept. It's in my dreams. Sparring with Jei wore me out enough to get a few hours, but other than that—I'm—shyte, I'm thinking about going back to Beryllia, even."

Cinta's ears stood up like exclamation marks. "You hated it there. You could not be yourself and Njande sounded far away to you."

"Yeah." She waved her wrist around again in a flop, almost

as if intoxicated, but Cinta smelled nothing but weariness. She sighed again and stood. "Yeah."

"What about asking Njande to—"

"You think I haven't tried that?" she laughed. Cinta's ears flattened back against his skull, offended; Jaika ran her hand over her eyes. "Sorry. I should at least let you finish your thought."

"I am going to bite you, is what I am going to do," Cinta grumbled. "You didn't even greet me when you arrived. You've been yelling at me about abilities I didn't even know I had, and when I try to help you, you just make me feel like a newborn cub."

"Well, you already bit me, so ..."

Cinta growled and turned to go. Jaika slid over in front of him: "Wait, I'm sorry. That was—*ratschica*, I'm actually sorry."

"Ich, and then you talk like that," Cinta threw a paw up at her use of the violent word.

"Cinta, it's just a word, for filk's sake!" She mixed Grenblenian with her Biouk now, apparently not satisfied with swearing in just one language. "Gah, can you *be* more ridiculous? I'm over here almost blowing out city blocks with my daytime nightmares and you're worried about my everloving *diction*?"

"You're what?" Cinta's eyes narrowed as he stepped back toward her, ears lowered by the side of his face now.

"I almost blew out all the power in Retrack City, okay? Hospitals, transports, communications, everything. I'm here trying to figure out whether or not—" She glanced up at the ladder up from the hold back to the main hallway, and lowered her voice. "I'm trying to figure out whether or not I need to take myself out of the picture before I get out of control, okay?" She threw up a palm before Cinta could speak his shock. "Not necessarily like that. Maybe I just go far, far away and live on some dust-moon somewhere. Maybe I just go on a crazy assassination mission against Bricandor and make sure I don't live long enough to filk things up. Or maybe it's a self-fulfilling prophecy, and that stuff's what does me in. I don't know until I know more."

Cinta pulled his ears down the side of his face, his stomach turning loops tighter and tighter as if someone had stabbed a roasting spit through his intestines and begun to twist as fast as they could. This was his fault. Njandejara had explicitly warned him not to make this a prophecy self-fulfilled by despair—he had orders to *only* tell her that she needed to cling to Njande to protect the universe. Cinta should certainly never have told Jei— he should not have scolded Jei at all! He had just wanted to stop the human from mistreating his sister, and the argument had grown out of hand, and his stupid mouth had blurted the truth, but he could not have *known*—well he *should* have known but he *didn't*—that Jei would *tell* her! Even at his very worst he had not thought the other Paradox Warrior so petty. "I am so sorry," he croaked.

"Well, it's not your fault any more than it is his. Or Njande-jara's, for telling you, in the first place. And the Accuser isn't your fault, either," she said. The gravel in her voice told Cinta she'd spent a lot of time considering who to blame, but not necessarily for this. "If I'm mad at you, it's not gonna be about you telling the truth. It's gonna be because for whatever reason I've got this nega-you Biouk part of me that's judging me for—I dunno. Hiding or holding something in. Did you make me feel bad about being human, when I was little? I don't remember it that way, but dayum."

"It was always you who didn't want to be human. That was not my fault."

"But like you were always so worried because I didn't have fur and claws."

"Yes, because you acted like you did, and almost got eaten on *several* occasions. A four-year-old human is like an exposed grub-worm that thinks itself a tiger." Cinta's fur bristled on the nape of his neck. "But even if the Frelsi hadn't taken you, we would have found solutions that fit your biology. I believed in you. I was the one who taught you to tree-run without claws; I was the one who said you didn't have to be Biouk to do everything I did, to be equal in Biouk life. I was always against you hiding yourself with the fur. That was *me*."

"That's true."

Cinta's fur relaxed a bit at her assent, even as his chest burned at her accusations. He could see suffering in her, and hear the hissing cloud circling her scalp, so he did not press her for an apology, but turned to more practical matters. "What has this Biouk question to do with you wiping out power grids?"

"Eh. I don't know." Jaika hid her eyes with her hand again, as if trying to wipe the tiredness away. "Hey, look, I'm sorry. I don't want to fight you or blame you. My head is—something's not right. Maybe I need to get a neurotransmitter check."

"Ebon Shadow has a neuropsychological evaluation system that can identify pharmaceuticals to balance cerebral chemicals," Cinta offered hesitantly. "But I do not think that will—I heard the voice you were talking to, and it was that ba-eater. You are not crazy."

"Dr. Loylan says there's no such medical diagnosis as crazy," Jaika pointed out. "And if you think about it, the two aren't mutually exclusive. I could have a brain thing going on, and a ba-eater. Or the ba-eater trying to cause the other thing."

"This is true. It cannot hurt to get a medical check."

The two stood in silence for a moment now. Cinta wanted nothing more than to beg her to talk to Njandejara with him, but if she did not want to, she would not hear the being anyway. Even two audible people from the same dimension would have trouble hearing each other if one had too much pain to listen; how much more difficult to hear if one spoke only through brain matter across time and space. Why had this happened? Would this have happened anyway, when Bricandor sent this ba-eater skittering over his ranks last year to hunt for anyone who might harm Stygge Sterba—and was this now that ba-eater's revenge for what Jaika had done to enter that sorceress' mind?

Or was this simply the scent of Jaika's discouragement after the Frelsi abandoned her, a signal of weakened resolve drawing the interdimensional vulture to circle, just waiting for her to collapse so it could begin eating her mind alive?

Or was she so valuable as a possible monster, and so dangerous as a possible hero, so loved by Njandejara that the other interdimensionals, jealous, would do anything to watch her suffer?

He wished to tell her this last thing—that she mattered, and did not need to feel alone, that the struggle itself only spoke to her value—when Jei Bereens burst into the hold.

"Lem, we gotta get to the needlecraft," he said. "Fort Tapiz just sent out a distress signal about mind control."

CHAPTER TWENTY-NINE
Jei

It wasn't a long ride from the *Huntress* to our hidden needlecraft, but every step toward the mind-control serum—and Diebol—seemed so real, so final, so crystal-clear, that I felt as if a lifetime passed between each bootprint in the sand. I'd stood in line waiting for execution before; that sense loomed over me again now.

We'd parked our needlecraft several days ago in the private hangar of a Frelsi-friendly citizen on the other side of town; we needed that ship now, and the paralytic serum it contained. My brain was already racing through scenarios as Lem and I ran across the quiet mud-brick garage, our soft boots loud in the evening courtyard. We could hear the soft whine of the *Huntress*'s engines in the distance as the mercenaries took off, leaving us to our work; as much as Cinta would have liked to come with us, he had orders to continue his crystal investigation.

And I had new orders, because the mind-control serum seemed to have arrived at the nearest Frelsi base. Diebol had all but promised to meet me on Forge—I was glad I'd heeded that, glad we were here, but that sense of death incoming would not lift ...

I breathed deeply as we took off; the needlecraft dipped and wove as I maneuvered between the dunes, staying low to avoid anti-air detection in case the Growen were closer than we knew. Steering the compuwall was like caressing a stove; the whole ship glowed hot from her stay in that low maintenance hangar without any environmental control.

"Do we know how they got—'mind control'—*in*?" Lem asked. She was behind me wrapping bandage tape over every skin cell, fortifying herself against any possible chemical touch.

"From the SITREP I got, a kid went missing around 0800 hours today," I answered Lem. "The squad that went out for him came back with his body—and then suddenly started attacking everyone in the fort."

"How do we know it's mind-control serum, and not like a planned betrayal?" she countered.

"Soldiers are turning on their companions mid-battle," I said. "Personality, affect, everything suddenly shifts. I haven't seen any footage; the wristband transmissions are chaotic. 'Walking corpse,' 'suddenly robotic,' 'like they're possessed'—lots of terms like that getting thrown around."

"And if it is Morda's serum, how's it getting delivered?"

"The turned squad have gas grenades, and specialized cartridges they're shooting at people. Leadership doesn't know whether it's the gas or the cartridges."

"Terrifying," Lem said without a shred of terror in her voice. There wasn't room for "terrifying" when you had bullets to count and weapons to strap to your thighs and chest. I got the feeling she had other things to fear these days; maybe the prospect of pure physical combat was a welcome relief. "So," she reviewed. "We're getting our blue goo to Fort Tapiz leadership so they can peacefully put down their own soldiers."

"Affirmative. They should have a water supply ready for us when we get there. You'll take the hose, right?"

"I don't wanna touch that shyte."

"I don't want to turn Growen."

She was quiet for a moment while I watched the blinking

coordinates in the corner of my compuwall; we grazed the edge of a blue dune, and dust plumed around my view.

"You're hoping if there's a problem I can just hose you down," Lem said. "But if I get hit with blue stuff, what happens?"

"You go EMP crazy and shut down everyone's weapons. That's a win in this situation."

"And if I get hit with mind control?"

"I got you."

Her uncertain hum carried zero confidence in that plan. I was kind of offended, but I couldn't blame her. I knew that feeling, that certainty that no one can help you. "I'll be at full power with more enemies, Lem. And you can keep me at your back so I can get the drop on you if I need to."

"I hate everything about this. We're so dangerous." Her hand muffled her sigh; it sounded like she was leaning on her fist behind me. "But I don't know who else they could call to shut down a horde of Frelsi zombies. And if Diebol's there, one of us has to take him down, so ..." I heard her shift in her seat, leaning forward into solutions instead of problems. "So we're wearing gas masks, and protecting our necks. That's where the turned guys are aiming, at the neck, right? And you've got an idea about how the turning's working?"

"Affirmative." I swallowed, swerving over the edge of a green dune, painting a gentle line in the landscape with the bottom of our needlecraft. This kind of fast, low flight was impossible for most people, but the precision centered me, made it easier to speak: "When she was alive, Mera had two separate biological abilities: one, a pheromone that prepared the target's nerves to receive her orders; and two, specialized cells that let her send out neurotransmitter signals to my—to her target's—nervous system."

"So if I were Diebol, and I wanted to mass produce that, I'd maybe have a gas to calm people down, and some kind of—tiny radio device or some shyte—that hooks into your spine. Something that can receive commands remotely, and then inject neurotransmitter commands into neurons directly," she mused. "I mean, you can't control someone with a gas. Gas can't tell you what to do."

"Exactly." I nodded. "The calming gas primes the nervous system, and then a specialized cartridge takes control. I'm thinking it's been difficult for them to replicate Mera's cell structure. I suspect they have to hit near the spinal cord, the higher up the better."

"So we need, like, metal collars or something. Do you still have those stasis fields?"

"Yeah, but I think anywhere in the spine—"

A glance in my rear mirror told me Lem had already pulled out the supply panel behind her seat. "I think we could rip out the wiring in your restraining collars," she said, rifling through what cargo she could reach in the needlecraft's tiny hold.

"Hey, I'm signed for those," I protested, trying to control the ship but dying to turn my head and stop her. "Anyway, they're too thin to cover anything substantial. You'd be better off with full body armor, and even that's got open kinks by the neck so you're not stuck in a vice unable to turn your head. Besides, the spine thing's just a hunch. The specialized darts still might turn you if they hit anywhere else. Mera could."

"Ech. I want a metal turtleneck."

"Just turn the collar off, then. Please don't break my stuff, soldier," I said.

"Acknowledged," she grinned, almost mocking the formality in her voice. She put my equipment away. "What's the word on standard Growen troops?"

"Incoming." I yanked a hard left around a larger dune and tapped my wristband with a throwing motion, tossing the information there up onto the front viewscreen. It scrolled transparently beside our view to the outside. "It would be stupid of them not to take advantage of this weapons' test to gain strategic ground."

"Well, hopefully we get there first. We sleep the turned Frelsi, and then we've got time to kill Diebol and take out the other Growen. Ah, shyte ..."

"What?"

My onboard map said we weren't far from our goal now; I heard Lem shift behind me, and a quick turn of my head saw her leaning on the window, one dejected palm on her forehead. "Eh, I just realize you're right. I should handle the blue juice. With your abilities, it's probably best to have you facing the Growen so you can power all the way up," she said. "I have more natural 'take you down without killing you' abilities, so I should focus on the turned Frelsi."

"Probably." The ship shook under me as I brushed another dune, my intake burning a trail of yellow into the red desert. "Let's stick together at first, deliver the juice, and then break off after, you toward Frelsi and me toward Growen. We need to be in close enough contact that one can power the other down if something happens, but I can work from a pretty decent distance."

"Roger," she said. The shuffling stopped behind me; she let out a relieved sigh. She didn't want to split up anyway. "I feel okay about this plan."

"Same." It took me a moment to shut my mouth; I tried to find another contingency. I didn't want to stop talking strategy ... but anything else would have to wait until first contact with the enemy.

The enemy ...

Yeah, this was why I didn't want to stop talking. Action felt good. Planning, details, logistics, I could do. But the silence forced me to acknowledge what we were about to do: battle Mera's legacy. My belly tickled with that same nervousness from ... ah, probably the first time I had to speak with a psychologist, when I first came back from my captivity as a nine-year-old. I remembered sitting outside the doctor's polymerwall with my arms wrapped around my knees, wondering what they would decide about me …

I hated waiting, back then. I'd just come back from several months of daily waiting alone in a cage—waiting to be hurt next, waiting and begging for the wait to end so it would be my turn and Diebol would have some relief. I'd wait, hoping he would return alive at all, wishing with all my will for him to be okay. Except for Njandejara, Diebol was the only good thing in my life for months: the only kind voice, the only playmate to bring back some semblance of the childhood we both lost in that cage.

Maybe my "thing" was powered by enemies because the people I'd loved most in my life were the people I also hated most. And now, like some molecular necromancy, we faced a weapon forged from *her* blood; her, the sky-dancer whose fingertips still lingered on my skin, buzzing up along my nerves with that painful jolt of control, my muscles moving against my will but my will driven mad by that sweet scent along her neck, that intoxicating desire to just drop my head back and let her mind conquer mine …

"Hey," I grunted.

Lem sat up. I could see her in my peripheral vision, leaning her elbows on the back of my seat. "Yeah, man?"

"Hey, kill me if I get hit," I said.

"No, I'll restrain you and take you to a doctor if you get hit, man," Lem said, a firm hand on my shoulder for just a moment. "Don't get any ideas, Jei. If Diebol's really managed to weaponize her ability, it's not going to be like seeing her again. You won't be love-drunk in her arms or whatever. It's just chemicals."

"Everything is chemicals, Lem," I murmured. "Oxytocin, adrenaline, NMDA, thyroxine—we're brilliant bags of chemicals, portals to other worlds created by molecular magic."

"Okay. But she's gone, and you're going to be fine," she said. "Remember you brought the building down, not me. You broke out."

"Did I?" But it wasn't really a question. I remembered that moment, that split second where I could sense the ship above and the only thing I could do, the only flailing motion my deaf and blind mind could muster, was to pull, pull to bring down the ceiling on all of us. It was Lem's ship, but my pull.

"Yeah. You escaped by thinking down. And I killed Sterba by thinking a question." The black cushions squeaked under her as she leaned back again, away from me, with a last pensive musing: "The little things that no one can prove are the things that matter the most."

CHAPTER THIRTY

Lem

JEI WAS RIGHT; THE GROWEN WEREN'T STUPID. WITH FORT TAPIZ belly-up and fighting itself on every street, Lem could see the distant hordes before the needlecraft even landed. As she and Jei circled the communications tower, calling in codes to enter the base, silver Growen land-runners sliced through the horizon, spiked wheels tearing up orange sand as if they made the planet bleed. Armored air-riders flanked these silver death-mobiles, and behind floated hulking prism-shaped transports that reflected the colorful dunes around them with such brilliance Lem had trouble telling where the desert ended and the transports began. An avid hunter of peacock-feathered guinea pigs back in the day, Lem was no stranger to seeing colorful things somehow manage camouflage, but the visual cacophony in the distance now was straight-up trippy—especially compared to the brick and stone, grey and auburn tones of Fort Tapiz around her as she and Jei deplaned.

"The Turned Frelsi will want to take down the EMP shield to let in the Growen," Jei said now, lowering his binoculars. He stood atop the needlecraft with one boot on the engine, leaning on his raised knee for just a moment longer before tossing the view-tool back into the cockpit and jumping down.

"So they'll send the Turned to the security tower," Lem nodded toward the rust-colored stone fixture in the center of the base. "If you wanna open the floodgates, that's where you do it." Fort Tapiz air control and central security lived in the tricked-out ruins of an ancient sailfin lizard prison—the most secure leftovers of the long-gone city on which the Frelsi fort was built. Lem strapped a black cloth mask across her mouth and nose and spun her mace over her wrist. "Are we go?"

Jei nodded, gripping the straps across his chest that secured the rucksack full of blue powder vials.

"Off to find the wizard," Lem said. They needed to meet their Frelsi contact, dump the powder, and get to work putting renegades to sleep.

Red horns blared from the old tower as Lem and Jei ran across the cobblestone parking bay. The place looked like it had once been a city plaza in ancient days, a center teeming with families and market stalls; now it was devoid of people except for security crews guarding the ships parked there.

"Wouldn't it have been awesome to see this place a thousand years ago?" Lem grinned, her head on swivel as she took in the squat square buildings, hodge-podges of ancient stone patched with modern polymerwall. In the sky above, the rainbow of swirling desert dust cast a slight shimmer on the EMP shield dome. Lem had never been able to actually see Fort Jehu's EMP shield, back on Luna Guetala, through the thick ivory polymerwall over the fort, and the clarity of the jungle air; the magical sheen she saw now enthralled her.

In the wonder of it all, she realized suddenly she felt good for the first time since leaving Beryllia. The blood pumping through her racing legs, the heated steam on her face under the mask, and the rasp inside her chest as her ribs plunged in and out in the exertion—it felt good. Maybe because no Frelsi fort had ever dealt with mind control before, so in this unheard-of emergency there was really no wrong answer. Everything was wrong, so nothing was wrong.

Well. Things could go wrong, still. A lot of things.

Thinking about feeling good suddenly Lem didn't feel good, again. Should she even be here? Shyte, she really could just make absolutely everything worse ...

But Jei's silence suddenly struck Lem as loud. She glanced over to see his lips pressed thin, and the muscle at the back of his jaw tightened: this was the face he made when trying to stave off memories, or just after that nauseating struggle they both shared with open spaces. All thought of feeling good or bad or ruining everything suddenly evaporated from Lem's mind. There was just this mission, and her sparring partner, and his ache.

"Jei, what's your wristband say about our contact point?" she asked. Her voice sounded gentler than she usually heard it; she couldn't take time and words to comfort the guy, not right before they plunged into combat, but she could see his eyes focus as her question drew him back to the moment. He glanced at the screen reflected on his hand, and his step picked up some perk.

"We'll meet one of the security squads at the base of the tower," he said. "They've got a team bringing down one of the mobile water tanks; we'll go with it to the main conflict site, keeping ourselves between the fight and the security tower. Depending on how that goes, we'll either stay there or move past it toward the outskirts and the Growen."

Lem nodded. As long as Fort Tapiz's EMP shield stayed up, vehicles would stay out, forcing Growen soldiers to dismount to enter. Both Paradox Warriors had agreed on the ride over that they couldn't go nonviolent with the Growen here, not with the dual-front conflict and limited blue juice, so Jei would need to get to a height where he could see the Growen and they could see him, and then quickly and kindly kill anyone who crossed the EMP shield on foot. His normal em abilities limited him to levitating objects about his weight, but they'd have enough enemies there to super-charge him to where he could throw buildings and shyte. Lem had her static shock to knock out Frelsi and her shield of sparks would protect her from getting shot herself.

Beyond their plans lingered the promise that if Jei's mind-channel conversations held any truth, Diebol was on his way, too. But Lem found herself looking forward to that, for some reason. Let him meet Sterba and the angry little Biouk, maybe.

Her fist clenched tighter on her mace as she swung it again, hungry for a fight.

JEI

Mera's fingertips gripping my hair, fist clenched at the back of my neck.

Her lips, parted millimeters from mine.

The sharp shadow under her collarbone, traced by those dangling beads tangled around my thumb.

There was no denying the horror of losing control over your body, but there was also no denying the sweet relief of despair, of finally just giving up. It was so much less painful to admit defeat than to keep fighting. Was that what she felt when she finally decided to obey her masters and just take command over me, instead of trying to reason with me and decide for herself? She struggled, before that kiss—by the time she started exerting full mental force over me she'd already died a thousand deaths. Lem would say, probably, that there was nothing left of "Mera" in Stygge Morda by the time we'd met, but Lem was dead wrong. The girl I knew, the sky-dancer who tip-toed through old temples and giant libraries thrown open before her wide-eyed mind as the wind of her powerful emotions rustled their ancient pages—

The traveler whose flighty, racing-hearted vision peopled the cold laboratories she explored with warm ghosts—

That girl knew better. She made mistake after tactical mistake in her struggle to control me, not because she was stupid, but because she couldn't bring herself to do what she was sent to do.

Because she *did* care, and *did* consider what loving me could look like; because her long, dark eyes could pierce mine and *see* what that possible future held. She couldn't get into my mind without stripping bare her own. The haunting beauty of her lashes, the perfect, scarred curve traced from under her arm to her hip, didn't compare with the folds and clefts of her grey matter, warm around mine, opening into elaborate mazes and colorful memories that were—just—

It wasn't fun being blinded, shocked, deafened, or manipulated like a puppet.

But being entangled with her thoughts, and the intimacy of that connection that was literally physically impossible with anyone who lacked her particular abilities—it—just—

I would give anything and anyone to have that willingly, purely, no strings attached and no Growen involved. I loved Mera long before she took control over me, and if she could have just waited, and listened, and let me find us a way out, we could have had the world.

Anything and anyone?

Yeah. Now, instead, she was dead, and I was struggling to untangle the biological thread of neurochemical addiction from my actual real and true feelings for her. A part of me wanted another hit of her power. A totally different me really loved her. And I was really filking scared that the first part would get me shot on purpose, because unlike all these other poor saps I had tasted surrender before, and it was so, so sweet.

Lem's voice brought me back into the moment again. We were at the base of the security tower now, within earshot of the skirmish just one street over. I was gloved up, loading a kilogram of dry L-42 sleeping powder into a huge mobile water tank wider than I was tall.

"It can't get you if it's not activated by moisture," I answered Lem; she was standing an unnecessary two meters away, holding the tank's fully-extended hose at arm's length, as if the tank might jump her or the hose might bite.

The sailfin reptilian with us chuckled nervously, flaring the nostrils at the end of his thin snout. Unlike the wide, thick Bont reptilians, the slender sailfins didn't show emotion with color change, but with the elaborate spined dorsal crests. This guy's sailfin stood up so straight on his back the slightest breeze almost blew his whole self away; he was clearly too stressed and excited to fold it down. He didn't look like much of a soldier in this state, but I didn't say anything. We hadn't seen the fighting yet, and even if we had, to us these were just some Frelsi gone rogue—to him, they were friends and family.

"It's chaos down there," he muttered, voice cracking as his vertical pupils darted down the street. Dust rose from behind the buildings that blocked our view, but we could all hear the gunfire and the screaming.

"All right, let's go." I screwed shut the cap on the tank and slapped the back of the thing like I was sending a mount on its way. The sailfin reptilian unlocked the brakes on the wheels and hopped onto the small chariot-shaped tractor pulling the tank. Lem jumped up behind him, standing on her tip-toes on the back edge of the chariot, and I vaulted up atop the water tank as the whole thing took off at breakneck speed. Dust splashed up around us like a liquid wake.

Explosions and clashing metal grew louder as the scent of smoke and acidic oxidizer fluid penetrated even the dust mask over my nose and mouth. We swerved around two corners, and then broke out into the chaos.

CHAPTER THIRTY-ONE

Lem

LEM HAD THOUGHT NOT KNOWING ANYBODY WOULD MAKE THIS easier.

It totally did not.

The street in front of her was a mess of multicolored camo fighting more multicolored camo. There were no tells—no puppet-like jerking or dead-eyes, or anything else like that— because she didn't know any of these people. She had no way of telling who was or wasn't acting like themselves. She assumed the people on *that* side of the street were trying to get on *this* side closer to the tower, but people were trading places and going down and yelling at each other and who could tell?

Well. There wasn't a ton of time to think about this, and the blue juice was nonlethal anyway, so hitting the wrong person wasn't the end of the world. Lem ripped the safety cap off the nozzle of the hose, pushed her way in front of Sergeant Braaap and his enormous sailfin—his spines had almost put out her eye during his maniacal chariot drive down the street—and squared her stance.

And then with a strong trigger pull she leaned back to fire a lusty azure stream across the street.

It was satisfying, actually, watching people bowl over, as the power of the hose bucked in her hands. She thought for a moment they might actually put this whole thing to rest in ten minutes—

Oh, now she could tell who the bad guys were. At least twenty heads jerked toward her in unsettling unison, as if someone who really didn't care about whiplash yanked their necks with invisible string. A shiver ran up Lem's spine, and for some reason it made her want to laugh. They seemed unreal, like clones of all different colors and size, as their weapons raised, and they fired—

Not at her, but at the water tank, and Jei had that under control. A power surge tickled Lem's left side and a rush of wind blew sand past her face as Jei's mace twirled into a forcefield to block the shots. Lem tapped Sergeant Braaap's scaly arm to get him to drive the chariot further forward, so she could reach more people with her sleepy stream—

The sailfin didn't budge. Lem turned to look—oh, shyte.

Sergeant Braaap's flared fin had completely relaxed, tucked down against his back, and his vertical pupils widened, then constricted again. His throat gurgled with an eerie, animal chatter as his tongue flickered in and out between his sharp teeth—

Lem didn't feel like watching the change ripple across his carnivorous muscles. She blasted him full in the face with a fire-hose-dose of blue. The force slammed him against the side of the chariot and knocked him over the side into the sand. "Sorry man," Lem said, whirling to see who'd turned him. There was a sniper behind her on the roof, a small human teen with wide eyes, maybe not even regulation fighting age. The little human made terrified, silently screaming eye contact with Lem, pigtails shaking as she jumped to her feet and fled toward the tower, ready to leap from one roof to another—

Oh shyte, can I reach …? Lem hurled a finger in that direction, thought *charge*, and forced a shock across the distance. The little girl shuddered as the electrical impact surged through her, and then she crumbled down on the roof, asleep.

"Oof, didn't like that," Lem grumbled. "I hope she's okay." She couldn't remember what Dr. Patti Loylan told her about how much voltage and current a kid could handle versus a full-grown blitzer, and she couldn't remember whether it was voltage or current that could hurt you, and it was hard to modulate between her two extremes of static only and knock-you-out shock. But either way, the sniper was out, and Lem was already facing the other direction, one hand hovering above the compupad controlling the chariot, and the other hand shaking with the force of the hose she still waved across the teeming crowd. She glanced down at the unconscious sailfin as she left him behind in the dust—a tiny silver dart was freshly embedded in the back of his neck, leaking blood around it, as his muscles twitched.

"We'll get you fixed buddy," she grunted. "Have a good nap." Then, over her shoulder to Jei: "Hold on!"

She briefly saw him throw a hand down to stabilize himself atop the water tank with an em-pull as she jerked the vehicle forward, plunging into the core of the crowd. A sea of hands reached for her all at once—she sprayed them down—behind her, someone aimed their gun at Jei—she threw a hand back to shock them out—

Jei emitted a growl of frustration. "Forget this, it's too messy," he grumbled. Lem glanced back to see him raise his right hand—

Everyone in the street floated in the air. The expressions of surprise reminded Lem of characters from children's books and holograms—nothing said "whoops" like wide-eyed pawing for a ground just out of your reach. Lem laughed, and blasted the whole street with blue juice.

"Nice," Jei nodded, gently lowering everyone back to the ground.

"This is fun," Lem answered. "I like it when things just work." She dismounted from the chariot, and with a rushed exhale ran up the wall of the building behind her to check on the kid she'd zapped while Jei called in to their mission coordinator in the tower.

A little puff of green dust scattered under the impact of Lem's boot as she landed on the short roof with a grunt. The preteen there seemed a bit dazed, but she'd begun to sit up already; Lem gave her shoulder a wordless pat with a wet, gloved hand, and let the blue juice relieve the little warrior of her frightening consciousness.

"Mom shot me," the girl muttered as her screaming purple eyes blinked shut. Lem's stomach twisted as the slim shoulders became heavy against her forearm, and she lay the girl down against the auburn stone. Shot? But a quick pat-down to check for blood only found another little oblong silver device embedded in the back of her spine. *Shyte, she was turned by a parent.*

Lem's throat began to tighten for the mother. Gah, hopefully she was unconscious, too. Lem wouldn't want to live if that was her.

"Yo, will they come sort their people out now?" Lem yelled over her shoulder, suddenly struggling to hold in something that came out sounding like irritation. How dare she feel okay, feel "fun," feel like kicking blitzer or Frelsi-zombie butt, when this happened. How could she not be miserable?

But if you were miserable, you got nothing done. Was it wrong that getting her blood going with combat was the only happiness she had recently?

Whatever. "Hey! Jei, what's up?"

Jei held up a finger as he spoke into his wristband, pacing atop the water tank with a shake of his head. Lem had always hated when he did that, that finger. She always let it go because you didn't have time to be up in your feelings with bad guys riding your butt. The sound of distant gunfire kept Lem from hearing what Jei's handlers said to him through his wristband, but he summarized finally: "There's a prison medical crew en route, but there are skirmishes all across the base—the first Turned squad split up so they could hit as many people as possible. Right now there's another mass of Turned forming two streets east."

"So we need to circle, but still stay in between the Turned and the tower."

"Sounds about right. We'll make faster work of the next bunch now that we've got a rhythm."

Lem nodded, and vaulted down the short, squat building to sprint back into the tractor-slash-chariot. With Jei still riding the water tank like it was a Pegasus from his home planet, she followed his directions to the next conflict. One hand steered, hovering over the horizontal compuwall that guided the floating chariot; the fingers on her other hand lingered by the mace on her belt. She heard her breath, felt the weight of the hose draped over her shoulder, listened to the sand in the breeze—but through it all she was still cognizant of the strong desire to smash something. They would see Diebol at some point, and she had so many words for him when they did.

And so they progressed in a slow circle through the base like this, rounding the streets around the transmission tower, always checking for stragglers at their backs as Lem ran crowd-control and Jei protected her and the water tank. Lem liked how he'd put it: a rhythm …

They soon hit their fourth mass of battling Frelsi—no match for two Paradox Warriors with a sleeping serum. The hose no longer bucked so much in Lem's hands. "I think we're about halfway out of juice," she called over her shoulder to Jei.

"Roger. We—"

"We what?" Lem shook the hose, leaning forward as she squeezed harder on the trigger.

She didn't hear an answer. Oh shyte.

As Lem turned to look, Jei swayed, closed his eyes, and then collapsed, bouncing with a clanging thud against the tank before he slid down into the sand.

CHAPTER THIRTY-TWO

Jei

BLOODSEAS, I THOUGHT I'D DEALT WITH THIS ALREADY.

I was back in the hallway in my mind, and it was tragically clean—all my graffiti scrubbed off left only gleaming ivory. Without the glow of my ancient verses woven through the gulf between hallways, dusk had fallen, cloaking all those hidden spaces in shadow again ... pearls and skeletal forms alike.

The idea of passing through that darkness was infinitely worse now that I knew how many times I passed all that terror without seeing it. I stood hesitant at the edge of my hallway, staring at the illuminated cage waiting for me in the gray.

"Come *on*, Jared!" I shouted. "Let me out and fight me in real life!"

"Where you have the shining advantage of god-like powers and supernatural allies? No thank you. I'll hold you here until we can get a spine-sucker in you and we'll go from there."

I couldn't see him, but I heard him. He had to be hiding somewhere down the curve of his hallway, or maybe in the shadow just beside the cage. I groaned. I needed to get him *out* so he couldn't hold me here with whatever force of will he'd developed during my time under Morda's spell. I could repulse him again with blankets of ancient words ... but how long would that take?

Shyte, I'd left Lem out there to manage the mind-controlled forces alone. What if she got hit? Bloodseas, what if *I* got hit, and ...

My throat closed, as if the fists clenched and trembling by my sides were wrapped around my neck. If they made my hands kill her, I would never—I'd done it once already, I'd felt that despair—

I trusted Lem on her own. She could handle the best of them. You don't lock your biggest gun away in the safe when it's battle-time.

But big guns were so *dangerous* in the wrong hands ...

My heartbeat echoed and pulsed in the walls. Bloodseas, what could I do?

I needed to cross over to the cage, find him, and kick his ass. I knew from a number of kicks and bruises that *I* could feel the construct of pain invoked in this space; maybe he could, too. Never mind that everything I saw before me wasn't real—just a symbolic representation my mind came up with to help me conceptualize the radio channel between Diebol and myself—it all still ran on electric pulses in the brain. And so did pain.

But as I tried to step out of my hallway, into the darkness, I tasted metal. My tongue dried—could I hear a hiss, a whisper, to the left corner, where the burnt skeleton hung before? Was she skittering across the floor on her belly, elbows jutting up like a lizard's, a death rattle waiting in her crushed throat? What *else* lay in wait for me, the product of my mind's illness, scars gashed across the neuronal tissue over and over again with each new loss?

My boot returned to the ivory floor, unable to enter the shadow.

This is cowardice, I told myself. *Get over there and make him let you out.*

My limbs would not move.

I never froze. Dr. Loylan taught us the three mammalian adrenal instincts were fight, flight, and freeze, and she'd taught us to learn ours early so we knew how to deal with them when they arose. Mine, I hated. Mine was flight—the instinct to jump back, to dodge, to dash away. I'd always wanted the fight one— the instinct to strike out, to snarl, to leap forward like a cornered predator, like Lem.

But freeze?

I didn't know what would happen if something from my past grabbed me in the darkness. I imagined myself insane, locked here in my mind forever, while outside my body stumbled around in horror as my fingernails raked over my eyes—

"They're closing in on you out there," Diebol remarked. His voice reverberated through the entire space. "Be patient. You'll be out of here in no time."

He shouldn't have said anything.

I rolled out my shoulder and sighed, awakened by the power of the same tongue that used to drive me blind. Ugh, that tone of *patience* and arrogant compassion—was I really so dumb, that once upon a time his words would've forced my next move? I wasn't interested now. They sounded—fake? No, not fake. Hollow, and pale. Like he needed to speak to give himself a sense of control.

His strength was his weakness.

I remembered that corollary, that *weakness is strength* whispered to me in a reflective mind-altering cell back in the Stygge training center. One of the clearest and strangest memories of Njande's voice, spoken if not in my ear, then in that neuron right inside the eardrum. I was vomiting on the floor on my hands and knees when I heard that one, if I remembered right.

Weakness is strength.

I shook out my wrist, scanning the darkness as I muttered another old archaeological passage to myself. "*Strengthen your weak knees, so that what is injured might not be dislocated, but instead be healed ...*" It slipped through my lips like a spell; my mind absently questioned why it came to me now, and what any of these things meant in the moment, but I knew they would clear up in time. They weren't thoughts to fight with right now, just details to observe, like the darkness, like the light, like the scent of sweat or the sounds of swishing clothes, or any other sensations you note when you're stalking a combatant. "Help me, help me find him, Njandejara," I whispered, still standing in my hallway, still scanning for my place to strike, still not relishing that first step into the darkness.

But—I wasn't the only one with a literal dark side in here. Diebol most likely didn't like that haunted cape hanging over him, and I couldn't imagine he'd want to sit next to my corpse of a memory. So he probably wasn't in our dark spaces. I didn't see him in the cage, or in his hallway, so—

My eyes scanned upward, and there, atop the wooden cage, crouched a familiar silhouette in the shadows. Aha.

And while I hated it, I knew I could deal with whatever monsters lay on my side—shyte, I'd done it already, and if this was all a construct representing something else in my mind, then bloodseas, I'd done this already in therapy, too. I didn't think Diebol had.

I cracked my neck.

"Let's enjoy some weakness," I said.

LEM

Lem crouched over Jei's body, shielding him and as much of the water tank as she could, shoulders hunched and chest expanded like a sabertoothed cat flaring its scruff. That cat snarled in her memory as its kits huddled against its ankles—Lem lashed out with the hose like a paw extended. Humans and lizards of all shapes and sizes collapsed under her swipe. But there were a lot of them. It was as if, like river sing-tooth fish swarming to blood, the masses sensed Jei's collapse, and they'd come to collect.

"Diebol isn't far off," Lem muttered—to Njandejara now, for the first time in a while. The waves of broken bodies kept trying to flank her to the left, around that awkward bend, to get to the water tank. The forcefield of her mace spinning in her right hand took so much—not focus, she could spin in her sleep, but— agility, energy, something drained from her nervous system as she scuttled and reached like a crustacean with a flaming claw, straining to keep her body over Jei and her back to the tank while protecting it from shots fired.

She could do this. She knew she could do this. She just needed to think. Wait it out. They were wasting bodies in her direction.

But she couldn't think of anything but the Growen forces now right outside the EMP shield. She could hear voices over Jei's wristband.

"It's like they've emptied every Growen camp from here to Mezclow, Mezclow, Mezclow!" a Wonderfrog voice crackled. "We need more forces around the periphery!"

So strange, a Wonderfrog here in these awful sands ... he shouldn't be here. He should go home to somewhere wet....

"I'm sorry, we're tied down here, croaker! We have to make sure the zombies don't get to the tower—if they do then you'll really have a Growen problem on your hands!"

They were arguing, all those voices, about where to direct their forces. If the Growen breaking through was inevitable, then you needed a greeting party at the edge of the city. But if it wasn't inevitable, if there was hope of keeping back the growing tide of turning Frelsi, you needed to stack power by the central tower. So on and so forth.

Blablabla, her inner voice chimed with the debate. Diebol was waiting out there. *Maybe in here already. Coming to collect his prize.* That was why there were so many Growen. They were here for Jei. For the super-weapon. For the one who mattered.

This is the end. What's the point, even?

Maybe the whole thing was a trap—summon them both here to Fort Tapiz just to get Jei.

But no, that wasn't true—Fort Tapiz was one of the biggest Frelsi settlements on this continent, a real infected cut on the Growen's heel. Of course the Growen emptied out their camps to take it out, now that they had a shot with mind control. Of course Lem and Jei couldn't have stayed away. All these people needed them....

"We're all going to be Growen weapons. This is never gonna end well." Lem heard her own grumble. Her voice sounded dead. It was surprising how close it was to her ears. She was feeling very far away. So many damn *people* crawling over each other to—

Focus. You need to focus.

There was another cluster of Turned down the other street to the left—she could hear, over the wristband, as they moved house by house toward the tower. Shyte, she needed to move the chariot to that cluster. Could she get there? She had basically no cover except her spinning staff; the Turned kept clambering over the chariot on her right, or trying to flank around her left, trying to shoot the tank, trying to shoot her, trying to hit Jei—it was humanly impossible to—be—everywhere—

With a ping, and hiss, a shot hit the tank.

"Shyte!" Lem's cry sounded so forlorn to her. This was it, this was the end, she was failing them all—

It's okay! The tank's only half-full, and the shot was at the top! Nothing's leaked, it's okay! A loud voice in her head broke through the panic—maybe Njande's.

"It doesn't matter, they're going to hit the bottom soon anyway." The Accuser's words replied in her mouth; more pings, more shots she couldn't block, punctured the tank behind her. This wasn't working. She needed to move. She was spraying and spraying and there was literally a pile of bodies stacked around her in a crescent, with more Turned climbing or using their fallen comrades as cover, and as the pile stacked up she felt her throat closing because she could hear the repressed fear in the wristband: "Shyte, they've broken into the tower. We need reinforcements here now!"

How *the hell* had this spread so fast? A lot of the Frelsi had armor protecting the back of their necks, with only very thin slivers of skin showing through. Every Turned soldier couldn't possibly be a crack shot! Unless the person controlling them was? But then, could the control person see through their vision? The Frelsi supposed to be on her side seemed to move so slow— she couldn't see them now—

"Repeat, we need reinforcements now!"

The thought of leaving Jei and running over to rescue the tower occurred to her, but only for a fleeting second, as a fantasy, in a world where she could move so fast Jei would not turn into a super-weapon for the Growen by the time she returned. But in this real world, right now, she heard more pings, she couldn't spray past the cover of the piled bodies, and there wasn't enough water pressure to hit the top of the pile with her spray, where more hidden figures were firing and firing and firing at her—shoot, that was a fully automatic—

Let's stop playing normal people games.

CHAPTER THIRTY-THREE

Diebol

A HOT WIND WAS PICKING UP OVER THE SHIFTING RAINBOW OF DUST when Diebol strode through the main street on the edge of Fort Tapiz with his hands in his pockets and a lightness in his step.

"You require aid, friends?" he smiled.

The tattered Frelsi soldiers lining the evening street wore grimaces of every sort—anguish, rage, terror—and they were such *different* faces, all of them—reptilians, humans, the occasional space-lemur—but as Diebol flipped one little silver control switch, they all saluted in unison. As one. No disagreements, no culture, no *differences*, just one.

"You resent it now, but in time you will come to appreciate your freedom," he cried out, a herald for the future of warfare. "There will be no more need to eradicate you. You are *welcome*."

And then, with his own grimace, he sent them back to their business. His fingers played along the wide black control pad with a deftness he would have recognized as talent had he been allowed video games as a child. The center of the control pad bore a top-down map grid which showed the location of each deployed unit. With mere button-presses he sent pre-recorded voice commands to entire units through the darts in the base of their skulls. For the most complex actions, he could select a particular unit with the touch-pad and speak to it directly; tendrils grew out of the silver darts to connect with the subjects' cranial nerves minutes after impact, so he could see through the subjects' vision if he needed to shoot with accuracy they could not manage. Of course, for the simplest actions—like walk in a straight line, auto-attack, or salute—different switches had been coded with different neurological programs already.

It was a waste of time to code a salute. And a waste of time to flaunt it now.

"Oh, please," Diebol muttered back to his Accuser. "After everything these fanatics have put me through, I've earned a moment to gloat. They need to feel my control." He waved his hand, as if that could banish his "father's" interdimensional pest, the flittering invisible creature that moved over the ranks to spy for Bricandor. It had taken a special interest in him after he'd disposed of Lem Benzaran last year. "Go bother someone else."

Eyes on the control panel, Diebol's black leather boots took him absently right down the center of the main street, flanked by Frelsi soldiers who had waited for him at the EMP shield. He'd channeled an em-push into a small, iridescent bubble around the control panel and his mace the moment he walked through the field to protect these sensitive electronics from damage.

But to bring in the rest of the Growen Army with technological advantage intact, Diebol needed his Turned Frelsi to take down the security tower that controlled the shield. His new friends limped or ran around him, dragged forward by the indomitable force of Morda's neurotransmitter soup, climbing buildings or watching his back as needed, while Diebol managed them *and* the Paradox Warrior trapped in the mind-channel. Anyone else but Diebol would have been overwhelmed by the stimuli, struggling to juggle two realities and now two hundred people at once—but whether due to the overactive electromagnetic brain waves, or simple and repeated war room training from childhood, Diebol was very comfortable in control. He felt deeply connected to each of these little people as they moved with his wishes, and he wondered for a moment if this was true, altruistic, platonic love, the unattached ideal.

Send this unit down the left street. Correct the aim on this soldier. Jei's still motionless in the mind hallway.

Diebol's eyes narrowed; the gas mask on his face misted gently with a sigh as he rose to a short building top, carried and assisted by his Frelsi companions. And then, as he looked to the city street below him, Diebol saw his true target.

Diebol had known he would find Jei—the fear he saw in the mind-channel, even now, assured him. Diebol's mastery of multitasking had blossomed in the past year with intense meditation, and when he took enough stimulant medication, he could control the mind-channel while still conscious in the real world. His own body, his own mind, were now just two more puppets for his will, two more sticks on the crude game board scratched into the cage floor between himself and Jei. This was all that game—that wager for his first friend's soul.

In the mind-channel, the Paradox Warrior stood paralyzed at the edge of his hallway, scanning the darkness for specters, while Diebol crouched atop their shared cage in the space between. *Watch the shadows from the cage.*

In the real world, dust sprinkled Diebol's black jacket with another gust of wind, speckling him as if he bled neon. Jei lay in the sand, crumpled as if in death, his face crossed with that same sadness he always wore when he slept, apparent in his eyes even through the clear panel of his gas mask. Lem stood over him, filthy with colors and overstretched in all directions, a violent concentration breaking in her grimace—

It *was* her. She was alive. Diebol *knew* she wasn't dead; Jei's brain waves had confirmed that she'd survived Sterba, that the Frelsi had canned her, and that her disappearance was entirely fabricated.

But the last sight Diebol had had of Lem Benzaran, unconscious and gift-wrapped for the Stygge Queen, still reverberated through his memory as if in the present. As if he'd really believed her dead. *You killed her, you killed her, you killed her,* the jeering Accuser cried …

Another deep sigh. Real world: *Send this unit forward. Help this soldier aim. You ten, on auto-attack, just charge at whatever's in front of you.*

Back in the mind-channel: *Jei still hasn't moved from the hallway.*

Perhaps he had killed her. This was certainly a different Lem than he knew. There was no confidence on her face, no overwhelming certainty that her interdimensional would come for her—ah, shyte, there was as much despair as the time he'd captured her adopted brother. Only now she gritted her teeth in it, eating it with every gasp, every reach, every blocking movement of her spinning neodymium mace.

"I have come to save you!" he cried, arms raised as his horde closed in on her like a rising tide after a storm.

LEM

Let's stop playing normal people games.

Reach, fire another electric shock.

You can't do this. You can't. Everything you do is wrong. You know that. Everything you do is wrong.

Another Turned sniper on the left, atop the pile of bodies—blast him with sleep-water.

Let's stop playing normal people games.

Stretch to protect the tank with her spinning mace's field.

Traitor. Traitor. Traitor.

Crouch to protect Jei.

What are you doing here?

Cry. Just curl into a ball and cry.

No! Lem stayed on her feet, but as her shoulders drooped, the tank took another volley of hits. Fluid began to ooze from a small hole in the upper side.

"It's okay, it's still not leaking much," Lem told herself. Shyte, her voice sounded so meaningless. "It's not meaningless." *Yes it is.* "Focus! Protect him."

And then her eyes met Diebol's.

At this angle, in the rapid moment she could spare for that upward glance, with the pile of unconscious Frelsi stacked up almost to Lem's height, Diebol seemed to stand on a mountain of people. But no—he was on a rooftop, across the street, raising a messianic hand to the sky. Lem heard the snarl rising in her throat, an echo of the last breath of a dying sabertooth cat. There was no hope. He had arrived, and she wasn't ready.

Stop playing normal people games.

Lem had a split second to decide. If the sleep-water had a paradoxical effect on her system, and powered her up instead of knocking her out; if the gas in the air was Morda's calming pheromone, that settled the nerves of her targets—

Don't do it. You'll lose control. It's weak, using chemical aids is weak. You'll hurt everyone. You'll fail.

"I've already failed. This is my last shot."

Lem ripped off her gas mask, and plunged her fist into the spray of blue.

JEI

Back in the mind-channel, my tunic rustled, the only sound in the dead silence as I leapt across the expanse toward Diebol's shadow.

He flickered out of existence, and I tumbled unceremoniously onto the top of the wooden cage. But before I could take that chance to wake, and return to the real world, he reappeared in his hallway, leaning on the doorjamb with his arms folded over his chest and a smug smirk across his cheeks.

"Let me out," I warned, throwing out my hand to threaten an em-pull. "You don't know what could happen to your mind if I kill you in here."

"You can't. You care about people like me too much," he laughed. "I didn't think it was possible—Cadet Commander Jei Bereens trialing a crowd-control approach to warfare? What will you do with all the prisoners?"

"You're doing the same thing."

"Ah, but my captives won't ever fight me again."

"There's more than one way to achieve that result."

He sighed, feigning an interest in his fingernails to appear nonchalant. "Fear, psychological warfare, diplomacy—even your chemical capture—I've tried all of it before," he said. "Trust me, there is only one way to ensure your enemy lives without harming you again. This is it." He held up a silver dart. With a squeeze of his fingertips it popped open, deploying six short metal claws from its sides and a tangle of long, many-branched tendrils from its center. "Get a good look at your new best friend."

I shook my head with a tight-jawed sigh through my teeth. The limp neurological tissue dangling from the dart was laced with blood—this was meant to scare me. He was stalling, and I'd already given him multiple chances. Whatever happened to him, and this place, whether he needed me or not, I couldn't stay here anymore.

I powered up my em-pull and Diebol's throat slammed into my hand, flying from across the room. He was light—almost inconsequential. I knew his weight, I knew the touch of his skin, and this was like paper. He was splitting his attention somehow.

Impressive, but doomed to fail.

My grip squeezed his carotids and trachea as I slammed his back down on the top of the cage. The wood cracked; we broke through it and fell—

"No!" he choked, coughing as much from my knee in his sternum as my grip. "You fool, you'll—"

"I'll attract attention," I said. I wasn't the only one with terror in my dark side. I jerked my other hand toward the shadows by his hallway, my em-pull fishing in the muck for—oof, it felt cold, and chilled my—shyte, I could see black shade creeping up my hand, decaying my fingertips with scattered ice—my breath crawled down my windpipe like those tendrils—

"Strengthen the weak knees," I muttered, and closed my other fist.

The floating cape dashed at us, bigger as it neared, flickering, teleporting like a nightmare. Bricandor's shadow fell over us, and my breath halted in my throat, my heart fluttering like it would fail. Shyte, I wanted to roll away, I wanted to run. I was little again—we both were—and it was *my turn next.*

"Let me out, buddy," I said through clenched teeth, gripping Diebol's throat with both hands, forcing him to stay here in the shadow with me. His eyes squeezed shut; he wheezed, struggling under me, fingernails raking blood down my forearms as his cheeks paled with terror. *Come on, come on!* I just needed him to blink back to the real world for a second, and at this proximity, touching him, I would be fast enough to return myself, too. "Let go," I repeated. "You're afraid, I can feel it. Let yourself out."

"You'll break first," he hissed hoarsely.

There was a familiar sting across my back. I withheld the yelp. The cage splintered around us now; our game pieces, sticks and stones, flew into the air around us like a tornado. I could feel Bricandor's eyes burning like red coals into the back of my skull. I remembered all of this. I remembered being forced to fight my only friend. I remembered giving up meals so he could eat. I remembered the first time he sold me out—the guilt, the rage on his face, and then the coldness that swept over his young eyes. The deep, confusing pain, as a child, under Bricandor's hand—

"Let us both out," I coughed, as if I were the one choking.

"I *will* save you, Jei," he wheezed. "I will never let you go."

CHAPTER THIRTY-FOUR

Diebol

DIEBOL COULD FEEL JEI'S GRIP ON HIS THROAT EVEN OUT IN THE REAL world, as real as the rising sand stinging the exposed sliver of skin between his gloves and sleeves—as real as the buttons clicking under his fingertips.

Choking didn't matter. Diebol was still maneuvering his legions through the streets and into the tower. He threw a couple units on auto-attack to just hurl themselves at any living thing in front of them, and tapped the cranial nerve view screen to focus in on the five soldiers that had reached the tower first. Up those stairs. Send two to overwhelm the first guard—that smaller child could slip through and climb the railing—and he himself now stood just meters away from Lem Benzaran, and the target she guarded.

In the mind-channel, Jei's grip tightened; the cold shade of Bricandor's cloak seemed to crack in spiderwebs across his skin. No. No! Diebol only had to push through a little longer. Handle the choking. Handle the sting of the memory of the whip on his back. Forget all that. "I will save you, Jei," he coughed, hurling another wave of turned Frelsi at the girl piling bodies in the center of the street.

As fast as Diebol's brain was moving, every moment seemed

slow, and long. Plenty of time to act. Plenty of time to suffer. He met Benzaran's eyes, and let her know in that glance he would kill her to get to Jei if he had to. His new friends broke into the tower control room, and the sky flickered red as the EMP shield went down. Benzaran didn't even look up at it. She was ripping off her gas mask.

Surrender? But her jaw was so set—

As Benzaran sprayed herself with the Frelsi sleeping serum, suddenly an enormous power wave knocked Diebol on his back.

LEM

Lem's electric blue bubble surged out like her own expanding universe, and this time she pushed it as hard and far as she could.

"Sorry hospitals or whatever, I hope you have backup generators," she muttered. "Shyte, I hope this works."

She glanced behind herself toward the security tower still visible through her wavering cerulean energy field. If she could raise her own EMP dome to *just* below the tower's top office, they'd still have electricity up there to try to get their own security field back up while she kept the Growen out of Fort Tapiz. Up—up—up—almost high enough—deep breath—familiar terror tingled down her back again, and she gritted her teeth in it, swallowing it like a meal into her pounding chest.

Eerie shadows flickered across Fort Tapiz as Lem devoured it, her chest squeezing tighter with each city block. For a few seconds the Frelsi around her ran, freed from Growen control and trying to help by putting as much distance as they could between themselves and her. She heard a few soldiers destroy their own weapons. Had her surge knocked out the mechanisms in their spines? Maybe—

No, hope was too good for her. Diebol had only fallen with

the control panel for a moment. On the roof across the street, he clawed his way back to his feet, gripping his throat as if choking. The Turned jerked back around to attack Lem, arms and necks yanked almost comically by inertia.

Except the five Frelsi closest to Lem. These, dazed for a moment, yanked their now non-electric rifles to mechanical bolt action function, and took up positions around her, facing their Turned comrades.

"Hey, can you hear me?" she asked the nearest sailfin.

"Yes, thanks," he coughed, his fin flat against his back in bitter resolve. There was no stun function on mechanical-only mode. He was aiming at his comrades to wound or kill. "I think these control-pellets draw power from the biological host somehow. Most of them don't seem to have failed with your blast."

"I can see that, yeah." It was like most modern pacemakers, maybe: depending on the model, they'd usually only fail if the EMP blast was very close, and very strong. "Go help the tower get the EMP shield back up, please," Lem said, eyeing Diebol again now as he positioned his puppets around them.

"But if you turn—"

"Can't be sure you're not gonna help make that happen, sorry," Lem answered. "If you wanna help me, get some distance between us first, then shoot that guy." She pointed her mace at Diebol. An iridescent bubble floated in his hands: he'd shielded his control pad from her field the same way Jei had shielded his pistol during sparring. But the *arrogance*, to bring that thing in here, this close to her, *while* he was holding Jei hostage in his mind?

"I'm getting filking tired of everyone underestimating me," Lem growled. A surge of static sparks shot from her palm around the mace, reaching like electric fingertips to grab the control panel—

And then the five Frelsi disappeared.

All the still-awake Frelsi disappeared. Lem was alone in her dome, in a world of empty streets and sleeping corpses. She heard the swishing of Sterba's robe, and the pitter-patter of almost-silent Biouk paws.

"Shyte, this thing again," Lem grumbled. Then, louder: "Anyone on my team better get the filk away from me, because I can't see you anymore, which means I am definitely going to hurt you."

"Are you fighting blind, then, dear Lem?" Diebol called from across the street.

"I can still see *you*," she muttered, listening for the fleeing footsteps. She could still hear distant explosions, and close by, the moans of injured Turned struggling against their mind-control bonds as they shuffled toward her. "You're a part of my nightmare world, Diebol, so you get to stay."

"I'm touched that you dream about me," said his teasing voice.

He didn't actually say it, though. She could see him, over there, blinking back a headache and playing with the control panel. He didn't have time to tease her. His voice, dancing around her head, first in this ear, then the other—she fought the urge to jerk and strike—this close voice wore Diebol's timbre like a cloak, but it wasn't him.

"Filking Accuser, this is impossible," Lem grumbled. She sprayed the hose in a blind arc around herself now, increasing the pressure with her fingers in front of the nozzle. She could hear bodies hit the ground under her blast—but she could also hear ringing and hissing as the shooting started up again and the tank took more hits.

She needed that control panel, and Diebol was within her reach.

"No, he is not—you are overextended and weak," said Sterba.

"You idiot, you should've had him by now, he's right there! What's wrong with you?" said the angry Biouk self.

"You can't hit me, because you dream about me, and you want to be ruled by me," said Diebol.

But in the clarity of Mera's calming gas, Lem could hear them all as they were—as shadows. Shadows that clawed at her belly, and made her want to weep and scream over the churning nausea and despair, but only shadows. She swallowed her bile and glanced over her shoulder again, checking that her field was steady at the base of the tower's top security office as she aimed her staff at Diebol—

No, if she fired energy off through the laser it would power her back down. Like at the end of the fight in Retrack City. She wanted more power, not less.

So she sat in the vulnerability, and let herself feel like shyte.

"Come on out and play," she said, dropping her mace and summoning the angry Biouk into her fingertips. Hot pain flashed in her midsection as she threw her hand forward. Lightning claws blasted toward Diebol. The control panel flew across the street and into her hand.

But Diebol came with it.

JEI

I broke free.

With an ear-splitting crack, the mind-channel shattered around me, and Diebol's hold disappeared.

I awoke into chaos. There was an electric blue dome over the fort, turning the red sky purple in sizzling waves. Lem was almost falling on top of me, wrestling with Diebol and screaming to some hidden sniper she apparently knew about to *shoot him shoot him right now* while Diebol yanked a black box of switches and buttons out of her hands, shielding it from her in an em-pull with a tell-tale iridescent bubble. He tried to get distance from her, but she gripped his wrist and voltage jolted through him, highlighting eye sockets and clenched teeth. We were surrounded by Frelsi who all seemed to be firing at me or the tank leaking behind me, and Lem's rapid blinking told me she was holding the sky up while her mind battled itself.

I felt a tug, and there was a woozy flash of cage and cape across my mind. But Diebol couldn't concentrate enough to pull me back into myself, and there were plenty of enemies around to power me up.

I reached out my fingertips, and felt nervous systems crackling in the storm.

DIEBOL

It was not fair to be a mortal battling the gods.

Diebol didn't care about the electricity she sent surging through him. He'd learned through torture to compartmentalize that pain the same way he compartmentalized everything else with his overactive neural tissue. It was data, and he processed it. Like the unfortunate datum that Jei was awake now, and super-charged by the presence of multiple enemies.

What was harder was processing the fact that Jei had just torn the tank of Frelsi sleeping serum in two, and was now sending the water toward Diebol and his allies like wet tendrils, perfectly controlling the complex polarity of the liquid like just another body part.

He could *do* that?

It's still just a kind of em-pull. Super-charged, or normal, that's all he does, wild em-pulls.

Meanwhile Diebol was straining as hard as he could muster to hold in focus the iridescent bubble protecting the control panel from Lem's repeated attempts to electrocute him and it as he weaved and dodged and flicked control buttons to send Turned Frelsi rushing at both Paradox Warriors with all the auto-attack frenzy of water-predators drawn to blood—

He couldn't draw Jei back into his mind. He himself couldn't get back in there, where the cape hung frigid over his shoulders, and Bricandor's fingers rifled through his grey matter—not while battling *the girl who could apparently create her own EMP shield when poisoned.*

"This isn't quite fair," Diebol quipped, flashing them both a wide grin. He had to grin. That was his last remaining advantage —the charm that had dictated their lives during imprisonment. Bricandor always said the tongue was the tiny spark that could set ablaze all the cedars of the Great Forest—

Diebol resisted the nausea that suddenly surged into his throat with Bricandor's name and the sudden realization, in the flood of memories long-suppressed, *that he had no idea where he had come from before life in that cage.* Before the whips and questions and forced fights with the eight-year-old who would become Jei Bereens. Diebol had no earlier memories. Only the cape, and distant screams. And he had never thought this strange.

Had he been a Frelsi child?

Vomit—he tasted vomit. Ah, what had Jei done to his mind?

Diebol had the entire fort on auto-attack against these two now, with no coordination, just chaos. He ducked another blast of clawed red lightning from Lem's fingers and threw up an em-push to re-channel the charges Jei threw at him to steal the control panel—

"You want this?" Diebol called to Jei, pretending to wave it nonchalantly while shielding it heavily with the strongest polarity shift he could muster. He almost tripped over some poor unconscious Frelsi fool, but played it off with a skip as if dancing in his taunt. "I suppose you might. You called her Mera, didn't you? I suppose this would be her brain."

It wasn't any such thing, not even metaphorically, but Jei's concentration broke at that name—the name the Growen had taken away and replaced with *Morda.* Jei's em-pull broke just long enough for Diebol to shift some of his own charge toward Lem, shoving her backward into a pile of rabid Frelsi.

"Careful, they'll tear you apart, beautiful," he crooned.

"Unless you kill them all first? I hear you're Frelsi enemy number one anyway these days."

Again, completely untrue, but the venom might divert her focus while he drew his pistol—*finally*. He fired a pistol shock toward Jei to power him down—

Ah, really? The shock diverted into a bit of torn metal Jei had orbiting him like a small moon. Diebol withheld the curse and the scowl he felt, dropped the pistol, and let it float after him while he ran backward. Another polarity shift in his neurons—send those negative charges to the back, positive charges to the front—and he sent four unconscious Frelsi bodies hurtling through the air toward Jei.

It didn't do much of anything—it was like throwing sand in the eyes of a Crajk beast, and watching it shake its mane and unsheathe its reptilian claws anyway. But enough sand could mask a getaway....

Diebol ducked down a narrow alleyway, throwing the colorful dirt of Fort Tapiz around himself like a tornado. He felt someone's em-pull wrapping around him, and saw sparks in the dust-cloud—

Let me help you, cooed Bricandor's filthy interdimensional. *I can help you. What can you do on your own, anyway?*

"Never." Diebol spat. He stuffed the control panel down his shirt, and gripped his pistol with both hands as he drew all the focus back from every area of the fort. No more horde control, no more mind-channel, no more multitasking. When super-charged like this, Jei could find him by feeling out neurological systems, and who knew what Lem could do. But every charge in nature had an opposite, and now Diebol closed his eyes, and focused on feeling the charges coming at him. Like a lady following a lead in a dance, where Diebol felt a push, he responded with a pull, and where he felt a negative, he responded with a positive. *I am nowhere*, he whispered in his mind. *I am gone.*

CHAPTER THIRTY-FIVE

Lem

"Shyte, I can't find him," Jei muttered.

Lem found herself laughing out loud. He couldn't find Diebol?

She couldn't find *anything else.*

There was sand swirling around her in the blue light. Water shot here and there like the tentacles of a hydromorph. She could feel fingers clawing at her, jabbing around her eyes, and blows, and now and again the natural energy field around her rippled with a cartridge or dart that just swerved before touching her skin—she was in a pile-up, of some kind.

But she could see no one. Not Jei. Not the Turned Frelsi. Not any Frelsi allies. Not even the Growen Army around the perimeter of the fort, or the Frelsi ships she could hear out there trying to carpet-bomb them. Even that sound was muffled, as if somehow the whole world had frozen, and only Lem and Diebol were alive in the ruins amidst stacks of unconscious bodies.

"You're not getting to keep that thing," she cried out, blasting all the invisible people off herself with an electric pulse. The EMP shield she held above the fort flickered for a second—for a second she saw a crowded street full of people—and then the shield returned with Lem's inhale. She raced down a sandstone alleyway lined with pillars to pounce on her prey—

"I'm not trying to get away," Diebol laughed, sidestepping her attack. "Wrong alleyway, by the way."

"Huh?"

He flickered out of existence, and appeared racing down a red-brick side-street. Was he—

Oh, so you're crazy now, said the Biouk she could now see crouched atop the nearest adobe rooftop. *Too much time pretending to be a human, and now you broke.*

"I'm not crazy," Lem muttered, knowing all the while replying to herself was pretty filking crazy. She ran down the side-street—

"Wrong again!" Diebol called, his voice echoing behind her.

It was so easy to keep the shield up. She was struggling to keep it from rising above the tower and shorting out their generator up there—*get your own shield up, please!*—she begged internally. Her heart was racing too fast. She was dying, it felt like. She had to be dying.

That's good, though. You can join me then, said patchwork Sterba.

"You were so pretty," Lem heard herself murmuring, her fingertips on the dead woman's chin. "We could have been sisters."

We could never have been sisters, and you know that.

Lem's boots didn't seem to make sound in the sandy streets as she chased Diebol toward the edge of the fort. Shyte, there were so many of him. So many memories. But why did the stupid exile trial keep playing in her ears? She had so many *much* more horrible memories to be traumatized over. Why did she care what Seria or some crotchety old armchair Colonel thought? She had so *many* worse memories. Diebol was everywhere.

"What could we have been?" she heard herself asking. Filk, she was dizzy. She was so terrified. He could have done anything he wanted to her in the training center, and she would have had no way to stop him. The helplessness and the cold floor and the chains splaying her out, stretched open, all seemed to be happening right now.

And the tender moment in the underground tunnel, and his fingers stitching up her wound, as they both hid from all the other electromagnetics out to kill them—Jei and Mera and Sterba and all the Growen politics—that was right now, too. Oh, that went so badly, but it could have gone so much worse! Sterba destroyed two planets' worth of Frelsi bases, but she could have —Lem's siblings faces didn't dare pop into her mind. She couldn't have that. It was all too terrible, what could have happened—in the weird, timeless haze, it seemed it to be what *could still* happen, and all the pressure of that mission crushed Lem's chest again. Diebol was the only respite from it all.

It was all too horrible, too horrible. There were too many of Diebol. Still somehow Lem knew he was heading toward the perimeter of the fort. She didn't know why, but she felt if she didn't catch him, the meaningless terror surging through her veins would kill her for sure, and there would be no relief in death.

DIEBOL

Things were bad, but not hopeless. The swirling sand seemed to be hiding Diebol from eyes, and his new electromagnetic canceling technique seemed to hide him from Jei. Lem Benzaran was steadily gaining on him as he raced toward the edge of the fort, but she kept running down side streets, and he began to realize those glowing, suddenly-blue eyes saw things that maybe weren't there right now. Maybe she was on something like he was.

But Diebol was proud of himself, in some ways, for his calm amidst the apocalypse. What he was doing, and what was being done around him, were all horrible things of epic proportions. Jei was at full power now, standing atop one of the taller buildings in the center of the fort, where he could see—and crush—the Growen vehicles outside the perimeter. The ancient reptilian ruins echoed with the screech of bending metal and the screams of the Frelsi hordes, a chorus Diebol knew would live in many people's nightmares on both sides.

But not his. He didn't dream. He only ached, somewhere deep within his core.

That wound was opening, though. Whatever Jei had done, this sick nausea didn't come from a Paradox Warrior's psychic injury. It came from some un-thought memory Diebol couldn't access, and never thought to access—a memory that now flickered just on the tip of his mind's tongue. Whose child had he been, before the cage? He knew he bore little biological resemblance to Bricandor—some, but little—and he knew the old man well enough to know many electromagnetic children had lived and died under that grizzled hand before he discovered Awakeners and created the Stygge Army. They had pretended to be brothers, Diebol and Jei, but biologically that was *almost* impossible, given their hair and skin tones.

What had Diebol been, before the cage?

It didn't matter. Why did he care? This was just another mental attack, like the Accuser he kept swatting away. Just something else to be ignored until later during meditation. Jei had broken something loose in there, something that rattled around Diebol's skull, but that something wasn't necessary for function. Legs pumping down the narrow streets through the clouds of dust, and taunts that reverberated off the old buildings—these things were the mindful now.

Diebol's chest burned with his expanding lungs—a good burn—as he ran, wet breath misting his gas mask. He wanted to glance at the control pad and take a closer look at his now-wild hordes, but he didn't dare risk a stray shot from Benzaran or an electromagnetic probing from Jei destroying it. Each "freedom-pill," as Dr. Sanders had called these darts, could only link to one control pad, and couldn't be re-networked without removal from the host, so if he lost this, there was no redundancy. No control panel here, no new Forge army, and the little reptilian child had died in vain yesterday. He would not have that.

But Diebol *also* could not have Jei crush the entire Growen force in this sector and leave all of the Growen comrades in the nearby bases open to attack. He needed to get Jei alone so he would be easier to power down. Or at least mostly alone.

I can help you with the other one. The Accuser's glee turned Diebol's stomach, and he peeled up the bottom of his gas mask to spit in the sand. He needed no interdimensional help. He could take care of Lem Benzaran on his own—he didn't know her buttons as well as he knew Jei's, but he did know something was wrong with her.

Could he get her away from the fort, too, though, so that his forces could get in? He could, right? The two Paradox Warriors couldn't risk him escaping with the control panel—they would both have to pursue him, if only so Benzaran could watch Jei's back to keep him from turning.

A green glow emanated from the elliptical windows atop the security tower—they were restarting their EMP field. Damn it all, if Diebol could just draw his control panel long enough to coordinate the Frelsi forces he had around the tower—

The moment Diebol reached into his pocket lightning shot toward him; he blocked with a stream of positive charges. It didn't completely absorb the shock—it still hurt—but the charge balance kept him from powering down and protected his control panel. Where—ah, there she was.

"As zesty as ever, my lady," he waved to the girl stalking him from the nearest rooftop.

"Not your lady," she said. Just said. Not snarled, or quipped, really. How unlike her.

"Well, no one else will have you, so I doubt you can afford to be selective," he laughed, sending an em-push her way. She tripped backward, but he made sure she saw as he reached the edge of her blue bubble and ducked outside, parting it like a waterfall with the canceling polarity of his hand.

The Frelsi EMP shield fired back up behind him as he left Fort Tapiz. Pity, that. But his dual armies, inside and out, still stood a chance if he could draw the two Paradox Warriors away, and those two truly had no choice but to follow knowing he had the control panel. Diebol ducked as a spiked land-runner sailed above his head and folded in on itself—holy shyte, he needed to get Jei away from his men.

He needed a filking vehicle though! Here, outside of Fort Tapiz, there was smoke everywhere and so much screaming. The scent of sulfur and blood stung Diebol's nostrils as his soldiers' utterly *helpless* stratagems shot through the sky with the flying fragments of shrapnel.

"The missile grid is still up—we can't hit him!"

"We have to storm in low-tech mode, weapons on mechanical settings only!"

"But without our vehicles and firepower—"

There was an air-rider just over there, as yet undamaged—Diebol shifted his protection polarity as he approached it, feeling for the push-back of Jei's reach—almost there—and perfect. Diebol swung himself up on the bike seat inside the narrow elliptical armor, threw on the pair of goggles dangling from the handles, and took off into the desert. A surge of negative charges at his back, pulling, pulling—he pushed positive charges with it, canceling, dancing—and he broke free.

It grew quiet quickly. The rushing wind drowned out the battle sounds behind him.

You're a failure. You've accomplished nothing.

Diebol refused to answer his interdimensional Accuser. He'd accomplished a great deal. It wasn't the sweeping victory he'd hoped for, but Fort Tapiz was in chaos, and Diebol still had a very good chance at coming home with a super-weapon or two. It wouldn't be long now …

Ah, there was that distant whine of air-rider engines. He glanced back over his shoulder: Fort Tapiz was now a shimmering cloud of dust on the horizon, and a lone air-rider carrying two people pursued Diebol into the desert.

A grim grin clothed Diebol's cheeks against the stinging sand. He would come back with Jei, or he would not come back at all.

CHAPTER THIRTY-SIX

Reise

REISE SPRINTED AHEAD OF NATHAN AND GIDEON, THE GRIP ON HIS boots squeaking against the ice. Left—right—right—left—he turned as many fast corners as he could, hoping this blasted maze of tunnels posited a challenge to his pursuers, too. At least they'd succeeded in luring the Growen slugs away from his little brother and sleeping mentor—Reise had found people wanted to kill you more if you'd killed several of their friends, so that was something.

"They're gaining on us," Nathan panted.

"I sure wish I'd stop skipping cardio," Gideon said back. "I keep telling myself, my dude, you're gonna regret doing only weights all the time...."

Reise grinned. There was no situation too bad for Gideon's mawkishly trite humor.

But it was a grim grin. Reise had never faced Growen capture before. Death, he knew, but bombings, fiery crashes, or taking a cartridge to the brain in battle did not faze him. What did faze him was the thought of an execution on his knees.

"Oh, shyte," he muttered. They'd reached a long, straight passage—no cover, no corners, and far too long. A death-trap. Could they turn around and take another—? Nope, here came the blitzers, their silvery orb-helmets shimmering light blue like the walls.

Filk it. Reise whirled, knelt, and shouldered his rifle. His companions could keep running if they wanted. He hoped they would. But he wasn't going to take a cartridge in the back. Breathe. Aim. Breathe. Tiny rotations of the sight—steady—flash of neck—fire.

He heard a whiz, and a thin *thunk* as a cartridge or bullet or something passed over his head, and hit—Gideon, from the sound of it. Reise didn't turn to look. The top rule in combat first aid was prevention via security. Aim. Breathe. The sight shivered a bit—hold it—neck flashed—fire. Another wet hard impact behind him. That sounded like a hiss from Nathan. He didn't know how he hadn't taken a hit yet, and he fully expected one in seconds, but right now the blitzers suffered from the narrow, cover-less hallway, too. Breathe. Aim. Breathe. Pull the trigger. Pop—hit only armor this time. He could feel his heart pounding slow and hard in his ears.

But then he felt a muzzle against his neck from behind him. What, how—

Reise turned his head to see both Nathan and Gideon aiming their weapons *at him*. Their eyes said they were as surprised as he was—horrified, in Nathan's case, and utterly stupefied, in Gideon's, as if he couldn't quite process what he was seeing.

"Don't move, or I will have your companions gut each other with their combat knives," a tinny voice shouted down the passageway.

The lurid detail was asinine, Reise thought: "You leave yourself nowhere to go from there," he muttered. But he didn't break eye contact with his companions over his shoulder, lowering his rifle to the ground. They blinked, their lips fluttering as if both wanted to speak, and couldn't summon the words. What—and also, why? Why hadn't anyone killed him yet?

"Stand up and turn around."

Reise could see the speaker now. It was difficult to tell,

without mouths, but in typical Growen fashion the person giving orders was not the person in the line of fire. He or she or it stood in the back, there, tucked against the wall.

Stand up and turn around? "No, just kill me where I am," Reise shouted back. He would not. He would not pull tricks like a dog. Heat burst up his neck, chin, and cheeks.

"Fine."

And Gideon shot Nathan.

"Holy—" Reise jumped, his heart in his throat, ears ringing— he'd been around guns all his life, it wasn't the close shot that did it, or the burst of blood from Nate's forearm, it was the cold, jerky way Gideon suddenly swerved, and the way Nate could barely manage a coughing cry of pain, and what *in the galaxy was happening right now—*

Rage—there was only rage, seething like bitter citrus at the base of Reise's tongue. Stand and turn around? Why? What was the point of any of this—the angle, the logic? *Just kill us already, coward.*

Reise looked to his older companion for some kind of clue, some kind of protocol from the guy who knew all the rules. But Nate's jaw had closed, and he looked away from Reise, clearly fighting to keep panic off his face as his nostrils flared, and he squeezed his eyes shut as a small trickle of blood ran down the flesh wound on his forearm. Gideon's face held no answers either, just pale, numb fear, staring, and hollow. No jokes. He loved Nathan, and that was clearer on his face now, in his moment without control, than ever.

Control. His companions could not protect themselves. There was really no choice, then. Reise raised his hands, teeth gritted, and let the power in his legs push him to his feet. "Is this just a power trip?" he asked. "You feel stronger giving orders to people before you kill them?"

"Shut up, puppet."

Hoarse breath caught in Reise's throat, choked by his fury as he turned, his face burning, to put his back to his enemy.

Cowards. *Cowards!* He would rather die than follow an order from an idiot, even a small one, but *this* was what they wanted from him: not his life, but his freedom. *Why, though?*

A sharp pain stung the back of his neck. Immediately something dug through his flesh, winding its way along his spine, pushing up under the flesh of his occiput with pulsing precision. He wanted to scream as it rooted through his nerves, but could not—*scream, scream, scream, please scream!* His breath would not flow—shallow, it flickered at the tip of his tongue, as only his eyes shrieked. He stood still, at attention, with infuriating obedience as the blitzers strolled over.

"Really? We're keeping all three?" asked a large, burly one.

The leader, in the back, nodded. "I haven't seen a sharp-shooter like this kid in years. We need that. Given the supplies at the crash site, they're likely on a medication run for the hidden settlement. We need that settlement eradicated for the project, so we'll do what's worked on Forge and use him for infiltration."

"And the other two?"

"It would be suspicious for a lone pilot to show up without a crew."

"But the skinny one's injured now?"

"It happens during crash-landings. Fits the story. And it's not that bad anyway, any medspider could fix it up. Stop asking questions and form up."

The blitzers didn't even speak to their prisoners. Reise felt his muscles jerk, and his legs took him marching into the queue. A burly, wide man like a refrigerator unit stood before him, and behind him, a tall, freakish thin one, like a ghost from a dream. Just a dream, a distant dream … Reise watched his own boots roll over the ice without his volition, heel-toe, heel-toe, soft squeak and crunch—even from back there somewhere, staggered in alternate formation between blitzers, Reise could hear the sawing breath of his frightened companions, blowing in his ears over his slamming heartbeat. He tried to remember the turns they took—to count the lefts, and rights—but lost count to the rhythm of the footsteps, the breath, his heart—

They arrived at a large ice wall with a tiny, dark, narrow tunnel through it. Reise's chest tightened. No. No, he would not go in there. He didn't know why. He didn't know if ursa-flies burrowed—if you would find yourself face to face in the darkness with a proboscis or something's striking fangs, unable to slither backward. That wasn't the only terror of tight spaces, closing in on the edges of his vision, pressing against his chest so he could not breathe—there were many ways to summon a nightmare, not all of them real.

His body carried him into it without leaving him the option to refuse.

CHAPTER THIRTY-SEVEN

Cinta

CINTA LIKED THE GLASS FACTORY. IT SEEMED A GOOD BACKDROP TO his disappointment.

Two huge iron doors loomed above him, set into a broad-based mountain-like tower with one central smokestack scraping the greying evening sky.

"They are not open?" Cinta's ears folded back against his skull, and his paws scrubbed his scalp with frustration—but not at this, so much. Yes, he needed this lead for the investigation: they still did not know why the Growen suddenly needed enormous amounts of untreated, non-industrial quality neodymium crystal, and the secrecy, the dead ends, the odd involvement of Growen-hired mercenaries, and his adopted sister's strange, fearful half-theories and desperation all twisted his bowels with something unsaid—

Therein lay his true disappointment.

In fact, the sum of "Lem's" entire current existence disappointed him, from the way she talked now, to the emptiness in the back of her eyes—and the fact that he could not cuddle her and fix it, and keep her little and safe, somehow made him angry both with himself and with her. Cinta kept his eyes off the horizon, but he would much rather face mind-controlled traitors at

Fort Tapiz right now than wait here for the dust to settle. What if she destroyed everything, or died?

"I cannot believe they are closed so early," he repeated.

"Not a problem, laddie," said Lark Scrita. "We din' need the old scientist anyway—just a chance to look around." The Bont mercenary had already begun unscrewing the laser projectors from her whip; with a loud click she snapped a projectile grappling hook in their place. Her partner, the Ebon Shadow, roamed his gloves across the metal doorjamb, hunting for DNA to copy into his suit for any access panels they might find.

"Mmm wait, we do not—well—" Cinta scratched his muzzle with his forepaw.

Lark thrust out a hip and laid a clawed-fist against it. "'Ey furry, did you hire us because we do Frelsi things, or because you need people who can break treaties?"

"That is not—we are in a Contested Zone anyway, so that is not the point. There is no treaty here. But this is a civilian factory and—" He leaned back, and saw a small figure rounding the corner toward what looked like a service door. "I have a better way."

He dropped to all fours and trotted toward the figure. Property damage to innocent people, they did not need right now, if avoidable. A small slippery entrance behind a sanitation worker who knew things—that would work. The short cloak and respirator disappeared inside before he could get a good look at his unwitting benefactor. Hurry, hurry—

Cinta arrived at the side door just before it closed, and a quick paw inside stopped its slam. He waited, listening for the worker's soft footsteps as he or she or it proceeded away down the echoic, metal halls ... with a cocked ear, he slipped inside.

The lizard and the human followed him. "Not bad, furry, not bad," Lark whispered. Cinta huffed—he found her tone patronizing—as his eyes adjusted. Rust coated the service hallway, and down its darkened shadows flickered a lone, outdated white fluorescent light. The whinging scent of iron and some distant chemical stung his nose, and Cinta thought he heard skittering.

"Shyyyyte this place gives me the creeps," Lark whispered. "Yup, they're definitely doing something for the Growen."

The Ebon Shadow sighed.

"'Ey, don't sigh at me. And no, I don't just think they're Growen because it's ugly in here," she hissed.

Cinta whacked her on the kneecap to signal silence. She jerked away from him with uncharacteristic fear, and he thought he heard her cry out something about discovery before he realized she hadn't said anything aloud. He looked at her for a moment, his mammalian pupils wide and perceptive in the darkness as her mind yelled something at him about backward knees and image projectors ...

Her secrets would have to wait until later. Industrial neodymium had many uses: enamels, computer hard disks, and powerful magnets fit for high-quality microphones or anything else requiring low mass with strong fields. This area on Forge lacked any kind of large-scale processing for those purposes— and anyway, the crystals in the Growen brief Jaika discovered on Beryllia seemed much more heterogenous. This old glass factory, however, recently had begun selling large quantities of its supplies on the side, and Cinta had it on good authority that at the very least, local Growen agents and third parties had made contact with scientists here. While he did not expect to find any sort of visitors' log, they could perhaps find a record of materials sales, or something useful in the laboratories. Cinta reached the corner, and looked both ways—

"Can I help you?"

Cinta's paws leapt to his holster. Scrita and the Shadow pinned themselves against the wall, covering him with their aim.

Soft eyes glowed in the shadows above a graceful muzzle draped in a black cloth respiratory mask. The tattered hood and weather cloak did not hide the outline of large, elegant ears, and

Cinta found himself face to face with what looked like a Biouk girl about his age.

"What is a neighbor like you doing on this dry planet?" Cinta asked in Biouk, ears raised and paw still grazing his weapon.

"I might ask what a neighbor like you does at all," the girl answered, flashing perfect, pointed teeth with a throaty laugh. "You, and—"

She looked up and saw his companions. "And the Ebon Shadow," she whispered.

She dashed for the other side of the hallway, her jaw set with determination as her ears laid against her back with fear. Cinta saw the alarm on the wall, and leapt in her path. They tumbled into the hallway, a ball of fur and heat; she snarled, and Cinta felt her claws slipping through the fur around his neck. He slid to the side to dodge; over her shoulder he saw Lark's aim swerve toward the maiden's back—

"Wait!" Cinta bucked, rolling them over so the maiden lay underneath him. "Wait, please." To the Biouk girl: "We are here only for information."

Her eyes strayed, not to the lizard's weapon, but to Cinta's paws. "You fight me with your claws sheathed?" she asked in Biouk.

He scrambled off her, hiding his clawless paws from her sight. "I mean you no harm," he said. Truth better than the truth of his tortured shame. A Biouk male without claws could not protect a mate.

"We need to look around," Cinta added, in more of an angry growl than he intended. He cleared his throat: "It's to protect the galaxy."

She laughed, eyeing the insignia on his pouch as she pointed at both of his companions. "Protect the galaxy? You're not in the most benevolent company, young Frelsi rogue."

"Young? I don't see your fangs, either, whelp—"

"'Ey, stop flirting already!" Lark interrupted. "Maid, do you speak Grenblenian?"

"I do," the girl said, in an accent-less speech that instantly made Cinta jealous.

"Tip-top, pleased to meet you, sweetheart. You know who we are, so—"

"Well, I know who he is," the girl pointed at the now-sighing Ebon Shadow.

Lark huffed. "You know me, too. I'm Lark Scrita, renowned Bont bounty hunter."

"I'm—sorry, but I—" The maid looked from Cinta, up to the disappointed lizard. "Is this important to you? I—uh—sure, yes! How could I forget. The famous Lark Scrita. You did that thing, that one time." She shot a look to Cinta that said she definitely had never heard of the lizard. "How can I help you, Lark Scrita?"

"We're s'posed to meet one of the scientists who manages plates here. If you can just point us to the neodymium-curing lab or whatever, we'll be outta your hair, lass."

The maid tilted her head. Cinta found his eyes straying to her paws, where the tips of her claws remained unsheathed, and if he closed his eyes, he could hear a soft chatter in Biouk as she thought. "Sheathed claws, and protecting me from his friend," she seemed to be saying. "How curious. Exciting and frightening, but curious! A Frelsi operative. But the Ebon Shadow ..."

Before Cinta could hear a more specific question, the maiden spoke aloud: "Mm. I can do better than that. Come with me." She turned left and trotted hesitantly down the hall, pausing often to look back at them. Did she think she might still have a chance to report them if she kept an eye on them?

"I'm the only one working today. Just cleaning." The metal walls reverberated with her high voice. "I can't leave you alone. You understand. We make some of the finest glass in the galaxy here, all the old way, and quite expensive. Of course I know you could kill me at any time. Your reputation, and all." She looked at the Shadow, who cast a rather intimidating specter in the blinking fluorescent light, his clean black armor reflective and almost formless as his heavy steps vibrated the rusted, blood-tinted floor. Cinta did not like having that otherworldly portal-monster walk behind him either, but the flicker of fear in the eyes of his fellow Biouk drew him to her side. He should not have begun so harshly with her, he thought. "I have some slight Frelsi sympathies. Let me be the one to show you around the facilities. Perhaps I can convince you that you're in the wrong place," she finished.

It seemed such a strange plan on her part, but like a hostage trained to reason with her captors, perhaps the young lady knew a pleasant demeanor would protect her from a fight she would otherwise lose. "You have questions yourself," Cinta found himself saying to her in Biouk.

"I don't imagine you can tell me what you're looking for," she said.

"I can, actually. We're tracking the flow of neodymium crystals in this area."

"I don't know why anyone would pay a mercenary like the Ebon Shadow for that," she laughed. Cinta closed his eyes again; in her suspicion-filled thoughts, it almost sounded like she had seen the Shadow before. "It's all right," she went on aloud. "I won't be able to believe anything you say anyway." She paused, and pointed to a heavy square door with a small, reinforced double-glass window. Ear-piercing beeps shredded the air as she entered a code into an old, old security panel. Cinta had seen no polymerwall so far. "I need my cleaning supplies, through here. You can follow me."

The storage room the maiden entered contained more than cleaning supplies: Cinta saw shelves and shelves of metal tongs, and beakers, and an array of other old tools he did not recognize stacked several meters back down a long room that could have fit a needlecraft. The girl pointed them out as she walked, explaining the differences between various glass blowing and pouring techniques. Beyond the storage room, she showed them a furnace room full of old, square kilns, and a long factory floor with high ceilings, imposing metal rafters, and a huge stained glass arabesque window facing out into the desert sky. Cinta found himself becoming bored, and in his boredom, his frustration returned. What an inane task. Find a supply chain for neodymium crystals, here? Meanwhile his sister could be destroying a town.

"You're doing good, laddie," Lark's breathy whisper interrupted Cinta's thoughts. "The local network in't very well protected, and Shadow's got the drop on their database. Their network passcode's the same as the combination for the door we passed back there. Your flirting works."

"She is not flirting," Cinta hissed back. "She is afraid of you."

"What was that?" The young lady in question stopped talking, her paw still resting on an unfinished stained glass window laying on the nearby workbench.

"Sorry, go on," Cinta shook his head.

The girl scratched her muzzle with her paw, removing her mask and hood with a tilted head. The arabesque window near the ceiling cast a soft glow on the maiden's uncertain face, her pale brown fur halo'd almost to yellow. Cinta found himself wishing he had his once-masculine claws, and his paws ached. "Go on," he repeated. "Is it here that they dope the glass with neodymium?"

"Mm, no." The maid shook her head. "But this is some of our trademark neodymium glass, here. It's highly prized by collectors and artists. Here's why." She held up a reddish-purple transparent panel shaped like a diamond, and carried it over to a small lamp at the end of the iron workbench. When she switched on the fluorescent lamp, the glass panel became a radiant blue. "Neodymium contains sharp absorption bands. Under trichromatic lighting, it'll even turn green. You can make a pure red by adding gold, or selenium. Artists like it because the color doesn't change depending on how you heat the glass—the color depends entirely on forbidden f-f transitions in the atom, not so much the chemical environment."

"You sure know a lot of science for a janitor, lass," said Scrita, running her claw along a glass frame shaped like a female sailfin.

"I spend a lot of time with the artists and scientists, when I can." The girl's ears flattened to the side, forming a sheepish, shy T with her head. "I make my own pieces and experiments when I'm here alone. Which I'm not supposed to be right now. Truth be told, that's why I'm hoping to get you in and out of here without raising an alarm. I would rather the foremen continue to think it's ceiling elves leaving them notes and recipes in the morning."

"Why wouldn't you want credit for your work?" The Bont's scales flashed a confused, almost irritated pink.

"They wouldn't like it, someone like me showing them up." The girl lowered her head, chewing her thin black lip as she trotted to the next room.

CHAPTER THIRTY-EIGHT

Cinta

CINTA AND HIS MERCENARIES FOLLOWED THEIR NEW GUIDE INTO another enormous factory room, this one wreathed in snaking copper-colored pipes studded with dials and valves. Cinta looked back behind him; the small doorways forced the Shadow to duck, and their contrast to the huge rooms would have seemed comical to Cinta if not for the lifeless, expressionless golem following him like an insistent black shade. Cinta knew the Shadow's deliberate, sinister movements allowed the hunter to record footage through his helmet, and the man also had penetration software running to break into the local database. That hidden work did not make his mechanical gait any less disturbing.

Behind the Shadow, in the workroom full of half-finished projects, Lark lagged, running her fingers over a shard of neodymium glass—

"Do you have to steal from them?" Cinta hissed.

"I do, mate," she whispered back, flipping the maroon triangle between her claws. It disappeared like a magician's performance beads. "Might need to analyze samples back on the ship. Also, it's pretty as filk."

Cinta sighed, and turned toward the Biouk cleaning girl, who had begun wiping a smudge off a length of pipe on the wall. He wanted to get out of here already. "Do your employers sell their excess inventory?" he asked. "Like if you have crystals you can't melt down into glass or however it works."

"Mm, it doesn't work like that exactly. But yes, with the economic downturn the factory takes any extra income it can get. It costs to run machinery and actually pay creators. That's another reason I don't want to bother them about an artisan salary." She fiddled with one of the dials on the wall, and the room began to hum. "I'm trying to think about why you'd care. About the kind of neodymium we use here, I mean. It's not processed enough for magnets and weapons."

"We're wondering that, too." Cinta slipped both paws into the pouch around his midsection and looked over at the Shadow for a confirmation they could get out of here soon. The human gave an almost imperceptible shake of his head. More time. More talking. Cinta might as well throw out a direct question: "Do any of your coworkers have Growen sympathies?"

"Some. Most people here just want to be left alone." The girl tilted her head; her ears twitched this way and that for a moment. "Neodymium has an unusually large specific heat capacity at liquid-helium temperatures. Are you doing work with cryocoolers, maybe?"

"No," Cinta said.

"Right. You'd still want something high grade. Right." The girl bit her lip again. "You know neodymium acts as an anticoagulant for mammals intravenously. And in fertilizers it promotes plant growth."

Cinta looked over at Lark. "What would the Growen want with thin blood and healthy plants?"

"Nothing," Lark said, tapping her claw on dials, running her fingerpads along pipe bends, and generally touching things she had no business touching. "That what you're talking about over there?"

"I apologize. We should speak Grenblenian." The maiden's

ears drooped a bit, and she smiled shyly. "It's been a while. Since I've met someone planetary, I mean," she nodded toward Cinta. He looked to Lark, internally begging her not to make him talk his broken Grenblenian in front of this eloquent science-janitor. The Bont lizard gave him a sassy nod—oh, precious jungles, that wasn't what he meant—and said:

"Well, Cinta's pretty hot, and planetary a-f." She crouched to slap his shoulders. "This mad-lad's got all the Frelsi ladies crazy about him—like fifty girlfriends, no lie, lass."

Oh, please no.

"I—all right, I guess," the maiden's eyes narrowed. In Biouk culture there was no better way to lower a male's real estate value than imply he had already broken multiple trusts before even reaching mating age. Why this? Bont lizards were known for being monogamous even after their gametes changed during half-life—was Lark assuming because Cinta was a mammal he was promiscuous?

"She is actually insane," Cinta stammered in accented Grenblenian, pointing at Lark, who did not get a chance to protest before Cinta cut her off: "I never had a lady, Frelsi or otherwise. Not that you care—about that—I—" His absent claws ached. "Not that—anyway, you are smart. You know other reasons someone might want neodymium crystal?"

The maiden observed Cinta's embarrassment with a shy grin before moving on. "Well—do you care where they came from?" she asked. "You can record neodymium isotopes in marine sediment to reconstruct historical changes in ocean currents, for example."

"Oh, maybe." Cinta looked over at the Ebon Shadow. "The Beryllian project wants very perfect records. Maybe it is a project about the past. Ar-kay-ology. He is very superstitious, Bricandor. You know. He tried to pay you for a sacrifice person, yes?"

The Shadow looked over at Lark Scrita, who hissed some curse about little girls and old men.

"If it's about beliefs," the Biouk maiden piped. "In spirituality folk healers use neodymium to draw out what they call impurities. Contaminations."

"There! There. The universe has a Contamination, he thinks," Cinta said. He stood up on his hind legs. "Something with where the crystals come from, and arranging them where they should be. Like an old lady wearing magnets on her wrists for her cancer. This, but for the universe."

"Eh, he's not going to mobilize an entire collection of crystals based on his weird beliefs," Scrita dismissed with a wave of her claw. The Shadow looked at her with his arms crossed, and Scrita immediately began to argue with his silence. "Look, nutter, just because he buys kids—that's not the same. Beans, this is a billion drachma endeavor. The Frelsi sure in't gonna pay for us to go back and tell 'em the old man's just crazy."

"I don't know what you're talking about, of course," the Biouk maiden demurred. "But I do know that it can be both. Something can have a real effect—like anticoagulating blood— and also a mystical effect in someone's mind. Neodymium is a spin glass, you know."

"What's that?" Lark asked.

"Well. Mm. Atoms magnetize because of their 'spin': they align so there's a slight net positive and negative difference within the element. Not a real charge difference—not like they've moved their electrons *away* or something, like in electricity, or voltage—but a partial pull in the material."

"The north and south pole of a magnet," Cinta remembered.

"Mm," the maiden nodded. "In normal magnetic and magnetizable elements, atoms line up in a low-energy organized lattice. It's called being ferromagnetic. You can look at it in an electron microscope. You'd see the atoms all like little soldiers facing the right way." The Biouk girl drew some stones from the pouch around her midsection, and aligned them on the floor into little boxes and diamonds, as if maybe her audience did not understand her simple words. "Now—" she held her paw up in a "pay attention," and tossed a handful of new stones, breaking most of her patterns with a clatter. "In a spin glass, some structures within it align, all ferromagnetic, and some do not, anti-ferro-magnetic. Broken patterns. The atoms get stuck in arrangements that aren't the lowest energy configuration—meta-stable, you see."

The Shadow spoke now, for the first time. "But every element aims for the lowest energy configuration. That's basic entropy."

"Yes," the young scientist smiled. "Neodymium is special. Unlike any other element on the periodic table. It would take more energy for it to find the lowest energy configuration for every atom. It lives in juxtaposition."

"Why does it make such powerful magnets, then? Wouldn't that weaken it?" Lark asked. "Like a compromise?"

"Mm. It breaks our rules of what a magnetic material should be, a paradox of heterogeneous diversity, at the same time chaotic, and at the same time ordered." Her eyes closed almost in a trance, and her voice carried a reverence Cinta had only seen in mystic ceremonies back home. "There's nothing more ordered than the inside of a strong magnet, and yet neodymium lives in a stable chaos state. What seems chaotic actually creates the *most* ordered polarity. So many possibilities for artificial neural networks, quantum computing, physics, chemistry, materials science—so, so mathematically complex inside, but so worth the pain for its secrets."

Lark's reptilian pupils constricted at the young lady's delight, and the hunter leaned in, her rough toothy metal mask centimeters from the soft halo'd face. Cinta's fur bristled; the huge lizard cast a hungry, sinister shadow over the gentle worshipper. "Alrighty, lass," Lark said, a smirk in her voice. The maiden's eyelids fluttered open. "Say a bad guy loves this paradox shyte as much as you. Where would he go to get it, and what would he do with it?"

The Biouk girl's ears twisted around her head, and she looked to Cinta. "So you really don't know what you're looking for, do you?"

"Sure we do, lass. Whoever buys natural crystals for the Growen and knows why, that's who-slash-what we're lookin' for," Lark answered. "And you seem to know an awful lot, mate."

The girl did not cringe away from the lizard, but her eyes remained on Cinta, twinkling with a ferromagnetic fear and anti-ferromagnetic bravery, to use her words, with a paradox in her gaze. Cinta closed his own eyes for a moment, listening to her say, "I want to see where this leads." He opened them again in time to see she had kept her mouth closed—he could hear her mind, and he could hear her on purpose, and that made her delicate face somehow even more fragile to him. "I am sorry for my intrusion," he said to her in Biouk, bowing, although he knew she could no more sense an intrusion than she could feel his heartbeat. "Thank you for educating us. You've been the most helpful person we've met here on Forge. One more question, please. Have you seen anyone unusual meeting with your supervisors, or hanging around this place, that you don't know?"

"Only him two weeks ago." She nodded toward the Ebon Shadow. "But you know that."

The Shadow shook his head, and Lark and Cinta both looked at each other. "He ask about crystals last time, too, lass?" Lark asked.

"Mm. He was more talkative then, though." She lowered her ears in remembered annoyance—Cinta was not surprised that the flamboyant Shadow-double offended her Biouk sensitivities, too. "My supervisor told him the location of our crystal supply mines are a guarded secret. After some threatening and whining, he left. He said next time he came back he wouldn't be so 'nice.' I thought that's why you came—or does he have amnesia?"

The Shadow interrupted with a tap to the side of his helmet. "The Growen know where their hidden mines are. This network's been accessed before."

"By 'you,' 'last week,'" Cinta guessed.

"Yes."

"Then aces to spades, they've already started collecting, boys." The tinny, garbling microphone in Lark's metal mask didn't hide the wide grin in her voice. "Finally we're getting somewhere." She pointed at the Biouk maiden with the butt of her whip, and looked to Cinta. "Whaddya wanna do with her, lad?"

"Nothing, I—what question is that?" Cinta scowled.

Lark laughed, shook her head, and then reached in one of the pockets on her utility belt for a sleek white business card. "'Ere miss. If you think of anything else about neodymium, strangers in town, or whether or not Cinta here's got a girlfriend—you call me."

"O—okay." Then, as a flustered after-thought: "My name is Masha."

"He's pleased to meet you, Masha," Lark winked. "We'll be in touch."

CHAPTER THIRTY-NINE

Laaru

LAARU BENT OVER THE BATHROOM SINK, RUNNING COLD WATER OVER his pale face. He still hadn't made a final decision on the scholarship Counselor Bricandor had offered him. He did know he wanted out of the work-study program as much as anyone else did. And he definitely liked Counselor Bricandor—the old man had met with him for lunch twice since the initial offer, and Laaru was pretty impressed that a busy diplomat would spend so much time mentoring students and sponsoring educational programs.

Still he couldn't shake that nagging inside—that fear that the galaxy's right and wrong wasn't what he thought it was. It didn't matter that every time Laaru played Pele's weird escape in his head, her warning sounded different. Xunst kept tugging at that anxiety: *"If a galaxy-famous diplomat wants to talk to you, it's because he wants something from you. There's no such thing as free face-time with someone that busy,"* he'd said. Over the past week, they'd become *much* less friendly, Laaru and Xunst. Lunch yesterday? Almost silent.

So Laaru *definitely* didn't expect Xunst to charge into the bathroom and grip his shoulders like a drowning man clinging to a branch in the river. "Laaru, do you still have a hidden passage open?" His straight black hair clung to his forehead, slick with sweat, and his almond eyes squinted above hot pink cheeks. He'd been—running?

"Yeah—yeah, uh, why?" Laaru stammered.

Xunst swallowed. "I'm Contaminated. And they're starting a Contaminated purge here."

"Whoa, uh why—why do you think that?"

"My school supervisor messaged me to meet with her, and there are Growen blitzers in the room where she's waiting. Maybe it's because I've been talking to you too much, and you're too valuable for Bricandor to lose." Xunst's eyes darted toward the bathroom polymerwall. "I know it sounds crazy, Laaru, but this is what these people do, and—"

"Xunst, these—'these people?' You're—Xunst, do you hear yourself?"

"Four people in the Contaminated support group I meet with got the same message. And I haven't heard back from them for the last hour. We know for sure one of them got arrested—Kym saw it."

"Wait, Kym's Contaminated?"

"No—or at least, I don't think so—she was the informant. Not on purpose, just—look, if I can avoid this meeting, and no one comes looking for me, then okay, that's fine, I'm just paranoid. You and Nevik can tease me about that forever. I'd just really rather not find out the hard way."

Laaru rubbed his forehead under his headband. He was starting to sweat himself. "Okay, so uh—how long do you want to hide, I guess?" he asked. "Just until tomorrow?"

"What, you have a checkout time? Not enough vacancies in hotel Laaru?" Xunst cracked a weak smile.

"I mean—if this is real then definitely I don't want anything to happen to you, just"—Laaru swallowed to keep himself from asking Xunst again if he was sure. Mistaken or not, Xunst was actually scared, and knowing his repressed personality, probably more scared than he looked. Just—"I've never had any reason to be afraid of the police," Laaru wavered. "Have you done anything, I mean? Or—maybe they want to just talk?"

"Maybe. Or maybe not fearing them is a luxury you get that I don't, Laaru." Xunst stepped back, running his hands over his face with a sigh. "Look, I don't want you to get in trouble— you're just the only person I can trust who also happens to have a hiding place. If you can't, you can't. It's your call." His voice wavered at the word "call" like a man actually about to walk to his death—like his pride had him struggling not to beg. Laaru had never seen anyone like this. It was simultaneously more stressful and yet somehow much less dramatic than he would have imagined from the lightchannel shows about evil armies. He would have felt better if Xunst had run in screaming with someone shooting behind him.

Laaru swallowed again. "We're across from my dorm room. You can get in this way," he said. He wiped his hands off on his baggy school trousers and poked his head through the polymer-wall, looking out into the stone hallway lined with soft evening lights. He looked both ways and saw no one: he still had about ten minutes on his night-time pass before the rooms locked, and he imagined Xunst probably did, too, but most people on this hallway made sure to be in their rooms by now. It was rows and rows of good kids here. It was laughable, almost, right? The idea that anything sinister would ever or had ever happened here? The smooth floor in this particular part of the hallway was even lined in red carpet, and each lantern dripped with ornate iron tassels.

Still, Laaru motioned to Xunst, and they darted across the hallway to Laaru's room.

"Why do you use the public bathroom when we all have bathrooms in our bedrooms?" Xunst wondered as they entered.

"I like keeping mine clean," Laaru shrugged. "Perks of being right across the hall." He pointed under his bed. "The tunnel entrance is down there. Are you—you going to need a blanket or something, or—why don't you just stay in my room, or—?"

"I don't want to be in here when they come to question you."
Xunst was already on his belly, shimmying under Laaru's bed
and kicking his carpet out of the way. Laaru yanked open the
oaken cupboard on the wall and got a spare blanket to stuff
down to him. He didn't believe anybody would come to question him—that sounded actually insane—but well, he didn't
want his friend to get cold ... right?

This was crazy. It wasn't—bad—right? His parents definitely
wouldn't get mad at him for helping his friend skip a meeting
with his school counselor. This was just—guy stuff, friend stuff.
*You know, that classic situation when your friend's paranoid that the
government's out to get him.*

Xunst had barely disappeared before there was a knock on
the door. Really? Laaru almost laughed. But something tightened
in his chest, and there was acid in his throat. This was so weird.
So—just not—this wasn't real life, right? He almost expected to
wake up.

Laaru stuffed his rug back under his bed, slammed his
cupboard, and then trotted to open his door. The same school
administrator from the other night stood there, her hand on her
hip. "I am not a messenger, you know," she started immediately.
"I have multiple degrees and I run an entire district here."

"Yes—yes ma'am?"

"You need to give Counselor Bricandor your text number or
something so he can invite you directly when he wants to talk.
This is the third time this week I've had to come get you. Come
on!" She snapped her fingers in the air, not even looking at Laaru
as she began to walk away. Laaru followed. Weird that she
thought he mattered enough to have a diplomat's direct communication number? This time she didn't even give him a chance to
change—*it's like she thinks we're on a casual basis or something.*

It really was like a dream. Laaru felt dizzy. Xunst thought
people wanted to *arrest* him? Laaru had never even seen a
soldier before this month. He had an imagination, too, but who
would ever want to arrest Xunst? Was the guy a danger to

himself, maybe? He definitely wasn't Frelsi or anything, and "Contaminated," for most people, just meant they talked to some kind of invisible person they thought existed or whatever. It was really weird, and kind of a bad thing to do, but pretty— harmless, right? Like taking illegal drugs? A victimless crime?

Laaru found himself standing in the same ornate office where he'd first met the counselor: four circled chairs on a burgundy rug in front of the same majestic stone table backdrop. The lights this time glowed a soft, cold blue that cast the Counselor's face in stern, sharp shadows, but the old man motioned to an uphol- stered stone chair next to him with a gentle smile.

"I'm so sorry to bother you this evening, Laaru, but as you know I am very busy during the day," the Counselor said. "I just had one question for you. Well, two, really. Or three," he chuck- led. It was an infectious chuckle, and Laaru couldn't help but crack a smile. Why was everyone so afraid of this man?

"Is something wrong, Laaru?" the diplomat asked.

"A little. Why—" He couldn't ask, though.

"Why don't people like me?" Counselor Bricandor finished for him softly.

"Uh—yes, sir." Laaru coughed. He could feel his cheekbones heating.

"Misinformation. People fear what they do not understand. Why does this school insist on acting as if Pele stole something from them when she left? They simply don't understand the situation."

"Is—is that why you've been here so long? Are you trying to clear her name?"

"Oh, she knew what she was getting into, and they won't ever find her." The Counselor waved his frail hand with such a snappy flick of the wrist Laaru feared it might drop off. "I can't blow her cover, either. She's our secret." His eyes sparkled as he laid a thin finger to his lips—Laaru remembered his grand- mother sneaking him sweet-oyster-cakes with the same grin. "I am looking for someone, though. There is a small group of disaffected youth here, you see, who have stumbled upon some—shall we say misinformation. They are a danger to themselves and others. Despite the best efforts of your school to protect their minds, they've been fed some silliness about super-slaves and so forth—they think I kidnap talented youth like yourself, and so they are trying to—well, it's an assassination plot." He gave Laaru a piercing look, and then laughed and looked elsewhere. Laaru's own eyes widened. A—what? Xunst was part of *what*? "Ah, what am I saying. You wouldn't know anyone like that, do you?"

"How would I know if I—do you think I'm that?" Laaru couldn't finish a sentence.

"No no no, of course I would never suspect you! These are strange kids, who talk about things that don't exist. I was just wondering because you're—well, look at me. I'm an old man. I don't know a lot of young people here, obviously, and neither do my bodyguards. I just thought perhaps if you heard talk like that —well, perhaps you would be able to let me know."

"I—what's going to happen to these kids? If you ..."

"I believe the confused youth just need to be re-educated. Sometimes people are too far gone, and self-defense is self-defense, but I think you can agree it's better to resolve things nonviolently if we can, no?"

"Of—of course." Laaru's mouth grew dry, and he found himself staring at the carpet. What—what should he do? Was Xunst part of an assassination? No, right?

He had promised to just let Xunst have one night in the tunnel. Did Counselor Bricandor have that kind of time, though? What if they killed him tonight? It didn't matter that Xunst wasn't a strong guy—anyone was stronger than this bag of bones sitting in front of Laaru now.

Laaru looked up to find Bricandor wearing an offended look; a wry grin, and then a gentle sigh replaced it as he scribbled something on his palm with a holo-pen. "What?" Laaru blurted.

"Oh, just needed to send a message to someone. I am busy, of course. I apologize for being rude."

"No—you—you made a face, sir. Did I—did I say something wrong?"

The old man smiled. "Well, you just seem frightened, you see. That does sadden me. Have I done something to frighten you, Laaru?"

"No—no sir." Laaru shook his head. "Can I—will you be safe tonight? And if I find something out, can I find you tomorrow?"

Counselor Bricandor smiled. "I do have bodyguards."

That was true. While Xunst could probably snap the diplomat's neck between his two fingers, any one of those space-soldiers could snap all of Xunst with a stare.

"Do you know something, Laaru?" Counselor Bricandor asked. That intent look said the elderly gentleman would forgive Laaru, if he did know.

Laaru scratched his head. "I—I don't know. I think I need to ask. I have some weird friends, but none—none that have ever said they wanted you to die or anything."

"I hardly imagine they would announce that."

"Well—I mean, with all due respect, sir, my generation doesn't have a lot of tact. Most of the people I know kind of say what they think." Although Xunst was a pretty reserved guy …

The diplomat looked up, and there was a booming clap outside the stone doors. Someone wanted to enter. "Ah, my captain is here," Counselor Bricandor said. He leaned in toward Laaru almost conspiratorially. "Did you know, Laaru, that in some countries they knock on the door, instead of clapping, to enter?"

"They—they knock here on Beryllia, sir."

"Ah, I see." The Counselor raised a shrill voice. "They knock here, Moulton! Come in."

"Sir, with the—?" The deep voice from outside sounded muffled through the thick stone door, and distorted through some kind of audio processor helmet. It cut itself off with an awkward pause.

"Yes, yes," the diplomat tsked impatiently. "Come in."

The stone gates cracked open, and a space-soldier entered—dragging Xunst by the wrists.

CHAPTER FORTY

Laaru

THE TEENAGER STUMBLING THROUGH THE DOORWAY OF THE conference room against his will looked like Xunst, but like someone had taken Xunst and tumbled him through a laundry machine. A tousled mess had replaced his normally proper, combed black hair; his always clean, pressed blue jumpsuit was torn at the shoulder, with dirt caking the knees. Was that a trickle of—blood—on his forehead?

The worst change, though, was the shocked betrayal in his eyes. *"You sold me out?"* didn't cross his pursed lips, but it didn't have to.

"I—I didn't say anything!" Laaru blurted. But remembering whose presence he was in—shouldn't have said that—

Laaru whirled back to the Counselor: "I didn't think he was the kind of person you were talking about! You know I wouldn't hide a murderer—but I didn't—I didn't say anything!"

"You didn't have to, Laaru. I heard you in your tunnels that first day, and your mind told me he was in them now," the diplomat said. The kind crow's feet hugged his piercing blue eyes in a gentle squint as he turned his soft gaze on Xunst: "Child, do you know where your 'graduate' went?"

How did the Counselor know their code term for Pele?

Xunst seemed determined to be obstinate and make whatever this was worse for himself. He pursed his lips together harder, and with a set jaw said nothing. Laaru wanted to yell at him to say something—but would that be worse ...?

The elderly politician didn't seem to mind the rudeness. He chuckled, and turned to the huge space-soldier twice Xunst's height and girth—the guy so big both Xunst's wrists fit in one of his hands. That guy? That guy stiffened as if afraid when the tiny old man looked at him.

"He doesn't know anything," Counselor Bricandor said to the space-soldier. "None of the other Contaminated did, either. Benzaran clearly didn't know about the project beyond what's publicly available. She wasn't even planting a new Frelsi cell here. Just lost, poor child."

"So—the Structure has not leaked, sir?"

"No. We are fine."

"What do you want us to do with these, sir?" the space-soldier asked, lifting Xunst's wrists in the air as if indicating a bag of groceries.

"They're just normal Contaminated children. You know what to do." Counselor Bricandor waved him away.

"What do we tell the administrators, sir?"

The diplomat sighed in frustration. "Assassination attempt, equivalent force, unfortunate tragedy, condolences. Don't be daft." He glanced at Laaru, and back at the space-soldier. "The truth."

That opened Xunst's mouth. "Hey Laaru, I've never tried to assassinate anyone. You know I'm harmless." To the diplomat: "Do what you want with me, but don't lie to him about it. He's got a right to make an informed choice about you."

"Harmless? As if the circle-blades in your dorm room are just for show," the diplomat smirked. *Wait, they searched his room?*

"Those are ceremonial, you racist. My family's handed them down for generations."

"Ech," Counselor Bricandor waved to the space-soldier with more wrist-cracking fervor, and the behemoth turned to go.

"Wait—please—wait," Laaru blurted. It surprised him, but the space-soldier stopped, and looked at the diplomat, who paused with his eyes on Laaru. "Are you going to kill—" Laaru realized that his own sudden fear answered his own first question. Xunst might die. Counselor Bricandor still looked as kind and gentle as ever, and the space-soldier still looked terrifying, but the fact that boring, quiet Xunst looked like a martyr—not like a crazy person, not a danger to himself or anyone else, just a disheveled hero in someone else's action story—that turned everything on its head. Laaru knew there wasn't logic in that thought; he couldn't make a decision based on who looked heroic or not. But: "I need time to decide—"

"Laaru, do you think I kill people?" Counselor Bricandor asked, folding his hands on his lap.

"I—know that you're in a war. I'm not naive, I don't think? If someone tries to kill you, you take them out, right?" Laaru held up both hands as if there were a gun pointed to his own chest. "But is there—you want me to join your army, right? Can he be pardoned or something if I do that?"

"That's not at all how scholarships work, young man," Bricandor shook his head.

"Hey, Laaru, shut up, you don't know what you're—" A huge fist to the side of the head cut Xunst off mid-protest. Laaru's world spun, and his chest squeezing in on itself, as if his rib cage wanted to choke him but couldn't reach his neck. Panic? Yes, this was panic, like before he had to give that one class presentation, but so much worse—

"Forget scholarship," Laaru stammered. "I'll just join, just right now. We can leave right now. Whatever. Don't—don't hurt my friend."

"You don't trust me to do what's right?" Bricandor asked.

"No, it's not that I don't trust you—it's—misunderstanding? Different interests from different people—that's all war is, right?

People don't really make decisions? You do what you're conditioned to do and Xunst does what he's conditioned to do and it's no hard feelings, it's just what you all do, but I don't want—anything—to happen to anyone. Look, sir." Laaru was on his feet now, his racing mouth finally still as he ripped off his glove and laid his palm on the stone chair behind himself. Laaru had talked about his ability with the old man, but he hadn't *shown* him, and maybe—

It was an instinct, more than a plan. Laaru shielded the old man with his own body as that feeling he hated so much surged from deep within his abdomen. The chair exploded with a loud *crack*; shards lodged in the ceiling and the walls; a shower of dust puffed over Laaru. Laaru whirled to lay a hand on another chair, to show he could do so much more, he was worth so much more—

"That's enough, Laaru," the wizened leader coughed, waving dust out of his face as he rose to his feet now himself. "I hear you. Moulton, lower your weapon. Laaru is just being loud, is all."

Laaru turned; the space-soldier at the doorway had a huge gun aimed at his head with both hands, shoulders square and legs spread like pillars lodged in the earth. Xunst slumped discarded behind him against the door frame on the floor, clutching his forehead with both eyes closed.

Bricandor whistled through his teeth for a moment and tilted his head, thinking. Presently he clapped his hands with a soft little *plat*. "Well, I think that's settled, gentlemen. We're leaving. Laaru, you can bring Xunst on the ship with us."

"No, definitely not," Xunst murmured, and stumbled from a crawl into a run. The space-soldier swiped at him, and missed—

Laaru darted out into the hallway after them. He couldn't see Xunst—there was a corner less than a meter away, and Xunst had turned it immediately. The space-soldier lumbered toward the turn—

"Kym, get out of my way!" Xunst's voice cried.

"Uh, guy, why are you running from the authorities?" her voice answered. "Just calm down and it'll be fine, stop freaking out."

"Kym, I don't want to hurt you, and I won't, so please just *get out of my—*"

The giant whirled right; time seemed to slow for Laaru as the soldier raised his weapon. There was a crackling sound, and a hiss. "I told you, just obey the police!" Kym gasped, and a rustling thud followed like someone had dropped a sack of vegetables.

Laaru passed out.

CHAPTER FORTY-ONE

Laaru

A FAMILIAR HUMMING AND A BACKACHE BROUGHT LAARU BACK TO himself. Golden-copper ceilings and a warm metal floor met him; as he sat up, his chest pressed against soft, silvery straps. Where—? He was in some kind of spaceship, much more ornate than the transport bus that had brought him to this sector. A brilliant light blue sky shone through the domed sky-light in the ceiling above; carved figurines molded right into the walls, all one fluid piece of art. The whole place looked like a sculptor's palm holding a svelte glass orb. Or maybe more like a mandorla or superellipse than an orb, with the two pointed ends, but that didn't—Laaru wasn't in school right now, and didn't need to identify the geometry.

"Ah, you are awake," Counselor Bricandor said. He sat on a plush, gold-weave couch, shimmering at this angle in the light. Multiple large space-soldiers stood around him at attention—or anyway what Laaru imagined from military shows must be attention. He had always preferred biopics himself. "I wanted to explain something to you."

Laaru unbuckled and sat up; the safety straps melted into the floor. Wow, polymerwall everywhere, too? Expensive. He couldn't—wow, he couldn't tell exactly where the pilot's cockpit was. Maybe underneath them? Where was—

Uh-oh. Xunst was in the back corner, wearing some kind of collar around his neck that shed a yellow glow across him. He winced like he had a terrible headache. But he was alive. *The soldier must have used some kind of electric stun bullet or something to knock him out.*

There was a woven silver muzzle around Xunst's head and mouth, gagging him and binding his jaw shut. "Why is—why can't he talk?" Laaru asked. He began to feel that panic again. What had he agreed to? What was happening?

"He carries a dangerous Contamination that will destroy the universe if allowed. It's airborne. Speaking, more than anything, spreads it. Touch can, too, of course, and fomites, but speaking is worst."

Laaru didn't ask what a fomite was. He was watching the mountains outside the window grow larger around them, and feeling a weight on his chest and arms that wasn't just psychological. Gravity was shifting from artificial to planetary. He'd probably woken up when they broke atmosphere. And he didn't recognize these mountains—not just like he'd never been here, but like he'd never seen anything like these stark blue granite walls on any map, history tape, video record, anything. He stood up, and walked over to the glass, ignoring the speed with which his breath rose in his chest.

Ooooooh man.

The whole landscape was a mess of canyons—like earth-worm tracks, before they dig down under the soil—just a tangle of round-bottomed, high-walled smooth canyons. As they flew lower Laaru could see, of course, that the canyons weren't really smooth, but even up close these giant ragged walls seemed patterned in rings. Canyons were usually formed by cataclysmic water erosion and giant rivers, and he couldn't imagine any kind of river that moved like that.

"Where—what—"

"They're carved by the giants that live here. Worms, or snakes, is what they look like—of course I have no idea what their biological taxonomy is, or what the humans here call them," Counselor Bricandor said. He was leaning on a fist he had propped up on one arm of his gilded couch. "The humans here don't have space travel, or contact with the outside world. They probably don't even know their ancestors came from space."

"Why are we here?" Laaru asked. His stomach was so heavy. Just so heavy. He hadn't even told his parents about his decision. He was going to be in so much trouble. They would want to know why he'd been scouted, and why he'd suddenly joined the military instead of finishing school. It was ridiculous.

"To teach you something. And it's on our way home, of course." The old man eased himself to his feet. Laaru realized they were bare as they plodded across the smooth floor under that swishing brown robe. "You have a brilliant future ahead of you, you know." The diplomat stood beside the student, hands clutched behind his back as they gazed out the window. "You have a quality about you that is more important than your skill."

"What—what is that?"

"Compassion." The diplomat didn't hesitate. Laaru didn't understand; the old man went on: "You don't trust your friend, and you don't trust me, but you were quick to try to protect the both of us from each other because you have compassion. And you were willing to demonstrate power and endure shame to do so."

Did—did the old man know his trigger?

"I know many things, Laaru." The old man nodded. "Oh, by the way. I have already sent a message to your parents. I told them your fantastic research project was selected by our scientists, and that at the completion of your research project Beryllia will automatically award you a diploma. They were surprised, and frustrated that you hadn't told them, but they quieted down when I told them what you'd be earning. They don't know about your gift, and they don't need to know."

"Th-thank you," Laaru said.

"I don't personally scout for the Stygge Army, you know. And I came upon you quite by accident. Most gifted people go to train on Revelon, under my son. Your friend Pele was the first graduate from that facility, actually. But you are special. You will work with me directly."

Revelon—and the Stygge Army? All real, then. And Pele hadn't been happy about that whole business. Uh-oh …

Bricandor placed a soft, wrinkled hand on Laaru's shoulder. "Don't be afraid. I don't want to lie to you, you know. But there are many things it will take you some time to understand and unlearn. Some things that are true, but not true. I want to save the universe from itself. I want to create a perfect peace. Do you believe me, Laaru?"

Laaru looked down into the piercing blue eyes looking up at him by his shoulder. They were so pure and earnest. "I believe that you believe that, sir," Laaru whispered. "Is that all right?"

"That is a good start." The old man patted his arm. "Now. Have you ever heard of a doctor cutting off an injured part to save a whole?"

"Cancer and stuff, yeah. I mean yes. Sir."

"Sometimes the compassionate thing to do is to put down an injured animal, yes?"

Uh-oh. "Please, sir—"

"I'm not going to kill your friend," Bricandor snapped. The annoyance seemed so fierce, so sudden, that Laaru almost jumped. "But just because he is your friend does not mean he can be allowed to continue to spread disease across the galaxy."

"Isn't Contamination just a word for like being superstitious, though?" Laaru choked. "What's the—harm—"

"No. And you do him a disservice by assuming he is merely a fool with an overactive imagination," the old man smirked. "No, what they do is real, and dangerous. Their mental communication opens a tiny electromagnetic portal to another world, and every time they do that they suck energy out of that world into this one. They, and their Accomplice on that side, are robbing the beings in that world of their rightful strength—and the entire process infuses an unnatural energy into our cosmos that throws off the balance of entropy."

"The—I—I don't understand." The pseudo-science was too —just—

"There is a natural life cycle to things," Bricandor huffed, a bit impatient, as if explaining things Laaru should already know. "Things live and die. There is Yin, and there is Yang. And eventually, everything cools, and there is peace. This is an ugly, hot universe, full of strife and death and suffering, and there is a place for that, for a time. But in the end, we need peace, and cool. All atoms in agreement, all matter in agreement, everything as one, everything at rest."

Laaru felt so dizzy. What did any of this philosophy have to do with Xunst? What—

"You will understand, eventually. For now understand that it would be very, very cruel to allow him to continue infecting others. They die horrible deaths, you know, the Contaminated Ones, and their lives are a misery. The beings from the Other plane do not appreciate their interference, and those beings can be *terribly* cruel. Understandably so, of course, and sometimes you must be cruel to be kind, choosing between two evils— anyway, all choosing and evil will end once the universe has reached nirvana." Bricandor returned to his seat now, waving his floppy wrist again as if to cut off his own ramble. A space-soldier guided Laaru backward away from the clear wall with one large, gloved hand and stepped in front of him, motioning one of the other soldiers toward Xunst. "Here, on this unmarked planet," Bricandor said finally. "Your friend will not be found, and he will infect no one of consequence."

Xunst's eyes widened over the muzzle. Laaru opened his mouth to say something, anything, but his throat seemed glued shut and he couldn't even breathe. There was a swooping feeling as the ship slowed, now just meters off the ground, and the window rippled as its permeability changed. With one hand a space-soldier removed Xunst's collar, and with the other, he threw him through the wall.

Laaru heard the thud and the tumble; he ran to the window as it solidified again. Seconds—it all took seconds. Here, then gone, and no goodbye. They'd already sped up and lifted off, and Laaru could barely see Xunst standing on the cliff, a tiny, forlorn toy looking around in shock and lonely wonder.

Laaru almost couldn't see. Everything seemed misty. Hazy. He felt a space-soldier guide him toward Bricandor's couch, and found himself sitting in stunned silence beside the old man on the soft, gilded sheets.

"This is the kindest thing," he heard that quiet voice say. "Killing him would be kinder, to spare him his future torment, but I don't think you could stomach that, and he is your friend. So this is the kindest thing. He will be all right. Rest, and do not fear. His invisible friend will take care of him. And I will take care of you.

"I will become like a father to you, Laaru, and you will replace the son I soon lose."

CHAPTER FORTY-TWO

Jei

WE TRACKED DIEBOL FOR ABOUT A DAY AND A HALF BEFORE LEM finally agreed to stop and rest. A small outcropping of rocks indicated something like a cave in the rolling dune sea. I leaned back against her, pulling the air-rider to a stop with my weight.

"The ride's doing all the work," Lem grumbled as the engine quieted. "Don't know why *we* need to stop."

"Sleep is a thing. Especially for mental health."

"I'm not crazy."

"Didn't say you were. Bloodseas, Lem." I was a bit grumpy myself. It was getting dark, and I felt hung over now that my energy boost had died down. There was no more electromagnetic "reaching": I didn't have Mera's electro-locating organ in my inner ears, so I could only "sense" other people's neurological systems when I was fully charged up—when their movements seemed to ripple against me in the fabric of the planet's magnetic field. Without that, we only had our eyes and the telltale signs of air-rider traffic drawn across the sand, and even Lem's Biouk training wouldn't help us much in the desert in the dark.

"It's like a taunt," Lem grunted, her shoulder flush with mine as we shoved the air-rider into the shallow cave formed by the jumble of boulders. I powered the air-rider's levo-pads off so it lay on the ground, and she flopped down beside it and ripped off her mask, pointing outside. "It's right there," she went on. "The path is right there, just a big old streak right off to the horizon. He's right there."

"He's counting on exhausting us so he can take a shot," I said. "That's the entire reason he led us out here. The control panel's bait. We just need to not lose him until the air squad can escape Fort Tapiz to bomb him and it."

"I'm not stupid! I know that! That thing is the bait that gets us taken, and we're the bait that gets him bombed. He can't go back to civilization with you chasing him or you'll power up, we can't get the control panel without risking you. Blabla, big filking clever game between you two. I was paying attention during your briefing call." She punched the side of the air-rider and a panel popped open; she reached inside and tore open a nutrient bar like it had personally offended her.

I gave her a nod of respect. Most Frelsi didn't know where the supplies hatch was on that air-rider model.

"I know because I was Growen, not because I'm smart," she growled, reading my look.

"You weren't Growen, you were undercover," I corrected.

"I was Growen," she snapped. "Had to get their stupid shyte all the way up in my head so Sterba or Bricandor or whoever couldn't pick me out. Had to believe it. Like the tentacles of that hydromorph, all up inside my brain." She extended her fingers in an upward digging gesture and hit me with a dark look—she was referencing the ba-eater that tried to possess me during our time in the Stygge training center on Revelon. "I hate that Cinta's got their same gift. It's gross."

"Or it's a phenomenal tactical advantage once he gets used to it," I said.

"It's gross."

I didn't reply. I didn't feel like arguing with her. I felt like lying down and taking a filking nap. My head throbbed, my neck ached, my eyes felt hot and strained, and every muscle pulsed with a dull, frustrating soreness. I'd taken out a *lot* of their force, and if I could've stayed—if it wasn't so damn important that we got that control panel—I could've demolished the whole siege. She wasn't the only one pissed off. I *hated* it when he did this. He'd put a piece on the board I couldn't ignore, and then I had to waste a turn stopping him instead of continuing my offense in whatever area I'd gained territory.

At least he wasn't going to be pulling me back into the mind-channel. I was in charge in there now. I hadn't checked, but I could feel the emptiness—it was quiet, quieter than my mind had been for years, as if for years I'd had radio static playing in the background and now I'd switched it off. I missed it, and that angered me, too.

"You just gonna stand there all night, or you gonna sleep?" Lem asked, looking up at me.

"I'm going to shoot you, is what I'm going to do," I muttered, sitting down and catching the nutrient bar she tossed my way.

She laughed, and sighed.

"What?" I asked.

"I know that feeling." She pointed her nutrient bar at me. "Where the other person is just so hopeless and grumpy and you want to punch them for it because they're sapping you. That's how I felt with you. With Cadet Commander Bereens." She leaned her head back against the air-rider and groaned. "Shyte, what's happened to me?"

"A lot. A lot happened. Hope gets tired."

"I guess."

I leaned back on the rock behind me. There wasn't quite enough space to stretch out—my boots pressed against the air-rider, next to Lem, and hers touched the rock next to me—but sitting this way we could both see out the small entrance. Neither of us wanted to lie down with our heads or feet facing the entrance—too vulnerable.

I closed my eyes for just a moment. A peace—there was a

peace there behind my eyelids, as if I could see Njandejara, or as if he was a soothing liquid that flowed from my eyes across my scalp. My soul became hungry—*your words, like home* ... I moved to open my archaeological texts on my wristband.

"Anything?" Lem asked. She apparently thought I was checking mission details.

"Just more traffic from Fort Tapiz," I told her, tapping through general messages not meant specifically for me. "Dr. Loylan's stationed there. Remember her, from Fort Jehu? She's trying to find a way to get the things out of people's spines without ripping out their nervous systems or getting electrocuted herself."

"Ooh, tell them some of the things turn off with a good EMP blast!" Lem pepped up.

"I did, as soon as you told me. When you were driving."

"Oh. That's not helping a lot of them, then." She deflated again.

"Unfortunately no. They've locked up and sedated most of the people we incapacitated, though. There is some talk about just killing all of them, but no one's really pushing for that yet."

"Shyte, it makes sense if they do. I'd rather die if I were going to—well." Lem looked away from me, out to the desert night. Stars twinkled above us now.

My chest seemed to sink around me. It was a soft sadness, but my voice came out with an almost angry gravel. "So. Even after that, you're thinking of doing it."

"After what? Doing what? What are you talking about?" Lem snapped.

"You were in full control back there. You saved the fort."

"Maybe, maybe not."

I leaned forward. "It's not an obvious or easy win—the rest of the Frelsi still have to do their own jobs. You can't save the whole world, Lem. But—"

"But I can destroy it."

"I was going to say but you did save the fort from being

overrun when the shield went down. Bloodseas, Lem," I sighed. I closed my eyes again. Shyte, I was too tired for this.

But I could feel her sinking. I couldn't read her mind or hear the monster flitting around her—but the stiff sound of her breathing, and the mental echo of her words—shyte, Lem.

I shifted my weight, crossing my legs so I could lean forward close to her, with a hand on her shoulder and my eyes locked in hers. If she didn't look so angry, I thought her rich umber eyes might melt into tears. She was tired, too—of everything.

"I don't know about the universe, but I do know my universe will be a whole lot worse without you in it, lady," I said. "Don't go there." I felt her deltoids soften under my palm, and I let her go.

"I'm a soldier, not a lady," she sniffled her grumble, looking away from me again. But her posture relaxed, and she knocked a fist gently on my knee to let me know she'd heard me.

"I know." I had avoided calling her soldier in case it triggered a memory of the fact that she was definitely *not* a soldier anymore. "I just figure you won't listen to me if I don't call you names."

"Shut up."

"I will if you go to sleep," I said.

"Shyte, man, aren't you tired?" She yawned mid-sentence. "See? I'm dying over here and I didn't just smash like a hundred tons of metal with my brain."

"No, you just held up the sky with your brain. Easy stuff, I know." I got a smile out of her despite herself, and shook my head. "Go to sleep. I wanna check something first."

"Hey, if you're awake working, let me help," she said.

"It's not work."

"Shyte, you have a diary about her?" she reached for my wrist with a wicked grin.

"What? No, people don't have 'diaries' *about* girls, that's not what diaries are," I laughed, jerking my arm away. She pounced over to my side and locked my elbow in hers in a modified arm-bar, peering at my wristband with a craned neck. I let her have it with kind of a sigh, glad to see some fire in her.

"Oh," she murmured. "It's stuff from Njande."

"Yeah."

She let me go, and squirmed away, back to her side. Her eyes strayed outside again.

"You want to listen with me?" I asked. "I guess I 'listen' with my eyes now, but you know."

She took a second to answer. "Why don't I want to?" she wondered. "Am I mad at him? Why?"

"Could be changes in your brain chemistry after trauma. Could be the—thing—altering it for you. Dopamine, serotonin—all that stuff can be played like a musical instrument."

She nodded, and curled up to face the stars with her back to me. "If it helps you rest, you should read to strengthen yourself," she said. "And maybe reading aloud will help push this thing away from me. So we can be in top form against him tomorrow."

It was very practical—not a lot of joy in it. Like a good luck charm or something. It bothered me. He was a person, not a—thing—and the whole point of the ritual of the ancient texts was to know him, not to—whatever. I couldn't really explain it, so I didn't. I was feeling kind of selfish anyway, and just wanted to coat the folds of my brain in soothing oil, whether she was part of it or not. So I did.

It was a particularly ancient and revered piece I had up on my wristband right now, something my Biouk scholar contact called the "Listen"—a simple verse supposed to hold the secret at the center of the universe. *"Shema Yisroel, Adonai Eloheinu, Adonai echad—v'ahavta et Adonai Elohecha b'chol l'vavcha, uv'chol nafsh'cha, uv'chol m'odecha."* I let my tongue savor the syllables, a long-gone human language somehow so much more similar to Biouk than to Grenblenian. "This text can be translated 'Listen, One Who Wrestles With The Power. The Master Who is Our Beings of Power, the Master is One. Love at the Master Who is Our Beings of Power. Love at the Master Who Is Our Beings of

Power with all your deep will, with all your life wind, with all your strength.'"

"Who is the 'One Who Struggles With The Power,' I wonder." Lem's muffled, sleepy voice floated back to me on the quiet night breeze.

"It's you, I think," I said gently. "And me."

"So is the Power bad?"

"No. The Power there is the shortened name for the Master Who Is Our Beings of Power. Our Njandejara. It's not struggles 'against,' either—it's a broader term, like 'with.' Struggles 'with' power can be against or alongside, both. Or like how you might struggle with an idea—doesn't literally mean it's your enemy, just something you're working through. The name 'One Who Struggles With The Power' shows up first during a sparring match between a person and Njandejara, where the person won't let him go until he blesses them. An enmity that isn't an enmity."

"A paradox," she hummed. She was already almost asleep.

She didn't know it, but we had already grazed the first two layers of meaning, the literal and the allegorical. My favorite layer, the historical commentary, rose now. I liked to intellectualize while I read; it felt like wine on the brain as I spoke: "There's a comparative text from the same time period that three sages later pair with this one: *v'ahavta l'reacha kamocha*."

"*Reacha* kinda sounds like the Biouk word 'neighbor' that we use all the time," Lem murmured. "You know, I always thought neighbor wasn't the best translation for it, in Grenblenian. The Biouk *reicha* could be the dude who happens to live next door, or it could mean your special, intimate friend. Or just like dude or 'fellow' or whatever."

"It's like that in the ancient language, too. Basically this second text means 'love the intimate friend, the satyr, the fellow person, as your own self.' So because the word was so broad, there was actually a debate for a while as to which meaning it meant." I paused. "Hey, actually—I've been wondering for a while why Biouk has so much in common with this language from literally eons ago."

Lem never missed a chance to talk Biouk culture, but her muttered, sleepy reply now escaped me, so I let it sit with a smile as she faded. I went on, my voice quieter: "Anyway the sages. One I read seems to say this 'Neighbor' text is the actual fulfillment of the 'Listen' text. Another I read says it's its second command. Putting them together, I think loving the intimate friend you can see is how you love the Otherworldly Being you can't."

Nothing answered me. I knew she hadn't slept well the last couple of days, and I was relieved to hear her breathing begin to slow, and see her back begin to expand like billows. I set a wakefulness charge on my wristband—just a little burst of temperature change that would fire off at random intervals and keep me alert—and an alarm for when it was my turn to pass out. I hated the rhythm of taking turns to sleep—just the unnatural *urgency* of splitting up sleep like a ration pack. Nothing beat the safety of letting the whole team conk out in a spaceship after a mission, hidden in the cradle of darkness and swaddled by stars.

I hadn't minded staying awake for Mera. I'd felt safer, even, watching over her. Even imprisoned together after she sold me out, I would wake up when she slept to make sure Diebol didn't hurt her when his lackeys came in to take her blood. It was something innate—no alarms needed.

My chest ached. Bamboo rustled in my mind. This small cave reminded me of the night I hid Mera in a snow-turtle's den on Alpino to protect her from Lem and Diebol. The tight fit in that burrow, like a sleeping bag, had made me afraid she would think I was taking advantage of a bad situation, and I had pressed myself against the cool earth as much as possible to give her as much space as I could. But there was no space between us, ever. Even later, in all her suffocating control, I never wanted space. I sure as shyte didn't want it now. My own freedom was pain to me.

"Don't let me go back to *Mitzrayim*," I murmured to Njande-jara. The land of bondage in the ancient stories. Many people who escaped from there wanted to return because of the plentiful food, and I had a hunger, still, for the old surrender Diebol now carried in a little dart. "For the first time in my life I want what I actually need—we're finally lined up, you and me—but that nagging memory won't leave. There's a secret here, in the center of the Listen, where your name is plural and singular at the same time. I saw that code you hid, you know, Master Who *Is* Our *Beings* of Power." I remembered a metaphor I'd heard once about the nature of the electron, both a particle and a wave, and it seemed so clear to me that the electron, and this plural, singular name, held the same secret at their core, a secret so fundamental to the fabric of reality it made all our struggles somehow utterly meaningless, and somehow also so much more important. "Just let me taste a little of that secret, so I'm not hungry for the wrong thing."

A memory from another text answered me almost immediately: *What you ask into my breath, I will give to you.*

I shivered in the desert night.

CHAPTER FORTY-THREE

Diebol

DIEBOL DIDN'T REALLY HAVE THE LUXURY OF SLEEP. HE HAD NO ONE to watch his back, and he was just fine with that. He knew meditations that would keep him awake. In the meantime, he steered his air-rider in a wide berth around the dunes, doubling back to hopefully get behind his two targets before daybreak. He was glad he had led them into the desert to keep Jei away from enormous forces that would super-charge his abilities; no doubt this flight into the dunes had saved Diebol's forces back at Fort Tapiz from certain death. Diebol had a much better chance of turning Jei out here. Still, if by some dim chance Diebol could avoid fighting both warriors at once—perhaps by creeping up behind them while they rested—he preferred that.

Diebol blinked hard and hissed through his teeth. Shyte, even through the cloth respirator mask, the goggles, and the leather hood, the sand here somehow managed to sting into Diebol's skin. It bothered him more than it should. Itching, itching ... whose child had he been, before? And why had he never thought about it?

It was time. Diebol flicked his holo-pen out of his pocket, drew a square on the windshield in front of him, and scribbled a code to call Bricandor. The summit room of one of their diplomatic ships appeared on screen—the one with that obsequious golden couch.

"Whose child am I?" Diebol snapped the moment he saw the old man's face.

"We are all children of the universe, and chance, my son. What has become of your tone?" The "Counselor" answered with that sickly sweetness that usually preceded punishment, but Diebol didn't care.

"We're past that," Diebol said. "I'll control the Frelsi in a matter of months. The new High Command are my handpicks. The two *witches* that you groomed to balance my power are both dead. When I return with the next Stygge superpower, you will cede control of the Growen to me."

The old man opened his bare-toothed mouth to speak, but Diebol interrupted.

"No. I alone have override codes for every mind-control module Sanders ships—on every planet. And I have no problem sending my new army of desperate guerrillas through every Uncontested Zone in the galaxy to hunt you—what do I care what the media think of the Frelsi, right?" Diebol set his jaw. Years ago, he wouldn't have dared to announce this, but he'd waited patiently, and now it was time to sink his teeth into the alpha's neck. "All your mind-games, all your 'diplomacy,' all your 'friends' mean nothing with all your old Generals dead."

Bricandor's thin lips pursed together. "It was you, then, last year. You had the girl kill the High Command for you."

"Benzaran. Yes." Diebol grinned. The memory of her existence pissed him off, but that had been one of the most enjoyable nights of his life. Blood, heat, a dance, and in exchange for protection from Jei she'd handed him the perfect, blame-free coup by wiping out a room full of frustrating bureaucrats he despised. When choosing between the lesser of two political evils, she had chosen Diebol over Sterba and Bricandor.

"Why him, and not her, then?" Bricandor asked, leaning back

in his seat with a curious raised eyebrow. "If you can bring back just one, why will you choose him?"

"She served her purpose. Now I need something with a little more raw power. He can't kill with a glance or read minds like you can, but his fully charged state carries more than enough power to rip you in half with an em-pull." Diebol tilted his head. There was no reason to hide anything anymore from the mind-reader. "And perhaps because of what you did to us. I've hated him on and off, but I've always hated you. Now if you step out of line, I can have him remove your spine. That seems like justice." Diebol's teeth gritted together. He was less in control than he wanted to be. His words were even, but something stirred in his stomach that hadn't moved in years. Not since the cage. Whatever Jei had awakened in there—whatever memory he could not access—was dissolving Diebol from the inside. Still, he kept his tone cool: "Now answer the question," he said. "Where did I come from?"

Bricandor chuckled, and leaned his head back against the couch with his eyes closed. "Let's see. How about I tell you *if* you come back alive to claim your throne?"

"It's already mine. As I said, the Growen armies under High Command, and the new Frelsi recruits, will all obey me over you in any dispute."

Bricandor leaned forward. "But you can't *kill* me without Bereens. Maybe you can't even kill me with him."

"My goal isn't to kill you. It's to control you." Diebol grinned. He could feel his teeth grinding. "Give you a cage in your mind."

"True control requires a survival threat."

Diebol looked away at the horizon and scoffed. He pulled his air-rider to a stop. "It seems you don't fully understand the situation."

"No." Bricandor's stare intensified. "It seems *you* do not understand, my son."

Diebol forced his jaw to relax. He had prepared for this

moment for years. This, not Jei, was why he had taught himself to balance other people's charges. The death-wish. Bricandor could shut down entire neurological systems with a desire. Diebol closed his eyes.

"What was it like?" he'd asked Jei last year.

"When your loving 'father' tried to kill me by looking at me?"

"Humor me."

"Like silence. Choking, cold, and suffocating, but not because anything was squeezing. It was like my brain decided it didn't need to exist anymore, so there was no use for air, or heat, or motion. My neurons were fine with becoming the same energy level as the air whether I wanted that or not. One with the universe. Not me anymore."

"It sounds peaceful," Diebol had joked.

"It was terrifying. Respiratory systems stopped first. The pain centers were last to shut down. You happy?"

He was now. Because this was the last hold Bricandor had on him.

A whisper. A whisper of Bricandor's scent, almost. Diebol couldn't feel the charges like he could when trying to balance Jei's reach or Lem's electron-laced tendril of shock. It was so, so subtle—not a breeze, not a tingle. Just a whisper over his neurons. It really was like Jei had said, like the universe was pushing in unbidden to erase him as he became a still, cooled part of a homogenous whole.

And instead, he was more of himself. *Breathe,* he told his lungs, and *beat,* he ordered his heart, not in words, but in balance, responding to each touch in the air with a touch of his own. If the whisper drifted left, he drifted right, and if it pushed in, he pushed out. His hands floated before him in slow blocking motions, like a battle with a slow, slow stream, or a dance with a lady frozen in time.

And then, as quickly as it had begun, it was over, and he heard a vicious curse. He opened his eyes to see Bricandor screaming at his guards to leave the room.

A cool rush washed over Diebol, and he laughed out loud. He had done it! He had decoded Bricandor's abilities. Had he doubted himself, knowing despite years of study he had only successfully canceled *anyone* just yesterday? Who knew, and who cared. He and Jei would trample their captor now, Jei the sword with the power of his violent pull, and Diebol the canceling shield. His vision almost blurred with joy, and he doubled over with an involuntary whoop of triumph he *knew* he had not made since boyhood.

"See!" Diebol cried. "See, it's *not* what you told me—that you can reach across the universe because you are 'one with it,' because you somehow 'feel every ripple in its fabric,' and you just have to push back in the right pattern to crush whatever's making the ripple. Ha! No, that's your mythology." Diebol laughed at the happiness in his own voice. He couldn't believe he was finally daring this. "Because if that were the case—if you could feel the whole universe—then why couldn't you just kill anyone whose mind you could read? Why not just"—He snapped his fingers.—"all the Frelsi leadership, shyte, Jei and Lem would be *long* gone." Was he calling her by her first name? Eh, momentary slip. "Benzaran *especially*: now that she's not cloaking her thoughts, with your disgusting energy-friend floating over her you should be able to feel her anywhere. No," Diebol leaned in toward the screen, unable to contain his excitement. "You need an eye-line because without help you can only manipulate charge as far as you can *see*. I don't know exactly how you learned it, but your death-gaze is just an expressive version of your receptive mind-reading: you 'see' what their EEG signals are doing. If Morda's specialized organ was in her inner ear, yours is in your optic nerve, and like waves out of phase cancel each other out, once you can 'see' the wave someone's putting out, you can cancel it out by emitting the inverse."

"Silence, you!" Bricandor hissed.

"Oh, I have listened to *plenty* of your lectures, now you can listen to mine. So for the 'without help' part. I admit, I was still a bit unclear on how you could kill at a distance, when you're on another planet. I thought perhaps your interdimensional scum helped you, like they help with your reading—yes, by the way, I know you can't read minds across space, I know they relay you messages. Just like I know about the dim-witted little rock boy you think you can mold to replace me."

"You—"

"Shut up, 'Daddy,' I'm gloating." Diebol fired his air-rider back up, and continued on his loop around the dunes. "Anyway, the distance-kills didn't make sense. But then I figured it out. We take wave forms and send them across the galaxy all the time. Right now you and I are talking because my sound waves are converted in the microphone, transmitted, and then emitted by your speaker. My image, too—it's a different process, but it's still a wave that's converted into electrical energy, sent, and then converted back. You send your phase-canceling waves the same way. *You* need a viewscreen to kill."

The sagging skin around Bricandor's sharp cheekbones tightened visibly as he ground his jaw. "Are you quite finished?"

"No." Diebol paused, and let Bricandor stew in that pause. "I know what you are now."

"What's that?"

"A feeler."

"A what?"

"You feel. You intuit, you listen, you empathize. Your ability and your personality revolves around what you can directly sense. Like Morda, which is why you listened to her at all even when she was absolutely falling for Jei."

"Don't compare me to that teasing little—"

"You whore yourself out with interdimensionals because they make you feel pretty, so the comparison is apt." Diebol forced himself to smile over this, but he knew he never really would get over the betrayal of first discovering Bricandor's secret. "You are a feeler. Sterba, meanwhile, was a thinker. I didn't appreciate her goals, but she did have a brilliant, overcharged mind—all that technological control came from *infinitely* fast, upcycled multitasking. She wrote it all as code, while it was happening! She was a thinker. That's why you needed her, and that's why you needed me. I don't have some special sense organ—I up-regulate my brain. I multitask, I strategize, I *think* my way through the very atoms that move to kill me. Any idiot can turn off their viewscreen and stay out of your eye-line, but I don't have to because I can cancel you out by unraveling who you are. You compare yourself to an alpha wolf, an impressive *animal*—but I'm a *man* and I have a gun."

Bricandor bared his teeth; spittle shot into the lens of his viewscreen. "You didn't stop me," Bricandor hissed. "I chose to stop because killing you would be a waste. You have the ability to override any of the mind-pads, and if some other Growen upstart decides to take control, he will come for you first. The Frelsi send more assassins after you than after me every year. People love me, and fear you. I let you live because for now you are an effective *decoy*." His fingers touched his throat in spasms, as if something there itched, or choked. "Because you serve the purpose of the universe still. And your wench lives for the same reason. My purpose. Your precious *boyfriend*? He only lived because I don't *care*. But now he lives because I know he will ensure you die."

Bricandor cut the transmission, coughing and cursing.

Diebol smiled.

CHAPTER FORTY-FOUR

Jei

"HE'S HERE, JEI."

Lem's tap woke me up; her hand pressed against my scalp as I jerked upright. "Watch your head," she said.

A lone air-rider hummed in the far distance somewhere to our right. We'd planned for Diebol to double back—that was partly why we'd waited to sleep until we'd hit our tiny cave. It was a lot harder to shoot a back that was against a rock, after all.

I blinked back groggy mist and swallowed the acrid taste of awakening as I reached for my mace and my lightning rod. I nodded, and Lem took up a position at the mouth of the cave with the right rock wall as cover, ready to fire electricity to power him off once we got him close enough. If we were extremely lucky, he would pass right by us, and we would jump him, but most likely he'd see the rock pile from a distance and one of us would have to actually go out to confront him.

"He may just rip the top boulder off us," Lem said to me over her shoulder. "He's still coming straight for us."

"I don't think he's quite that strong," I said, closing my eyes to try to summon as much strength as I could.

"I mean, I can do it," she said. "It's that em-hance shyte you made fun of me for that first year. Using the extra verve in your action potentials to improve the contractility of your muscles and shyte."

"Verve. I like that word," I murmured. I was digging in my mind to prepare for the fight. Focus on the color green … ready … there was no mind-channel anymore. It was strange, and it saddened me. After twelve years, just like that, it was gone? At any rate, he couldn't drop me unconscious now. But without a horde around to feed me off the energy of their action potentials, I couldn't crush him with a finger, either. It was going to be an old-fashioned fight with normal em-pushes and pulls and the lethal heat of mace against mace. "I'm sorry, old friend," I found myself saying. Friend? It surprised me that my words didn't surprise me.

The distant hum stopped. I opened my eyes, and looked to Lem. When the air-rider engine started again, it began to grow quieter instead of louder.

"Shyte, he's turning away. Toward that dune cluster," she said.

"He knows we're here. He'd rather we chase him in the open," I said.

"I really thought he'd do a straight fight right here."

"Against the two of us? Never. He wants to take us out from a distance." I was already dragging the air-rider out of the cave and firing it up. "Come on. We have to get close fast before he's in the dunes so he can't kite us for a clean shot."

She swung up behind me as I pressed my palms on the windshield to take off. Diebol's air-rider was still visible, but small and blurred against the rising sun.

"Can you reach him from here?" she asked.

"No. Can you?"

"Go faster."

"Thanks."

My stomach churned, just a little, inaudible over the muttering engine beneath us. I thought about eating—just one quick nutrient bar for some extra energy before the big day—but

I couldn't make myself do it. My muscles twitched, ready to pounce, and I could feel the energy of anticipation pulsing in my chest.

"This is it," Lem said. She felt it, too.

"This is it."

I pressed hard, urging the air-rider forward. Diebol didn't get any nearer. We were about the same speed: he'd reach the dunes before we reached him. They waited, little red and maroon bumps in a landscape streaked green and gold. I steered us in almost a perfect trace over the blue streak left behind in the sand by the levo-pads of Diebol's air-rider. The bumps grew to hills. My stomach tightened.

As we entered the dunes, Lem's palms gripped my shoulders, pinning me to my seat; I held still as she used me to balance and turn herself around on the air-rider. Her back pressed against mine as she squeezed the seat beneath her with her legs, and I felt a small flash of heat as she activated her mace, ready for when he'd attack us from behind. A slight sting tickled my spine, and out of my periphery I saw sparks: she was "on" now, her involuntary forcefield as instinctive as the hair rising on my forearms.

I took a deep breath, and forced my jaw to loosen as I calculated. We were following a figure eight around two dunes. He'd be behind us with the next loop. Instead, I shot off to the right, breaking away from the trail to circle round a third dune, drawing another clover leaf to his design in the sand—and then I cut across the top of the dune.

There he was. We barreled down the hill, on top of him in an instant almost before any of us could react. Too fast to stop. All right then. With my jaw set I gave one last press into the windshield to buck the vehicle forward faster, aiming it like a missile toward Diebol.

"What the filking—!"

"Gah!"

Lem and Diebol both screamed; just before the crash my

elbow swung back to hook Lem's side and knock us both off our air-rider. We tumbled into the sand with a scratching thud as the explosion lit into a blue orb that swelled and then disappeared, leaving burning fuel and metal behind.

Sand bit my hands as I rolled off Lem and scrambled to my feet. "Did I get him?" I wheezed as smoke billowed around us. Where was—

"No!" Lem's crawl dove into a charge, head-down like a bull. I barely saw Diebol's silhouette as she slammed into him weapon-first. Sand swirled up to hide them; her red mace flashed against his ultraviolet black. I leapt over the smoldering wreckage toward the sand-cloud—

An em-push met my chest. He wanted me to stay back. No cheeky taunts? No clever mind-worms to throw us off balance? A gust of wind blew away the sand between us, and Diebol's eyes met mine as he blocked another two-handed, club-like blow from Lem.

There was a finality in his gaze. He, too, knew that this was our last fight.

This is it. I pressed against his em-push with one of my own. Lem fired lightning at him from her fingers. I felt him relax his push against me to … was he redirecting or balancing her charge somehow? Why didn't he power down? Lem had mentioned this happened during the fight at Fort Tapiz—

Whatever it was, Diebol's focus on Lem weakened his push toward me. I slipped my flayer pistol off its holster, let it load, and fired a volley of death shots at him. Another sudden push from him knocked my weapon to the side before the shot fired. My cartridges careened toward Lem, and then swerved around her sparkling personal shield. She tossed me a little side-eye for shooting at her, but she could deflect a few near-misses.

Diebol tried to push me again. "Back off, Jei," he hissed, teeth clenched.

But I was in close range now. I drew and swung my green mace at his head. He dodged. Lem circled around to his side; she slashed high while I slashed low. He blocked her and jumped my swing, dodging backward with a glance over his shoulder toward what looked like a canyon in the distance.

"Don't run, man," Lem panted. She fired more electricity at him; he cursed, and as he focused on her again I gritted my teeth and reached an em-pull toward his throat to snap his neck.

"Back. Off." Diebol dropped his mace, letting it float beside him to block another blow from Lem as he threw both hands toward me. A wall of air and sand knocked me skidding backward, waves of dust in my wake. "I don't want to kill you, Jei."

Lem laughed—a dark, full-throated laugh. "Looks like you're the Chosen One, buddy," she smirked in my direction, eyes burning.

"If you're jealous, witch, you can turn around and I'll take you, too," Diebol teased. But his words lacked their normal —"verve." My stomach tightened; I saw his jaw clench. Shyte, we were really doing this. I'd killed other people before when I had to, and I'd thought about his death a thousand times, really believing I wanted it, but now, hunting and cornering him like this—

Diebol blocked my staff with his still-floating mace, throwing it to block me as he dove under Lem's mace to strike a clawing blow at her throat.

"You can't do it, can you?" he asked me as Lem blocked him with an uncertain fist, stumbling backward. Another electrical surge burst from her knuckles, dancing down his arm, but again he didn't power down.

"Hey, why doesn't shock turn you off?" Lem panted. "I want some of that."

"Won't do you much good dead," he answered.

"Why the shyte you want me to die? I'm the one who set you up to be king, man." She swiped his feet with her boot, knocking him backward onto the ground.

Both Lem and I were on him in an instant, staff-end of our maces on his throat. His em-push resisted us, holding the burning sticks centimeters from his carotids as we pushed, pushed—my muscles shivered as I tried to plunge my weapon through air that felt like stone. Sweat spilled across my forehead, and Diebol tilted his head back and roared as he fought to live. Shyte, I remembered this, remembered him as a kid, that same head tilted back and screaming, and I wanted to *save* him not kill him—!

My breath was too heavy in the cloth mask, and I ditched it as Lem ditched hers, letting it flutter away in the burning wind. Lem shot another tendril of electricity.

"I need you to stop that," Diebol groaned.

Suddenly he rolled to the right, smashing into Lem's legs. She fell into me, over top of him; both of our staffs plunged into the sand. It was a cluster of leather and hair and skin and punching and clawing, and by the time we untangled Diebol had drawn his pistol and fired randomly. A shot rang out, and Lem hissed in pain.

We all made it to our feet, standing in a triangle facing each other. Lem cursed, shaking out her hand; the spark of her innate shield was gone. He'd powered her down.

A grim smile crossed Diebol's face.

I threw an em-pull to snatch his neck again as he reached toward hers; he closed his eyes and wiped a palm toward me, and instead of feeling the resistance of an em-push-back, it felt like my pull had just disappeared. Shyte, what the—

His hand closed around her collar, and he slammed his other fist toward the ground, hurling them both backward away from me and into the air with an em-pull that blasted sand into my face. I blew out and shook it off—but by the time I was charging after them again, he was already on top of her, his lips pressed into a tight, determined line as he stabbed his mace toward her chest.

She bucked him off; he kept a grip on her collar as they both fought to their feet, and as soon as he got his footing he lifted her up and slammed her to the ground on her back, forcing a cry of pain from her lips. He followed it up with a pistol-whip. *Lem!* I was on them again. I wanted to scream, to order him to leave my partner alone, but we were past futile words: he needed to kill her and take me home. I dove for him, mace out-thrust like a spear; he pushed her backward, sidestepped me, and—

Oh *no*.

I heard the report of the gun, and felt a sharp sting in the back of my neck.

CHAPTER FORTY-FIVE

Lem

"Shyte, no—"

Lem's scream came out more as a groan; sticky blood was spilling down the side of her face, and while Diebol hadn't had a good swing when he whacked her—just glancing across her skull, not enough to kill, or incapacitate—for a split second everything shook, the whole world a blur. Still she shoved herself forward in one last desperate grab for the control panel now in Diebol's hand because her partner, *oh no, man*—

Jei stepped in front of her and kicked her in the stomach. Air burst out of her in a grunt, and suddenly Diebol's pistol was in Jei's hand, and Jei was grabbing at her shoulder, trying to turn her around so he could Turn her, too—

She elbowed him, thrashed, and fell, rolling backward to get as much distance as she could. Dizzy, she teetered at the end of the roll, and landed splayed on her back, panting.

"Shyte," she murmured to the sky. Jei kicking her didn't shock her like she'd thought it would. She'd fought Jei plenty of times, with and without abilities.

But he was shaken. She could see it on his face as she rose. They had a moment of respite as Diebol breathed a shaky sigh of relief, visibly almost tearing up with a hand on his forehead.

"It's done," he gasped. "I just have to take you home, and it's finally done. Everything will be okay."

Shyte, he hadn't believed he could do it.

But filk him, it wasn't done. Jei was gritting his teeth, eyes squeezed shut as if he thought he could fight it. "You got this, buddy," Lem muttered, staggering to her feet. "Or I got you."

As if in answer, Jei opened his eyes and raised the pistol toward her; a soft blue glow let her know he'd clicked it to kill. He grimaced and his eyelids fluttered as he tried to block his own vision, maybe to throw off his aim.

"I will offer you a boon, Benzaran," Diebol said, composed once again. "You're powered off. You can't block a bullet. You can't shock me and damage my control panel. You can't shock him in the dim hope that his implant might malfunction—and I can promise you, it won't, not sheathed inside the electromagnetic powerhouse of his biology. So you can fight us, and die." He took a step forward, and his tone changed. "Or—Lem—you can *live*, take a small dart in the spine, and be taken care of for the rest of a *good life*. I've trapped Bricandor—I am in control now. You know my ethics. You know once I have you on my side, I won't let anyone touch you. You'll be treated like a queen on your off days, and I will help you figure out and enhance your powers. When you're working, you will get to mow your way through the galaxy taking out the people who *dumped* you. I won't make you kill your family. You will crush the unbelieving fools who testified against you between your fingers, Benzaran."

Lem wanted to argue with him, but she couldn't. Her mace lay near him in the sand. Her head pounded, and she was so dizzy and tired and unbearably *sad*. A heaviness poured over her head, and shoulders, and as her heart rate slowed and the adrenaline dropped she really began to realize what had just happened to her friend. Shyte. Shyte, she'd just doomed everyone. She'd known she would. Her breath began to shudder and heave within her. Oh, no, oh no …

Lem glared at Diebol, and for once in her life said nothing.

"I have to kill you, then," Diebol said. "You know that. And you know that I no longer feel bad about it."

"I do," she answered, voice hoarse. "And damn it sounds *so good*. You have no idea how tired I am of thinking my own thoughts. Of trying, shyte—of living. Either option sounds good right now."

"So might I suggest you pick Door B?" he said softly.

At his gentle tone, the dam burst. Lem wept, and he let her weep. She wept for what had happened, for the family she missed and never saw anymore, for the parents who were always in danger, for the treetops and Mali and Pali and Cinta, for Jei and his lady that she'd killed, for Fort Jehu that she hadn't been able to save from Sterba in time—shyte, she wept for Sterba, who truly had understood her, in dreams, in life, and in death. And Lem wept for what could have been—for the softness in Diebol's voice, and his fingers sewing up her shoulder back in the tunnel on Alpino, and the cool rage in his eyes when he protected her from his soldiers years ago, and the aching struggle in his voice as he gripped her wrist back in the cold, cold torture room where he first entered her nightmares.

And as she raised her hands and turned, head bowed, she cried for what would be. For all the different little things they would destroy together.

Wait.

Lem was still wearing a child's dancing ribbon around her boot.

Love, One Who Wrestles With Power, with all your last strength.

She heard Diebol flick a switch on his control panel.

She gritted her teeth; her arms trembled just a bit, and her heel tapped nervously.

One short. One long. One short.

She heard Jei switch the pistol from kill to control.

Before he could fire, colored sand burst up in lovely, patterned fireworks behind Lem, thrown up by the tiny repulsion fan in the toy on her heel. Jei and Diebol both coughed, blinded for a moment by the gritty spray. Lem whirled, ran, and dove for the gun, sending a smashing side-kick into Jei's gut to loosen his grip. He let go and doubled over. She tumbled into the sand over top of the weapon, hugging it to her chest.

Momentum carried Lem's roll to her feet as she sprinted for the cliff Diebol had looked to earlier. Heart pounding, she untied her tunic, and the moment she began to feel the slightest tug of an em-pull behind her, she let that tunic fly—it fluttered behind her as someone's pull grabbed it, instead of her. She didn't turn to see whether or not it hit someone in the face. She was almost at the cliff. And before her pursuers could reach her, she threw herself forward and chucked the gun off it. It disappeared into the depths, clattering, gone before anyone could see to em-pull it back up.

"That was stupid," Diebol hissed, catching up. "Now I have no hope not to kill you, and you have no weapon. We have three staffs *and* Jei's pistol between us."

"Well, it's hard to think when you've been clocked in the head," Lem muttered. Sand stung everywhere her tank-top and pants didn't cover as she crawled to the cliff's edge. Shyte, it was jagged down there at the bottom, as spiked as if someone sat down and actually designed it for impaling. But there was an ivory-reddish outcropping and what looked like a ledge under it, not far below her. She breathed hard twice to psych herself up, and dove.

Lem landed on the outcropping with a painful *crunch* in her shoulder. Whatever was damaged, she didn't have time for it— she swung herself under the outcropping to the ledge below, squeezing her back against the canyon wall to hide under the shadow of the stones.

"I know where you are," Diebol yelled down. "You won't be able to get back up without your powers."

"So give me ten minutes, then, and we'll have a fair fight," Lem shouted, knowing full well it would be more like twenty or thirty before she recharged. Her voice didn't reverberate through the gully as much as his did, and it sounded small, and weak to her. "How come there was only one em-pull?" she asked. "You don't know how to control Jei's abilities through that thing, do you?"

There was silence for a moment.

"So I'm right, then," Lem called, squeezing her eyes shut against the new pain in her shoulder and the pounding of her head.

"Give me ten minutes," Diebol answered, echoing her words. "It's like learning the controls to a new game. Or the same game, on a new level."

"Glad it's fun for you," Lem shot back. Oh, filking shyte, her shoulder! She tried to rotate it; it screamed at her, but she could still move it, and nothing was hanging off it. Shyte, at least it wasn't the same one she'd actually dislocated on Retrack City.

In the quiet that followed, the wind whistling through the canyon carried with it whispers she didn't want to hear. "Shyte, leave me alone, please."

Look what you did. Look where you are. Don't you need to end this, end you, *before it gets worse?*

She ignored it. Man, why didn't Diebol just climb down here and fight her already? She scooted to the left edge of her little standing ledge and leaned out, trying to see past the rock jutting out protectively over her. "Guess if he makes it to the outcropping I'd have an advantage to just reach up and knock him down, from here. Not a lot of space for two people, much less three."

Maybe he's just left because you're not worth killing.

Lem narrowed her eyes. She was beginning to have trouble telling between the Accuser and her own thoughts. Either way, she was pretty sure Diebol needed to kill her. She'd never let him get away with Jei if he didn't.

Unless they're getting away right now.

Shyte! Lem craned her neck, trying to see up, or look for handholds as she patted along the canyon wall—shyte, it was pretty flat and chalky, she really couldn't get back up until her nervous system balanced or recharged or whatever it did to make her power come back. Were they leaving? Almost involuntarily, she cried out for Jei.

"I'm here, Lem," he answered, his voice ragged and low.

"Wait, you can talk already?" Diebol asked. "It usually takes people about an hour to acclimate."

"It—isn't as strong a hit as the real thing," Jei said. As Mera. Something wistful floated down with his voice in the wind.

Shyte, man, hold on, Imma figure something out.

CHAPTER FORTY-SIX

Jei

THERE WAS SOMETHING LITERALLY ROOTING INTO MY SKULL, PICKING its way through my neurons. It didn't matter that the tendrils had surgically nonlethal accuracy—the headache still sucked, and nausea swelled in the base of my throat as Diebol messed with the sequences on his control panel. Everything he did made it worse.

"You were not prepared," I groaned, trying to lean back to stabilize the sick feeling. Instead of leaning back, my hand rose, and pain swelled in my palm. "Ah, shyte!"

"Sorry. I am prepared, actually," Diebol said. "I have a sequence of programs most likely to mimic the brain patterns Morda used to use on you, and I'm just running through them now. It took her weeks to learn your moves—I think you can give me an hour."

"Ten minutes," I corrected.

"She's not going to figure her way up here in ten minutes," Diebol laughed. "I doubt she recharges faster than thirty."

"She's not patient enough to wait an hour."

"True. And she shouldn't. Once I've got you up and running, she's dead." Diebol looked up from the panel in front of him to make eye contact with me. "I'm sorry about what's going to happen, by the way. Well. I'm not going to regret it. But I'm not happy about making you suffer." He looked back down to his console. "You know what I mean. I'll let you close your eyes when the moment comes if you want."

I didn't answer. Part of me reacted—something deep inside that screamed in terror at what I'd be made to do—but the rest of me just refused to panic. I had to figure this out or she died—along with a whole lot of other people. I wanted to convince him just to leave with me, instead of keeping us camped here waiting to crush Lem, but if we did leave, it would be much harder for her or anyone to break me loose, and how many people would die in the meantime?

It really was now or never.

I glanced down at my hands folded politely in my lap, trying to see if there were any more messages on my wristband about Dr. Patti Loylan's emergency research on implant removal. If Lem could destroy the control panel, could I maybe make it back before some other control panel picked me up? I closed my eyes —I could do that, voluntarily, and after a few minutes I'd been able to speak. What else could I do? I opened my eyes to focus on a finger, willing it with the same mental muscle I used to trigger an em-push …

It didn't do anything.

I needed to understand my new limits, and I knew better than to ask him directly. "Is this really you, Jared?" I asked. It took so much effort to speak, like an iron band tightened around my chest whenever I said a word. "You said so much about how we destroy the universe with our Contamination. And I can still talk. Are you really telling me you're okay with having me around you, Contaminated, for the rest of my possible life?"

"Which is going to be much longer now, thanks to me. You're welcome," Diebol said, tapping behind his ear with his holo-pen, and then glancing over the cliff to check on Lem. An iridescent bubble of energy floated around the control panel, protecting it from shock in case she did power back up in time. "Advanced programming will make your Contamination go away, eventually. This is only a start. But after Morda you can't hear him anymore, correct?"

I looked away—or I thought I was going to, but didn't. I was stuck facing him. "I didn't think I told you about that," I murmured.

"You didn't. I guessed, based on some of her reports, and the fact that you're obsessed with reading old bits and pieces dug up in archaeological finds." The uglier side of him came out now in a sneer: "It's pitiful. You're lapping up crumbs scattered through the ruins of history—on old vases, papyrus, sheep's skin, pressed trees—trying to find a taste of your space-lover like a dog chasing a bitch in heat."

"Your metaphor sounded badass until you said space-lover," I pointed out.

"I'm sorry, it's hard to focus on quips and insults when I'm trying to reprogram a human mind. Forgive me for my lack of erudition."

He was right, though. I knew he couldn't actually ever take my sweet and strange interdimensional friend away from *around* me—my dear whatever-he-was cared about me too much to just leave. But a lot can happen to a human mind. If I couldn't perceive him *at all*, not even in my mind or my dreams, would he still—well, he would still exist, but how much would I believe that, over time?

Nothing will separate us. Nothing. I repeated his promise to myself—a promise found on an old letter buried in the ruins of an ancient tyranny. It didn't do much to calm my pounding heart. I didn't want to live like that. I already hated not hearing.

"I think that was genetic. I have a genetic predisposition from my dad, and Mera just triggered it," I said, as if he cared.

He looked up. "You have *never* mentioned having a father."

"When, in all our history of trying to kill, capture, or convert each other, do you think it would *ever* come up?"

Diebol shrugged, still focused on his work. "Was he terrible?" he asked.

Was he terrible?

I didn't know how to answer that. Even before I stopped talking to him over Lem's exile, we had already been on pretty cold terms. For years, ever since I came back from my first imprisonment as a young child, I'd had the feeling he avoided looking at me. Perhaps it was too painful for him, I realized suddenly. Perhaps I reminded him of the love he'd lost and of his inability to protect me—and maybe her, too—from the enemy. That wasn't an excuse, but—well, perhaps that was the reason.

"He's never tried to kill me, or torture me, if that's what you're asking," I said. Bloodseas, what a time to be having revelations about my dad that I couldn't do anything about. Maybe if I lived I would call him.

"You should tell me who he is, and then you won't have to kill him," Diebol said.

"I'll still have to kill him," I said. "He's an admiral."

"Ah." Diebol nodded. "That's unfortunate."

"Yeah."

I chewed my lip. That I could do. It seemed like I had more control of everything above my top cervical vertebra, which made sense, given the general locations of the cranial nerves. But ... based on what I understood so far, even with this device's slight anatomic limitations the neurotransmitters released into my cerebrospinal fluid could probably cause enough imbalance to alter function in my brain. Like an anti-psychotic medication given to someone who doesn't need it. Diebol had always hated the idea or concept of mind control, but perhaps that was before he saw me in love with Mera.

Bloodseas, would he even have experimented on her if not for me?

"Is this my fault?" I wondered. "Did I doom the galaxy?"

"No," he said. "If it wasn't you, she would've picked

someone else, and I would've gotten results all the same. Not results specifically tailored to you, mind you, so maybe the fact that I'm almost done figuring this out is your fault."

"Thanks." I hated the idea of her picking someone else—and in this moment that seemed really dumb of me to hate. I had other worries. What could I tell Lem, without messing her up further or giving away whatever semblance of a plan we could somehow put together from up and down a cliff? I looked back at my wristband. I could barely make out a new message blip— probably asking me to check in with my handlers back on Alpino. I'd technically left Fort Tapiz on an "unauthorized" pursuit, although I knew the leadership there had explained what had happened. Again, there were bigger problems. Why couldn't I think straight?

Another sharp pain shot up my arm, this one like burning heat. I cursed, and Lem cried out for me again.

"It's ... fine," I groaned back. "He's testing programs to see if they work on me."

"So he might not be able to use your powers at all?" she called back.

"He seems pretty confident he can in about an hour," I shouted. I punctuated my sentence with a yelp as a cold sensation shot down my back. I wanted to scream at him that he was messing with my sensory system, not the motor systems he probably wanted, but I figured he didn't really need my help.

"Be quiet," he hissed, pressing something on his control panel. My mouth felt heavier ... but after closing my eyes again, and focusing, I could still speak.

"I told you," I coughed. "I've got a tolerance."

He reached for a gas canister on his utility belt and puffed air from the tubing into my face. "How about now?" he asked.

That was the feeling I remembered. Mera's overwhelming calm—the sensation that you were just sinking into an ocean of silk for the best rest of your life. Every skin cell tingled with a quiet, pleasant comfort. I tried to shake my head, or blow out, but I couldn't, and bloodseas, I didn't want to. *Help me, Njande-jara. Please.*

"I hate that you can do this," I croaked, wincing.

"Shyte, you can still talk? Your whole face is so relaxed you look like you might start drooling."

I hated that. I blinked hard. I didn't want to be like this in front of him. I didn't want him to be able to do this to me. It felt absolutely wrong. I dug down, and tried to hold on to that sensation—the disgust, the wrongness—to fight the toxic peace. My body begged me to let go. Why be disgusted? This was what needed to happen.

"You do realize what you're doing, right?" I fought not to slur. "I didn't ask for what's happening to my biology right now."

He stiffened. "Death and taxes are the same," he muttered. "No one consents to those, either. No one questions them in war."

But I caught the tension in his voice, and he blinked oddly after he spoke, shaking his head like a Pegasus shaking off a stinging fly. There was a moment, in this sequence of tics, where he glared into space with his lips pursed, and cleared his throat with a growl—and the iridescent bubble around the control panel *flickered*. "I want you to not speak," he said.

It wasn't just me he was talking to.

"Bloodseas," I murmured. I called to my partner: "Lem, he's got a ba-eater."

"I do not," he hissed. "I do not *have* some interdimensional scum. It pesters me because Bricandor is too weak to tear me down himself these days. Because he is weak, and I am strong!"

Lem's voice carried such a curious pause I could imagine her a Biouk with one ear cocked. "It tears you down?" she asked.

"I'm not going to talk about it with you!" he roared.

The protective bubble flickered again. Shyte, we could work with this. "What does it say to you?" I asked, knowing the question would make the answer swirl in his mind. *Please, Lem, be ready when the bubble drops …*

"Silence!" He blew another whiff of pheromone into my face, and my scalp seemed to melt right off my skull in utter relaxation. Bloodseas, I could remember her skin. I was the only person in the universe currently breathing this pheromone who *actually* had the owner's synapses written across mine, and as her lips seemed to touch my neck I wanted to lay my head back and just live in the memory. *Please. Please help me. I can't. I want her back so much. Please.*

I needed to hear my invisible friend. You can't break a desire with asceticism, by punishing or praying it away with sheer force of will—the strongest desires only bow in the face of a sweeter longing. I needed to hear him, to desire justice and freedom, and I could not—and my brain was too fuzzy with the glory of her gaze to quote parables and poetry to me.

"Is it because of what Lem said in the—the training—center?" I found myself asking. Some part of my brain was still fighting. "That you don't like to remember forced biology?"

Diebol ripped out his gas mask—still holding the control panel in his protective field. He donned the mask with a vicious glare and dumped the entire canister of pheromone at me. His protective bubble around the control panel was visibly breaking, and I wanted to yell for Lem to move now—but I was so, so fine. Everything was fine. Everything was perfect. Why would Lem need to come up here and ruin the perfection? *Help. Me.*

"What was it Lem said, back then?" I asked, my tongue heavy with the memory of Mera's taste. "When you forced her to eat those weird mind-meds years ago? About bodies, and autonomy … why did that bother you?"

"Because I would never do *that thing* to her!" His screams were so loud they were blowing out the speakers of his mask. "To anyone! That is a boundary I never cross, because that *disgusts* me. All of this disgusts me, the whole war! It always has, and you know that! Because of you, and because of Bricandor, there are no other ways to save this galaxy, and I despise all of it! All of this is evil *you all make me do!*"

Please, Lem, now is your chance, please—

"I have to be fine with what I do. I have to!" He visibly trembled as he looked down, trying to focus on the code he had been running, actually pawing for the control panel as it floated in his diminishing field. He tapped his holo-pen against the panel, and behind his ear, clearly trying to focus on its blue glow. Still his bubble dimmed to clear. "We almost have everything within our grasp."

"Who's we?" I heard myself ask.

"You know what?" His pen ground against the surface of the panel as his teeth gnashed. "I can do this, too. She 'has' the same one I do. It's stronger when she's around."

"Maybe—it's not stronger when she's around because she has it." Shyte, words were hard. "Maybe—it's stronger because —you feel guilty about hurting her."

"Thank you, brilliant scientist, I just couldn't figure that out. I know it doesn't *create* guilt, you imbecile, any more than it causes cancer or mental illness. It takes what's there and morphs it into venom." He gripped my wrist. "You keep looking down at this. What do you think is there? Oh, look, it's a bereavement notice on a feed you've been monitoring. Benzaran, looks like two or three or whatever of your little brothers are dead or captured. Bloodseas, how many siblings do you *have*? Well, two or three less, I guess that's how many."

He tossed my wrist back into my lap; my jaw dropped.

"What?!" Lem's incredulity echoed across the canyon.

"It's on his wristband, beautiful, it's real. You're welcome to come up here and check." He put my pistol in my hand, and I found myself holding a steady aim at the edge of the cliff. To me, he hissed: "I was going to put her out of her misery without this emotional shyte but if you want to play mind-games, I can play better." And to her: "They're on Bijou. Cold little planet with almost no livable landmass? I think the report said one of them's been sharpshooting Frelsi, so it sounds like Jei here isn't the only new member of my team who needs saving. Why don't you go try to save your brother? If I give you a choice, between saving him, and bothering me with Jei, who will you choose?"

"Are. You. Really. Trying. To pull this *filking* hang-my-family-over-me shyte again?" Lem roared. "Are you really serious?"

"Why change what works?" He grinned at me and clicked a button on his holo-pen. It didn't matter that his protective field was thin, now, and torn as if clawed open by a beast.

Because my stomach dropped as I felt a tiny em-push leave my fingers.

CHAPTER FORTY-SEVEN
Jake

JAKE GRIPPED BOTH HANDS OVER HIS OWN MOUTH. HE'D LAIN SO long on the ice his back burned—he hadn't known until now that cold could feel *hot*—and he could still hear the grays walking back and forth around the abandoned campsite. The dead bug-bear-creature his older brother had killed weighed on him, stink plunging into his nostrils with every silent inhale. Every single rise of his ribs terrified him. *Stay still chest, stay still!*

Above all, he did not want Lev, lying beside him, to wake up. *He'll freak out if he finds this thing on top of him the moment his eyes open ... oh no, oh no ...*

Every second dragged on forever. He didn't know how long it took for the blitzers to move all the boxes of medication. He didn't know why they would care. Weren't the Growen, like, really rich? His legs ached. Why did he want to kick *so badly*? Had he never really sat totally still in his life?

He was thirteen. He was regulation fighting age. He had to do this. In some periods in history, people his age got married and had *kids*.

But ... in other periods they played in their bedrooms on video games, or went to school, and everyone treated them like babies.

That thought distracted him for a while—the other lives someone like him could have lived in some other time—but not long enough. He didn't shiver—he had more meat on him than his skinny older brother—but he wanted *so badly* to roll off this ice. Even the bear-monster-thing was going to get cold eventually. Why was it taking them so long? It had taken Reise like what, a couple minutes, to move all these boxes on his own? And he was not very strong, even!

Bootsteps neared. Like, really near. Jake didn't turn to look. He couldn't. His neck just wouldn't turn. Maybe he was going into a fight, flight, or freeze again. And he was actually happy about that. If he just pretended it didn't exist, and didn't move, it didn't matter.

The boot stopped by his ear. He could see it out of the corner of his eye.

"What's this ugly thing?"

"Maybe why they crashed." The boot kicked the carcass. Jake clawed tighter at his mouth, stifling the squeak as he felt the impact. He would've jumped, but the bear prevented that—even that solid kick hadn't shifted the carcass. He squeezed his eyes shut, and felt something wet trickling down the side of his left cheek. *Please go away. Please go away.* His breath was sawing now in his chest, fast, and—if he didn't keep his mouth shut—so loud—

"I think it's migration season or some shyte. My first deployment here last year, on recon? None. Now it's like these monsters eat through a ship every week."

"Maybe they're smart. They've learned ships mean somethin' yummy inside."

"Maybe. Why the hell you think the Frelsi cut it up like this?"

Jake couldn't hear the garbled answer from the other speaker. Oh no. Would they check beneath it? *Please don't look here. Please go away—*

"Disgusting," he heard, eventually.

The boots left.

Oh they were gone. They were gone. Oh it was so cold, but he needed to wait. It was cold, and they were gone and he still had to wait.

The natural light had faded to a dim blue glow by the time Jake squirmed out from under the monster and heaved it over so he could see Lev. The squad leader still slept, the reddish ridges on his face faded to a sick, pale pink that flushed with every slow, slow breath. Even through Jake's gloves Lev's skin felt cold. Jake reached into the man's makeshift fur-wrappings and reactivated the medspider on his arm. It hummed and lit up with soft yellow vitals—nothing seemed better from before.

Jake couldn't stop looking over his shoulder—would they come back? It was so empty now: just the burnt spot left by the fire, and the blood from the creature smattered around the icy cave. He shifted his crouch to put his back to the wall so he could see down the dark hallway. What was he going to do? Really, what? Was Reise coming back? He tapped on his wristband to call Nefesh.

She answered right away. "Is he any better?" she asked.

"Who?" Jake whispered. "I—uh—Lev?"

There was a pause, like his uncertainty either angered or worried the other squad leader. "Jake, I want a SITREP," she said, her voice stern.

Jake tried to remember the formula they'd been taught. There was a way you were supposed to report this stuff. Nefesh was worried about her mate, so like—should he start with that first? Jake was much less worried about Lev than about the others right now. "He's—breathing?" Jake heard his own statement come out like a question. "Nefesh, the Growen came. The other three led them away. I hid with Lev. That was—" He checked his wristband. "An—hour—ago?"

"I can see their vitals. They're all stable. Heart rate's up on Reise and Nate ..." Her voice lowered into a hum. "That's weird. They're still moving away from you, but not running. That's a *high* heart rate for you not to be running, Reise ..."

"Small spaces," Jake said. "He's scared of small spaces. There are a lot of them here."

She had a snorting laugh. "You have no problem ratting your brother out, do you?" Her voice grew serious. "No, I mean I think they're injured."

"It was a lot of Growen," Jake said. His own voice sounded kind of dead to him. He cleared his throat. "What do I do?"

"You need Lev to wake up. We don't have a location on the secret settlement there. Their encoding technology's too old to risk sending that data across space, which is why they were supposed to meet and escort you. That should still be the case."

"What if the settlement's dead?" Jake asked. "There were a lot of Growen ..."

"Calm down, Jake. Nate's wristband is indicating proximity to a medspider. Someone's fixing him up, and your crew only had the one spider left, so that means our boys found friendlies. I've never heard of the Growen fixing anybody unless they're an electromagnetic super-weapon, have you? And we all love Nate, but he's not a super-weapon. Sit tight, and they should be coming back for you."

Jake wanted to say "yes ma'am" or "roger" or something, but his throat stuck. Nate hadn't been injured when they left. Reise and Gideon were killing machines, and Nate could hold his own, but still, Nate was—Nate was gentle and soft. Jake didn't like to think about anyone hurting him.

Nefesh seemed to pick up on his fear through his silence. "It's gotta be something very minor. There isn't enough blood volume loss to register on the wristband. Probably a cut. Or a cartridge grazed him. What I want to hear from you is that you'll watch Lev and obey the medspider."

"Yes ma'am."

"Is there a hiding place where you can monitor the spot without leaving it too far?"

Jake glowered at the dead ursa-fly-thing-monster. "Yes ma'am."

"Is there a strong chance the Growen will come back? Anything valuable left there?"

"No. Someone cleared out all the supplies. They left the dead monster. I—" Jake took a deep breath, and gripped his knife. Lev looked almost glow-in-the-dark in his paleness. "Reise was trying to get the poison sac out of its face for the medspider to analyze. To fix Lev. I'm going to try to do that."

Nefesh paused; Jake heard something kind of like a sniffle, and a harsh cough. But when she spoke, her voice still sounded as calm as an onboard computer: "Good. Stay concealed. I'll keep trying to get in touch with them. And I'm coordinating a return vessel for you."

"Yes ma'am."

Jake stared at the mangled face near his lap for a long time after Nefesh broke contact. This was the kind of thing people would say someone with a childhood brain injury like his shouldn't do. He'd never heard of a surgeon with a limp and seizures. He was the only one here, though.

Jake's hands shook. He couldn't have them shaking. He couldn't cut the poison line by accident. Wherever it was, in that jumble of blood and stringy stuff. Reise had cut in such a way that he could follow some kind of tube from the proboscis back into the muscle of the face. It was weird, this flayed, hairless face, with one bit of hairy outside nose still attached. More than weird. Like the kind of stuff that gave soldiers nightmares, maybe.

You know why I sleep like a baby when all the other Frelsi have nightmares?

Something like that. Nate had said something like that.

"There is only now," Jake muttered, swallowing. There was no future screw-up, or past screw-up. There was only right now, and doing the best he could right now.

Jake slipped his blade under the poison tube and followed it into the face, letting the edge gently cut through the red strings of tissue. Reise had already smashed out a lot of the bone in the faceplate. Jake picked those out of the way, laying them on the ground next to him like pieces of puzzle.

And he found it. This had to be it. It was definitely a sac. Like a holding bag, like a face-scrotum or something, surrounded by muscle.

Jake took a deep breath and disconnected the medspider from Lev. He tapped the part of its back that glowed with the toxin read-out, and it gave him an option to analyze poison for antidote synthesis. Jake pressed that, and a small needle protruded from the bottom of the spider with a small, sucking hiss.

Jake's hands shook more. Oh man, he really didn't want to break the poison bag. He lowered the medspider toward it—he could not stop shaking. He gritted his teeth. "There is only now, and now Lev needs an antidote," he growled. He felt a soft pop as the medspider punctured the thin wall of the face-sac ... His glove left a bloody fingerprint on the medspider's back as he pressed analyze.

It took about an hour for the medspider to come back with a result, and another five minutes or so for it to disinfect itself before it could jab Lev again. Jake waited.

He waited as the dark grew full of hissing sounds.

He waited as no one answered him on his wristband.

He waited through a tense night of squirming behind the ursa-fly.

And when Lev woke up, they both waited, because apparently there was now a Growen blockade around this nowhere planet for some reason, and no one could reach them. Lev would have taken Jake to look for the settlement, but apparently command needed them to wait some more, because all Frelsi locations were on lock-down following the reveal of some Growen mind-control bug, and Reise had been spotted sniping locals.

By the time Jake realized he was going to be stuck on this planet for a very, very long time, it had been a week of eating nasty bear, hacking off ice for liquid, and digging a more "comfortable" hiding place in the wall behind its body. Lev didn't talk much. He probably missed Nefesh, Jake thought. The man always smiled when Jake made eye contact with him, but honestly he seemed pretty mad, and every now and then he'd look at his wristband and hiss between his teeth. Once he walked away a bit to talk privately to leadership, and Jake heard him argue until his throat got hoarse. Lev vomited a lot, moved slowly, and after a while Jake noticed he looked kind of yellow. One day, after the medspider flashed something about "liver function tests," Lev stopped letting Jake see it.

Jake spent a lot of time hugging his knees and rocking just a little, letting himself fall into thought-pictures of mazes and lines, as if one line at a time he could little by little erase his brother and his friends from his mind. "Now" was taking a very, very long time, and it was nice that there also was something other than now. Maybe that was one of those paradoxes. There is only now, and there is not now, maybe.

He was relieved the day a very orange and tight-jawed Lev put a hand on his shoulder and nodded for him to follow. He didn't care that Lev didn't say anything—not what they were looking for, or why. Maybe they were looking for food, or power. Jake didn't know, and they didn't walk far that day, anyway. It wasn't even because of Jake's leg: he could've gone for a lot longer, but Lev gripped his side and needed to lean on him as they came back to their hidden camp. Over time, they explored their area more, and dug more of their hiding place.

"How long until our wristbands run out of power?" Jake asked one day.

"Six months," Lev smiled. "You should know that. You shouldn't worry. Everything's going to be fine."

"How do you know that?" Jake asked, an eyebrow raised. He didn't want to point out that he knew Lev was hiding how sick he still was, and he knew they weren't allowed to get to safety because they themselves might be a threat to the settlers. He hadn't gathered exactly what his brother was doing for the Growen, but he'd heard enough to understand that stragglers on their way to the gate got turned. Lev might never see his girl again. Jake might not—

Jake realized suddenly that his face was wet. His stomach hurt. He was so cold. He'd been so numb for the whole week, and everything from it blended together, and now suddenly something deep inside him hurt and he felt more afraid than he'd felt the moment before he took the knife to that monster's face. His hands shook. The wet on his face—not tears, he told himself, just wet—burned.

"How do you know?" He repeated. "That everything's going to be fine?"

"Because after all of us are gone, space will still be singing about us," Lev said. "In the meantime, we're going to do things that are worth singing about. And then, when we're asleep in that vibrating space dust, we will be fine, too."

CHAPTER FORTY-EIGHT

Cinta

CINTA HAD BEGUN TO REALIZE MORE AND MORE THAT EVERYONE around him lied. Perpetually.

Lark Scrita, to begin with, could not really belong to a reptilian species. Beyond the matter of her humanoid clothing—which would irritate most reptiles with sensitive thermoregulation—her color changes always delayed after her emotions, as if she selected them instead of expressing them naturally like a Bont lizard would. In most Bont lizard cultures, pairs mated for life, even after their temperature-triggered sex change in mid-life, but Lark's mindset seemed more akin to a human or a cat. Cinta would have dismissed all of this as quirky individuality had he not overheard some odd anatomical thoughts he wished he did not while standing outside the lavatory waiting for her to leave the factory. He was not Bont, but he did have some certainty they did not possess mammaries.

Of much greater importance, the Ebon Shadow, Carl Hampt, had begun to run out of funds, despite his appearance of infinite resources from his days working with the Growen. He could not afford to keep a prisoner sleeping in suspended animation in the *Huntress*'s hold indefinitely. The medications he used were costly. They needed information and an ethical disposal method soon.

Finally, Masha the glass factory maiden was with child. Now that they had left the factory, and the tension of escorting the Ebon Shadow had worn off, her … fetal pup … constantly occupied her thoughts. This disturbed Cinta, as without adult fangs she seemed about his age—while technically viable, still at least twenty years shy of normal Biouk mating age. Something had gone wrong in her life.

So, as Cinta and his mercenaries followed their new guide into the crystal caverns outside of town, Cinta became quite certain he did not like the ability to overhear minds. There were many stressful, odd, or distasteful things he did not need to know. He swiveled his ears instead to focus on real sounds.

The dripping in the caverns somewhere deep below them. The crunching footsteps on jagged rock as the four descended. The grunting, and occasional skidding slips as the Bont and the Shadow struggled with the forty-five degree angle incline while their height forced them to bend over in this side-tunnel clearly designed for much smaller people. The sand-laden wind whistling at the small, circular entrance behind them that still shone with the light of the sky.

"Storm's coming. Rain and sand," said Masha. "I never used to be able to tell as a cub. But people who live here long enough just know."

"How?" Cinta asked.

"I don't know."

Another clattering rustle of pebbles and shards—Cinta put back a paw against Lark Scrita's shin, behind him, to keep her from sliding forward on top of him. She cringed at his touch again—still hiding that secret human identity—and panted as she tried to find a non-sharp place on the tunnel walls to stabilize herself.

The earth rumbled with distant explosions. Cinta looked to Masha.

"Mmm, there's a better blasting and drilling site a few kilometers north for lanthanide ore. That's how most industries get their neodymium. We use that site, too. But my employer likes the rare earth crystals, instead of the ores, because of their artistic applications. There's a large node here." She scampered ahead with comfortable ease, her large ears folded across her back not because of stress, but to protect from scratching on the serrated walls. Cinta's time on Revelon with Jaika and Jei had not left him with great love for small places, and the damp mineral scent in here suffocated his tree-dweller nose—but at least he could fit.

"I'll let you know when to turn your head-lamps off," Masha said in her perfect Grenblenian. "This tunnel opens up into a large cavern. There's a front entrance to that cavern big enough for vehicles. If your Growen have begun work here, we should see them there."

"We need to switch so you're not in front, soon, lass," Lark interrupted with a grumble. "In case you're leadin' us to a bloody trap."

Cinta suspected Scrita was actually annoyed because she had said such a cool, cocky goodbye—business card and all—and then Masha had decided to come along. Scrita cared a great deal about any and all exchanges involving her business cards—which, she insisted constantly, she had kidnapped a woman to make.

Masha did not seem to mind. She obeyed, and as her lithe, smooth pelt wriggled past Cinta's side he missed the family nests back home very much. The Grenblenian "excuse me" did not exist in most Biouk dialects. "All right," she said. "Just turn off your head-lamp when I say so we're not caught."

Cinta did not like being in front, but whatever scuttling shades populated his underground imagination, they could not very well surprise him in a straight tunnel with no twists, turns, or corners. Leading the line he could pick up the pace, which he did, because he grew tired of this mission already and wanted answers now so he could go help his sister. The merce-naries protested his speed with grumbles, but Masha kept up easily.

"She makes a good point," Cinta said to her in Biouk. "Why are you still helping us?"

"Well, neighbor, I'm very bored. Not many other neighbors in exile."

Cinta did not ask why she was in exile. He had grown up in a gentle tribe, but some, like his cousin's, had strict sanctions against pregnancies before fifty revolutions. Still, no one should have known unless she told them—she did not have the scent yet.

"My clan lives here. Dispute after one of the smaller Moon Wars. We failed a coup," she explained.

Oh—so not the pregnancy. "You don't spend much time with your clan, though," he ventured. "Always working … kind of different from everyone else?"

"Yes …" Her ears flattened tighter against her back. "Do you have a different question you want to ask? I see your ears, neighbor."

Oh dear. Cinta caught himself with his left ear tilted in awkward curiosity toward her, and tucked it back in line with the other ear. "Ehm," he coughed. "I don't know how to say this. But I know. About the … pup. That's why I am being—strange. I am sorry. I should not know and I won't tell anyone."

Her ears rose so sharply she almost hit the top of the tunnel. Cinta put out a paw to protect her from scraping, then kept running. She trotted after him. "I'm not going to deny it," she said. "But. It's not what you think. It's a parthenogenesis."

That Cinta did not like. Why make something up? Something had happened—either she had made a choice, or someone else had made a choice—so assign or take responsibility and then move forward. He had a biology background; natural self-fertil-ization had never been described in their species. Cinta kept his ears neutral, but trotted on ahead with irritation.

Two things happened very suddenly as he reached the edge of the tunnel.

One, the tunnel opened into a hole high up in the wall of a huge cavern lined with glittering brown, yellow, and lilac facets. Blitzers and workers droned about the floor, picking out sparkling rock and slicing it out with whirring diamond saws and lasers to load into floating carts.

Two, the rocks on the opposite cavern wall spoke to him. Their speech was so clear, and so *loud*, that Cinta would have turned around to see if anyone else had heard if he wasn't entranced by what looked like violet, iridescent eyes hidden in the wall, like a nebula contained in crystal.

"Take care of your new friend," said the stones. "I'm trusting you with the magic of her science."

"I—I just met—magic of the science the—what?"

"Also, try not to be a dick."

Then, with a blink, Cinta reached the end of the tunnel again.

What? It was as if time rewound. He was walking through the inclining tunnel with his companions again. There was no giant cavern. There was a small, rusted door with a biometric scanner that Masha unlocked with her paw, and that small metal door opened into a cleaning closet seated high in the wall of a cavernous office. Masha slid open a tiny panel in the closet door so the others could look out, and below, in the office, blitzers mulled about with holomaps and docuscanners. Masha pointed to a door at the other end of the office, and through that door Cinta caught a glimpse of the actual crystal harvesting operation.

"They're not supposed to be in here," Masha was saying. "This whole area is closed to outsiders. It looks like they broke that outside door. Why do they need the office, anyway?"

"To keep their discussion away from the lower ranking workers moving the crystal, mate," Lark was saying.

Cinta was still reeling from the time skip. *Njandejara?* He asked.

"Yes?" answered the clear voice only he could hear.

What was that?

"You heard me. Pay attention. Holomap, far left corner."

Uh—yes, okay. Cinta prodded Masha's shoulder, interrupting her, and pointed to the red glowing orbs in that corner. "I see a map of our galaxy with markers on specific spots for some planets," he said. "What do you see?"

"Looks like one o' the old astrology charts the dancing girls'll show you at casinos to improve your luck," Lark said.

"That alignment hasn't occurred yet," the Ebon Shadow said. "It's in two years. The coming gravitational change alters a number of important shipping routes and treaty zones."

"Half those markers are on nowheres-ville moons though," Lark said. "So it's not like that's their strategy guide or some shyte."

"A better explanation than your magic astrology crop circle," said the Shadow.

"Look, I'm not saying—"

While the two humans bickered and whispered at each other, Cinta watched Masha, and waited for her answer. She held peace for a moment, then: "Mm. That's the atomic structure of a neodymium laser diode."

"So they're turning those solar systems into a giant weapon," Lark said. "Rad beans, now we know. The Frelsi'll prolly want us to go disrupt some of these spots. There's one on that moon near the Bont homeworld—that's not too far. Can you copy the readouts from here, Hampt?"

The Ebon Shadow tapped the side of his helmet and nodded.

But Cinta watched Masha, and saw her head tilt as her eyes traced the diagram. "If that's a weapon," she asked in Biouk. "What's it pointing at?"

A mournful howl in the upper tunnel—the storm, it seemed, had come.

CHAPTER FORTY-NINE

Lem

LEM STOOD SEETHING ATOP THE DUSTY OVERHANG, HER BACK pressed against the ragged canyon wall as her chest heaved. She was straining inside herself as hard as she could to build up spark around her body again—breathing, pushing, breathing, pushing to birth power. She needed to build up static cling so she could climb the cliff face and shock the control panel while Diebol was still upset.

He wasn't the only one upset. If Diebol was telling any kind of truth, her younger brothers had just been on a simple supply run when they got *got*. Reise, as comfortable in combat as on a game console, and Jake, wide-eyed and full of possibility ... there'd still been hope for them that this filking worthless universe wouldn't mess them up. How *dare*—

If you hadn't left the Frelsi, you could be there protecting them, right now.

Could she still? Could she climb down the cliff, run south or some shyte, find transportation, and beeline it to Bijou? It wasn't like she was going to actually get Jei back, not in this state.

"Shut up." Lem clenched her teeth and inhaled, standing on tip-toe to try to breathe just a little bit of Mera's pheromone floating over the canyon. Calm down, and get control. Jei had been right: the gas had really helped, back at Fort Tapiz, to quiet a bit of the self-doubt and discouragement the Accuser liked to prey on. She needed that little medicine right now.

"What do you think, Benzaran?" Diebol taunted. "Save your brothers—likely very doable—or save your partner—likely impossible?"

Shyte, *so young*. Reise had already been two standard revolutions old when Lem came back from Biouk life, but she'd held Jake as an infant. He was the first baby human she'd ever seen, all furless and screaming like a choking day-lizard, little wrinkled fist flailing in the air. He was regulation fighting age now? But he was just a baby. Her chest tightened. Oh, *no* ...

Breathe. With another inhale Lem found enough charge to stick her hand to the canyon wall. "This is extremely stupid," she yelled. "You've already tried the whole 'oh no your family' bit. You don't think I'd drop this in a heartbeat if I could, and go smash nuts on whatever unit commander you've got holding the control panel on Bijou?"

"Lem, so violent! I thought you were trying for pacifism." Diebol's voice bounced from rock to rock with the echo of a laugh.

Yes, sure. She was shyte as a "good guy." "I have a mission," Lem growled back. Breathe. Both hands. She could start climbing. She didn't let herself look down behind her at the sharp, gaping slit of death below her overhang. Two quick breaths to psych herself up—then go, fast. Diebol probably had a weapon primed to shoot her up top, so she needed to build up enough electricity to throw a hand over the cliff edge and shock everybody and everything before she emerged ...

"Just your mission?" Diebol asked. "What happened to your rebellious heart, your passion?"

Yes, she had changed. Shyte, she hated what she was becoming. One of her hands began to slip—

No. Breathe. There was calm in the air. Halfway up now. Getting close. She needed charge. She rubbed the wayward hand against her forearm, reminding her body what it was, what it could do. The Frelsi didn't need her and Diebol didn't think she was really worth stealing, but dammit she had capacitors on her nerve endings and she could shock people. Sure, she couldn't actually em-push—her static worked just fine. Shyte, she even had some new ability they didn't understand, too, to make giant EMP shields or whatever—not that she knew how to trigger that in any useful way right now without the blue juice back at Tapiz. Seemed like she'd run out of energy for that. But point was, she *was* worth something here. It wasn't impossible.

Right?

Inhale.

"It's your *family*, Lem."

Yeah. She was a shyte sister. A shyte *person*, really. Erratic, and undependable. Jei was an idiot for breaking her out from Beryllia. Why would he or anyone else want her around? Just bad judgment. Even Cinta was disappointed in her.

Njande, why am I here?

Hear, One Who Wrestles With Power: Love l'reacha.

And there, there was why. There was a central rule above family bonds, above biological mate loyalties, above charity or justice or right and wrong or any other rule. All those things flowed from that central rule, but none mattered apart from it— and *it was okay just to follow that one rule.* To love, and be okay with loving.

"Jei is my family right now," Lem muttered, something like shame blooming across her cheeks as she approached the top.

"What was that?"

"I said, Jei is my family right now!" Lem roared. She swung herself upward, electricity blasting from both hands. Jei fired at her, but the shot swerved around her innate field. He, Diebol, and that stupid, stupid control panel all lit up with blue arcs of lightning. *Diebol didn't even have his field up over the panel?* Lem fell half-off the cliff, stomach on the edge and legs kicking to try to push herself the rest of the way up—

"Die, witch." White light flashed in Lem's vision as Diebol stomped her in the face.

"Oh, *shyte*—" She clawed at the sand as she fell backward, suddenly flailing in the air—

Jei's familiar hand latched onto her wrist, and Lem slammed against the side of the cliff instead of tumbling to the spikes below. Pain jolted through her bones, but she looked up to see him give her a quick smile. His pistol clattered into the crevasse behind her, knocking against the small overhang on its way down.

"I hit the control panel," Lem breathed.

"You hit the control panel," he panted.

"Move." Diebol kicked Jei in the ribs and Lem saw the blinding black-purple of an ultraviolet staff come stabbing down toward her face. Before she could react, she found herself yanked left, out of its path, as Jei kept his painful, rug-burning grip on her wrist and twisted his body to kick Diebol's legs out from under him.

"I'm right here, you idiot," Jei snarled. Lem bicycled her boots against the cliff face, clambering up as Jei yanked her to his side. Dust and pebbles rained down beneath them. "Can you stop targeting her now, maybe, since I'm free of your shyte spine-sucker?"

Lem flopped back up onto level ground with everyone else. It took her a second to recognize the blood dripping from her face down into the rust-umber sand.

Diebol jumped back to his feet; so did Jei. Lem struggled to rise behind Jei's boots, her shoulder, ribs, and head screaming at her as she tried to push her chest off the ground.

She collapsed when she saw Diebol throw out his hand and summon her mace to his side. It orbited around him in the air as he gripped his own with two hands.

Shyte, after all that, Diebol wasn't powered off. Jei was. Diebol had still managed to neutralize some of her shock, and even though Jei had been training to decrease his own charge time from an hour to twenty minutes, that still meant twenty minutes against a fully-powered Diebol. Lem would've liked to take a second to aim and make sure she *just* hit the control panel. But she hadn't been able to take the risk that Diebol might succeed in protecting it and send Jei after her with his abilities intact.

You hit the panel by chance, you know. His protection bubble only weakened because Jei and I distracted him. What a warrior he is, against the three of us!

"But I did hit it," Lem tried to mutter back, ignoring the implication of friendship with the Accuser. "Fort Tapiz has a chance now."

It doesn't, really. As long as you're alive, no one really has a chance. You and I will ruin everything.

Shyte, she couldn't do this anymore.

CHAPTER FIFTY

Jei

I STOOD BETWEEN LEM AND DIEBOL WITH MY ARMS SPREAD. MY black tunic rustled. Wind whistled through the canyon to my left. My mace glowed emerald in the sand beyond us; Diebol left it there. He'd made the mistake years ago of attacking me with my own mace, and knew better now than to give me an opportunity to take it from him.

Only the owner of a neodymium mace can actually touch its surface unscathed.

Lem heaved on the ground behind me. She was bleeding; head wounds always gush more than you'd expect. Nothing fatal, but I didn't know how much more she could take. With Diebol treating me like a glass figurine through the whole first fight, I was almost unscathed. Very dizzy and high now, but unscathed.

It worried me that he still didn't want to kill me.

"Move," he said.

"Try me," I said.

He growled and swiped his hand right. I felt his em-push trying to knock me aside; I followed its force, and instead of resisting I spun clockwise, rolling with that force right back into his right side. He stumbled, yanking his mace away to keep from hitting me—I slammed into him, snatching in the air at Lem's.

"Stop, you'll burn your—"

My palm sizzled as I touched it—that sear on the sensitive nerves of my fingers hurt worse than any mace blow I'd ever taken but I kicked off Diebol's knee, and then his chest, getting height and breaking his concentration so I could tear that burning death-stick out of his orbit. The magnetic field resisted me, then gave. I hurled the mace down behind me to Lem.

A stream of curses erupted from my mouth as soon as I let it go. Diebol was yelling something at me; Lem, behind me, was yelling something, too. I could hear neither of them over how pissed off my hand was at me.

"Shut up, both of you!" I roared, gripping my wrist.

For a split second, they did shut up. Lem, still on her knees with one hand on the ground, held her mace in the other as if raising her hand to speak. Diebol was recovering, still stumbling backward from my chest-kick knocking him off balance.

"Jared," I growled. "Back *off* her. So help me, no amount of electromagnetic ability powered down or up or filking *sideways* is going to save you if you keep going after her."

"Are you serious—she's a threat I have to take out, why would I—"

"Shut up, I'm not done! And you—" My words to Lem came out more like a snarl than I intended, but with Mera's loss still swirling around my brain I was struggling to care about anything at all except my shrieking hand.

"Me?" Lem stammered. "What did I—"

"You're a fool, is 'what did you.' We just gave Fort Tapiz a chance, and you're yelling at me for a burn? What are you both, my parents who won't let me touch a stove?"

"Do you not understand what you're worth?" she scoffed.

"I know what I'm worth. You don't know what you are."

DIEBOL

Diebol had a headache. He'd never turned his new brain implant on before now, and by all that was good in the galaxy, this buzzing had better stop when the device finished charging up. Jei's temper tantrum certainly didn't help.

What a weakling you are—you let your concentration drop and got your panel fried. You got so mad when little Jei poked your buttons—how cute! Look at him, taking his turn now.

The Accuser *also* didn't help.

But what really didn't help was that Jei was charging and striking, fully aware that Diebol wouldn't run him through. Diebol wasn't going to tell Jei *why* he still didn't want to kill him, but Diebol also did not want to be taken out by a bare-handed idiot while he himself held a weapon. He thought he had about an hour until Jei powered up again—that was how long it had taken when they measured his limits during Morda's captivity. Plenty of time to finish this fight. Diebol tried to side-step around the angry warrior to strike the tired girl on the ground still clutching her staff like she didn't quite know what to do with it—

Jei wasn't falling for the side-step again. He moved with Diebol, stepping diagonally past him to—*gak*—clothesline Diebol's neck on his forearm. A fist to the face followed.

Diebol threw himself to his feet and backward with a solid em-push on Jei's chest. Diebol's left brow pulsed with pain; he tapped it, and found blood. He'd muffled the blow with the push, but damn, Jei.

"Are you planning on beating me to death without a weapon?" Diebol laughed.

"I don't know. Are you planning on coming back with us in a stasis collar?"

"You're *not* in a place to negotiate." Diebol held one hand to his ear, trying to silence the buzzing as he raised his other hand.

If he was precise he could em-pull beyond Jei, maybe, and drag Lem over to impale her on his staff—

You would do it that way.

Oh, not more of this.

I wonder why you really got mad at little Jei's biology review. We both know why, right?

Jei helped Lem to her feet, wrapping an arm around her shoulder for support as she raised a hand, her head drooping as she fired another jolt of electricity at Diebol.

It's not because you're so righteous and idealistic.

Diebol took the shock, balancing the charge without so much as a wince. It stung but he could out-last Benzaran—she shuddered backward after shooting as if her electricity had a recoil.

You aren't mad because controlling their bodies disgusts you. You would willingly do that to her. You like hurting people. You used to get a little rush when they'd take little Jei out of the cage, remember? You tell yourself it was a rush of fear, but we both know that's not true.

"You are disgusting," Diebol growled.

Didn't you say I only work with what's already there?

"Well, I know that's not there, so I guess I was wrong." Diebol took a couple more steps back to make sure Jei didn't charge him again while he prepared. "Unless you and Bricandor put it there, maybe." He dug into his pocket for the last two amphetamine doses he'd saved for himself. It was time to unlock that thinker multitasking he'd boasted to Bricandor about, the terror of Fort Tapiz. He popped the pills, and as he waited for their effect he evened the playing field a little: "Lem, dear, what's our mutual enemy saying to *you*, right now? Because—to answer that nagging internal question I know you have—yes, we know the same Accuser. You know he's usually right about you, don't you?"

That's quite flattering, but then what about you?

Lem winced as something played in her head; she leaned back wearily against Jei and spoke to him, not Diebol: "Hey—

hey, Jei, I can't exist anymore. And I think I can take him out with me if I—"

Diebol could just barely hear Jei's interruption. "Nope, not an option, we're ahead right now," Jei muttered in a low voice near her ear, his hard gaze still fixed on Diebol.

What Diebol *could* hear very clearly was the crackling sound of something going wrong with the sparkling field around Benzaran. If he had to guess, it probably wasn't healthy to medicate yourself into holding a shield over a fort and then less than twelve hours later take a bunch of blows to the head. He just needed to land one more really good one. Or—because the two "Paradox Warriors" didn't know they were on a clock—he could just wait for this *infernal thing in his skull* to finish charging ...

Jei was clearly calculating, too, trying to figure out whether or not he could risk stepping away from Lem to charge Diebol, or perhaps to run for his mace still laying several meters beyond them. Still at least fifty minutes until he powered up again.

Look at him, so cute. He's going to be so unhappy when she dies. Hey, do you remember the first time you sold him out? The first lesson Bricandor taught you? I know you like to say you were just a little kid, and it wasn't your fault, but—

"Do you wish you had stayed on Beryllia?" Diebol blurted to Lem. His words came out more strained and desperate than he intended. "It was quieter there, wasn't it? And you had friends, too. Wasn't there a boy learning his powers? Wait, let me recall—did you help him, or ...?"

Oh, this is just mean.

Lem shook her head, and shoved herself away from Jei, clutching her temple with one hand. She still kept a firm grip on her mace with her other—Diebol didn't dare try to yank it from her with Jei still halfway between them.

"Ah, right, you did *not* help him. You went gallivanting across the universe with Jei. Your little trainee is with Bricandor now," Diebol said. "He's supposed to become my replacement."

Jei looked confused; Lem's face died.

Look at that. No more emotion in that ever-expressive brow. Doesn't that hurt you? You know if you hadn't tried to train her two years ago, she would never have become such a problem? She could have died happy, maybe.

"I only tried to save them," Diebol hissed. To Lem: "One of his friends was Contaminated. Was that your doing? That one's dead or marooned or something now."

You destroy everyone around you.

"It's almost like everyone you run into is doomed," Diebol said.

Hey, that's my line.

"I don't know what you're talking about," Lem said. But he knew she did. She raised a hand to fire another jolt—

Jei made a break for his mace.

You know why I want you to die?

Diebol dropped his own weapon into orbit around him and thrust out both hands: one for an em-pull to drag Jei back from his mace, the other to feel and balance Benzaran's shock. *Ccch*, it still stung. He rotated his wrist like turning a knob—his energy switched from balancing, to a pull. Lem's mace came flying toward him.

With her attached.

Because you are a snake. Bricandor did everything for you.

Lem swiveled at the last second and threw both legs forward. Diebol got boots in the gut before he could block—

"What, you think I was just going to let go? After you burned his hand?" Lem muttered.

"Fair enough." Diebol clenched his fist; everything was becoming clearer now again, and at the same moment as Diebol blocked Lem's next mace blow, he switched his pull to grab Jei's mace and hurl it off the cliff, leaving Jei to stumble and fall as the force on him released.

Just a scared little boy, in the end, willing to sell everyone out for his "greater good."

"Shyte—" Lem coughed as she tried to block Diebol's side-smash—toward the shoulder she'd fallen on. She couldn't maintain her grip.

"It's going to rain," Diebol heard himself remark.

Maybe that's why you don't know where you came from. Imagine a little boy, caught by the Growen, scared into revealing where the rest of his family is hiding …

A hot wind rose. The sky darkened. Sand blossomed around Diebol with the twitch of his fingers, and here, he called the creature's bluff with a grin. "I remember every awful thing I've ever done. I'd remember that. You've run out of fuel, pest. Why do you really want me dead?"

"Who the bloodseas are you talking to?" Jei's voice, by his ear —biceps wrapped around Diebol's throat for a goose-choke.

Diebol roared, and ripped his hand toward the sky. "Tell. Me. Or I kill the old man."

Do you think I will let you?

"Do you think you can stop me?!"

Jei went flying behind him with an elbow and an em-push. Diebol tripped Lem and stabbed the butt of his staff toward her chest—her weak block only deflected it into her arm.

You will die. Bricandor will accelerate your Universe's heat death and send all that delicious energy back to my dimension. The Traitor will weep as his disgusting meat-consorts freeze.

"The Traitor?"

Njandejara. You're a lot like him. Torn between two terrible choices, not because you're powerless, but because you're so idealistic you won't let go of either. You betray your kind to save your enemy. It's not me or Bricandor who put you in this situation. It's you and your delusions.

Diebol found himself laughing. "So you want me dead because I'm not on team end-the-universe?"

Yes. But I'll still give you a last bit of help. Tell her *you won't allow the universe to end and see how she takes it.*

Diebol looked down at Lem as Jei charged him again. He threw an em-push to keep his old friend back; Jei pulled the same tunic-trick Lem had to keep coming, but Diebol pushed again.

Below him, Jerusha-Lem Benzaran was so tired. She could barely lift her head to meet his gaze as she struggled to get up, her left shoulder a meaty mess at the end of his staff and her face covered in crimson, flecked with lilac sand. As rain broke it drew patterns across her face like war paint.

Jei charged again, this time trying to roll around the em-push like he had earlier. Diebol sent another. The buzzing from the implant was beginning to quiet.

Lem probably knew the Accuser wanted to use her in some way, Diebol realized. Perhaps she was supposed to live, and go insane. She probably did have to die for the universe to survive, and her eyes begged only for Jei's life anyway—she'd lost desire for her own.

"No," Diebol said to the mind-worm. He would tell her nothing. In honor of what could have been, and in rebellion against the leeches that sought to end his dimension, his last words to Lem Benzaran were not taunts. "It is amazing weather here," he said to her.

"Yeah," she croaked. "It is."

No kings, and no gods. Only man.

CHAPTER FIFTY-ONE

Jei

IT WAS RAINING IN THE DESERT.

A whirlwind of colored sand swirled around us with Diebol at the epicenter.

As the sand rose, it left rocks behind, all blood-tinted ivory like the rest of the cliff.

I found two, rough and cold in my palms, as Diebol raised his mace above Lem again.

Her boot was *right next to his*. It didn't matter that I was spinning like the sand, trying to weave around his em-pushes to gain only a meter at a time, and it didn't matter that I didn't have powers or that she was running out of strength. Her boot was right next to his and neither of them saw it. I cocked my arm back, and shouted a memory to draw her eye: "The levels are designed with a way out!"

She looked up.

I hurled both stones, and dove forward.

Diebol sent em-pushes to block the rocks, and stop me in the air.

Lem kicked his boot.

As Diebol stumbled forward, his mace hit stone, not Lem; he

released his push against me just long enough for me to tumble over into them again. I wedged myself between them, picked up the nearest rock, and smashed it at his head.

He threw me away again with an em-push, diverting my blow to his shoulder blade with a cry of pain and knocking me back several meters—but I brought Lem with me, my arm wrapped across her torso. We skidded along the ground at the edge of the whirlwind; she drooped, barely holding on to my shoulder.

We needed to regroup. I yanked her outside the whirlwind's eye, squinting against the stinging dust—

Bloodseas, even out here the sand was starting to fly. The clearing at the center of the whirlwind may have been Diebol's doing, but we were also in the middle of a real desert sandstorm now. I dragged my partner behind an L-shaped boulder at the edge of the cliff. It looked like part of the cliff face—like a false edge—and with any luck, it would buy us half a minute to plan. As the wind rose around us, the entire landscape disappeared in the vortex of colored sand, and for a moment, in this niche in the rock, it seemed like Lem and I were the only people in the whole world.

Lem vomited off the cliff and then slouched next to me, her eyes staring off into the distance. The rain was washing away the blood of her head wound, and her shoulder was mangled, but not fatal. Still, her head drooped like something was really wrong in there, and I had no idea about other injuries from her fall. The sparks around her had died down. "The levels are designed with a way out?" she murmured. "I said that, didn't I?"

"First thing we fought about in the training center," I nodded. I looked over my shoulder, resisting the urge to look over the edge of the boulder. I could hear the wall of sand approaching.

"I was wrong," she said.

"Maybe. Maybe not. It's a paradox." I checked her pulse, and surveyed myself. Bloodseas, the skin on my right palm had flaked away in ugly blackened boils and cracks. Had I really thrown a rock with that hand? Now that the adrenaline had dropped a little, those nerves were *shrieking*. That hand didn't want to do anything anymore ever again.

Lem still had her mace, though, and we just needed to survive until I powered on again—which wouldn't be long now, I hoped. Diebol was likely estimating something like forty-five minutes, from back during my last captivity, but it was actually more like five minutes. I motioned for Lem to turn off her mace to hide—she did.

But Diebol's voice carried beyond the storm. "Valiant effort, Jei. But time's up."

Suddenly, my hand that didn't want to do anything did something.

It raised in the air as if I wanted to be found.

Ah. And here I'd thought we might both live.

Lem dropped her head in her hands. "He has a backup drive," she moaned.

"You're still on the clock, Benzaran," I said. "Help pin me down." She wasn't a small woman, and she could at least physically keep me from standing up like I apparently wanted to do now. She turned to face me from the side and locked my knees over one of her legs, placing the other across my lap as she gripped my wrists. She was shaking her head.

"My implant's just an extension of my control pad, and not as nice," Diebol went on, his voice nearer now, but still muffled by the rising wind. "It's only linked to one person—you—and I can't see through your eyes. Still, it'll work; each dart only links to one control panel, so once I got you I couldn't really risk losing you. I've been working on this back up since the day before Morda died." He suddenly corrected himself: "Mera. And I'm Jared. Bricandor's naming rules don't need to apply anymore. We'll use normal names working together. It will be okay. I promise."

He promised, huh.

"All three of us do entirely too much talking," I remarked to Lem. Everything was suddenly becoming very clear to me. I could move now only until he gave my body its next command—sit, stay, stand, whatever. If he couldn't see through my eyes, that meant he was just waiting until he could see me before he gave that next command so he didn't accidentally run me off the cliff. But the moment he found me, it would be me and him against Lem.

And I couldn't hide forever. We couldn't climb down the cliff and run away—even if we could have reached the bottom in time, as soon as I got near an area with enough people to super-charge me, Diebol only had to make me em-push and I'd be knocking over buildings whether he could see me or not. And I wasn't going to make it very far to begin with if he ordered me to sit.

Worse, even without super-charging, I would power back on normally in a few minutes. When that happened, I was going to kill Lem even before Diebol saw me. All it would take was one wild em-push to smash her against this rock or hurl her off the cliff.

"Can you power me down again?" I asked.

"Are you—? Oh, shyte." Lem closed her eyes, and I could feel her grip tightening on my wrists. Her chin tilted back as her teeth clenched and hoarse breath escaped her throat …

A tear rolled out the corner of her left eye.

She couldn't.

"Hey." I knocked my knee against her leg. "It's okay. Stop."

"I'm sorry," she whispered.

"It doesn't matter. Even if you could, I'm pretty sure I could kill you without my abilities right now."

She leaned the side of her head against the rock. "Let me die."

"No," I said. "Help me call my dad."

"Why?"

I didn't tell her why. I didn't have to.

"Jei, please," she whimpered.

"Lem, there's a mind-control implant in my spine. Right now, in the present, your apocalypse is still only theoretical. Mine isn't."

"Let me take him with me," she said.

I answered with a shake of my head. She couldn't kill him right now. Yesterday, maybe. We were all tired, all three of us, but she couldn't even walk straight. If she tried to drag him off the cliff, he'd just kick her off him. And if Diebol really was done with Bricandor, that meant there was no power balance against his High Command—no more toxic eccentricities slowing the Growen down. It was about to become one streamlined force. I could have told her about my certainty that Diebol wouldn't hold out against the Accuser as long as she had—he didn't have help—and I could have said something psychological about the fact that if Diebol let anyone kill him, it would be me, or that I knew I was never going to escape him as long as I lived. I didn't go on, because even if we had time, she was too hurt to hear any of it.

"I'm going to try to get us both out of this," I said. "But you need to understand that what happens next is my choice. It's not your fault. It would have gone worse without you. And we're probably not both coming home."

LEM

The Admiral did not answer when Jei called.

As the sandstorm worsened, and Diebol's search for them drew nearer, and Jei kept trying to stand, Lem had to hold his wrist up to his face for him to leave a message. He forgave his dad for something Lem didn't quite understand—something it seemed he himself didn't quite understand. He talked about his mom, and how he hoped to find out what had really happened to her, and he told his dad he'd like to meet for lunch if they saw each other again.

"That's probably not going to happen. I'm sorry for—not knowing you. I hope you start hearing again. Njandejara misses you. Good—uh, goodbye. Dad."

She'd never heard him call the Admiral "Dad."

They had three minutes until Jei's powers returned. Maybe more, maybe less. Lem's stomach tied itself into a knot so firm she thought she'd vomit again. She didn't know what Jei planned to do, but she knew it involved using a force Diebol couldn't mind control out of him. Probably gravity. She couldn't see straight. Her breath wouldn't slow down. *Please, please don't do this. Please let me just try.*

"Jei, it has to be me," she whimpered. "Look, I'm not what I'm supposed to be. I should have been born a Biouk. I am a shyte human. I want to re-roll, start over. Mulligan. I need different cards."

Jei winced as he tried to rise again. "That's not how death works," he said.

"How does anybody know?" Lem cried.

"No one does." He was so quiet. So … peaceful. A soft grin flickered over his lips. "But Lem, remember a couple years ago, we talked about Njande's proposal—that there's a way to transfer our sentience to his pocket dimension, or like a place in the future, when we die?"

Lem shook her head violently. "Jei, we don't know if it works. There were criteria, and they were impossible for us to fulfill. A bunch of synaptic changes and shyte, Jei!"

He shifted his weight, leaning sideways so his forehead almost touched hers. "I've been thinking about that," he whispered. "I think there's something that's going to happen very soon that fulfills the criteria. There are hints about it everywhere."

Diebol's voice penetrated the wind again—he'd walked past them, but now circled back around. Jei paused, listening—Lem couldn't hear what Diebol said.

"I'm ready to roll the dice," Jei went on. "Mera really messed me up, and I really miss hearing Njande, Lem. I'm not unhappy about the idea of maybe finding him by protecting you. You know I calculate everything. I'm not just going to take a shot without thinking it through. And I know what I'm worth. I'm maybe happier with myself now than I've ever been. I'm—ready, is all."

They could hear footsteps now. Jei tried to stand up again; they both struggled to keep him down. He cocked his head, listening, then turned back to Lem: "Don't let me go until I say, okay?"

Lem didn't want to let him go at all. They'd been to death and back again a hundred times and she'd *never* worried about him, but something was so different right now, and this differentness was the most terrifying thing she had ever experienced. "You said you didn't want a universe I'm not in," she whispered. "What about me? What if I don't want one without you?"

"Well, today, Lem, you don't get what you want." He bumped his forehead against hers, gently. "But thank you. I love you, too."

At that, a heaving sound Lem hated escaped from her throat. *We wouldn't be here if you weren't such weepy weak trash,* said that other voice. She gritted her teeth, focusing on the pulse in Jei's wrists under her fingers, his knee warm against her leg in this bitter, stinging wind, and his firm forehead. No. She shook her head. This couldn't happen. What was he waiting for? She should charge out there. She should charge now.

Jei's left hand twisted around to grip her wrist. "I know you can't hear this right now, Lem. But you *are* worth keeping alive."

She shook her head. She couldn't—she couldn't—

"Look at me, please, Lem. For once in your life, don't fight me."

She looked, and she couldn't stop crying. Why? What was wrong with her?

His emerald-blue eyes seemed to glow against his dirty face. Shyte, he was ... happy. "Maybe we're all destroying the universe in our own way, Lem—one butterfly wing at a time. But I know your *go'ali* lives. The one who buys your hope back after everything's gone. It's not me. I can't really explain how I know, or who it is. But Njande's going to send someone. Maybe it's him, himself." He nodded for her to let him go, and then, as he rose, whispered a promise in her ear. *"Va'ani yadati go'ali chai, va'acharon al-afar yakum."*

And he was gone. Lem tried to crawl to the edge after him, but his words, Njande's words, were a safety net that she could not pass.

JEI

It didn't matter that we'd closed the mind-channel. I knew two presences better than any other in the universe: his, and hers. And the moment he was close enough, before he could see clearly enough to decide what to do with me, I dove for him.

He didn't see me until I slid into his knees and knocked him to the edge of the cliff. I felt my body trying to obey his order —*let go, stand up!*—but the momentum carried us both over the edge. Diebol's mace fell on top of the cliff, teetering on the edge above us—my hands shot out instinctively and grabbed the rock next to it, sending blood and pain down both palms.

Diebol latched on to my boot with an em-pull. "I am *never* letting you go," he growled.

"I know." Too bad—I had hoped maybe I could just knock

him off and go home. *Sorry, Lem.* My fingers tightened their grip on the cliff under Diebol's order—*don't you dare let go*—as he started to pull us both back up. My palms twitched—he was trying to get me to em-pull, too. My ability wasn't back on yet, but in another second—

Give me strength just one last time
And I will pull the temple down.

I obeyed him, and I em-pulled.

I em-pulled Diebol's teetering mace harder than I had ever pulled anything in my life. It shot into me, through me, and into him, as we fell into the canyon.

He lost control for a split second but despite the searing agony between us he *still* tried to pull up to save us both, he *still* ordered me to pull, stealing my breath with a cry I didn't recognize, but he was disorganized in his shock and now we were spinning, and as he fired my powers, he only made me pull on the ground below. His body collided with mine, still skewered on the staff; a flash of fear ran through me as I saw the spikes approach; he tried to push, and he lost control of me. I rolled over to face the sky, and bucked backward. I would not let him die looking down.

There was an instant of horrible penetrating pain as the spiked rocks pierced through him, into me. His wrist twitched against mine, and I thought I heard him say something; I know I heard Lem's voice echo through the canyon. There was brilliant color; Mera's sigh; and then it was over.

And in that infinite, closing moment, I had the sudden realization that this was what I'd asked for. I asked to find the secret at the center of all things, and taste the desire that made all other flavors bland in comparison—the longing that would break me free from all my other masters. Hinted at in every human pleasure, every glint of glory on every blade of grass, and in that one rule I'd read to Lem; not everyone had to die to find it, but everyone who ever found it eventually died at least once. I could hear again. I could *see*. My dearest friend was no longer invisible, and when he greeted me with his hearty embrace, he was completely the opposite and yet exactly the same as I expected. And it was all worth it. He was worth it.

And that, Lem, is where my story ends.

The End.

INDEX OF TERMS AND CHARACTERS

Air-rider: Single or double-rider hovering transport vehicle, popular among civilians and Frelsi warriors for its low cost of construction, safety profile, and ease of operation.

Alpino: Neighboring planetary system to Luna-Guetala. Its various biomes range from arctic tundra to temperate zones, but due to extensive landmass, with oceans comprising less than 50 percent of the surface area, much of the planet is covered in volcano-strewn prairie or cool desert. Bereens's home planet. Contested Zone.

Ba-eater: A Biouk term for an interdimensional being that devours the human psyche. Used to describe gods and demons of multiple religions.

Bangla: A species of wide, many-trunked, vine'd tree common to Luna-Guetala jungles.

Baricella: A species of bipedal mammal characterized by long, black, fuzzy growths around the mouth that resemble the pedipalps and legs of spiders. Habitat includes Luna-Guetala jungles

and the moon of Baricel orbiting Gas Giant 3; small colonies
were transported by Growen slavers for cheap labor to the
Northern Continent of Alpino. Visual spectrum includes high-
acuity infrared but does not include much of the color spectrum.
Communicate verbally with an extremely high-pitched
language, most of which is outside the range of other
mammalian hearing; emotionally, communicate with motions of
the growths around the mouth.

Bichank: This people group, called "land-walruses" by many
humans, bear more similarity to a sentient grizzly with tusks.
Habitat includes the Luna-Guetala jungles, but actually likely
originated on the cooler planet of Alpino. Culturally similar to
Biouk peoples, communicate verbally with a throaty, roaring
language, and emotionally with eye movements and wrinkles of
the muzzle, like humans.

Biouk: See space-lemur.

Blitzer: Member of a Growen heavy infantry unit, characterized
by silvery armor and large, reflective, space-capable orb'd
helmets.

Bricandor: Leader and supreme diplomat of the Growen Unification Forces. Human in appearance and appetites; rumored to
have appeared in the galaxy, or at least developed his Stygge
powers, after the Black Comet.

Burbura: Independent planet with over 90 percent of its surface
area under water, a condition many scientists attribute to a past
global warming crisis. Highly technological trade, media, and
political hub home to most of the sentient species in the known
universe—"where Burbura goes, so goes the galaxy." Independent planet/uncontested, with both Frelsi and Growen diplomatic presence.

Cadet Commander: The highest rank available to a child in the Frelsi guard, preceded by Cadet 3, 2, and 1, and Enforcer. Followed in adulthood by Lieutenant 2 and 1; Sergeant 5, 4, 3, 2, and 1; Captain 3, 2, and 1; Colonel; and Admiral. Unlike the Growen Unification Forces, which separate rank into three chains—Officer, Enlisted, and Stygge—the Frelsi separate rank only into the child and adult chains.

Captain Rana: Wonderfrog officer over the Eighth Combined Battalion in the refugee base at Fort Jehu, overseeing both children and adults in self and community defense. Former commanding officer for Lem Benzaran, Jei Bereens, and Lem's siblings. Contaminated.

Cinta: Space-lemur from Luna-Guetala, 28 revolutions old, currently studying interspecies biomedical science to become a healer. Formerly a pacifist, joined the Frelsi Unification Forces last year after capture by the Growen. Lem Benzaran grew up as his little sister for a few years, and they have since remained close.

Contaminated: A derogatory term for a matter-based, sentient being who speaks to interdimensional energy beings such as, and usually specifically, Njandejara.

Contested Zone: The areas not covered by the Spaces Treaties. On Contested planets, the Growen and the Frelsi fight for dominance. On Independent Planets in the Undecided or Uncontested Zones, neither is authorized outright displays of force. The Growen hold that all Frelsi allied-planets fall within the Contested Zone, but that Growen-occupied planets do not.

Dr. Patti Loylan: Physician assigned to the Eighth Combined Battalion at Fort Jehu. Also supervises the biological research program to improve artificial habitat compatibility, travel comfort, and optimal combat ability of diverse species. Shy. Not contaminated.

Ebon Shadow: Bounty hunter alter ego for brothers Carl and K'arl Hampt. The most feared mercenary in the galaxy, the Ebon Shadow was often hired by the Growen for plausible deniability with assassinations or kidnappings that would otherwise break the Spaces Treaties. Following the events of the Battle of Bioumatta, chronicled in *Neodymium Exodus*, and the presumed death of K'arl, the Ebon Shadow began exclusively accepting anti-Growen contracts, working in tandem with the young Bont bounty hunter Lark Scrita.

Electrogenic: An electromagnetic being that can generate electric charge, similar to the electric eel on the rumored human homeworld.

Enforcer: The second-highest rank available to older children. See Cadet Commander.

Firebase: The largest Frelsi base on Alpino, located in the South Central continent about three hours' journey from Growen South Central by air-rider.

Forge: Generally habitable arid planet orbiting the second sun in the Bioumatta system. Resource-rich, but characterized by generally toxic colorful sands throughout much of the planet's atmosphere. Some portions of the planet are terraformed, or are only habitable underground, due to the planet's proximity to the sun and certain past meteorological events.

Fort Jehu: One of the larger Frelsi bases on Luna-Guetala, about an hour's journey by air-rider south of Retrack City.

Frelsi: Conglomerate of militarized special interest groups and refugee bases organized to protect people groups punished for refusing to join the Growen Unification Project.

Gideon Horn: 16-year-old male freedom fighter, ward of the Frelsi refugee system. Orphan. Special skills in ground combat and weightlifting. Known for cheerful, occasionally insensitive demeanor. Best friend of Nathan Peter and Reise Benzaran. Contaminated.

Gray: Frelsi slang for members of the Growen Incursion under the Growen Unification Forces.

Grenblenian: Common trade language throughout Luna-Guetala, adopted by most planets with a mammalian presence.

Growen Unification Forces: Interplanetary social organization forcefully uniting all sentient beings under one centralized government. Supported by various economic and social causes, including interest groups that propose eliminating Contaminated people to defend the universe from interdimensional invasion through their brains.

Jake Benzaran: 13-year-old male ward of the Frelsi refugee system, below fighting age. Brother to Jerusha-Lem, Reise, Juju, and others. Special skills not yet known. Sustained significant childhood injury leaving him limping, and prone to epileptic attacks; as a result, can be quite skittish. Contaminated.

Jared Diebol: 23-year-old male soldier in the Growen Unification Forces, advanced early to commander status due to his Stygge training, electromagnetic abilities, and unusual voracity. Specialized knowledge of the Frelsi electromagnetic pair due to his close mental relationship with Jei Bereens. Not contaminated; obsessed with curing contamination.

Jei Bereens: 20-year-old male freedom fighter, ward of the Frelsi refugee system. One of two known electromagnetic humans in the Frelsi forces. Highly trained, with specialized knowledge of Growen systems and technology due to his childhood in Growen captivity. Arch-enemy of Jared Diebol; Paradox Warrior partner of Jerusha-Lem Benzaran. Contaminated.

Jerusha-Lem Benzaran: 17-year-old female freedom fighter, ward of the Frelsi refugee system. One of two known electro-magnetic humans in the Frelsi forces. Highly trained, with specialized knowledge of Biouk space-lemur society due to childhood living among the space-lemurs. Contaminated.

Juju Benzaran: 11-year-old female ward of the Frelsi refugee system, pre-fighting age. Quiet, with talents in early communication, and an unusual protection spell from Njandejara. Sister of Lem Benzaran. Possibly contaminated.

Land-runner: A sleek, heavily armored, spiked vehicle that uses wheels to move along a planet's surface, most commonly employed by the Growen.

Lark Scrita: 18-year-old human living her life as a famed sixty-year-old Bont bounty hunter. Not contaminated, but the child of a contaminated couple killed by the Growen. Unallied.

Lechichi: A fruit common to Luna-Guetala jungles. Grows in clusters of small, translucent white orbs with rough reddish-purple husks.

Lieutenant Seria: 22-year-old female freedom fighter, ward of the Frelsi refugee system, highly trained in communication and investigative skills. Not contaminated.

Lift: A floating platform with one solitary railing and a compuwall for light transport of goods and people within a short distance.

Luna-Guetala: The only known habitable binary or "double-planet" system, differentiated from a simple planet-moon system by the sheer size of the smaller celestial body. Luna, the smaller, more temperate twin, is often mistakenly called a moon by LG inhabitants. Neighbors the Alpino planetary system.

Masha: Exact age unknown; between 28 and 30. Sanitation worker at a large neodymium glass factory on Forge. Artistically and scientifically talented, but limited because of her gender and social status. Pro-Frelsi. Highly contaminated.

Meat-man: Frelsi slang for perpetrators of sentient trafficking, whether through slave trade, brothel ownership, or actual sale of sentient beings for edible consumption.

Mera: Deceased at 20 years old. Female soldier for the Growen Unification Forces, thought to have been originally rescued from abuse as a sky-dancer by Diebol. Graduated from the same Stygge training program Lem and Jei rejected. Tasked with solving the problem of Jei Bereens when he becomes super-charged. Special skills in tracking electrical fields with a sense organ similar to the ampullae of Lorenzini in sharks; releases a calming pheromone and neurotransmitters that allow her to control others' minds. Outgoing, insecure, warm. Not contaminated. Diebol experimented with her biology to produce a mind-control dart for mass production.

Morda: Diebol and Bricandor's name for Mera.

Nathan Peter: 17-year-old male freedom fighter, ward of the Frelsi refugee system. Recent orphan. Special skills in compassionate organization and negotiation. Known for small size and quiet voice. Best friend of Gideon Horn and Reise Benzaran. Contamination status unknown.

Njandejara: Interdimensional energy being interested in befriending matter creatures. Differentiated from other energy beings by existing outside time, as well as outside space; rumored to be the ancient origin of all life. Considered a mental illness by Growen scientists, and a dangerous invasion force by Growen philosophers.

Reise Benzaran: 15-year-old male freedom fighter, ward of the Frelsi refugee system. Brother to Jerusha-Lem, Jake, Juju, and others. Special skills in sharpshooting and piloting. Known for unusual, highly educated speech pattern. Contamination status unknown.

Retrack City: Large, cosmopolitan area occupied by the Growen forces during latter period of the Growen-Frelsi conflict for Luna-Guetala. Most populated and culturally celebrated space-port on LG. About an hour's ride by air-rider north of Fort Jehu.

Revelon: Planet in the Uncontested Zone with fairly low gravity, mostly cool climates, and thin mountain ranges, inhabited by tall mammalians with keratinized, thick, rock-like skin.

Skraeli: Any of a number of sentient life forms comprised of complex carbon-nitrogen clouds. Require extreme gravity to maintain protocellular oxidation and life, and must wear atmosphere suits on the lower-gravity planets inhabited by most sentient beings. Language comprised of flashes of color punctuated with occasional sounds; emotions often communicated with scents.

Space-lemur: The human slang term for the Biouks, a sentient tree-dwelling race of omnivorous mammals characterized by small stature about half the height of an average human, enormous ears often as large as the head, powerful claws, a lack of tail, fangs that extend to the chest in adult specimens, and an extended lifespan often over a hundred Luna-Guetala revolutions. Divided into "moon" and "planetary" subspecies, with the "moon" species dwelling on the Luna twin of the Luna-Guetala twin planetary system. Language comprised of harsh, throaty sounds and snarls; emotions often communicated with ear movements.

Sterba: Deceased at 30 years old. Female soldier for the Growen Unification Forces. Trained and tortured by Bricandor to force an artificially strong bond with Mera, who is viewed as her sister. Special skills in heightened concentration and cognitive processing allow her unprecedented control over computing and machinery with incredible range. Cold, perfect. Shared nightmare bond with Lem Benzaran, who still feels deep connection with her. Not contaminated.

Stygge: A person gifted with electromagnetic abilities who has allied themselves either with the Growen, or with another force bent on eliminating the Contaminated.

Suns: There are two suns locked in an unusual binary system, one much larger than the other, which almost orbits it. These two suns support all known life in what is called, by Biouk scholars, the Bioumatta system. Luna-Guetala, Burbura, and Alpino orbit the first sun at the same rate as the second sun follows beside them, allowing for an almost-perfect temperature alignment from both sides. Forge orbits scorchingly close to the second sun, yet still at a distance to sustain some life, and the Bont homeworld close behind, with its many moons. Revelon, a larger, cooler planet—and smaller, with less gravity—orbits further from the second sun, passing between the two suns into proximity with Luna-Guetala every few years. Further out, orbiting the entire double-sun system, is the resource-rich gas giant Skraeli, and beyond that, Bijou.

Undecided Zones: The areas protected by the Spaces Treaty; also known as Uncontested Zones. See Contested Zone.

Wonderfrog: The human slang term for the Bwangam people, a semi-amphibious sentient group with a body plan similar to a human-sized frog. Native to Luna-Guetala, but population range also includes the Burburan swamp systems. Language comprised of rounded, guttural sounds, with frequent repetition; emotions communicated with changes in skin color and aggressive, expressive body language.

TRANSLATOR'S NOTE

The manuscript you have read was translated from a time-shifted language that appears itself to be a Biouk translation from the original Grenblenian. Therefore, the reader should understand that many idioms such as "Prince Charming" or "homework-eating dog" may not exist in the original, or if they do, they exist in rather different contexts.

The entire work caused a number of us a great deal of trouble. The original manuscripts of these chronicles appear worn and aged, but dating with radium, argon, and carbon produced wildly inconsistent and unusual values, and electron microscopy revealed the presence of compounds and genetic material not in existence on our planet. The original joke in our lab—that these volumes came here from the future, or perhaps another dimension altogether—eventually became less of a joke, and more of a conclusion, especially once it was revealed how, and at what cost, our lead obtained these documents. Nevertheless, no one in our laboratory felt comfortable publishing our results as fact.

And so, I have brought them to you, as fiction. I hope in this under-standing you will forgive any apparent anachronisms in the text.

ABOUT THE AUTHOR

Jen Finelli is a world-traveling sci-fi author who's ridden a motorcycle in a monsoon, swum with sharks, crawled under barbed wire in the mud, and hiked everywhere from hidden coral deserts and island mountains to steaming underground urban tunnels littered with poetry. She was once locked inside a German nunnery, and recently had to find her way through swamp-filled Korean foothills dotted with graveyards on Friday the thirteenth under a full moon without a flashlight. On her quest to rescue stories often swallowed by the shadows, she's delivered babies, cradled the dying, and interviewed everyone from prostitutes to Senators. If you want cancer-fighting zombie fiction, dinosaur picture books, scientists jumping into volcanoes, or talking cars and peyote legislation, you might like Jen. You're welcome to download some of her stories for free at byjenfinelli.com/you-want-heroes-and-fairies, or join her quest to build a clinic for the needy at patreon.com/becominghero. Jen's a practicing MD, FAWM candidate, and sexual assault medical forensic examiner—but when she grows up, she wants to be a superhero.

Byjenfinelli.com

facebook.com/neodymiumuniverse
twitter.com/petr3pan
instagram.com/becominghero

OTHER WORDFIRE PRESS TITLES BY JEN FINELLI, MD

Neodymium Betrayal

Neodymium Exodus

Our list of other WordFire Press authors and titles is always growing. To find out more and to shop our selection of titles, visit us at:

wordfirepress.com

 facebook.com/WordfireIncWordfirePress
twitter.com/WordFirePress
instagram.com/WordFirePress
 bookbub.com/profile/4109784512